THE UNDEAD DAY NINETEEN

RRHAYWOOD.COM

RR HAYWOOD

CHAPTER ONE

Day Seventeen

'BOMB...'

Howie jumps into view with his trousers round his ankles and in any other setting it would be almost comical, except the expression on his face removes any trace of humour. As one the lines of youths, men and women all burst away in every direction.

Lilly had heard the crackled static filled radio transmission between Marcy and Howie and by the time she had brought the others back in the boats so Lani had descended into madness, gripped by the infection that surged through her body as the shock rendered her weak and helpless.

Lilly saw the bodies of Jagger, Darius and the other children left lying where they fell. She heard Mo Mo shout *ambush* and saw Maddox take aim on Lani and in turn she saw Lani aiming straight at Howie.

In that instant she felt the tension in the fort become a real tangible thing that made the air feel thick. Every second was dragged out and her heightened senses became acutely aware of the tremble in Maddox's hands and the look of absolute pain on Mo Mo's face. She watched as Nick and his team moved out into a line as chaos erupted when the youths who had been made to kneel, suddenly scattered to run in every direction.

Maddox screamed for everyone to get down. Order was clawed back and all that was left was Lani standing in the middle, alone and armed with her weapon aiming at Howie and in that profound silence she heard Howie utter the words *I see you*. Lilly knew he was talking to the thing inside Lani. Everyone knew it and everyone watched in awe as Howie stalked towards Lani seemingly without fear.

That image seared into Lilly's mind. The view of Howie unafraid with Meredith at his side. Her head held low and showing her teeth in clear recognition of a thing sworn to be killed. Not one person looked away or dared speak, even breathing seemed too noisy for fear of doing something to spark an action.

She watched as Howie stalked his prey into the armoury and heard the muffled thumps, grunts and bangs coming from within. Confused glances were exchanged and Dave went to move forward until the banging developed a very rhythmic and very obvious cadence.

'They're not...' Paula muttered in disbelief, breaking the silence punctuated by the sound of a table being thumped against the floor

'No,' Clarence said slowly, 'They wouldn't...'

'What?' Dave asked.

'What?' Clarence said.

'What wouldn't they do?' Dave asked.

'Er...' Clarence said, wincing at the sound of the table banging harder and faster.

Lilly blushed. Even she knew what the sound meant. Everyone did. Apart from Dave who stared round and looked back at the entrance of the armoury with his blank expression somehow managing to convey confusion.

It didn't actually go on that long. It just felt like it did. The table thumping getting louder and faster. Donk. Donk. Donk. Donkdonkdonkdonk.

Desperate to look in another direction Lilly glanced over to the new woman, knowing instantly it must be Marcy simply from the description Nick had given her. He'd said she was pretty but Marcy was not pretty. Marcy was beyond pretty. Marcy was beautiful with perfect cheekbones showing through golden skin framed by lustrous dark hair cascading down her shoulders and thick dusky pink coloured lips pursing with a foul look at the noises coming from the dark room.

The banging, growing faster by the second, suddenly stopped. What followed was more grunts and muttered oaths making everyone unsure if they should be doing something to stop it.

'DIE,' was the word they heard screamed by Lani before Howie appeared jumping from the doorway with his trousers round his ankles.

CHAPTER TWO

'**B**OMB...'

No further warning is needed and as one the lines burst apart with everyone scattering in a desperate attempt to find cover. Lilly ducks back towards the gates intending to run round the edge to Billy but nothing happens. Seconds go by all filled with near on silence until Howie stops and turns back to stare at the armoury. A dull thud comes first and a sense of relief that whatever bomb Howie was shouting about wasn't that big. Then the big explosion comes and Lilly watches as the walls to the armoury blow out sending a shock wave that rips Howie from his feet sending him metres through the air to land in a crumpled heap.

Masonry rips out shredding human forms with sickening thumps. Twisted shards of metal lacerate and amputate. More explosions, more detonations, grenades going off one after the other in rapid succession. Rounds in the magazines of the stacked weapons go next. Pinging off the sides of the rooms and out into the fort proper. Those already hugging the ground are mostly spared but anyone left on their feet is either shot or struck by flying debris.

Flames scorch out deep across the ground then up into the sky. A wall of heat rams into Lilly sending her staggering back as a hand whips up and pulls her off her feet. She goes down hard landing on Maddox who rolls himself over her body, giving her protection against the bricks, stones, metal and bullets turned into missiles. Screams pierce the air. Howling pain filled wails as limbs are shorn off. Beneath her body the ground rumbles and overhead the skies fill with thunder that rolls for miles.

Lilly looks up just in time to see a flaming comet shooting across the ground that slams into a young girl trying to run away. The speed of the projectile removes the girl's upper body leaving a pair of legs that fall silently to the floor. A life gone, snuffed away in the blink of an eye. The flaming debris lands within the fort igniting the dry tents, canvas and materials left in the open air. Secondary explosions still pummel her ear drums and her eyes fill with flames and the silhouettes of people running without the sense to get down.

'MOVE AWAY,' a voice filled with anger snaps her attention over and she sees Howie on his feet with his face ablaze as he strides through the crews grabbing them to be pushed away from the danger. 'MOVE BACK...MOVE...DAVE...GET THESE KIDS MOVED...'

Dave on his feet in an instant, drawing breath to bellow in a voice that belies human origin, '**MOVE BACK NOW.**'

Clarence staggers to his feet with a child in each hand wading through the bodies to dump them on the far side. She spots Nick getting to his feet and staring round as though looking for someone. She surges up, pushing Maddox away and knowing Nick's eyes search for her.

'BLOWERS...COOKEY,' Howie yells, 'GO WITH NICK.'

The three lads sprint past Lilly still struggling to get up and head towards the far side and the children cowering by the vehicle ramp. She goes after Nick, screaming in warning as a flaming chunk of masonry lands right in front of him. In the confusion of noise, Nick doesn't hear the warning but vaults the object and pushes on, desperate to find the girl.

'Howie,' Maddox mutters sprinting from her side to slam bodily into Howie as a chunk of wall sails over their heads. Lilly spins, seeing Marcy shielding a young girl with her body. Roy and Paula on their feet dragging children up and forcing them away. Lilly turns again trying to see Nick but he's lost from view in the chaos exploding around her.

'Lilly,' Maddox grabs her wrist turning her round to face him, 'get the injured to the hospital...' he spits the words out with a mask of pain etched on his face and limps off to drop down as he tries feeling for a pulse on the body of a child.

She snaps to the now. To the overwhelming savagery of pain and hurt caused by the detonations coming from the armoury. Fires everywhere and spreading so fast from tent to tent.

Howie runs past holding an unconscious boy in his arms that bounces with the motion causing more blood to drip from his ears. 'DOCTORS...DOCTORS...' Howie shouts ahead slamming his foot into the door and he disappears inside. Clarence, Paula and Roy all holding injured children run in the same direction.

Lilly looks round spotting a black clad youth writhing on the ground just metres away. She rushes over dropping to his side and gently pulling his hands away from his stomach. No blood so something must have impacted his mid-section. She scoops him up, becoming very aware of how light and frail he is. These kids were brandishing weapons just a little while ago and looked frightening in their black clothes but suddenly they're just kids again. Little kids with high pitched voices crying for help with thin arms and legs bruised, cut and bloodied. She runs behind Roy holding the boy in the crook of her arms and pushes through into the medical bay and if it was chaos outside, it's worse in here.

Doctor Heathcliff Stone covered in blood from a broken nose tending to a young girl laid out on a bed. Doctor Lisa Franklin the same, her own nose bent out of shape and the front of her white lab coat soaked crimson and wet from the beating given by Lani.

'Here,' Doctor Anne Carlton shouts to Lilly, motioning a table top swept clear of objects to make another hard surface on which to work. Lilly rushes over to ease the boy down.

'Where's his injury?' Anne asks staring down as her hands start working from his skull down his neck towards his body, feeling for broken bones or fractures.

'His stomach,' Lilly says, hiding the wince as Anne yanks the boy's top up to reveal skin already a deep purple.

'HEATHCLIFF...crush injury, mid-section,' Anne shouts without turning.

'Risk of toxic shock,' Heathcliff shouts back without stopping his own work, 'Get Penicillin into him and work to stabilise the vital organs.'

'Into the back,' Anne looks up at Lilly, 'the meds are all stacked in order...look for Apsin VK...'

'Apsin?' Lilly asks.

'Brand name for Penicillin...quickly go...'

'Lilly, bring me more gloves,' Doctor Andrew Stone shouts as she rushes past.

'Gloves,' Lilly says back, 'Apsin VK...gloves...'

'I need more dressings,' Lisa shouts pressing firmly on a bleeding wound of an unconscious man.

Lilly gets into the back room and stops stunned for a second at the order and precision of everything laid out so neatly and in such stark contrast to the chaos outside. Bottles and boxes of medicines stacked on a table and she works along, muttering the names on the labels before finding a box marked Apsin VK 250mg. She grabs the box and turns to see the gloves stacked in the corner in size order from small to extra-large. Who shouted for gloves? It was Andrew. He is average size so best take the large. She grabs the box marked large then thinks again and takes a box of each, stacking them in her arms before grabbing a roll of sterile dressings and heading out into the room now so full of wounded children and adults.

'Here,' Lisa shouts at her.

'Gloves,' Lilly drops the box marked large next to

Andrew who yanks a pair out. 'More gloves,' she calls out placing the other boxes on a central table. 'Apsin VK,' she holds the smaller box out to Anne before darting over towards Lisa.

'Gloves on, open the packet and be ready to wrap him up,' Lisa says grimacing with the effort of squeezing the man's arm.

Lilly nods and without panic she goes for the medium sized gloves and pulls them on her hands before ripping the plastic bag open to get at the white dressing within.

'Start just down from my hands...' Lisa says, 'That's it, wrap it tight, tight as you can. We'll tourniquet it for twenty minutes...'

'Tourniquet?' Andrew shouts from across the room.

'Arm injury, going on now,' Lisa shouts back.

'Mark the time,' Andrew calls back, 'Lilly, you got a watch?'

'I have.'

'Twenty minutes from now that tourniquet needs to be loosened, mark it.'

'Okay.'

'Lilly, once you've done that come to me,' Anne calls out.

'Okay,' she winds the bandage round the arm working to cinch it as tight as possible thereby freeing Lisa's hands so she can take over, breathing noisily through her mouth and wincing every few seconds from the pain in her broken nose. 'Are you okay?' Lilly asks in genuine concern.

'Do I look okay?' Lisa's reply is sharp but it only serves to harden Lilly who stiffens and moves off to Anne, 'What do you need?'

'We need triage, find someone who can do it.'

'Does she know what triage is?' Andrew calls out.

'I know what triage is,' Lilly replies looking round at the youths lying on the beds, the table tops and being lowered gently on the floor by the men and women carrying them in.

'Lilly,' Andrew gains her attention counting under his breath as he works CPR on the bare chest of a boy, 'if they're screaming they're alive. The urgent patients are the quiet ones or the ones bleeding out...'

'Got it,' Lilly says.

'This one is dead. Are we recording life extinct times?' Andrew stands back grimacing as he rips the gloves off.

'No time,' Anne shouts, 'Lilly, find someone to remove and stack the bodies. We can do formal identifications later.'

'How the hell can we do this without blood?' Lisa snaps pulling her hand away from the dead lifeless neck of the man she just finished tying the tourniquet on.

'I believe that's what got us in this mess, wasn't it?' Anne points out with a glare at the other three doctors. 'Locking Lani in here for her blood...'

'Not now, Anne,' Heathcliff growls.

'Lani made her own decisions,' Lisa says flatly, 'next? WHO IS NEXT?'

'Lisa!' Anne snaps at the harsh shout.

'This boy has stopped breathing,' Lilly says calmly, feeling for a pulse on the neck of the boy Howie carried in. Thick lines of blood from his ears stain his neck and shoulders.

'Let me see,' Lisa pushes in at her side to place the flat round end of her stethoscope on the boys chest. She pauses, closing her eyes while her fingers work the same area as Lilly was, feeling for any signs of life. A few seconds and she opens the boy's eyes to shine a small torch at the pupils, 'dead, get him stacked.'

'Shouldn't we do CPR?'

'Save energy and time for ones with a chance,' Andrew shouts.

'Lilly, get more help in here,' Anne adds her voice to the shouted orders. The young woman strides and pushes her way past the groaning children spraying blood and vomit over the floors and walls and yet more coming in, helped along by adults and older uninjured youths.

'Maddox,' she calls his name, seeing him rise from depositing a child before turning back to the door. She rushes over to follow him out to a fort now ablaze with flames shooting high from the tents and structures within. 'They need more people in there...'

'Get what you can,' Maddox stops mid-stride to assess the damage and chaos in front of them, 'the adults looking after the young children....use them,' he fixes her a quick look full of intensity and she detects the pain in his eyes and the tremble of his hands. How he's still walking after being tazered so many times is incredible. Then he's gone. Walking purposefully into the devastation with a calm voice giving clear orders.

With her arm up shielding her face from the heat of the fires, Lilly runs round the edge of the fort. Skirting the blaze in the middle, dodging people who run screaming and panicked. She picks the long slope of the vehicle ramp out with ease and notices the children being shepherded up towards the ramparts at the top, away from the heat and harmful fumes and smoke billowing to fill the enclosed fort.

'LILLY!' She spots Billy waving and runs faster as he breaks free from the adult trying to catch him and runs down the ramp.

'Billy, go back up,' she shouts waving her arm but knowing he won't stop until he's got to her. She sprints hard while knowing that a few seconds of being lower in the fort won't hurt him but just the sight of her brother injects a fresh burst of energy into her limbs. 'Are you okay?' She drops down at the last second, absorbing the impact of his small body flinging into her open arms. His head instantly nestling into the crook of her neck as she envelopes him with a tight squeeze of maternal affection that would see her kill to protect him. Billy doesn't answer but clings tight as he's lifted and carried back up the ramp.

'Everyone up...come on,' she calls out using her free hand to guide the slower children up the slope, 'That's it, fast as you can...'

'Lilly, what's happening?' A woman shouts, panting heavily from running up and down the steep incline.

Too much to explain, too little time to say it all. 'Not sure,' Lilly opts for the best answer, 'The hospital is full, they need help in there...'

'We need help up here,' another woman shouts, 'what about these children?'

'HAHA! Lilly and Billy and Milly,' a young voice squeals out in delight as Lilly feels a fresh pair of arms wrap tight around her legs, 'Pick me up, Lilly...where's Clarence? Can I go with you? Are they having a bonfire?'

Fighting to stay upright, Lilly goes to reply but finds the young girl spinning round with another squeal of delight at the cold nose and furry head pushing into her neck. Releasing Lilly she lunges out to wrap her arms round Meredith's neck, burying her face in the deep fur.

'Is that dog safe?' A woman asks, hefting a stick with a menacing intent that has Meredith flicking her top lip up with a low growl warning of the danger of holding a weapon near her little ones.

'She's fine,' Lilly blurts, 'Honestly, she's completely safe.'

'Her name is Meredith and she hates CATS,' Milly informs everyone with an arm looped over Meredith's head squashing her ears flat. The dog is enormous, dwarfing the tiny girl clinging to her and her soft brown eyes flick over the faces of the children almost as though checking each one of them. So many of them too. Boys rescued from the house that Billy was rescued from. Others brought along by survivors threading their way to the fort. Orphaned, destitute, terrified and now once again being rushed from another point of danger.

'Billy, I have to go and help the others,' Lilly says lowering her brother down close to Meredith and Milly, 'Stay here with Milly.'

'Come with you,' Billy clamps on harder, refusing to be torn away from his big sister again.

'I have to help the others,' Lilly says softly, 'Look, Meredith is here, give her a big cuddle.'

'You can cuddle Meredith if you want to,' Milly says in such a gentle tone it brings tears forming to the back of Lilly's eyes, 'She likes cuddles but she doesn't like cats. We went to the zoo. Do you like the zoo?'

'Billy, I'll be back soon. I promise,' Lilly says gently prising his arms from her neck and half turning him so those arms can wrap around Meredith instead. He takes the invite and sinks into the deep hair of the dog that shows no reaction to the two children now clinging to her, other than the two eyes that stay fixed to the top of the vehicle ramp and her ears now pricked back up alert and ready. Meredith lowers her backside, planting herself between the top of the ramp and the children behind her. Nothing passes. Nothing gets through without being seen and checked. A tendril of understanding sweeps through Lilly. The dog is staying. The dog will protect. At any other time Lilly wouldn't even notice that sensation but these are different times and there isn't time to question it, just an instinct.

'How many adults have we got up here?' Lilly stands up sweeping her eyes over the taller adults and counting as she goes. 'Who knows first aid? Medical training? I need two of you...'

'I did first aid at work,' a young woman stands up from the middle section of the children.

'What's your name?'

'Amy.'

'Amy, who else?' Lilly asks, looking round, 'The hospital is full of injured children...'

'Yeah I can come,' another woman says reluctantly when no one else volunteers, 'I did my certificate a few months ago.'

'Thank you,' Lilly says genuinely, 'Please come with me. Billy, I'll come back as soon as I can,' she bends to kiss him on the forehead with another quick hug before rushing off with the two woman following behind. 'Forgive me but I don't know your name,' she says to the second woman.

'Hannah,' the woman says politely with a tight grimace, 'How bad is it?'

'Bad,' Lilly says dipping her eyes for a second, 'they don't have time to remove the bodies and do triage on the children...'

'Bodies?' Amy asks, cutting in with an audible swallow.

'Some grenades exploded in one of the rooms...' Lilly explains, selecting her words carefully, 'the debris caused multiple injuries and several fatalities. Stay to the edge,' Lilly speeds up to get past fires still burning. On the far side she sees Howie and the others wrenching water pipes from the walls to fight the flames and more figures beating at the tents to get them away from the walls. She leads them through the mess and the heat that wafts over their faces with a stench of chemicals and thick smoke that stings their eyes. Hands over mouths and staying low they get quickly to the door and through into the complex of rooms full of screaming, writhing children holding broken limbs, shattered ribs and clinging to mates that lie silent and unconscious.

In the blink of an eye Lilly can see all order has been lost as the doctors rush from patient to patient while glancing constantly to the rest of the wailing children. Heathcliff sways on the spot from the pain in his nose and the sheer pressure of the situation. Lisa scowls, suffering her own pain and a thrumming headache that refuses to ease off despite the pills she's swallowed.

'Lilly!' Anne shouts clapping eyes on the three women.

'What first?' Lilly asks seeing Amy and Hannah stare round at the confusion within the main room.

'Fucking bodies,' Lisa shouts, 'Get them moved, we're tripping over them.'

'I need dressings,' Andrew twists round with fresh blood spattered over his face.

'Hannah,' Lilly says turning to the woman on her left, 'Go into the back rooms, find bandages and bring them to stack on the main table. Amy, they need the deceased moved...can you do it?'

'I er...'

'Just bloody get them shifted,' Lisa screams with such fury it sends a fresh spurt of blood pumping from her nose.

Amy nods, swallows and seems to square her shoulders with an attempt at firming her resolve and into the mess she heads. Moving to the bodies pushed from the beds onto the floors as the doctors rush to give aid and treat the next patient. She grabs the wrists of a young girl, no more than nine years old and starts dragging her down the central aisle past the injured kids to dump the corpse outside. A sound of retching and she comes back in wiping her mouth with the back of her hand.

'Where does it hurt?' Lilly heads to the first in the line waiting to be seen.

'Arm,' the boy says through gritted teeth.

'Do you feel sick?'

'No, jus' fuckin' hurts, you get me?'

'I do,' Lilly says softly, 'just stay still and we'll help you when we can, okay?'

The boy nods with rapid breaths blasting through his nose. Lilly looks down the line seeing the ones that are moaning and gripping limbs, looking past the screaming ones, looking beyond the ones swearing and crying. She heads to the first silent child. An Asian boy with thick dark hair and the first signs of a wispy beard showing on his chin. Fingers to the neck. Fingers to his wrist. She opens his eyes trying to see if his pupils dilate from the light.

'I think this one is deceased,' she calls out.

'FUCK IT,' Lisa roars spraying more blood from her nose, 'WE CANNOT WORK LIKE THIS.'

'Get a grip,' Anne hisses, 'Lisa...LISA.'

'This is insane,' Lisa mutters stepping back from the bed holding the patient she was treating.

'Lisa,' Anne calls out in a softer tone, 'Triage with Lilly...we'll do these. Lisa...LISA!'

'What?'

'Do triage with Lilly, we'll do the patients...'

'Triage?' Lisa asks confused as her mind starts closing down.

'I need your help,' Lilly rushes to the doctors side, grabbing a soft dressing from the table she places it in the doctors hand and gently pushes the same hand up to stem the blood dripping from her nose. 'Help me...I think that boy is dead.'

Lisa nods and allows herself to be pulled gently down to the Asian lad while holding the gauze to her face.

A simple task now. Check for life. She can do that. She checks the heart first, using her stethoscope. She feels for a pulse in the neck and wrists. She opens the eyes and shines a light.

'Deceased,' she says flatly.

'Amy, this young man needs to be removed,' Lilly says holding Lisa's wrist to move her down the line to the next silent child, 'Check this one.'

Lia nods again. Stethoscope. Neck. Wrist. Eyes. Light. 'Dead.'

'Amy, this one too. Hannah, can you help Amy please...we've got more bodies than I realised.'

'Dead,' Lisa says at the next one and reels back on her heels shaking her head at the shock of it all

'Dead.'

'Dead.'

'Dead.'

The bodies mount up. The corpses carried or dragged down the room to be piled outside to smoulder and singe near the flames and heat.

'Dead....NO,' Lisa freezes with her eyes wide, 'Alive...she's alive...ANNE.'

'Coming.'

'Lilly, move over,' Lisa switches back to her skills and training to gently lay the girl out as she first runs her fingers up the spine checking for back injury. 'Okay, lift her up...easy now...'

'Over here,' Andrew calls out while heaving a boy from a bed to a chair, 'you'll be fine, just sit still,' he says as the boy screams at the pain in his broken leg being jarred from the motion.

Broken arms. Broken legs. Crushed skulls. Bones fractured and dented. Crush injuries. Burns and scalds. Teeth knocked out and gunshot wounds from rounds sent flying as they detonated from the armoury. As the bodies are removed so Lilly, Hannah and Amy set to applying pressure on wounds and holding children steady as the doctors reset broken bones or dig into flesh to remove the bullets and fragments. Blood sprays out. Vomit is brought up. They mop and clean. Spraying anti-bacterial spray on the floor and wiping down the beds and tables as best they can. Gloves should be changed between each patient but such is the pace that gloves are only changed as they remember to do so.

Heathcliff sways constantly, his legs seemingly weak but he pushes on, using his years of knowledge and expertise in orthopaedics. Stitches are given. Wounds cleaned and those not at risk of instant death are sent away. Antibiotics, Penicillin and pain-relief are given out like smarties with Lilly, Hannah and Amy becoming dispensing chemists.

'Take these.'

'Drink this.'

'Go outside, up the ramp and wait with the other children.'

In the chaos order is clawed back. Painfully slowly and at times they lose more than they save with crush injuries left longer than the prescribed time and deadly toxins flooding the young bodies. CPR done time and again, chest compressions and one of the girls pumping the balloon on the mouth mask in a vain effort to get the heart working again. Death is called more times than life is saved and those young are dragged and carried to be stacked to smoulder and singe near the flames and heat.

CHAPTER THREE

Slowly. Gradually. With sweat pouring down faces and minds frantically learning as they go so the odd one or two sent to traipse up the vehicle ramp become a trickle to limp along and up past Meredith lying down with a young boy and girl curled round each other sound asleep at her side. The women with the children on the top of the wall receive the once armed kids with warm smiles and soft words. Bringing them back into the world of maternal instinct as the adults fight fires below and bellow with deep voices that have broken from the maturity given them by the years they have lived.

'...go outside, up the ramp and...'

'Yeah I got it, I heard you before,' a boy says trying to smile at Lilly but showing a grimace of pain instead.

'The painkillers only take a few minutes to kick in,' Lilly smiles and touches his thin shoulder.

'Yeah,' he nods and stands up, 'Thanks,' he says almost surly but too hurt, too tired and too confused to sound anything other than near on helpless.

Lilly stands up stretching her back and turning slowly to see Amy rubbing her eyes and Hannah sagging against a wall. The three look at each other with eyes that have now seen all there is to see of the human body.

Lilly checks the floor. No more corpses to be moved. The worst of the blood and gore has already been sluiced and washed away. A quietness starts to settle, from sedatives given as freely as pain relief from doctors who know that a sleeping body repairs faster than one awake and crying. Heathcliff slumps in a chair looking deathly pale. Anne tends to a young girl, smiling with eyes full of care and a gentle hand that strokes the skin of the child as she falls slowly to sleep. Lisa works like a robot, rubbing salve into the burns of a woman given morphine to numb the incredible agony of her scalp nearly melted away. Murmurs sound out. Bodies twitch and jerk. Bodies that lie in beds, on tables and on the floor. Those at too much risk to be sent out and held back in whatever space they can find to monitor.

'Coffee,' Anne says quietly, easing back from the now sleeping girl, 'I need coffee...'

'We need blood,' Heathcliff grumbles from the chair, '...we need radiography and nurses trained in trauma...we need beds more beds...yes,' his voice trails off with a long exhalation of air, 'We need many things.'

'But we can start with coffee,' Anne says staring over at the older doctor, 'Lisa, get some rest. One of the girls can do that. Lisa?'

'Huh?'

'Go rest,' Anne says wincing at the amount of salve applied to the burn and realising Lisa had once again switched off to work on auto-pilot.

'I'm fine,' Lisa says, irritated at being disturbed.

'You need to rest.'

'I need you to stop telling me what to do.'

'Lisa,' Andrew says sharply, 'Enough, take five.'

'But...'

'Just bloody rest,' Heathcliff booms then grunts from the pain radiating through his nose into the back of his skull, 'And someone get me some blasted codeine.'

'You need anti-inflams,' Andrew says glancing over at him.

'Can't. Guts got acid,' Heathcliff says darkly, placing a hand over his stomach.

'Jesus, Cliff,' Andrew says rolling his eyes with a heavy sigh, 'You're a doctor from the bloody dark ages. The back room is packed full of Omeprazole.'

'My grandfather used to take that,' Amy says, recognising the word.

'I think half the population were on them,' Andrew says.

'That and anti-depressants,' Anne mutters.

'I was on anti-depressants,' Hannah says then shrugs when the doctors look over at her.

'Which ones?' Anne asks.

'Sertraline.'

'We've got loads if you need some,' Anne offers.

Heathcliff snorts with disdain, 'Anti-depressants during the apocalypse? That'll help.'

'I'm fine,' Hannah says recoiling as she takes the senior doctors words as a slight against her, 'But thank you.'

'Oh don't you worry,' Heathcliff continues, staring into the far distance, 'Let us know if you feel down or anxious. We've got pills for everything. Just don't get injured...or burnt...or break a bone... What happened out there anyway?'

'Lani blew the old armoury out,' Anne says before Lilly can reply.

Heathcliff snorts again with his favoured response to hearing anything he doesn't like, 'She turned then.'

'I don't know,' Anne says looking at Lilly, 'Lilly? Did you see?'

Lilly thinks before answering knowing full well that Anne was right there tending to Maddox as Lani heard the radio message and started the descent into madness. She looks at the doctor trying to fathom the reason for the evasiveness but Anne focuses on rolling the dressing in her hands and doesn't look up. 'I'm not sure what happened,' Lilly says, making out like she's thinking about it, 'Lani just snapped...but I went over in the boats to bring the others back.'

'Snapped or turned?' Andrew asks.

'Did you see her eyes?' Heathcliff cuts in.

'It was dark.'

'Lani was screaming at the kids,' Hannah says taking a step closer into the conversation, 'We all heard it...she was hitting them with her gun then she shot Darius and Jagger...like just shot them for no reason.'

'Is that true?' Andrew asks, looking at Lilly.

Lilly pauses, knowing she has to tread carefully, 'Lani did that yes. Like I said, she sort of snapped...but then I know from talking to Nick what they've all been through together...'

'But she was murdering innocent people, is that right?' Andrew asks and Lilly feels the pressure of the room weighing down as every pair of eyes focus on her, waiting for her measured and calm reply. Even Lisa stops and stares over with a baleful expression, almost as though she wants to hear Lani turned.

Again Lilly chooses her words and makes sure to look at Andrew then round at the others as she replies, 'I think we need to be careful about the terminology we use. Saying Lani murdered innocent people is factually incorrect and, I would respectfully suggest it is also inflammatory. I wasn't there at that point, I was bringing Howie back in the boats but if Lani shot people then those people had been armed just minutes before and had been holding her team captive.'

'How old are you?' Heathcliff asks, recoiling slightly.

'Fifteen,' Lilly says, adding some confidence to her voice. 'I do not know if Lani succumbed to the infection or if she simply snapped from the pressure of everything they have done.'

She stops speaking and holds her head high while feeling awful for lying. Lilly hates lying. One lie leads to two and on it goes with a web of deceit that threatens to catch you out at any second. Lani *did* turn. That was fact. Lilly saw the way Howie stalked at her with the dog at his side. She watched, hardly daring to breathe or make a noise for fear of sparking something as Howie walked seemingly without fear towards someone he loved who was now infected and holding a rifle aimed at him. She felt it too. The energy pouring from the man. Something primeval that was both dark and light. *I see you.* She knew Howie said that to the infection and not to Lani. *I see you too.* The infection, the disease, the thing inside of Lani said that. It wasn't Lani speaking. Or was it?

'It's hardly relevant,' Anne says with an air of resignation, 'I think perhaps we were trying to focus on something we know nothing about instead of...'

'Instead of what?' Lisa asks.

'Instead of doing what we were brought here to do,' Anne says.

'I thought we were brought here to help them understand the virus,' Lisa says with an edge to her already bitter voice and a glance at Andrew and Heathcliff.

'We're doctors,' Anne says, addressing the other three, 'Not scientists. Not virologists. Not haematologists. Medical doctors. We should stick to what we know. Bloody hell, Lisa. We injected blood from one patient into another! An old man lying on a patch of ground with a gun pointing at his head. Where's the science in that? We knew nothing of either patient's history or medical background...'

'Research has to start somewhere,' Heathcliff says defensively.

'No,' Anne says, shaking her head and folding her arms in an effort to telegraph her firm belief, 'Besides...'

'The old man survived didn't he?' Lisa says.

'He did,' Anne concedes, 'So on that basis we can simply take blood from Lani, Howie and the others that show immunity and inject it into anyone that feels sick or poorly. Is that right? We've got a hospital full of seriously injured people,' she says sweeping her arm round the cramped room, 'why don't we start now? Go on.

Someone go and ask Howie to come and bleed all over our patients.'

'Anne,' Andrew says with a sigh and a tired hand rubbing his tired face.

'No, Andrew. That is exactly what we did with Lani and that old man and on the basis, as Lisa put it, that he survived, then surely we have irrefutable scientific fact that everyone here will miraculously heal.'

'We're not saying that,' Andrew says tightly.

'No? What about this woman with third degree burns to her scalp? Surely we can try her can't we? Lilly, go find a gun to point at her head while we drip blood down her throat.'

'Anne...' Andrew's voice rises as the point she is making strikes home.

'Ah I know,' Anne says with malicious delight, 'Lisa, you've got a broken nose and no doubt a thumping headache and probably some concussion going on...'

'Stop,' Lisa says quietly.

'Put yourself as the next test subject in our scientific study. See if it takes the pain away or makes your nose get better.'

'Anne, stop it. Please just...'

'Why not, Lisa? You were more than happy to sacrifice the life of an old man. You're injured now. Or we can use Heathcliff. How about it Doctor Stone?' Anne says, staring hard at Heathcliff.

'Good God, Anne! Let it rest. We're all tired and this is not the time...' Andrew cuts in.

'Then look at yourselves,' Anne says firmly, 'Look at what you did. You took a young woman and tazered her when she wasn't willing to do as you wanted. The fact that she was electrocuted may have been the action that made her bloody snap! Have you thought about that? The shock and disorientation of being forcibly separated from her group? That she was isolated. Sick. Alone. Shocked? Have you any of you considered for one second that by playing God you caused this?'

Lilly watches the other three go to reply but something in the words spoken by Anne and the firm tone of the doctor make them stop. One by one they absorb the implication and the defiance starts to slip. A night of hell, of watching children die one after the other and dumping their small bodies on the floor to be dragged away and just the suggestion that they played a part in what made that happen is enough to sap the already dwindling energy from all of them.

Anne sees it too but there is no gloating from the sudden victory of the argument. She doesn't look smug or satisfied but as tired and exhausted as everyone else. Silence descends. An uneasy reflection on the actions they have taken. Lilly can see how it happened too. Hospitals have protocols. Everything has protocols with fail safes built into processes so that if one person makes a poor decision others will stop and rectify it. Everyone is account-able for their actions, or rather they were accountable. Now there are no processes. No fail safes. Three medical doctors decided to do something, so they did. They believed they were right and sought justification from each other. The fact that one of them did not agree did not stop them. They did it anyway.

Maddox chose a course of action but there was nobody to oppose him either or tell him he was doing the wrong thing. Or did he do the wrong thing? Lani did turn. Does that mean Maddox was right? If Lani had stayed in the hospital would any of this happened?

Easing away from the doctors, Lilly folds her arms and walks slowly down the main aisle to the door with too many strands of thought whirling round her head with each one of them screaming to be taken as the most important.

That's not our way. Nick's words float through the confusing fug. *We have to do the right thing.* Maddox *thought* he was doing the right thing but Howie would have *done* the right thing. Paula, Clarence and the others would soon tell him if they thought he was wrong. That's it. That's why they work so well, because of the collective experience and Howie's respect for that experience and knowledge coupled with an ability to make sound decisions under pressure. Find Howie. He can't leave. He has to stay and get this place safe.

As the decision is made so she steps through the door into the world shifting from night to day and a sky already lifting with the first rays of the sun highlighting the mess inside the fort. The ground runs sodden and filthy with blackened water. The fires now extinguished but with wet heat hanging in the still air. She looks over to the old armoury and the gaping hole in the wall. Even from here she can see through to the sea on the other side.

She looks round, sweeping her eyes along the perimeter to the new armoury, searching for Clarence's bulk to use as an identifying marker for where the group are. She's tired. Her eyes sting so she closes them for a few seconds and tries again. The first thing she sees are the bodies dragged from the hospital stacked on the ground. People walking slowly along the edges of the ruined mess of burnt tents in the middle. Her eyes scan each person, each group, each section and the first seed of worry starts to sow. She can't see Clarence. No Paula and Roy. She can't see the lads or Nick anywhere. No Howie and Dave.

She moves off, heading for the police offices and constantly blinking then rubbing her eyes. Movement at the main gate and she turns to see Maddox walking back in. He spots her and inclines his head. She stops and waits as the realisation dawns. Maddox is coming back inside which means he went outside. The only reason he would go outside is if someone was arriving or leaving.

She looks round again and this time sees the doors to the new armoury are wide open and the gap inside tells her some of the cases have been taken.

'Lilly,' Maddox says, getting closer and seeing the almost frantic look on her face

Her heart sinks, her stomach flips.

'They've gone,' Maddox says, coming to a stop just feet from her.

'I know,' Lilly replies, hiding the emotion from her voice. She looks at Maddox, at his red eyes and the grime smeared over his face. His hands still tremble but he holds her gaze steady and without expression. Lilly instigated the fight back with Lani. She took the box of grenades and made everyone drop their weapons. She sided with Lani and thereby opposed Maddox. She did it to save Lani and Howie's team. She did it knowing Howie would protect her, and if she died then she knew he would protect Billy and the children.

Except he's gone. They're all gone. Clarence. Paula. Nick. Nick has left. He didn't say anything. He didn't try and find her.

'Lani's dead,' Maddox says in a surprisingly gentle tone, 'She's in there.'

'Where?'

'Old armoury,' he says nodding at the ruined wall through which they can see the water gently lapping at the wall.

Nick didn't say goodbye. He didn't say anything.

'Are they coming back?' She asks, whispering the words out.

Maddox doesn't reply, doesn't do anything but stands and watches her for several long seconds, 'we agreed they'd stay away... be seen somewhere else,' he stops on seeing the fleeting look of confusion on Lilly's face. 'They left quickly,' he adds with the sudden recollection of Lilly's connection to Nick. 'We didn't know where you were.'

'Hospital,' Lilly says automatically, 'helping.'

'Hospital,' Maddox says, nodding slowly, 'You okay?'

She nods in return but stares down at the ground willing the tears not to spill from her eyes.

'About last night,' Maddox says, lowering his voice another notch.

She swallows, blinks and looks back up at him, waiting and

expecting the worse. 'Just don't hurt Billy...please...I'll go if you want but...'

'I don't know how to do this,' Maddox says.

'I can leave,' she rushes the words out, 'I'll take Billy if you want...I'll go but please, Maddox, don't hurt Billy...'

'S'hard,' Maddox whispers with a gentle shake of his head. 'You get me.'

'Maddox,' the tears stream down her cheeks, 'Please...Billy's lost everyone...'

'All those kids have lost everyone,' Maddox says, turning slowly to stare over at the vehicle ramp and the shapes of the children and adults gathered at the top.

'Maddox, please...he's my brother,' she holds the sobs inside but the tension in her throat reflects in her voice made rough and hoarse. 'He's my little brother...don't hurt him. Hurt me...shoot me...he didn't do anything. I did it.'

'Shoot you?' Maddox looks back sharply with eyes that take seconds to focus.

'Do it outside,' she nods, almost urging him. 'So Billy doesn't see. Tell him I left. Tell him I died in the fires but please don't let him see...I won't try and run...'

'Lilly,' Maddox says stepping closer, 'I'm saying I don't know how to do this,' he waves a drunken hand at the mess and destruction around them, '*this*... all of this...not shoot you. I know...how...I can shoot but...what?'

She blanches, showing confusion and terror on her face. Her hands wringing in front and her eyes constantly glancing to the ramp and her brother at the top. Maddox closes his eyes, trying to think clearly but his own mind whirls with as many strands of thought as Lilly's. A fug inside his mind. His muscles ache like hell from the repeated shocks of the tazer. It hurts just to stand up. He tries to remember what he was saying but falters and sways on the spot without realisation of his own motion.

'This is mess.'

They both look at Lenski stood with her arms folded across her chest. The defiant Polish woman glaring past them to the filth, 'This is mess. Everything. Everything is mess.' She tuts, shakes her head and tuts again with an angry blast of air pushed out through her nose. 'How we fix hole in wall? Where we put bodies? The burnt tents, they go yes? We get new tents yes?' She nods while speaking, asserting her decisions on the other two with equal glances between Maddox and Lilly. 'We no give children guns, yes? You have gun,' she nods at Maddox then taps her own chest, 'I have gun, Lilly have gun. No one else have gun.'

Lilly have gun? Lilly blinks in surprise but stays silent and watchful.

'If new people they come. You see them,' she says to Maddox. 'We no give guns to children. The Bossman not here now, yes? The children they all die now. Dead. Darius is dead...'

'I know...'

'No crew chiefs. No crews. No number one number two number three number four...no more, Maddox.'

'Okay,' Maddox says quietly.

'Howie is gone, yes?'

'Yeah.'

'Lilly, you stay, yes?'

'I er...'

'Good. This is good. We fix this. We fix mess. Lilly, you shoot gun?'

'Pardon?'

'You shoot gun, yes? You know how gun works, yes?'

She nods, 'Nick showed me...with a er...with a handgun...'

'Maddox. Give Lilly gun. Give me gun. No one else has gun.'

'Okay,' Maddox says, nodding at everything she says with a look of relief washing over his features.

'Small gun,' Lenski barks, 'Lilly and me we have small hands. Not big hands. We have small guns. We fix this mess.'

'Lilly?' Maddox says, purposefully widening his eyes as though fighting sleep.

Lilly watches him. Studying his face and manner. She sees a man not many years older than her.

'We make decisions together,' Lilly says with a glance at Lenski, 'All three of us have to agree...'

'Yes,' Lenski nods instantly, 'This good thing. We do this.'

'I...' Maddox goes to speak.

'And Doctor Carlton too,' Lilly cuts in.

'We do this,' Lenski says agreeing with a curt nod, 'Maddox do this,' Lenski says in such a tone it leaves nothing else to be said by Maddox who just dips his head.

'Okay,' Lilly says, blowing air through her cheeks, 'Okay...'

'Not okay,' Lenski says, 'look at mess. Look at work. We have hole in wall.'

'I meant okay I will stay and help,' Lilly says.

'I know this,' Lenski says bluntly, 'I know you stay. Maddox, get guns. Small guns.'

'I think we only have one size...' he stops at the glare sent his way.

'Good. Get gun. We have meet yes? We decide, yes?'

'Meat?' Lilly asks.

'Yes. We meet. We meet to decide. Three decide. Get Doctor.' She waves a hand between them.

'Oh, a meeting,' Lilly says.

'Meeting? Meet? Is same thing. We meet. Maddox. Get guns. Small guns.'

'Okay.'

'Now, Maddox.'

'Okay,' he says again, blinking heavily as he goes to walk off and stumbles.

'Take other guns from children.'

'Maddox, are you okay?' Lilly asks watching him sway further round in a drunken circle.

'Lock place where guns are.'

'Okay,' Maddox breathes the word out fighting to stay upright and keep the blackness at the edge of his vision from closing in. Everything hurts. His legs can't hold his weight and his neck creaks like rusted hinges every time he moves his head.

'Small guns, Maddox. Small hands.'

'Small guns,' Maddox slurs.

'Maddox?' Lilly steps towards him, watching as his legs simply buckle and down he goes, dropping like a stone to lie crumpled on the ground.

Lenski tuts, shaking her head with a mouth pursed and thin, 'Kurcze!' She looks over at Maddox and round at everything else that lies broken and ruined, 'Mess. All mess.'

CHAPTER FOUR

The room would be pitch dark if not for the gas lamp hissing softly. The back rooms of the medical complex do not have windows and no natural source of light can penetrate the thick walls that deaden the sound and smells of the fort.

He lies on his back on a hastily made bed of blankets stacked on each other to provide what degree of comfort they can give. The room is cool and bathed in the muted orange glow of flame burning within the glass casement.

'I know of one,' Andrew says with a sigh, 'Chap in London got tazered ten times and survived.'

'Anecdotal?' Anne asks, glancing over the form of Maddox to Andrew.

'No,' Andrew says, his voice a whisper in the darkness. 'Medical journal reported it for trauma doctors in the cities after the police started equipping their officers with tazers.'

'He not die?' Lenski asks bluntly, her emotionless face staring down.

'He's stable,' Andrew says, 'vitals are okay, heart rate, blood pressure...he's young, fit and strong,' he stops to pull a face with a tired shrug, 'Hopefully...only time will tell.'

Lilly shuffles forward, clearing her throat politely as a precursor to speaking, 'The man who was tazered ten times? He was okay?'

'He had mental health issues,' Andrew mutters, 'whether that has any bearing on his ability to withstand the shock is something I do not know. Any person exposed to that level of shock to the body can have very serious health implications...look, all we can do is monitor him and let his body rest.'

'How long?' Lenski asks, as blunt as ever.

'Jesus, how do I know?' Andrew says glaring up at her.

'We don't know,' Anne says, rising to her feet with a grimace at the pain radiating in her knees from being knelt down for so long. 'Who wants this?' She picks the pistol up taken from the back of Maddox's belt and holds it out to the two women who stare at the squat black weapon.

'Can you make him awake?'

'Lenski,' Anne says softly, 'Maddox is unconscious, there is nothing we can do to...'

'Adrenalin,' Lenski says quickly, 'I see this on television. They give the man the adrenalin and he wake.'

'No,' Anne says as Andrew gets to his feet, 'it doesn't work like that...'

'He needs rest,' Andrew says.

'We no have time for rest,' Lenski says.

'You have to listen...'

'No!' Lenski snaps, cutting Anne off with an angry glare, 'Maddox he strong. Maddox he...he strong...we need Maddox now.'

'He is unconscious,' Andrew says through gritted teeth.

'He no be this thing. He no be. He wake. Maddox... MADDOX...WAKE UP!'

'Lenski, stop it...' Anne says imploringly.

'He has been shocked what...six...seven times?' Andrew asks, shaking his head at the panic in the young Polish woman. 'He needs to recover.'

'How long recover?'

'Lenski, we've told you this. We do not know.'

Lilly watches as Lenski snorts air through her nose while pushing her hands through her hair. A rare show of worry and panic showing on her face.

'Kurcze...' Lenski mutters, throwing a worried look at Lilly. 'Take gun...you know to shoot? We move quick yes?'

'Pardon?' Lilly asks, blanching at the sudden rush of words.

'They see. They see Maddox go down. They see,' Lenski says reaching over to take the pistol from Anne. 'Take it...take gun...you know to shoot?'

'Nick showed me,' Lilly says, hesitating before taking the pistol, 'Lenski...I don't understand.'

'Show me you know to use gun,' Lenski demands, nodding at the pistol in Lilly's hand.

'Lenksi...'

'Show,' Lenski orders.

Lilly looks at the doctors who shrug and show as much confusion as she feels. With a sigh, Lilly holds the pistol in two hands and moves closer to the lamp. She presses the button on the side of the butt, releasing the magazine which she slides out into the palm of her waiting left hand. She pockets the magazine and slides the top back, turning the weapon over to drop the chambered round out onto the low table. With the safety on she puts the pistol down and pulls the magazine from her pocket. The bullet from the table gets slotted back into the top and she presses down, remembering every word Nick said as his hands worked over hers, showing her the movements. *Push the top bullet down, feel that? More pressure means the magazine is full, less pressure means it's not full. Yeah?* He smiled when he said that. His white teeth framed in his tanned face and that strong jawline. His eyes so hard. The eyes of a killer but vulnerable, wounded and brave all at the same time. She could have stared into his eyes forever. *Always check though* he said, nodding at her as he spoke and moving closer so his broad shoulder was brushing against her. *Always check, take them out and put them back in so you count the rounds...Dave said we have to do that...so we know when we'll run out.* It feels a hundred years ago now. The warm sun on them. The heat of the streets and the fear knotting in her stomach that Billy was in danger but somehow Nick made it better. It was the worst time of her life but the best too. Those snatched minutes with him. The kind way he spoke and how he kept trying not to swear and then apologising when he did swear. He said he would save Billy and he did. *How do you do it?* She asked him, having already seen him slide one out but wanting to keep his hands on hers for as long as possible. *Like this.* Together they slid the rounds out, counting them off until the last one popped out and into his rough calloused hand that was so gentle in the way he touched her. *What now?* She asked and he smiled that shy grin. *Put them back in.* They did it together and she knew Nick wanted to let her go so she could do it herself but she also felt his reluctance to release her hands.

'Eight,' she says sadly into the dark room with the glow from the lamp reflecting from the glistening tears in her eyes that blink quick and heavy. 'He'll have another magazine.'

'Will he?' Anne says, dropping down to gently roll Maddox as she feels the outline of his pockets, 'yep, got it, here.'

'Thanks,' Lilly takes the magazine, pressing the top and feeling the pressure. The actions harden her resolve. She picks the pistol up, slams the magazine in, yanks the slide back and holds it out to Lenski, 'Loaded made ready, safety on.'

Lenski blinks. An almost imperceptible nod. 'You keep. We go quick.'

'Lenski, I don't know what you mean,' Lilly says, lowering her hand holding the weapon.

'They see...they see Maddox and...'

'Who?' Lilly asks.

'Crews, they see. They see Maddox go down. They see Howie leave. There no number one now...'

The implication hangs heavy. The realisation hitting Lenski as the weight of the situation grows heavier.

'What?' Andrew asks, his voice showing irritation at the garbled almost coded way Lenski speaks.

'The crews,' Lenski whispers, 'They no have number one now...Maddox is number one...Darius number two. Maddox is...is here...Darius is dead...Jagger is dead, Mo Mo gone with Howie. Howie not here...I not number one. They no see me as number one. They see Maddox as number one...They take the guns...they see who number one now...'

'They'll take over?' Anne asks, a disbelieving tone in her voice. 'Tell them Maddox is fine and just needs a rest.'

'They see,' Lenski says louder, 'They not stupid. They see him...his hands do this,' she shakes her own hands imitating Maddox's tremble. 'They see him shit in pants...they see Lani do this...they see weak and they take...we go quick,' she says, switching her gaze to Lilly. 'We get gun for me and we go quick. We strong. We no be weak now.'

'Lenski, what...' Lilly falters, trying to understand what Lenski is trying to say.

The Polish woman curses softly. The intricacies of the crews, the way they are, the hierarchy, the power vacuum created and the need for one of them to take control...she can see it, feel it, she knows it but she cannot translate it.

'Kurcze,' she purses her lips, thinking hard, 'Maddox he see the Bossman and...'

'Who is the Bossman?' Andrew asks.

'Stop interrupting, Andrew,' Anne says with a warning tone to her voice.

'The Bossman he make kids like this. He sell the drugs yes? He make the drugs and he sell the drugs...he make kids be this way... Maddox was number two to Bossman yes? Bossman attack

Maddox. Maddox kill Bossman. Maddox number one now. Maddox strong. He clever. He clean. He no use drugs. He think smart yes? He see kids and crews and bad way and he know to change but he smart and he know to do it...slow...yes? He change and make better. The dogs in desert yes? What you call these...'

'Dogs?' Anne asks.

'The dogs that do laughing. They take weak and...'

'Hyenas?' Andrew says.

'Yes. These. Crews, they these animals. They no have...they no go school....they no loyal or...they no Howie! Yes? They young and what they know is bad...the Bossman he make them this way...'

'They're all bloody dead,' Andrew points out. 'Or lying back there cut to bits...'

'No. Many they left. Many older that quick and run when Lani blow up. Sierra. She out there. She see Maddox go down. She see Darius head shot open. They get guns. They take over. We go quick. We no weak,' she looks to Lilly, nodding rapidly with the fierce determination of knowing what must be done. 'You shoot them...like Lani...yes?'

'What? No!' Lilly steps back with disgust evident on her face.

'Yes! We do this. We strong. We no weak. They see weak they take. They dogs laughing. They take weak.'

'They're just children,' Anne says.

'No. One on own is children. They together they not children. They kill many times. We go quick. I get gun. We no let them have gun. We wait for Maddox to be awake yes?'

'Lenski,' Andrew says, closing his eyes as every minute of this new day just gets worse, 'Maddox might not wake up...'

'He wake,' Lenski says, growling the words out. 'He strong. Maddox no die. He strong. We go now.'

'Lenski,' Lilly blurts, running after the woman who turns to stalk out of the room, 'Lenski wait...'

'We no wait. We quick. We get guns...'

'Lenski I cannot shoot a child...I don't know if I can shoot anyone...Lenski, wait...'

Her words are ignored as Lenski walks briskly through the rooms. Adrenalin starts to course and thrum through Lilly's limbs. A shuddering sensation of pressure building. Of one danger passing as yet another presents itself. *I'm fifteen. I can't do this.* 'Lenski, please wait...'

'We go quick,' Lenski repeats without turning. 'Get guns...lock guns...fix hole in wall...'

I can't shoot a child. I have to look after Billy. Why me? Why do I have to do this? I wish Nick was here. I'm only fifteen. I'm not an adult. The speed of the walking makes her mind flit back to the time spent with Nick and the field in which they kissed when she offered herself to him. His lips. Soft. His hands and arms. Strong. His manner. Gentle. His eyes. A killer. He could have taken her. She would have let it happen but he didn't. *That's not our way. We do the right thing. Mr Howie said we have to do the right thing otherwise none of this is fucking worth it...shit! Sorry, Lilly, I keep swearing.*

That warm feeling inside when she thinks about him vanishes at the sudden rush of reality at the building pressure of a confrontation yet to come. She has seen the crews and the pack instinct is within them. The way they only take heed of each other and those they perceive as stronger than they. The deference they hold for Maddox and Howie's team but the sullen skulky way they stare at everyone else. The way they suck their teeth and curl their upper lips as they spit and look aside with disdain and disrespect.

Down the main aisle she rushes after Lenski. Watching the Polish's woman back and knowing inside that everything Lenski said makes sense. The children on their own are nice, even polite sometimes. Lilly knows, without vanity, that she is pretty and has seen the difference in reaction at the way the boys are to her in contrast to their reaction to others but that physical appearance won't hold sway now. Individually she could talk to them, maybe get them to understand and comply with consent but together? While they have that pack instinct and false bravado running through them? No way. Not a chance.

I can't do this. I can't. I wish Nick was here. He'd be strong and they'd see his hard eyes that are never hard when he looks at her. In the old armoury she took them coffee and mops to clean the dog mess up. She kissed him then too. When Maddox was coming and Howie and the others all scooted back. She grabbed Nick and kissed him with an effort to give pretence to why she was taking so long. Only it wasn't pretence and she felt first his shock, then his acceptance and finally his yearning for her. *Nick. Come back. Please come back.* She knows Howie's team have lost Lani and must be reeling from the pain and shock. The sheer exhaustion too of everything they have done. Of all the battles, the fights, the running and never giving in. Doing the right thing. Do the right thing. *That's our way. Nick's way. It can be my way too. I can do the right thing. I must do the right thing.*

Resolve comes back. Her back stiffens. Her eyes harden and the knuckles of her hand turn white from the pressure applied to the gun held ready. *Do the right thing. Those children cannot be allowed to take control.*

'We be quick,' Lenski says, slowing briefly as she reaches the exit door and turns to look back at Lilly, 'you be ready, yes?'

'Yes,' Lilly mutters the word, nodding once and firm. *Whatever it takes. Do the right thing. I wish Nick was here. I wish Mr Howie and Clarence were here. Paula, even Cookey would know how to do this. Any of them would. But they are not here. I am.*

Into the strong light they go. Into the outside world of death and filth. Of bodies still lying where they fell. Of tents still smouldering and a hole in the wall gaping through to the sea on the other side.

Behind Lenski she steps out and looks first right to see a youth wearing black ramming a magazine into an assault rifle as his mates adjust the slings on theirs. She steps further out to see three girls yanking the bolts back on rifles and Sierra striding through the fort with a group gathered round her handing out the guns taken from the new armoury.

Too late. They're armed. Her eyes scan the perimeter seeing the numbers of potential opposition. Too many. Everything balanced on that knife edge again. Every action taken could spark a devastating reaction. Her mind in overdrive. Thinking. Planning. Calculating the paths ahead and which one to take.

Movement to her left. An adult woman with dark hair who was up the top with the children on the wall now standing and looking sadly down at the bodies of those taken from the hospital.

Lilly glides behind Lenski, using the Polish woman to shield the sight of the pistol in her hand. The youths see Lenski and that recognition spreads as they stop to stare over.

'Too many,' Lilly whispers behind Lenski.

'Gun. Hide it,' Lenski mouths, turning her head a fraction.

Lilly moves quickly to the woman with dark hair, passing the gun from her right hand to her left to hide it from view.

'Hey,' Lilly says, naturally and softly but her eyes lock on the dark haired woman and pass a message so clear and evident. The dark haired woman blinks at the penetrating gaze locked on her. 'You okay?' Lilly asks, glaring fiercely with an expression that conflicts with the soft tone of voice.

The woman nods, unsure of what to do as Lilly closes the gap and leans in as though to hug her. The woman can't move back as the bodies of the dead children are right behind her. She stays still, feeling as Lilly reaches her right arm up and round her shoulders to draw her close.

'Take it....hide it...' A whisper in her ear and something hard pressed into her hand. With instinct she grips onto it, knowing instantly what it is. Lilly pulls back, that yearning in her eyes, 'Hide it...'

The woman nods quickly and shoves the pistol down the back

of her waistband before pulling the tails of her filthy checked shirt over to hide the shape of the gun bulging out.

'Go up...don't let anyone see it.'

The woman nods again. A small almost frantic motion of her head bobbing up and down. She swallows and looks past Lilly to Sierra and the youths all ranging out dressed in black with guns held in their hands.

'Lenski,' Sierra calls out, stopping metres away and her voice sounds rough, hard and cold. 'Where's Mads?'

'See you up top,' Lilly says at normal volume moving back from the woman who quickly turns away.

'He sick,' Lenski replies, sullen and staring.

'Sick?' Sierra asks. Everyone listens. Everyone watches.

'He was tazered several times,' Lilly says, moving to Lenski's side, 'He passed out...the doctors are with him now. I think he'll be fine...just needs a rest. Is anyone else hurt?' she asks looking round at the youths, 'the doctors can check you if you need it.'

'We's fine,' Sierra says. Holding her ground with some of the crew chiefs gathered round as she stares over, glowering and full of menace but empty in her eyes that have seen too many things. The image of Darius's skull exploding right in front of her replays over and over. His brains coating the front of her shirt. The shards of his skull sticky on her hands as she wept silent tears.

'Good,' Lilly says, taking care to keep her tone neutral. 'We need to get that hole in the wall fixed and the children up there need food and water...and this place is a complete mess.'

'We'll sort it yeah,' Sierra says, her tone flat.

'So much to do,' Lilly says, papering over the cracks and the tension mounting as everyone watches to see the power game play out. 'Bodies.'

Sierra scowls, a fleeting expression that wanes as quickly as it came, 'Bodies?'

'Where do we put them?' Lilly says heavily. 'We can't leave them here. What was Maddox's orders with the bodies?' She slips it in without confrontation. A reminder to all that Maddox is the one who gives orders. Maddox is number one.

'In the sea,' a youth calls out. 'With rocks and shit so they sink down, you get me?'

'I see,' Lilly says politely, letting her accent play off against the youth in a playful gesture. 'Well, the sea it shall be then. Lenski? What's first?'

The tension rises again as Lilly draws Lenski into the conversation, waiting to see if Sierra will accept what the woman has to say.

'We do wall first,' Lenski says with a deep sigh as she folds her arms. 'This mess. All of this is mess. Sierra, we need guard yes? On wall and on gate, yes? I fix wall you guard, yes?'

'How you gonna fix the wall?' Sierra asks, still not blinking or moving.

'I not know this. I not builder. We find the people in here who know this. We fix wall, we clean mess.'

'I can go and find someone,' Lilly offers, 'if that helps? Sierra? You okay with that?'

The girl flicks her eyes from Lenski to Lilly. The gun held tight across her chest. A curl of her lip and her head inclines an inch, 'Liam, you take the gate yeah?'

'Yeah,' Liam says from the side.

'Zayden, you's get a few watching that wall,' Sierra adds, 'where's Maddox's gun?'

'Pardon?' Lilly asks, stepping forward as though to hear better.

'His gun. Where is it?'

'No idea,' Lilly says, glancing over at Lenski, 'I didn't see it... maybe he dropped it or it fell out...'

Lenski shrugs with a gesture both non-committal and disinterested.

'Could be anywhere, Sierra,' a girl says looking round at the ground by her feet.

'Whatever,' Sierra says and the tension breaks as she looks away.

'Right, I'll go and see who I can find to fix the wall,' Lilly says. 'Lenski? Are you coming with me?'

Lenski shows no reaction as Sierra walks off but simply stares hard with her arms folded tight across her chest.

'Tense,' Lilly mutters.

'No. We fix wall then tents.'

'No I meant it was tense.'

'Yes,' Lenski says finally taking her eyes from Sierra to look at Lilly, 'I know this. We fix tents later.'

CHAPTER FIVE

I t feels like every pair of eyes is on her. It even affects the way she walks. Her arms swing unnaturally and she yearns to reach back and check the gun is still there. She knows it's there. She can feel it. What if it falls out? What if it slips? Everyone is watching her. Every single pair of eyes in the fort are scrutinising her every step and they can tell just from her gait that she is guilty of something.

The worry knots in her stomach as she starts the incline up the ramp and curses as the gained height means she'll be even more visible. She wants to turn and hand the gun back to Lilly. Why did she take it? She only went down to see how bad it was and if they could get some food and drink for the children. Oh god. Everyone is staring. She knows they are. The urge to turn and look is so strong but she walks on with heavy legs and arms that swing weirdly. Like at a comedy show when you try and sneak out for the toilet and the performer stops the show to call you out. That's how it feels. Like everyone is watching and staring.

She does turn. The urge is just too great and she risks what she hopes is a casual glance back, as though she is simply looking round from benign curiosity.

No one is watching. Nobody. Not one person is actually looking in her direction. They're all fixed on the stand-off between the hard looking girl with the rifle and Lilly and Lenski. Words are being said but the distance and the blood pounding past her ears blots them out.

Relief washes over her and she lets a long gasp of air out, closing her eyes and thanking whatever deity is watching over her. Reaching the top she looks over the forms of sleeping children and those injured and sent up who stare with eyes made slack from the sedatives and pain killers given out by the doctors. Bandages everywhere. Limbs wrapped in clean dressings so stark against everything else covered in grime, filth and shit.

She threads a path through the bodies, nodding at the other men and women until she reaches her spot. The spot she claimed when they ran up to keep the children safe. By the low wall that Howie and the others fired from when Darren led his army against them. She wasn't here when that happened. None of these people were. They didn't see the sacrifices made to keep this place safe and give their species a chance to survive.

She slumps down to rest her back against the wall and instantly adjusts position to stop the pistol digging into her spine.

'What?' Sam asks

'What?'

'Look on your face,' Sam says.

'What look?'

'What's going on, Pea?'

'In a minute,' Paula whispers, 'just act normally.'

'You are bloody joking I hope,' Sam chuckles without humour while edging closer to her friend. 'What's happening?'

'In a minute.'

'Paula bloody Gabriel...' Sam says, adopting a stern expression.

'I hate it when you call me that,' Pea whispers, ignoring the stern expression.

'Paula Gabriel.'

'Stop it.'

'Paula Gabriel.'

'Sam, stop! I'll tell you in a minute.'

'Paula Gabr...'

'Fine! I've got a gun...'

'What!?'

'Shush,' Pea whispers, waving a hand at her friend.

'Why have you got a gun?'

'Lilly gave it to me.'

'Lilly?'

'Yes, Lilly. The blond girl...'

'I know who Lilly is. Why did she give you a gun, Pea?'

'I don't know,' Pea exclaims then winces at the volume of her own voice, 'She just did. She came out of the hospital with Lenski and just stopped when she saw that girl...'

'What girl?' Sam asks, desperate for more detail.

'Er...she was with Darius...Escort or...Focus or something?'

'Sierra,' Sam says, rolling her eyes, 'you did that on purpose.'

'I did not.'

'So did,' Sam says.

'I forgot her name.'

'Yeah right, anyway...so go on...'

'Well, Lenski and Lilly came out and Lilly was holding the gun and they just stopped when they saw that Ford girl...'

'Pea!'

'Okay, they stopped when they saw Sierra, she's got a big machine gun by the way.'

'Who has?'

'Sierra, I just said that.'

'Oh right, yeah I'm with you now. So?'

'So Lilly hid behind Lenski then rushed over to me and slipped the gun into my hand and told me to take it and hide it.'

'She never did?'

'She so did,' Pea says, nodding earnestly.

'Why?' Sam asks, lowering her voice again and leaning even closer.

'Don't know,' Pea says, 'I don't think she wanted Ford girl to...'

'Pea...'

'Fine! I don't think she wanted Sierra to see they had it.'

'What about Maddox?'

'Oh god I didn't tell you that bit.'

'What bit?'

'Maddox got carried into the hospital.'

'Why? What for?'

'He passed out.'

'Well that Lani did tazer him like a hundred times,' Sam says, 'so it must be Maddox's gun, right?'

'Might be,' Pea says, shrugging.

'Where is it now?'

'Down the back of my jeans. You'd better take it.'

'Me?'

'Yes you,' Pea says leaning forward ready to tug it out but finding a hand pushing her back against the wall.

'I'm not taking it,' Sam says in panic, stopping her friend from leaning forward.

'I can't bloody keep it.'

'Don't give the bloody thing to me.'

'Sam, you're better at things like that. You take it.'

'Better at hiding guns? When have I ever hidden a gun?'

'You hid that joint in school.'

'Pea! That was over twenty years ago.'

'You still hid it,' Pea says reaching back to tug the gun free.

'Pea, no...put it away...I'm not taking it...'

'Take it...quick before someone sees.'

'No! Put it back in your pants.'

'Put it in your pants,' Pea says, thrusting it into Sam's lap, 'you know I can't hide things...I always get caught.'

'Pea, it's a bloody gun.'

'Remember that time you went on a date and I told your parents you were at my house?'

'Oh that's not fair.'

'Take the gun.'

'Pea...'

'Quick, someone's coming.'

'Shit,' Sam says, tucking the gun down the back of her waistband, 'Where?'

'What?'

'You said someone's coming.'

'Yeah, er...no, I just said it. But you got the gun now.'

'Fuck's sake,' Sam tuts. 'But you...you can do the whole face thing better than me.'

'The what?'

'The face thing...the resting bitch face...I can't do that.'

'What on earth has that got to do with anything?' Pea asks.

'If anyone asks us...I'll go red but you can do the whole resting bitch face thing.'

'Leave my bitch face alone.'

'I've got a gun now, I'll shoot you.'

'Do you know how to use a gun?'

'No. Do you?'

'No.'

Silence, pursed lips and furrowed brows. 'Don't you just pull the trigger?' Sam asks.

'Probably a safety switch or something,' Pea replies, 'like on the movies.'

'Oh, yeah probably,' Sam says.

Silence again and they sit shoulder to shoulder leaning their backs against the wall. Both exhausted, drained, filthy, hungry and thirsty. Sam stretches her legs out, sighing audibly as she adjusts to stop the gun digging into her back, 'What if it goes off?'

Pea looks over at the serious expression on her friends face, 'Go off?'

'Yeah, what if it goes bang?' Sam says and snorts a dry laugh at Pea's slow grin spreading across her face. 'You've caught the sun,' Sam says looking at Pea's darkening olive skin.

'Is my hair frizzy?'

Sam looks up, cocking her head to one side as if in contemplation, 'yeah,' she says slowly, 'it's really frizzy.'

Silence again but not awkward. A silence between people who have been best friends since childhood can never be awkward. They grew up together. Went to school together. Dated boys and went to each other's weddings. They helped raise each other's children and had lives entwined with the deep bond that can only ever come from a shared life. Nothing was ever left unsaid between them and a glance or the lift of an eyebrow was often all they needed to convey a whole raft of emotional messages.

They were together when it happened. At Pea's house watching a scary movie. On the sofa with snacks. Popcorn, crisps and red wine. While the world tore itself apart they watched actors tearing themselves apart while laughing and giggling. Then the movie just stopped and the technical error message came on the screen. That was funny too as it was right at the climax of the movie. They pressed buttons and even turned the satellite box off but the movie never came back on.

Instead they learnt, as so many did, of what was happening in the real world. They both had husbands and children but neither families were ever seen again. The one thing they had was each other. The darkest of days and the even darker nights when they wept and hid. When they held each other through the grief. When they ran and fell only to stop and help the other up to keep running and keep hiding.

It was the not knowing that was the worst. The displacement from their homes. The separation from everything that was familiar. The running. The constant struggle just to stay alive, all of those things were hard but not knowing what happened to their families was the worst of all.

Somehow. Through either divine miracle or pure luck coupled with a spirit inside that refused to curl up and die, they kept going. A whisper from another survivor. A fort. A man called Howie. It was a fragile rumour but enough to give light in the darkest of those nights. The next morning they headed south and joined the straggling lines of people threading their way to the fort.

If they had ever been separated it would have been over but they weren't. They had each other. They still have each other.

Pea looks down at the feather tattoo on her friends foot and the sadness rushes back in. The sight of something so familiar to her eyes and it reminds her of all they have lost. Sam senses it, feels it. She nestles closer and reaches a hand over to clasp Pea's with a squeeze. Words are not needed and in silence they wait.

Lilly reaches the top of the ramp and stops. Her mind whirling as she turns round to see Lenski is still coming up behind her. Another glance down to the fort at the black clad youths, now so fewer in number but all armed to the teeth once again.

They were too late. Lenski was right. Lilly blames herself for not understanding fast enough what Lenski was trying to say. Without Maddox here the youths have once again turned into the sullen child soldiers showing disdain to everyone else. She can see they're shocked from their drawn faces and hooded eyes. From the way they keep looking to each other for comfort and how they cling to everything Sierra is telling them and that hierarchy they have been taught shows true as they see her as the next number one. Why not Lenski though? She isn't one of them, that's why. It's not race or the colour of her skin, or even the fact she's Polish. The kids are made up of every ethnicity, race and culture. Lenski just isn't one of them. She's not from the estate. She hasn't been forced to fight to survive and run from the police and have well-meaning patronising social workers giving out colouring books when they attend state funded counselling. The crews would take orders from Howie and his group but only because they've seen how tough those people are. Lenski is strong in mind but she hasn't fought with them. She hasn't smoked weed, got drunk, had scraps or proven herself in the pecking order.

Billy is fast asleep and Lilly looks down with a fresh surge of worry at Milly and her brother curled up in the space vacated by Meredith. The thought of Meredith makes the pain in her heart so much more acute. The dog's mere presence somehow soothes the children around her, but Meredith isn't here. Nick isn't here.

'Look worse from here,' Lenski says, falling in beside Lilly as they stare down into the fort.

'We can fix it,' Lilly says with a tone firmer than the belief inside. She turns round, scanning the heads until she spots the dark haired woman at the far side sitting next to another woman. Both of them leaning casually against the wall and trying not to look at Lilly or Lenski.

'She have gun?' Lenski asks, seeing the dark haired olive skinned woman.

'She does,' Lilly says.

'You know this woman?'

'No.'

'She been here for some of the days yes?'

Lilly goes to reply but stops, hesitating as she tries to find order in the memories within her mind. Everything seems so different. Time is different. Like it's moving faster. *How long have I been here? A week? Longer?*

'How long have I been here?' She asks in a voice rasping from exhaustion and the filth of the fires hanging in the air.

Lenski shrugs, showing that same poker faced non-committal gesture, 'Two days? I think two days.'

'Two days,' Lilly murmurs, closing her eyes for a few seconds in a vain effort to reset her perception of time. 'Would you get Milly for me please?'

'Milly?' Lenski asks, watching Lilly squat down to lift her sleeping brother into her arms. 'This girl yes?'

'Please.'

'Who are you?' A sleepy Milly asks, peering through heavy eyes on being scooped up by the Polish woman.

'I Lenski.'

'Do you like chocolate?'

'Yes I like.'

'Night, Leski'

'Lenski.'

'But...it's not night time now,' Milly says staring round suspiciously at the bright day.

'Shush, go sleep.'

'Do you like sleep?'

'I like sleep. Go sleep.'

'Okay Leski.'

'Lenski.'

'Hi,' Lilly whispers on reaching the two women, 'Can we join you?'

'Sure,' Sam says with a glance at Pea.

'Thanks,' Lilly waits politely, like waiting for someone to move up on a train seat. The virtues of societal politeness and etiquette that held civilisation together. Sam and Pea move up. Not that they needed to move up as either side was empty but it shows the same politeness in an act done to overtly show their own politeness. Around them lies death. The stench of it hangs as strong as the smoke from the fires but the three nod and smile and make appropriate noises of gratitude as Pea takes Billy from Lilly and waits, holding the sleeping boy until Lilly sits down.

Lenski just sits down. She doesn't nod or smile or show any outward sign of emotion. Even when Milly slides down to a more comfortable position in Lenski's lap and rests her head on Lenski's bosom she shows no reaction. Whatever she feels, whatever she thinks is locked inside.

'Lilly,' Lilly says leaning forward to look down at Pea and Sam.

'Paula,' Paula says.

'Sam, hi,' Sam says lifting a hand.

The three look at Lenski who looks back and shrugs, 'What?'

'That's Lenski,' Lilly says after a second.

'Paula,' Paula says.

'Sam, hi,' Sam says lifting the hand again, 'She's Pea.'

'What Pea?' Lenski asks glaring at Sam.

'Paula is,' Sam says.

'No no it's fine,' Pea says quickly.

'What fine?' Lenski asks now glaring at both of them.

'She prefers being called Pea,' Sam says, ignoring the glare.

'I'm happy with Paula though,' Pea says, very aware of the glare.

'Pea?' Lenski asks, 'this your name?'

'Er...well,' Pea smiles, 'my name is Paula but...'

'What Pea then?'

'I think,' Lilly says diplomatically, 'This lady is called Paula but her nickname is Pea. Is that right?'

'Yes,' Pea says nodding rapidly at Lilly.

'Oh. I see this yes?' Lenski says with a curt nod, 'Pea.'

'Yes, Pea,' Pea says.

'Like the food or like the urine?'

'Er...' Pea freezes.

'Like the food,' Sam says, 'P E A...you know...The Jolly Green Giant?'

'...'

'The Jolly Green Giant,' Sam says at Lenski's blank look, 'you know...the adverts...HO HO HO GREEN GIANT,' Sam says affecting a low deep voice.

'I Polish,' Lenski says.

'Oh, don't you have the Jolly Green Giant?'

'It's fine, honestly,' Pea says blushing furiously, 'and the Jolly Green Giant was sweetcorn, Sam. Not peas.'

'I...' Lenski hesitates with a glance at Lilly rubbing her forehead and smiling politely.

'It was an advert for peas,' Lilly says.

'Peas,' Lenski says.

'Sweetcorn,' Pea says.

'Oh,' Lilly says, 'It's very nice to meet you both,' Lilly adds.

'Father Christmas do the ho ho ho,' Lenski says.

'So did The Jolly Green Giant,' Sam says.

'Honestly, it's fine,' Pea says, wishing the ground would open up from the protracted discussion on her nickname.

'Pea yes?' Lenski asks, looking at Pea who just nods and blushes again.

'I am sorry for doing that,' Lilly says, 'giving you the gun I mean…we didn't want them to see we had it?'

'Honestly, it's fine,' Pea says again.

'You have it?' Lenski asks.

'I gave it to Sam,' Pea says looking at Lenski then looking away from the intensity of the stare coming back.

'I've got it,' Sam says, 'Do you want it back?'

'Would you mind keeping it for a little while?' Lilly asks.

'Yeah sure,' Sam says.

'It's fine, honestly,' Pea says again.

'What's going on?' Sam asks, so direct and to the point it makes Pea wince.

'I mean you don't have to tell us though,' Pea adds quickly, 'it's fine, honestly.'

'Stop saying it's fine,' Sam says reaching a hand out to squeeze her friends. A gesture seen by Lilly who smiles warmly at Pea.

'Maddox wanted to disarm the children,' Lilly says, whispering carefully, 'but he passed out from being tazered and…well, Sierra appears to given them all their guns back.'

'Aren't you in charge of them?' Sam asks Lenski. 'Can't you just tell them to put them down?'

'I no say this,' Lenski replies. 'I not in charge like this way.'

'And now we've got armed children in here again,' Lilly says, 'but without Maddox's authority to tell them what to do.'

'How is Maddox?' Pea asks, 'is he okay?'

'He fine,' Lenski says instantly.

'Er,' Lilly pauses, choosing her words carefully. 'The doctors said his vital signs are good but...well they don't know really. He's had a back shock so...'

'He fine. He wake up soon.'

'But er, but just in case he doesn't wake up...' Lilly says.

'Maddox not die.'

'Oh god no, I never said that. I mean...no of course he won't but... well, just in case he doesn't wake up for a while...' Lilly says as both Pea and Sam nod in understanding.

'So what now then?' Sam asks, 'It's a right mess down there...is Mr Howie coming back?'

'I don't think so,' Lilly says, dropping her gaze.

'Sierra is alright though isn't she?' Sam asks.

'She see Darius shot.'

'Darius was her boyfriend,' Lilly says in explanation, 'and she didn't seem that fine a minute ago.'

'Shock,' Pea says, 'maybe you could talk to her. You know, like tell her she shouldn't be in charge right now?'

'This no work,' Lenski says.

Pea watches the two women. Lilly so young yet full of a natural authority and the way she speaks makes her seem so much older and mature and Lenski, stern faced with a coldness in her beauty and behind that mask Pea can see pain and deep worry in the Polish woman's eyes. 'You two look exhausted,' Pea says softly, 'it's still really early...you should rest.'

'We have much to do,' Lenski says.

'You both look knackered,' Sam says, agreeing with her friend, 'you two can rest here with us...we'll keep a watch for a bit.'

'We should get on,' Lilly says but her body responds to the suggestion of rest and she seems to sink further into the ground as her body relaxes with Billy's body curled round her. Too many problems. Too many things to do. The hole in the wall. The children need water and food. The mess in the fort needs cleaning up. The night has been pure hell and the day before was long and hot. The pressure building and never relenting. The heat sapping the strength from her body until it felt like she had nothing left to give. The frantic hours in the hospital and the bodies of the dead now stacked that need to be moved. She breathes out heavy and hot from the heat of her brother's body. Sweat on her forehead again.

'Let me take him,' Pea says softly, warmly, almost maternally. 'You rest now.'

'But...' Lilly flicks her eyes open, not realising they were closing.

'It's okay,' Pea says, seeing and sensing the worry in the girl. 'He's your brother I know...I have children. We both do.'

The tone makes Lilly wake enough to see the two women properly. Both of them are late thirties, maybe early forties. The maturity is there to be seen. The experience of lives lived and the sadness of loss so evident. There is safety here. Lilly knows this and smiles weak and tired.

'He is very hot,' she whispers, 'would you mind...I don't want him to wake up and me not be here though.'

'I'll stay right here,' Pea says, nodding earnestly. 'I promise you.'

It's too much. The kindness of the words, the soft brown eyes of the woman and the sadness of it all. She can't speak for the lump growing fat in her throat and the tears spill down her cheeks tracking clean marks in the grime.

Pea doesn't say anything. She doesn't have to. She smiles sad and warm and full of love all at the same time. As Sam gently lifts Milly from Lenski, so Pea shares the burden of a girl now crying silently. She takes the boy into her arms, leaning back and sensing the pure desolation of days of having to be tough and strong flow from Lilly who now feels so alone and lost.

'Come here,' Pea whispers to the girl. Holding back her own

tears she gently eases an arm round Lilly's shoulders who sinks into the hug. 'It'll be okay...everything will be okay.'

A mothers words. A mothers tone. A mothers hug and Lilly sinks into it, sobbing hard as the pain knots in her stomach. The arm squeezes, pulling her closer from a woman she doesn't know who now holds her brother in her arms. 'Shush,' Pea says soothingly, 'sleep now, it'll be okay...everything will be okay...just rest...'

CHAPTER SIX

'You's a builder then?'

She wakes with a start. Eyes batting open and instantly closing from the glaring sunshine.

'No, no I'm not'

'What bout you yeah? You's a builder?'

The heat is incredible with a crushing humidity. Pain in her head from lack of fluids. Her body aching from having slept on the hard ground leaning against a hard wall.

'One's of you's a builder, you get me? You's want food yeah? You's want water then's you gots to be a builder, you get me?'

She swallows. Her throat is dry and sore from the fumes of the fire inhaled. Cognitive function comes slowly and she clings to the image of Nick smiling at her in the dream.

'You done the DIY yeah? You's built shit, you's a bloke. You must have built shit before.'

'I'm a computer programmer.'

'You's look like a builder, you know how to build a wall?'

They were in the field but in the dream Billy was safe. Everyone was safe. It was just her and Nick walking hand in hand through the long grass. Nick was smiling at her. Telling her everything will be okay and how they have to do the right thing and he will come back but she didn't understand what he meant by that. Come back? From where? They were together so why would he come back?

'I'm really not. I'm sorry, I don't know the first thing about building a wall.'

'You's learn then yeah?'

Forcing her eyes open she looks across to one of the older youths standing at the edge of the group holding an assault rifle with two smaller children behind him.

'You's want food?' The older youth calls out in a rough rasping voice, 'you's lot want water you got's to fix the wall innit.'

'Is he okay?' Lilly asks the woman next to her still holding Billy.

'He's fine,' Pea replies but her expression doesn't relay the same message as the words, 'he woke up a little while ago saying he was thirsty but…'

'Haven't they brought any water up?' Lilly asks.

Pea shakes her head as Sam leans forward with Milly still in her arms, 'It's so hot,' Sam whispers with a grimace.

Lilly nods and reaches out to wake Lenski. A hand on the Polish woman's knee, a gentle shake and Lenski snaps awake. Her eyes open and staring at nothing. 'What? What happen?'

'Look,' Lilly whispers, pointing at the armed youths.

'Don't fink you's lot are listening,' the older boy says, unsure of himself and trying to mask his nerves with false bravado. 'We's got a hole in the wall and needs someone to fix it yeah, you getting me or what?'

A huff from Lenski and she clambers to her feet, 'Zayden, this enough. You no speak people this way.'

Zayden blanches at the sight of Lenski appearing at the far side of the group of people still hiding at the top of the wall. He didn't know she was there. Sierra just told him to find someone to fix the wall and get them working.

'Sierra said...'

'What has been done?' Lenski cuts him off threading through the crowd to peer down into the fort. 'It is same,' she snaps, glaring at Zayden, 'why no work done?'

'Been busy,' Zayden shrugs, 'Sierra said we's got to eat and drink yeah? Said we's tooled up now and in charge so's we got to guard everyone and stay alert so's we get food first.'

'We need water up here,' Lilly calls out, using the wall to pull herself up. 'It's hot. These people will be at risk of exposure and dehydration in this heat.'

'Hey, Lilly,' Zayden says, offering the pretty blond girl a big smile. 'You's can get some water yeah.'

'Thank you,' Lilly says, forcing herself to return the smile, 'but everyone needs water.'

'They's get water when they work, you get me?'

Lilly thinks quickly as she looks at Zayden. He's fourteen, maybe fifteen at the most. Big for his age too. Broad framed with pimples pushing through the first wispy hairs on his chin.

'Zayden,' Lilly makes herself smile broadly and hold her blue eyes on his dark brown and she notices the sudden self-conscious shuffle of his feet. 'I am sure we can get everything done and fixed up just the way Sierra wants but it's so hot,' she makes a point of wiping the sweat from her forehead. 'You can't expect people to work without water and food.' She walks round the group of women and children sitting in front of her as Sam reaches behind her own back to grip the butt of the pistol. A movement that makes Pea tense and hold Billy close.

'Tell you what,' Lilly says, still smiling just for him, just for Zayden, 'we'll get everyone some water and food then we can get everything cleaned up and fixed. Is that okay?' Womanly charms present for the first time in her young adult life. No. She did it once before with Nick in the field. *You can have me if you want.* Nick was different though. Nick wasn't Zayden now looking her up and down with his eyes pausing on the swell of her breasts.

'Sweet,' Zayden says, his voice lower, rougher, hungrier, 's'good wiv me, Lilly.'

'Thank you,' Lilly says, making her eyes squint a bit in what she hopes is a look of genuine flirting. A dull pounding in the back of her skull. Her mouth feels so dry but she follows Lenski to the edge to look down. 'Gosh,' she says clearly. 'There is a lot to do.' She turns back, locking eyes on Sam leaning slightly forward with her hand hidden behind her back. A gentle shake of the head and Sam brings her empty hand round with a single nod as Pea breathes out the tension.

'There is tap,' Lenski says, 'bottom of ramp. They use tap. Wash and drink.'

Lilly catches the way Zayden stiffens at being told what to do by Lenski. His eyes hardening as his chin inclines with a retort forming on his lips.

'Is it working though?' Lilly asks, blinking heavily as she looks at Zayden and the two other boys, drawing their attention back to her. 'I know some of them were broken last night, shall we go and check?' She asks, her eyes lingering on Zayden.

'Yeah alright,' Zayden switches instantly, his mouth forming a smile that shows chipped and broken teeth already stained brown from lack of brushing.

'We shall be right back,' Lilly says, making her voice loud enough for everyone to hear. 'I'll call up, Lenski and you can start sending them down. That's okay with you isn't it, Zayden?'

'S'good wiv me,' Zayden says, staring at Lilly's backside and turning to nod with a grin at the other two smirking boys.

She feels like shit. She feels the worst she has ever felt in her life with a thirst that borders on being dangerous but if she feels like this then so must everyone else, Billy included. She walks along the edge of the crowd with Zayden and only looks back when they reach the top of the vehicle ramp. Pea and Sam staring after her looking intensely worried and Lenski stood with her arms folded as the two boys glare and show that surly disdain.

'It is very warm today,' Lilly remarks as they descend the ramp.

'S'hot as fuck,' Zayden says.

Nick would have apologised for swearing. He would have blushed and said sorry with that shy smile. Instead she looks at Zayden smirking and staring into the fort to make sure the others can see him walking with Lilly.

They reach the bottom and the tap fitted to the wall. 'I do hope it works,' Lilly says, more to make conversation. 'I am so very thirsty,' she twists the spoked top and offers a silent prayer when the cold water rushes out, 'oh that is good,' she says, smiling at Zayden.

'Get some yeah?' Zayden says, ever the gentlemen as he nods at the tap, 'you's take as much as you want, Lilly.'

'Aw, you are sweet,' she says. She bends over realising the instant she does it that he can see down her top and she fights every instinct not to turn round. You do what you have to do. He even shifts position to get a better view. That smirk on his face as she glances up and no attempt to hide the direction of his eyes. She drinks. She is thirsty and water is water. The cold fluid fills her mouth, instantly easing the parched feel and soreness in her throat. Drink while you can. She sucks on the flow, pulling mouthfuls in to drink down into her empty stomach. The water runs off her chin, down her neck and glides towards her cleavage. She knows this. She can feel it and she hates it. She hates every second of being gawped at in this way.

'Gosh,' she stands up feeling genuine relief wash over her, 'that was very nice.'

'Yeah?' Zayden asks, mesmerised by the rivulets of water gliding down her golden skin.

'Lenski,' Lilly says softly, waving towards the top, 'Lenski? LENSKI?' She shouts but softly, womanly and watches as Zayden turns round.

'SEND 'EM DOWN YEAH,' Zayden booms, his voice cracking and breaking showing his real age and immaturity.

'I think that did it,' Lilly jokes, feeling her way on pure instinct. The first adults and children appear at the top. Coming slowly at first as though afraid but going faster as they see Lilly waiting and smiling at the bottom.

They start drinking. Gulping water down as adults get the children to the front to drink like slaves under the watchful eyes of an armed guard. Drinking thirstily to ease the headaches and fight the fatigue brought on by the sapping heat.

'Zayden,' Lilly calls his attention, not that she needed to as his eyes haven't left her for a second. 'There's another tap just down there, is it working?'

'I's check it,' he strolls off, the big man with the big gun and casually twists the spoked top. 'S'working, you's lot, get down there and drink yeah.'

More come down. They all come down. The lure of water too great and even the most terrified make the move.

'Hey,' Pea says as she and Sam come down with Lenski, the two armed boys following the last of the people down the slope. 'He's asking for you.'

'Thanks,' Lilly takes Billy into her arms and walks down to the second tap with the others. Zayden having walked off to boast at the two boys at seeing Lilly's breasts as she bent over to drink water.

The children drink first. Billy and Milly reviving themselves with long gulps under a flow that soaks their heads and hair. Pea and Sam stand side by side, watching the two kids as Lenski remains sullen with her arms folded.

'I check Maddox,' Lenski says, nodding at the tap to show she will drink then check on Maddox.

'Okay,' Lilly says quietly, 'Have you still got it?' She asks Sam.

'In the back of my jeans,' Sam says and casually turns round, 'Can you see it?'

'No it's fine,' Lilly says.

'This is shit,' Sam says, muttering under her breath.

'It is,' Lilly says.

'Lilly,' Pea says quietly, 'listen, this is a shit thing to say...but that boy can't take his eyes off you.'

'I know,' Lilly whispers, showing the sadness in her eyes.

'Use it but don't push it too far,' Pea says, checking the vicinity around them, 'just...just be careful.'

'I will.'

'We should stay together,' Sam says, looking at Pea and Lilly.

'We'll try,' Lilly says, 'I know these people a little bit but if I get separated...' Her eyes fill with fresh tears at the thought of her brother alone in the fort without her.

'Hey, we'll stay with him. I promise,' Pea says quickly, her hand reaching out to rub Lilly's arm.

'I'll shoot anyone that goes near him or Milly,' Sam says firmly, 'but on that note...how *do* you shoot it?' She asks with a quick grin.

'Thank you,' Lilly says to both of them with real feeling in her heart, 'There's a lever on the side, above the trigger. It shows a red dot when you push it forward. If you can see the red dot the safety is off, then you just point and shoot but the recoil is immense. Hold it with both hands.'

'Got it,' Sam says and looks at Pea, 'you'd better be careful now, Pea. I know how to shoot you.'

Humour. Weak and pathetic but something to cling to.

'I can still run faster than you,' Pea fires back with a wink at Lilly and a wince at the sadness in the girls eyes, 'hey, it'll be okay. Maddox will wake up or...or Mr Howie might come back.'

'They take many ammunition,' Lenski says, pushing her hands through her soaked hair, 'Mr Howie yes. He take many. Maddox he say no come back.'

Lilly's stomach tightens again. Another knot on top of the brick that sits in her gut.

'Rinse your head love,' Pea says to Lilly, 'You look flushed and hot, get some on the back of your neck, it'll cool you down.'

'What's your name?' Milly asks, wide awake and no longer thirsty.

'Pea,' Pea says, smiling down, 'And this is Sam.'

'HAHA! Pea...' Milly laughs, clapping her hands in delight, 'Do you like peas? I like peas. Mr Howie likes peas and Clarence likes peas. Billy, do you like peas?'

Lilly rinses her head and Pea was right. It takes the heat from her head and the icy river running down her neck sends pleasant shivers through her body. She rubs her hands over her face, sluicing the sweat and grime away.

With her eyes closed, Lilly stands up and reaches her hands to push through her hair, pulling the strands back ready to be fastened in the band held on her wrist. Her vest top rides up, showing inches of stomach.

'Christ love,' Sam moves in front of her, tugging the girls top down at seeing Zayden staring fixed at Lilly.

'That boy's not healthy,' Pea remarks, moving in front of Sam and Lilly to break the line of the sight from the sullen armed youth to Lilly. Zayden blinks and scowls. His face hardening. 'He's coming over,' Pea mutters.

Lilly's own resolve hardens. These people need food and shade. The fort is insecure and that means her brother is in danger. You do what you have to do. You protect your own.

'Hey,' Lilly steps round Sam and Pea to smile at Zayden, disarming his sulky countenance, 'that feels so much better. Right, what shall we do first? We need builders for the wall, right? Well,' Lilly says, moving closer to him, 'I was thinking we should get some of these people clearing this mess up,' she waves a hand at the broken burnt and ruined tents in the middle of the fort, 'And obviously the bodies need moving and while they're doing that I can try and find out who knows how to fix a wall. Did you find anyone when you were asking, Zayden?'

'Nah,' the boy says, mesmerised at the attention Lilly is paying to him, 'S'like...nah.'

'Oh well,' Lilly rolls her eyes, 'I'm sure we can find someone. Have we got some of our brave people guarding it now?'

'Yeah, like...Sierra got someone on it.'

'Great! You are very organised and that's good. Where is Sierra now?'

'In the pig office.'

'I'm sorry, the what?'

'The feds office, the pigs...'

'Oh the old police offices, got it, right yes, sorry, not down with the street talk. You'll have to teach me. Right, Pea, Sam. I shall go and see Sierra. Are you okay here getting some people organised to clear this mess away?'

'Sure,' Sam says, her head cocked to one side.

'Billy, you stay here with Pea and Sam, Milly, you too. I'll be right back.'

'Want me to ask about for someone to fix the wall?' Pea asks.

'That would be lovely, thank you,' Lilly says then looks at Zayden, 'if that's okay with you of course, Zayden.'

'Whatever, s'fine innit.'

'Zayden,' Lilly says, lowering her voice a notch as they walk round the edge of the mess, 'Is Sierra okay? I mean, she saw Darius killed right in front of her. That must be an awful shock for anyone. How is she coping?'

He shrugs, more interested in the smirks and nods from the other lads watching him with Lilly, 'She's good.'

'Do you think so? Poor girl, she must be devastated. We must do what we can to take the burden from her. What do you think?'

'Yeah, like...whatever.'

'But we mustn't be pushy,' Lilly says as though thinking out loud, 'No no, we must be decent and nice. Poor Sierra, I do hope she is okay.'

'Yeah,' Zayden nods, not giving a shit whether Sierra is okay or not, 'So's like, you got a boyfriend then or what?'

'Me?' Lilly asks, blinking at the unexpected question, 'Gosh well, I mean...' Think, Lilly. Think fast and tread carefully. 'No, no I do not.'

'What about that Nick then?' Zayden asks, 'Like, Mads said you's was kissing.'

'Oh that,' Lilly says, forcing a tight chuckle, 'Nick was just upset and I gave him a hug, that's all.'

'Ah yeah,' Zayden says hopefully, 'so's like, he's not your boyfriend then or sommit?'

'Nick? Gosh no.'

'S'good. I don't like him.'

'You don't? Why ever not?'

'He's a cunt.'

'Oh...oh right.'

'They's all cunts that lot. Sierra said they was. She said they's put everyone in danger and it was them that killed Darius and made Mads get tazered by that cunt Lani'

Forewarned is forearmed. Swallow the shock and be prepared.

'Yes, it has been an awfully confusing night, Poor Sierra.'

The police offices reek of tobacco smoke that hangs thick in the air. Choking Lilly as she walks in behind Zayden. The room full of youths leaning back on chairs, smoking with their feet up on desks. Like a classroom that's gone very wrong. Sierra, at the end in the central position staring blankly at nothing with an assault rifle across her legs. Lilly swallows, realising it's just girls in here. She recognises one of them as a girl called Skyla. The rest she doesn't know but she spots the scraped back hair and faces full of spite.

'What?' Sierra mutters, blinking slowly as she adjusts her gaze from staring at nothing to staring at Zayden.

'S'Lilly innit,' Zayden says.

'So?' Sierra asks, her eyes now unblinking.

Cans of soda, bags of crisps and chocolate bar wrappers adorn the table tops. Ashtrays overflowing. Dirty mugs left unwashed.

'What?' Zayden grunts, confused at the response.

'What's she want?' Sierra asks, refusing to look at Lilly but taking her in all the same. Blond haired, blue eyed, clean and healthy looking.

'Dunno,' Zayden says, shrugging.

'Why bring her here then?' Sierra demands, her voice quiet but full of malice.

'I'm sorry, Sierra,' Lilly speaks out politely, 'I asked to come and see you, please, it was my fault.'

The new number one continues to stare at Zayden. A show of power that she will look where she wants when she wants. The shock has hit hard. The sight of Darius's brains blowing out and his body slumping over. Maddox being tazered and everyone else made to kneel on the ground. Darius killed. Just like that. Dead. Shot. Never coming back.

'What?' She finally looks at Lilly, hating her, hating everyone, hating everything but too numb to action those emotions.

'I wanted to talk about how we should...'

'We?' Sierra cuts her off with an icy low voice, 'ain't no we.'

'Of course,' Lilly says, acquiescing instantly, 'I meant how we, the people out there, how we are to get cleaned up and fix the wall.'

Sierra goes blank, unfocussed, seeing only Darius's brains bursting from his head. She blinks back to the now and stares full of hate at Lilly. 'Just get it done.'

'Yes we will, we most definitely will. May I ask, is it okay to...'

'Don't give a fuck,' Sierra says, glaring at Lilly, 'just get it done, you get me yeah?'

'Of course.'

'You's speak like that all the time?' Skyla asks, adopting the new number one's cold expressionless manner.

'I do, yes,' Lilly says, sensing the tension rising.

'So's like, you go to private school yeah?'

'I did for a while but then I went to a normal...'

Skyla tuts, and rolls her eyes, 'Yeah whatever. Like don't go on about it,' she looks disdainfully away as the other girls snigger and glare. All apart from Sierra who's unfocussed gaze goes through Lilly to something unseen by anyone else.

'Get out,' Sierra whispers, not watching, not caring, not listening.

'Of course,' Lilly dips her head, almost in a bow to show she concedes the authority of the girl barely a year older than her. Out the door in a second and the room behind her cackles with teenage girls delighted at the posh girl being brought down a peg.

Outside and the humidity hits her as hard as the impact of the confrontation inside. The savagery of it. The brutal non-compliance to order or thought for others. Young people with no education seizing power without any concept of what that means and suddenly the future looks bleak. Maddox has only been down a few hours and may wake up. Mr Howie only left this morning or late last night. If it's this bad now what the hell will it be like in the days and weeks to come?

Thoughts whirl. Options that present to be considered and weighed with every variable given equal consideration.

Should she leave? Get Billy, maybe Pea and Sam and just get out. Take Milly and whoever else wants to go. Stay low and find somewhere close by to wait for Mr Howie to come back. She knows too well just how dangerous the world beyond these walls are and that's the question right there. The offset by comparison to the danger inside against the danger outside.

Sierra is in shock. That is obvious. Shock and grief goes through stages. Denial. Anger. Numbness. Let those emotions work their course, keep your head down and hope Sierra comes back to being a decent human being. Was she a decent human being before this? Lilly doesn't know the girl.

Holding that thought in her mind she then adds the next ingredient into the mix, that of the other girls in the room. Skyla and the others. They've obviously clustered around Sierra immediately on seeing Sierra as the new number one. They'll feed her power. They will sycophant over everything she says. They'll laugh when she jokes and test the boundaries with how far their own power extends. That just happened not a few seconds ago. Skyla was testing. She was seeing if Sierra would accept her passive insults to Lilly. Lenski's words come to mind, *number one, number two, number three*. Who will be the next number two? The power vacuum extends beyond Sierra. Every child carrying a gun will now be jockeying for position, and there's less of them now too. Over half were either killed or injured enough to take them out of the running. What does that mean? More competition? Less competition? Crew chiefs trying to exert control over their youths who are intent on becoming crew chiefs? How did these kids get this way? How did society fail them so much that as soon as the imposed law and order was taken away they evolved so quickly into being like this?

Lilly's awareness of the way Zayden watches her and responds is acute. If a boy was the new number one she might stand a much better chance at guiding him, manipulating him. That's what it is. Manipulation. Cold and disgusting but necessary. You do what it takes to protect your own.

She looks round as though assessing the damage and spots Liam keeping watch with a few other youths at the broken wall to the old armoury. At the back she sees another cluster hanging about the stores where the ammunition and weapons are kept. Another group down by the gate, milling about talking, drinking cans of coke, eating crisps and smoking cigarettes. There must be another group outside on the narrow shore. Liam has only four with him. Three at the back guarding the ammunition. Four inside the gate. Maybe four or five on the shore. Zayden and his two younger boys. A few more dotted about the fort. Sierra and four girls in the police offices. Thirty at the most. She glances over to the stacked corpses dumped outside the hospital. Most of the civilians were at the far side of the fort and only a few got hurt from the explosions. The youths were all close and too slow to duck, run or take cover. So many of them were killed or seriously wounded.

Thirty then. Thirty armed kids now running the fort all under the control of Sierra. The adult survivors outnumber them vastly. They could take back control. No, these children have automatic weapons. They'd slaughter the survivors without blinking then laugh about it after. Lilly has seen the rate of fire from automatic weapons, their power and the ease of pulling a trigger to take someone's life.

A new emotion joins the many already running through her heart as shock and guilt kick in. Shock that she's even contemplating a course of action that will result in further loss of life. The guilt she feels is misplaced and mistaken for the initial belief that she is merely trying to take control and power to have it for herself but her intelligence soon dismisses and works that one through. The control wouldn't be for her. It would be to protect Billy and the other children.

Thirty.

Zayden slips quietly next to her. His own face morphing as he tries to work out what just happened. He fancies Lilly but Skyla and the other girls were rude to her and he wanted to say something in the room and defend Lilly but he didn't know what to say, and anyway, Sierra scares him. He wants to say something now, an observation on the behaviour and manner of his friends so she'll think he's nice but he lacks the education, emotional maturity and intelligence to translate those thoughts into words and it quickly becomes too confusing and too difficult. Instead he looks at Lilly. Uncaring and unbothered to the fact that she can feel the intensity of his gaze. The way he looks at her skin that is so smooth and unmarked, which is so different to the other girls he knows who have acne, pock-marks and scars. Her blue eyes too. Some of the other girls have blue eyes but Lilly's are different. They're expressive but Zayden doesn't know what expressive means, just that Lilly looks different.

His eyes drop to her chest. Lingering again on the swell of her breasts, the narrowness of her waist, the gentle curve of her arse.

Sixteen years old and his prick stiffens in response to the view his eyes take in.

'Got a room,' he grunts.

'Pardon?' Lilly flinches, absorbed in her own thoughts.

'I got's my own room now, you get me.'

She pauses, hiding her revulsion at the lust in his face, 'I see, well...I am sure you will be glad of the privacy after...'

'Wanna see it?'

'Your room? Well yes of course I do but you know, I'm looking at this terrible mess right now, Zayden and thinking where the best place to start is. May I ask? How do we dispose of the bodies of the dead children? I mean, some of them must be your friends? Is that right?'

A mean but necessary manipulation to deflect his attention but it works and his expression transforms as he flicks his eyes over to the corpses nearby.

'Yeah,' he twitches, again unable to voice his feelings, 's'fucked up.'

'Then we should prioritise the disposal of the deceased. Do you think so?'

He doesn't know what prioritise means but he thinks she means they should get rid of his dead mates first. He nods, trying to look like he understands.

'This must be very sad for you,' she says softly, showing pity on the outside while feeling something else altogether on the inside. A hardening. A revulsion for all that he is. A wish to be away from him and his kind. A desire to repel him and get him as far away as possible. She saw the bulge in his trousers when he turned to look at the bodies and knows exactly what he is thinking. The reaction is so strong and for that briefest of seconds she wishes she had the skills of Dave or Mr Howie. She's not the only young woman in the fort. There are plenty of teenage girls hiding down amongst the survivors. Girls in their early twenties too. Full breasted women that will soon get the eyes of the boys carrying guns and the cackling of the girls in the police office.

The Lord of the Flies and the primeval desire for power with youths driven by chemicals pumping through their immature bodies forcing them to grow into men and women. Testosterone. Oestrogen. Raging hormones that swing moods from buoyant and wild abandon to downright evil with an utter disregard for the needs of anyone else. Too immature to grasp the concept of having half their own group killed but mature enough to have erections and sexual desires.

'We must stay busy,' Lilly mutters, voicing her thoughts. 'I mean, we should make a start and...and...'

'See my room later then yeah?' Zayden asks, giving warning of a dogged determination.

'I er...I think...er yes, yes that would be lovely.'

Nick. You have to come back. You must come back. Please, come back.

CHAPTER SEVEN

'Look at him,' Sam mutters, stepping closer to Pea, 'He's like a dog on heat. How old is she?'

'Fifteen,' Pea says.

'Where do you want us?' A woman asks making both of them turn round.

'Hi,' Pea says, 'you've had a drink?'

The woman nods as she casts a worried look to the two armed boys standing nearby, 'Any food?' She asks, dropping her voice for fear of being heard. 'My lot are starving.'

Sam looks past the woman to her group standing a few feet back. Young children clinging to grandparents already frail and weak but doing their best to show resilience and a stiff upper lip.

'Not yet,' Sam says sadly.

'Okay,' the woman says dully, 'Where do you want us? Someone said you're organising the work parties?'

'Er yes,' Pea says, exchanging a glance with Sam, 'you've got young children?'

'Three.'

'Can you start with the tents please?' Pea asks. 'We've got bodies to clear but...'

'But we'll ask people that don't have children,' Sam finishes her sentence, sensing Pea struggling to say the words.

'Children?' The woman asks, showing confusion.

'The bodies,' Sam says. 'They're mostly kids.'

'All kids,' Pea adds, dropping her gaze.

'Oh,' the woman sighs heavy and long, 'tents then,' she says with an air of resignation, 'where are we putting them?'

'Gates?' Sam asks, nudging Pea.

'I think so, get them stacked ready to take away.'

The woman moves off with her head bowed and heavy legs that trudge back to her group. Everyone is the same. Heads down. Eyes averted. Conversations muted and whispered.

'She needs to be careful,' Sam says.

'Careful?' Pea asks, staring after the woman, 'Why? What's she done?'

'Not her brainache,' Sam says with a tut knowing Pea won't take offence, 'Lilly.'

'Oh, that boy.'

'Yes that boy and he's not a boy. He's a walking erection with a gun.'

Pea can't help but snort a dry laugh and glance that quizzical look that Sam knows so well.

'Well,' Sam says pointedly, 'He bloody is. Trust me, I've got boys...I know what they're bloody like.' Her own words reach her ears as they come out. The reminder of her family, of her sons and husband. Of the life she had before this.

'Sam,' Pea says, whispering the word sadly.

'Forget it,' Sam says darkly, 'We need to keep an eye on her,' she drops her voice as Lilly approaches with the walking erection at her side.

'Hey,' Pea says, forcing a bright tone, 'Everything okay?'

'Fine,' Lilly says, mimicking the same bright *everything is fine* tone but her eyes translate the message, *everything is not fine. Everything just got more shit.*

'Great,' Pea smiles at Lilly then at Zayden. 'We've got a few work parties moving the tents.'

'I can see,' Lilly says, stopping to look round, 'Lenski back yet?'

'Not seen her,' Sam says, making herself not glare at Zayden and fighting the urge not to twist his ear from his head for staring at women's boobs that way. If ever a boy needed a spanking.

'But er,' Pea hesitates, 'the bodies...nearly everyone here has children and we were trying to find someone who doesn't have kids...you know...'

'Yes, yes of course,' Lilly replies heavily wishing Zayden would bugger off for a few minutes. Pea is right. It's unfair to ask people with children to shift the dead bodies of other children. 'I'll do it,' Lilly adds.

'No you won't,' Sam says.

'Miss?'

They look round to an old man waiting patiently with his quavering hand shielding the glare of the sun from his eyes. 'The deceased?'

'Deceased?' Sam asks.

'Over yonder, deceased children. You need 'em moved?'

'Er well yes, yes we do,' Lilly says, 'but...' she takes in his wispy grey hair and thin mottled skin. His hands so aged and gnarled. 'I'm sure we can...'

'I'll be doing that then,' the old man says, 'deceased don't bother me none, Miss. Undertaker for forty years before I retired. Mind that was a few years back now but the dead don't change now do they.'

'Undertaker?' Pea asks, offering a rare silent prayer of thanks for this glimmer of goodness in a world of pain and hurt.

'Aye, was,' the old man replies. 'Where's you resting them? They being dressed or anything?'

'May I ask what dressed means?' Lilly asks.

'Prepare for burial or cremation my love,' the old man explains, 'you know, according to the wishes of the next o'kin or…well, whoever knew 'em really.'

'I think,' Lilly says, 'that we are er…disposing of the deceased at sea? Zayden? Is that correct?'

'Huh?'

'The deceased? Are we disposing of them at sea?'

'The what?' Zayden asks.

'Your dead friends,' Sam snaps.

Zayden eyes harden instantly. His frame stiffening automatically at the perception of an older person trying to exert authority on him. 'Fuckin' speak to me like that.'

'It's hot,' Lilly blurts, moving in front of Zayden, 'it's so hot and we're hungry…it makes people get a bit snappy…Sam didn't mean anything.'

'She didn't,' Pea adds quickly, 'Sam? It's just the heat isn't it?'

Zayden glares. His nostrils flaring and his eyes locked on Sam who for an instant glares back with the pressure of the pistol digging into her back. Common sense kicks in. The instinct for survival and she lowers her eyes, 'yeah it's hot. Sorry.'

'Eh?' Zayden says, still glaring past Lilly.

'I said sorry,' Sam says, keeping her head bowed.

'Zayden, are we putting the dead bodies into the sea?' Lilly asks, smiling at his brown eyes and ignoring the white headed zit poking between two thin strands of hair on his chin.

'Whatever' Zayden reverts to sulky non-compliance.

'I think that's best. I'm sure it's what Maddox will tell us to do once he has recovered,' Lilly says, 'and we don't want to go against Maddox's wishes do we?'

'God no,' Pea says, getting the subliminal message that might as well have been hailed through a megaphone with a plane dragging a message behind while fireworks went off.

Zayden just shrugs. The subtlety missing its mark.

'I'll be getting on with it then,' the old man says, 'but if you putting 'em in the sea you'll need to weigh 'em down so they don't float up. Don't need much for that. Some string and some rocks will do it,' he shuffles round to view the debris scattered across the fort, 'plenty of material here for that. Tell you what. I'll get 'em out onto that shore first. Out of sight is out of mind. The living don't like to see the dead you see. Upsets 'em it does.'

'You'll need help,' Lilly says as he starts walking off.

'Ah never mind that. I got a bit of strength left in me yet.'

'Ask for Hannah and Amy in the hospital rooms.'

'Okay, Miss. Hannah and Amy it is.'

'Zay, it's Skyla. You getting' me?'

'Yeah, what's up?' Zayden answers his radio feeling important and making sure Lilly can see him.

'Sierra said you's got to get that fuckin wall fixed yeah? Said them's bitches should be doing that first.'

Zayden nods, not realising a nod into a radio can't be heard or seen. Sam and Pea look at Lilly who makes sure her face betrays no emotion.

'Zay, you dumb cunt, you get me or what?'

'Yeah,' Zayden answers sulkily.

'We's need more drinks in here too.'

'Get 'em then.'

'We's planning. We thinkin' and plannin' and shit. Sierra said get some fuckin' drinks yeah.'

'Whatever,' Zayden sucks his teeth, a sound like a long tut.

'Perhaps we can go and assess the wall ourselves?' Lilly says to Sam and Pea. 'See what the damage is?'

'Sounds good,' Pea says.

'You's two,' Zayden barks at his subordinates, 'get some drinks in the pig office, you get me?'

'Why's can't they get them?'

'Cos they planning and shit, you's get 'em.'

'Yeah whatever,' the first boy replies, sucking his teeth. They lope off, clutching assault rifles and glaring at anyone foolish enough to be in their way.

'Sorted,' Zayden says, feeling pleased with his ability to delegate in this new forward facing role of customer service and delivery. 'Wall then yeah? I's come with you yeah.'

They head off through the slow activity of hungry, hot, exhausted and emotionally drained people shifting through the squelchy black mess. Every pile of slag disturbed sends a waft of new stenches into the air. Fibres that lift on the thermals with ash and choking dust. Hands get covered in grime and filth and a woman cries out on finding a burnt corpse lying hidden in the debris.

'Like the holocaust,' Pea mutters, not realising her thoughts are being given a voice.

'It is,' Lilly takes the observation instantly. The old footage of the war and Jews being forced to work in shit under order of death. The people here aren't starving yet, or emaciated, but they have that same stunned appearance. The spark of life vanishing quickly. Youths dressed in dark clothes that are only too quickly gaining a sense of superiority.

Boulders, rocks and bricks lie thicker on the ground the closer they get to the scene of the explosion. The inner wall of the old armoury blown out far and wide.

'These poor children,' Lilly says in conversation to Sam and Pea, 'I think an awful lot of them were injured or killed last night.'

'Yeah?' Sam asks as Pea tuts sadly.

'I think they're down to about thirty now,' Lilly says, letting the words hang in the air.

Pea stares ahead, her heart beating faster. Surely Zayden would have picked up on that message but he looks blank and only interested in Lilly.

Sam stares round. To the few at the back by the new armoury, then down to the gate and back ahead to the youths standing about by the broken wall who are meant to be keeping watch. Thirty? So few.

'Zay,' Liam tilts his head back trying to adopt a soldier's stance of legs planted wide and his gun held across the crook of his arms. Sam bites her tongue and the motherly instinct to tell him to stand properly and to go and have a wash and brush his teeth.

'Liam, what's up?'

'Nuffin', you?'

'Nuffin'. What's you doing?'

'On watch innit.'

'You's watching out here?'

'Yeah stinks as fuck in there.'

'Yeah,' Zayden snorts, too stupid to think of what to say.

'May we go inside?' Lilly asks, taking care to look equally at Zayden and Liam.

'You's asked Sierra?' Liam asks, showing a greater intelligence than Zayden within the first few seconds.

'Yeah, she said we's got to fix it,' Zayden replies.

'How's you gonna fix it then?' Liam asks, 'it's a big hole. If they come now we're fucked. Are you three gonna fix it?'

'Oh gosh no,' Lilly smiles at him, 'we are going to assess the damage and work out the best method to get the room secured using the available materials. Once we have established the extent of the damage we can try and identify the people with the best skills to...'

Liam's eyes glance at Zayden who stares mesmerised at Lilly. Lilly is fit as fuck. Zayden is spotty as fuck. No way will she let him shag her. No fucking way.

'...If that's okay with you, of course,' Lilly asks.

'Whatever yeah,' Liam says, smiling at Lilly.

Zayden scowls and casts a dark look at Liam. Liam has shagged two or three girls already and once got his hand up Skyla's top so he knows he'll try and score with Lilly. He looks at Lilly smiling at Liam then back to Liam with a pulse of jealousy pricking his insides.

'I got's my own room,' Zayden tells Liam.

'So have I,' Liam replies with a cheeky grin.

'Yeah? Where?'

'Where's yours?' Liam asks.

'Dunno yet, Skyla said I'll get one though.'

'Me too,' Liam says with a smirk. 'Lilly, you getting a room then?'

'Me?' Lilly asks.

'Yeah, you must be like a crew chief now,' Liam says, flashing the smile that helped him get his hand up Skyla's top when she was pissed and for the simple pleasure of winding Zayden up.

Zayden glowers. Sensing Liam using his magical charm. 'I'm working with Lilly now, bruv.'

'Yeah?' Liam asks.

'Yeah.'

Liam squints and leans forward to stare at Zayden, 'Bruv, you's got a massive whitehead on your chin.'

'Fuck off,' Zayden growls, glowing crimson with a surge of temper at the smirk on Liam's face.

'May we go inside?' Lilly asks.

'Yeah,' Zayden grunts.

'Carry on,' Liam says, smiling politely.

Lilly leads the way. Stepping over the fallen masonry and into the main room where she kissed Nick. Blackened piles on the ground where the table and chairs were. Everything flammable reduced to ash and chunks of burnt material.

The epicentre of the blast and the damage in here is significant. Deep holes gouged in the concrete walls from rounds ricocheting. Blast marks from the grenades. The inner wall smashed down with only the corners and far edges remaining in place.

It stinks of smoke, wet ash, chemicals and burnt human remains. Like a foul stench of rancid pork.

'You gonna try and fuck her then?' Liam's words float into the room, snapping Pea's and Sam's heads round.

'Maybe,' Zayden is sulky with an aggressive edge to his voice.

'Fit, bruv,' Liam announces, thinking his voice quiet and muted but knowing full well the women can hear him. 'You fancy her?'

'Dunno,' Zayden mumbles.

Sam glares at the door. Her mouth pursed. Pea grimaces with a wince showing as she reaches out to touch Lilly on the arm, 'hey, ignore it.'

Lilly nods. A small motion but her heart beats harder. Hearing herself as the topic of conversation in such a way makes the brick in her stomach twist round and drop further.

'Yeah,' Liam gloats, 'might have a go on her, you get me?'

'Whatever,' Zayden's voice, sulkier, harder.

'You's don't mind yeah? We's bro's yeah? We share, you get me?' He asks, goading Zayden with a malicious grin that goes unseen.

'Said whatever.'

'You go first if you want...or we can spit roast her...'

'Sam,' Pea shoots her hand out, grasping her friend by the wrist, 'stop it...Sam!'

Lilly blinks and moves purposefully away to distance herself from the voices of the young men. She goes through the ruined doorway into the next room with the broken outer wall and stares through the gap to the blue sea outside. The humidity is crushing. Intense. The filth is worse. The stench. Her eyes fill with tears but she blinks them away, clenching her jaw and making fists at her sides while Pea hisses at Sam and drags her into the room with Lilly.

'This is shit,' Sam growls, her voice low but ready to climb up, 'I mean fucking shit. How dare they...'

'I know I know,' Pea says quickly, quietly, trying to calm her friend, 'they've got guns, Sam. Machine guns. There are children here...'

'I've got a bloody gun too.'

'Sam, no. They're boys boasting, that's all,' Pea says, knowing they are not just boys boasting.

'Lilly,' Sam reaches out to grasp the girl and pull her in close, 'you've got to take the gun...'

'No, gosh no,' Lilly says, 'If they see it...'

'They won't. Just take it...'

'He keeps staring at my bum,' Lilly whispers, 'He'll see it.' So wide eyed and innocent Sam and Pea could either cry or laugh but crying isn't an option.

'Come here,' Sam sighs, pulling Lilly into a hug, 'you have to stay close to us, okay?'

'You must,' Pea whispers, 'at all times.'

'I'll try.'

'You'll do more than try, young lady,' Pea whispers firmly, thinking of her own daughter.

That mothers tone hits hard. The brick gets heavier. Harder. Twisting more, 'I'll be fine. I will...gosh it's hot today.'

Pea goes to tell her not to change the subject but stops herself. These are hard times. Dangerous times and Lilly is switched on. Instead she turns away, full of the sadness of everything and feeling that sadness only increase at the sight of the body. 'Oh Christ,' she groans.

'What?' Sam asks, looking in the same direction. She closes her eyes at the sight. Hardening her resolve.

'Oh dear,' Lilly sighs a long breath. Lani dead. Lani still clutching a blackened knife with her guts strewn out now half cooked. The once beautiful silky black hair all gone. The skin blistered deep red. The skull showing in places. They take in the utter viciousness of the final act and as one they slowly look up to the wall above the corpse.

'He is coming,' Sam reads the words in a low whisper.

If anything, the sight of the body and the words serve to harden Lilly. The reminder of Nick and Mr Howie. Of everything those people have done and everything they have been through. There is a bigger game going on here. Something bigger than all of them. Nick said they'd killed tens of thousands, maybe hundreds of thousands. He'd said they'd fought every day and every day the infection sent more against them and every day the infection lost.

A surge of guilt at feeling self-pity when Nick didn't say goodbye and the realisation that he is part of something so much bigger than any of this. His life is in danger every second of every day. He fights to keep his group alive so they can defeat these things and give everyone else a chance to live. What did Lenski say Maddox had told them? *Be seen somewhere else.* That was it.

They went out knowing the infection is hunting them. They went to draw it away. Almost sacrificial in mission and intent.

Suddenly the bragging sulky tones of two teenage boys seem insignificant and trite. What Nick is doing is big and important.

'Who is coming?' Pea asks.

Lilly doesn't reply but smiles at the memory and the complete lack of fear Mr Howie had. *I see you. I see you too.* The sight of him and Meredith stalking at Lani who was turned and armed. Whoever is coming will lose. They will be beaten by men and women who hold strong and show no fear. What they have, that *thing*, that bond and motivation that keeps them together and keeps them moving touched her too. She wasn't with them long but it was enough for her heightened senses to grasp the goodness of the understanding. *None of this is worth it if we don't do the right thing.*

A new energy settles inside her. A forged resilience. If Nick and his small group can face such odds and persevere then so can she. There *will* be a fort for them to come back to. There has to be.

'How do we fix it,' Lilly switches her gaze to the outer wall.

'No bloody idea,' Sam says, shaking her head.

'Bricks and mortar I guess,' Pea says as Sam turns to look at her, 'What? I saw it on Grand Designs or something. Don't look at me like that, Sam.'

'Never said a word.'

'You don't have to say a bloody word,' Pea says, 'it's bricks and mortar.'

'Yep but we don't have any bloody bricks...' Sam stops as Pea lifts an eyebrow, 'yes okay, we do have bricks but we don't have mortar...what is mortar anyway?'

'Cement I guess,' Pea says, 'you make it from er...from sand, er...water...and, bugger, probably cement powder. There's enough men here to know. One of them will know.'

'We've asked,' Sam says.

'No,' Pea replies, 'that zitty little walking erection asked, *we* haven't asked...we're women, we'll ask.'

'That's so anti-feminist,' Sam tuts then grins, 'but I like it.'

'Zitty little walking erection?' Lilly asks, tilting her head to the side in contemplation. 'That is perhaps, the best description of someone I have ever heard.'

'Oh that's mild,' Pea says, 'wait till Sam gets angry, then you'll hear some descriptions.'

'Really?' Lilly asks.

Sam just nods and stares at the wall, 'twatty fuck face twat magee is one of my personal favourites.'

Lilly smiles in response. She hardly knows these two women and yet that magnification of time once more plays with the concept of perspective. Up until a few hours she'd maybe shared one word with them. Possibly not even that. She had seen them in the fort but now they stand either side of her, maternal, protective and full of common sense.

'Come on,' Pea nudges the young girl, 'let's go find a builder eh?'

'We need to move Lani,' Lilly says, looking once again at the remains of the Thai girl.

'To the shore with the others?' Pea asks, after a pained silence.

The idea of Lani being stacked with the other corpses doesn't feel right, but then nothing feels right now. 'I think so,' Lilly says. Dead is dead. It's not the body that counts but the memory and the essence of them that you hold in your heart. The essence of her father and mother. Her friends, family and everyone else.

Lilly moves to the corpse and drops down, fighting the urge to gag. She's seen violent death more times than anyone should see such things, but it's the smell. The sheer ripe stench of the foul half cooked rancid meat. Flesh that has been heated and left to rot in a room full of water that steamed to evaporate and the high humidity has worked to advance the rate of decomposition far faster than it normally would.

It must be done though. Lani has to be moved. Not Lani. Lani isn't here now. This is just a body of organic matter. That's all it is. A collection of molecules held in a certain order and no different to any other organic matter.

With one smooth motion she reaches down, grips Lani's ankles and stands up as the seared flesh tears from having adhered to the concrete ground. She grips harder, forcing the body to peel away. The skin under her fingers sinks in and rips open. Soft fat oozes out to slide thick across the backs of her hands and drip onto the ground.

The disturbance releases gases that expunge noisily and bodily fluids leak, seep and drip from orifices but still Lani remains stuck to the ground.

'Fuck,' Sam grunts and moves to Lilly's side to reach down and take a wrist. That too tears under her grip. The flesh parting like soft fruit. Pea comes next, grabbing the other wrist and together they pull back as the body sucks gloopily up from the ground.

The protected flesh on Lani's underside remains less cooked, less crispy and it rips open leaving chunks stuck on the floor. Liquid drips out. The smell of cooked shit fills the room. Lilly gags first, hacking as she turns her head to one side. Sam follows suit. Yacking and gulping air in short hard breaths.

'This was a fucking stupid thing to do,' Sam gasps, turning her head to the side and immediately regretting talking as that means she now has to breathe back in.

'We're...we're here now,' Pea's eyes water with tears that stream from the stench, the noises and the sight of the body falling apart with every foot they move it.

They drag the corpse across the ground and through the door into the main room. A wet slick left behind in their wake with Lani's skull bouncing dully on the ground.

Sam pukes first. A dry heave and the water she only ingested a short time ago comes thundering out. She manages to twist her head enough for the spray to mostly miss Lani.

'Oh no,' Pea groans. One action invokes another and at the sight of Sam puking Pea feels her own stomach heave and contract. With a gargled yell she vomits down at her own feet adding the fine aroma of hot sick to a rotten corpse of burnt flesh leaking shit, piss and blood.

'Fuck,' Liam dances back from the door with a look of revulsion twisting his features at the sight of the three women dragging the ruined corpse out. Sam pukes again. Retching but refusing to release the body knowing she wouldn't summon the courage to touch it again.

Zayden just stares. Too stupid to move and he notices the off-white fat oozing between their fingers and the gooey trail smeared behind that brings the smell to his nose.

'Urgh,' he gags first then pukes hard with half-digested Doritos spewing out with bits of popcorn floating in a marinade of 7up.

Liam is made of tougher stuff though and refuses to vomit. His eyes water. His face contorts. A vein in his neck stands out, throbbing at the denial of the natural reflex. Instead he forces a casual look at the mutilated cadaver and sucks his teeth, showing perfect disdain that just makes Zayden hate him that little bit more.

'No sweetcorn,' Pea grunts.

'Eh?' Sam grunts back.

'Sweetcorn,' Pea yacks, and widens her eyes, 'no...no sweetcorn in the puke...always sweetcorn in puke...'

'...Even, oh shit,' Sam turns her head up in an effort to draw clean air, '...even when you haven't eaten sweetcorn...s'always sweetcorn.'

'Wasn't though,' Pea gurgles, 'or carrots.'

'Didn't see any,' Lilly mutters trying with all her might to breathe in through her mouth but that just means the stench is converted to flavour that coats her taste buds. 'I'm...' She fails in the warning and heaves to vomit on the patch of ground next to her.

'God!' Pea heaves with puke streaming from her mouth and nose.

'Pea!' Sam chastises her friend but like a yawn the action is seen and copied, 'urgh,' she yacks to the side, spittle and drool hanging from her chin.

'Argh,' Zayden heaves again, puking hard with projectile vomit splattering the ground. His hormone addled mind too dumb to realise he's walking in Lani's slipstream with every ripe smell going straight up his nose.

Like an orchestral movement the action sets them off, one in turn of the other. Zayden's greater stomach contents triggering Pea who triggers Sam who triggers Lilly. Mouths stretching. Stomachs contracting. Drool, spit and bile sliding down chins to dangle and sway on strands that coat bare arms.

They walk fast, praying the body doesn't disintegrate and fall apart. Seconds go by. None of them puke. Hope builds with the front gate now firmly in sight. Hands sliding over the limbs grip harder as the flesh slides from the bone but Sam can't hold it in. The back of her throat pulls down. Her mouth fills with saliva and her stomach heaves with a mighty contraction. She bends double, entirely given over to the urge of her body demanding she expel the noxious gases coming into her mouth and nose.

Pea follows suit. Once again triggered by Sam. She heaves, turning her head to yack and a split second later Lilly takes her turn. All three women yacking, heaving, retching but refusing to drop the body.

'Think...' Lilly gasps between heaves, 'think he...oh gosh...think he urgh,' she heaves and draws quick shallow breaths, 'think he fancies me now?'

Sam blinks through misted eyes to the sight of Lilly's bright red face and her chin covered in stands of puke. She snorts a laugh that blows a snot bubble from her nose that sets Pea off. The snot bubble bursts. Pea laughs harder. Her cheeks wet from tears. Lilly starts giggling with an action as involuntary as the vomiting. The sheer barbarity of it. The degradation of her mind at handling the ruined corpse of someone she actually knew. Zayden still heaving and still too dumb to move away.

Near hysteria grips with all three desperately avoiding looking at each other for each time they do so they snort and laugh harder. Guffawing braying that hurts their stomachs as the tension finds a way out.

'Stop it,' Pea pushes the words out with a cackle of laughter that just makes the other two laugh harder but that tension nears breaking point with real sobs starting to sound between the laughs. Genuine noises of abject grief in response to the staggering heat built so high and trapped within the high walls. Pure misery created by man, made by man and continued by children armed with assault rifles.

Trapped in the micro-bubble and they don't notice the skies darken. They don't take in the clouds rushing overhead that hang so heavy and low.

As Howie and Marcy run hand in hand through the fields in a village so far away, so the first drop of rain falls to land heavy on Lani's burnt face and it rolls like a tear released from her cindered eye. Another falls. Another and more follows with a pattering that draws the attention of the others working to clear the mess and the old man who stops to ease the ache in his bent back from shifting bodies after a decade of retirement.

The skies open. A literal thing of almost prophetic scale and suddenly the air distorts with a haze of grey from sheet rain hammering down.

The three stop. They stop and turn their faces to the heavens and let the corpse slide from wet fingers and they don't hear the slump as the body comes to rest for such is the incessant drumming now filling their ears.

Blessed relief is given instantly and they stand with mouths held open as the purest of rain cleans the sick from their chins. The dust, fibres and chemicals hanging in the air are pushed back down by seemingly infinite tiny droplets of water that combine to form an army that gives grace back to the air they inhale.

It comes harder. Drumming with the beats of a marching band. Rain that builds with intensity. Sheet rain. Driving rain. A solid wall of water that seems to hang in the air. Every soul in the fort stops and looks up. Old men and women blink and let the water slide between their thin lips. Men and women just stand to feel something other than misery. Children stare in wonder for never before has such a thing been seen or felt. Rain but more of it than any of them thought possible.

Every other sound is blotted out. Every other sense dulled until each person becomes the centre of their own universe. Held in stasis in a river coming from the sky.

Lilly exhales slowly with a long release of air that escapes from her now clean lips and she lets the water pour over her. Not a thought given to anyone else. Not a flicker of memory of anything other than being right here.

Yet the rain comes harder with an intensity that seems angry. Like someone up there is offended by the mess made by the mortals scrabbling about amidst the blood and shit.

Still she remains static, rock-like and unmoving. So they all do. Every inch of skin is cleansed. Mouths held open to drink and gulp with the delight of innocence at something so wonderful given so freely.

Pea's frizzy hair becomes slick against her scalp and neck. Her eyes closed and she, like Lilly, feels nothing other than the splendour of this second.

Sam is the same. Lost in the moment. Drawn to another place in reality but harder it comes. The rain lashing down with a sensation close to stinging exposed skin.

Lilly reaches up with a slow lazy motion to push her hands through her hair. Feeling the filth wash away and as the pelting rain comes harder so she starts to think. She lowers her head. Looking round to see Zayden doing the same as everyone else and staring up with his eyes closed. She turns, slow and casual. Liam the same and every armed youth within sight copying everyone else.

She can't see the back of the fort for the greyness of the squall blots her view. She can't see the far side either for the same reason and if she can't see them, they can't see her. Go. Move now. Don't hesitate like you did before. Take the gun from Sam. Ram the point into Zayden's mouth. Take his rifle. Give the pistol to Sam or Pea. Disarm Liam and move like a demon. Move like Nick would move.

She grunts. Hardened and ready as the explosive retort of a single shot fired from an assault rifle robs that urgency and she turns to see Sierra striding from the police office with her girls ranged out behind her. Sierra fires again. Pointing the rifle into the sky and it recoils with the single pull of the trigger, thudding into her shoulder.

'YOU'S WORK,' she screams with a ferocious animation pulsing through her that belies the inert girl that stared slack at the wall only a moment ago. A third shot and someone screams as the world comes back to the harsh reality of the now.

'WORK,' Sierra screams. She aims for Lilly with unseeing eyes and slams the girl aside. 'WORK,' a hand lashes out slapping Pea hard in the face. Lilly is hit again. Skyla shouldering through her with a snarling scowl of scraped back hair and a mouth chewing a piece of gum.

'Work, posh bitch.'

Through the rain Lilly sees Sierra heading malevolent and furious towards the vehicle ramp and the direction of the children. Lilly goes to move after her, her mind filled with images of her brother but Skyla looms snarling with the butt of the rifle slamming out into her stomach, making her bend double with an explosion of pain. A second blow to the back of her head sends her crumpling to the ground.

'Ain't so posh now, bitch...you's down in the mud like...'

'Skyla...'

'What?' Skyla shouts at being interrupted by Zayden.

'Leave her yeah,' Zayden says petulantly.

Pea rushes towards Lilly only to get hit from behind by another girl ramming the butt of her rifle into the bottom of Pea's spine. A yell and she slumps down beside Lilly in the deep puddles already formed from a ground too hard to soak the water.

Another scream and Sam goes down twisting as she falls to lands on her back to protect the sight of the pistol.

Lilly sucks air. Forcing her stomach to relax and let the pain ease away. Through the noise of the rain she hears angry shouts coming from the direction of the vehicle ramp. Terrified screams of pain as more brutal hits are given out. She looks up to see Skyla glaring at Zayden then back down at Lilly as her scowl slowly morphs into a smirk. Her eyebrows twitch and the corners of her mouth flick up in delight at reading Zayden so easily.

'You's fancy her,' Skyla makes the connections and bursts out laughing. A soft almost gentle noise that would be sweet at any other time, 'you's hear that?' Skyla calls to the other girl that hit Pea, 'Zay wants to fuck the posh bitch!'

'No...no that ain't it,' Zayden flusters angrily, his face flushing a deep red that sends Skyla cackling louder.

'Zay, you dumb cunt,' Skyla shakes her head at him, a young girl trying to appear full of wisdom and maturity, 'She ain't ever gonna let you shag her...'

'I said that ain't it...'

'She's posh as fuck, Zay...she ain't gonna let no pimply boy be her baby daddy and anyway, you's ugly as fuck, bruv, you get me?'

Power corrupts and absolute power corrupts absolutely. Skyla stands tall. The water pouring down her face and dripping from the assault rifle held in her hands. Three women cowering in fear at her feet. Two of them older, like the social workers, pigs and teachers that used to tell her what to do and the other like someone from the movies. Refined, polite, cultured, educated and intelligent. The polar opposite to everything Skyla is. A reminder of the roots of her life. She'd never heard anyone like Lilly in real life. Bitches only spoke and acted like that in films.

She smiles. Teeth white but uneven and chipped. Her hair scraped back from her face showing the blackheads on her forehead and in her own mind she looks beautiful and full of glory as she stands over the nasty bitches and makes them cower in the water.

Power corrupts and she twists the events to justify her own actions. Lani killed Darius and made Howie escape. Lilly helped her. Lilly is one of them. One of the fuckers that made her go to counselling. One of the cunts that made her get kicked out from school. One of the fucking witnesses that made statements that led to her being convicted at court and sent on a youth offending programme where she learnt to be harder and tougher.

She is right. They are wrong. People like these three had all the power before but not now. Skyla has the gun. Skyla has right on her side. Skyla is number two.

Power corrupts and she revels in the feeling. Holding still to drag it out longer but something else lurks in the back of her mind. A feeling of discomfort. Of grief. Her friends being killed. Seeing their bodies blown apart. Watching them being dragged from the hospital to be dumped like trash. The upheaval of leaving the compound and coming here. The change in Maddox as he slowly stopped using their language and started becoming more like one of these fuckers crying in the rain at her feet. Emotions she can't understand and is too young to deal with. Like Sierra she masks it, swallows it, ignores it and lets it channel into behaviour that she knows.

Power corrupts and her eyes see pimply stupid Zayden. Big for his age. Broad shouldered but dumb as shit. Too stupid to do anything other than follow orders. Poor Zayden. Fancying someone way above his league. That thought makes her flinch. That Lilly thinks she is too good for Zay. Zay's thick but he's alright. Who does she think she is?

'You's not ugly, Zay,' she adds in a voice made softer by the conflicting emotions raging through her heart and mind, 'this bitch thinks she's too good for...'

'Get 'em up,' Sierra strides back into view, seething with rage that shows in the twisted features of her face. 'Where's that posh bitch?'

'Bitch is here,' Skyla calls out.

'Lilly?' Sierra hisses the name, powering towards them with a hand already held out ready to grasp Lilly's soaking wet hair. Her fingers clamp on, scrunching and twisting the strands. Lilly screams in pain at feeling chunks of hair being ripped from her scalp. Her own hands shoot up, clamping on Sierra's as she's wrenched up to her feet to be sent flying by a hard kick to the back of her legs. She goes down again. Yelping as her knees hit the ground first, jarring her body. Another kick to her ribs and she rolls away, sliding through puddles of filthy grime. Sierra seethes with an anger she has never felt before. A tangible real thing driving her on. Heedless of the rain, heedless of the cries of the girl scrabbling to get away and holding the assault rifle one handed she kicks again and again at Lilly.

'Sam no!' Lilly catches sight of Sam reaching behind her back but the words get muffled as her face slams down into the muddy waters.

'Stop...please stop,' Pea runs at Sierra, 'Sierra, stop...please...'

'Fuck off me,' Sierra twists away from Pea trying to grab her wrist.

'Stop, please...Sierra, look at me...look at me...'

Sierra does look. She turns snarling with eyes blazing and her fist clenching ready to punch and hit until blood flows and people die. What she sees is a woman old enough to be her mother. A woman of mixed race with darker skin and hair frizzy and wild. She sees brown eyes pleading with tears that stream to mix with the rain sliding down Pea's cheeks. In an instant the rage is quelled and abates but to back down fully will make her look weak. She glares, refusing to show emotion but wanting only to sink down and weep and curl up and cry forever.

Her nostrils flare. Her eyes glower as the veins in her neck bulge. She looks down at Lilly and inclines her head with a grunt.

'Work,' she speaks low but the words carry. 'Or you's don't eat. No one eats till it all gets done.'

She walks off into the grey sheet rain that hides the tears now coursing down her own cheeks.

CHAPTER EIGHT

W*ork or you don't eat.*
        Sierra meant what she said. They work. They do not eat.

The rain is relentless. Driving incessantly forever towards the ground where it gathers and forms deep pools.

There is no shelter and no place to gain a reprieve. Doorways are used by the kids armed with assault rifles that smoke and swig sugary drinks. They eat crisps, chocolate bars and stay dry.

Those in the middle work. They do not eat.

They drag the burnt and broken remains of the tents and structures to the front to be stacked in the middle section between the inner and outer walls. A place already filled with burnt cars and vehicles that were stacked before the sea made the fort an island of misery and death.

The children become quiet and withdrawn. Those too tired to work are left to huddle at the sides under rainfall that makes them shiver with cold from the lack of movement to keep them warm. Empty bellies rumble so they drink the water coming down simply to fill the void.

'Stay together, huddle up close,' Lilly tells them, pushing Billy and Milly into the middle with Pea, Sam and the others all working like sheepdogs to herd them together. 'Cuddle up, stay warm.'

'Hungry.'

'Starving.'

'Will we eat now?'

Pitiful voices that pull at heartstrings. They've been through so much. Seen too many things and now to sit hungry in the rain is too much. Children rescued from the stately home where Billy was taken. Orphans already. Murmurs ripples through the people. Muttered comments. Angry glances. Fists that clench and mouths that purse but the fear is too great to do anything.

The broken jaw of an old woman hit by the butt of a rifle swung by Sierra is testament to that. The fractured arm of a boy too slow to move when shouted at by one of girls. Black eyes. Hand prints across cheeks. People kicked to the ground who then had the barrels of assault rifles pointed at them and those girls with the scraped back hair came back. They strode through with scowling faces and mouths chewing gum. They glared at everyone and made sure the crews were doing their jobs.

'Work or you's don't eat.'

Those words are said time and again. So they work but they do not eat.

Cold hands grab at broken poles of tents to drag them out from the mess. Canvas made heavy by the water gathering in every crease and dip. Bodies made slick that are dropped with muttered curses.

Lilly stands holding the wrist of a dead boy and waits for Sam to grab his legs while Pea takes the other wrist. They share a glance but no words are spoken. Sam nods and they lift, heaving the literal dead weight up from the sucking water and on they go, trudging, wading and splashing through deep puddles.

They breathe heavy. Grunting from the effort. Hair plastered down over scalps. Clothes clinging to their frames. Lilly's head hurts from being hit by Skyla. Her ribs hurt from being kicked. Her stomach hurts too. Everything hurts but inside is calm. Deadly calm. Blue eyes that flicker back and forth. Watching. Scanning. Always watching, always scanning. Waiting for an opportunity and the next time she will not hesitate. No matter what it means she has to do. A coldness settles inside. An act of preparation to do a thing that must be done.

Pea and Sam watch her closely. Both sensing and seeing the change as the girl got up after the beating given by Sierra. A coldness now projected that is only masked when she stops to check on Billy and Milly.

Zayden stays close. His eyes hardly ever leaving Lilly's body. Watching her backside and the way she moves. The swing of her hips and the outline of her breasts straining against the sodden material of her top. Her bare arms so golden and slender. Her hair wet and slicked back.

Sam nudges Pea, nodding at the slack jawed idiot. Pea nods back but there is nothing they can do. He speaks softly to Lilly but everyone else is treated like shit. The fool doesn't even have the intelligence to think to be nice to her little brother or the other children shivering in the rain.

They go through the gate into the middle section and dump the body with the others that were meant to be taken out and buried at sea but Sierra banned anyone from using the boats and put another small team in there to make sure no one went near the outer gate.

The sun starts to wane. Evening approaches. The hours of darkness lie ahead and in the space of one day everything has changed. The outside world doesn't exist now. Just here in this place. Just the misery of being soaked with fingers that become wrinkly and puckered from the water.

Sierra sits in the police office. Back in the chair at the head of the table with her assault rifle across her legs. Her crew remain close. Talking, boasting, eating and drinking. They smoke non-stop until the air is thick and disgusting with the stench of cigarettes.

The table top and floor is strewn with empty cans, bottles and the wrappers from the junk food that has been gorged until they felt sick.

The same office where Sergeant Debbie Hopewell drew lists of survivors and their skills ready to be used. The same office where Ted gave comfort with his experience and calmness. The same office that saw Sarah rushing about with Terri as they struggled to bring order and peace to the lives of the few that made it to the safety of the high walls. Now the chairs are occupied by girls who sense something is very, very wrong with Sierra but are too inept to deal with it.

She stares vacant for hours at a time. Her mind stuck in a loop of Darius's brains being blown out and the aftermath of his death. The hatred she feels for Lani twists and grows to become a thing that mutates everything else. She pays no heed or thought to Maddox or Lenski but by the minute she is increasingly consumed with a need for a revenge that cannot be taken. Lani killed herself, and there the loop stops to replay from the beginning. Over and over.

In life there would be grief counsellors and adults ready to draw that pain out. With words of comfort, hugs and gentle touches they would encourage the emotional reactions to unwind and follow their natural course. She would be able to cry, weep, shout, rage, bellow and collapse until exhaustion took over. Then she would be allowed to sleep and rest and let the slow healing to begin.

People are mortal. Death is certain. Everyone dies. Everyone grieves. Everyone feels pain but the mark of a civilised society is how that grief is handled, but this grief is left to fester in the mind of an already warped teenager armed with an assault rifle and a gang of sycophantic followers who wouldn't dare challenge her. Monsters are rarely born but are shaped and made by their environment.

Her breathing comes faster as the replaying loop builds the

pain to a point that she cannot simply remain still and inert. So she explodes up. Sudden and full of purpose as she snaps back to the now and with a flinch she realises the sky outside has grown dark. How long has she sat there?

'They's working?'

'Yeah,' Skyla stands with her, nodding in reply, 'they's clearing the shit from the middle.'

'What about the hole?' Sierra demands.

Skyla pauses, casting a glance to the other girls, 'we ain't done it yet. Like...you never said nuffin bout the hole.'

Lani blew that wall out. Lani killed herself after killing Darius. Lani went in with Howie and Howie ran out with his pants round his ankles. Lani probably fucked him then blew the wall out.

'Sierra?' Skyla asks, watching the new number one standing by the table staring into space again.

'What?' Sierra snaps.

'You's okay yeah?'

'Yeah,' Sierra scoffs and grins with a distinct lack of humour in her eyes but the simple action of twitching her lips makes the other girls grin back. Picking her rifle up she walks purposefully from the office into the pouring rain with an involuntary shiver rippling through her body at the cold water hitting her exposed skin. For a second she stands still with her face turned up. It feels nice. Cleansing somehow. She feels tired. Drained even. The long hours of introspective fretting have worn her mind down to the point she now feels numb. She was raging a few seconds ago but that's gone now. Now she is numb.

Lilly watches her. Hidden further away towards the edge of the wall and she watches Sierra bathed in light from the offices behind her and how that light spills out metres into the fort. Sierra steps out, further away from the doorway and Lilly counts the girls that come behind her. Four girls plus Sierra. Five of them. Zayden still close with his two. Liam further up by the old armoury with his four. Three behind her by the gate. Too many. Wait.

'Zayden,' she turns to the youth, 'I've got a headache, can I get some pills from the doctors please?'

Pea flinches, watching the girl closely and the sudden way she turns to Zayden with the softness of her tone.

'We've worked all day,' Lilly says, stepping closer to Zayden. 'I am very tired,' she says, staring up into his eyes with her own eyelids fluttering heavily. Sierra has four. Zayden has two. Liam has four. Three by the gate. More outside the gate. Thirty. Nick isn't coming back. Howie isn't coming back.

'Yeah,' Zayden nods eagerly, 'you's get some pills yeah.'

'Thank you,' she whispers. 'I am so cold and wet...will we get food tonight? What about the children, Zayden? They need to go inside somewhere and get dry. They need food too.'

Sam stares hard, her heart beating harder as Pea shuffles a step closer to Lilly talking in a weird tone to Zayden. Like flirting but with an edge to her voice.

'Zayden?' Lilly says again when he doesn't respond, 'the children need food and somewhere dry. We all need food and somewhere dry.'

'Lilly,' Pea says in a low warning voice, 'we should get back.'

'Zayden?' Lilly says, her voice firmer, 'I asked you a question.'

Sam swallows. Her hand inching round her hip towards the gun wedged down her waistband under the sodden and filthy shirt. She blinks the rain from her eyes.

Zayden shrugs and offers a hard glare to Sam and Pea before trying to smile at Lilly, 'you's can come to my room tonight yeah? You'll dry up and have food.'

'What about the others?'

'Lilly, we should go,' Pea says again, flicking her eyes over to Sierra standing outside the offices with her crew.

'I will ask Sierra myself then,' Lilly says, walking off with Zayden running to catch her up.

'Lilly,' Sam hisses, moving after the girl. 'Lilly, come back right now.'

'Sierra,' Lilly calls out, snapping the girl's head over to her. Skyla moves out to intercept her with her rifle already moving ready to lash out. 'We have worked all day. We are wet and tired. The children are...'

'Shut the fuck up, posh bitch,' Skyla stalks at her with a snarl.

'The children are freezing, Sierra. They will die if they don't get dry and have food.'

Lilly stops a few metres away, pulling her arm free from Zayden trying to pull her back. Skyla stops in front of her. Scowling and ready to slam the butt into her gut again. The other girls move round Sierra, all of them glaring balefully at Lilly.

'We have worked,' Lilly says in a voice loud and clear enough to carry through the fort. 'You said work or we don't eat. We have worked.'

'Lilly, come back here,' Pea hisses, trying to get round Zayden who pushes her back.

'The children will die. The old people will die. There are weak people who have worked all day in this rain and they will die if they do not get shelter and food.'

'Hole,' Sierra says, staring expressionless at Lilly.

Lilly breathes out slow and steady. 'I was trying to fix the hole when you beat me into the ground...'

'Lilly, shut the fuck up,' Sam whispers frantically.

'You told us to work. We cleared the bodies. We cleared the mess. We cannot do anymore tonight. There are no torches. No lights. It is pitch dark and raining.'

'Hole,' Sierra says again, her eyes locked on Lilly.

'I am sorry, Sierra. We cannot fix the hole tonight. Will you give the children food and shelter? If not us then you must feed and protect the children.'

'Fix the hole and you eat.'

'We cannot fix the hole tonight. Will you give the children food and shelter? They will...'

'Who you talkin' to bitch?' Sierra snaps, animating back to life with her head cocked to one side, 'you talking to me?'

Lilly nods, her eyes clear and unblinking and the rain pouring down her face, 'yes I am talking to you, Sierra.'

Sierra pulls her head back and looks round at the other girls, 'she talking to me?'

'She is,' Skyla says, pulling her own head back disdainfully.

'Will you feed the children and give them shelter?'

'Someone tell this bitch to fuck off before I hurt her.'

'You's can go now,' Skyla says, gripping her rifle harder.

'Lilly, for God's sake,' Pea calls out, 'enough...we'll fix the wall.'

'We cannot fix the wall tonight,' Lilly calls out, 'some of those people will die if you leave them out in this without food.'

Sierra explodes out. Striding past Skyla with her rifle swinging back. Lilly sees it coming and lets it happen. It has to happen. It must happen. It will hurt but pain is just pain.

'Cunt,' Sierra slams the rifle into Lilly's chest, forcing her back into Zayden. Lilly hisses with the pain but keeps to her feet. She gasps and blinks fast before standing upright.

'Will you feed and give shelter tonight?' She asks, looking back at Sierra.

'Oh you's a dumb cunt,' Sierra shakes her head and smiles at Lilly as she takes a step back, 'Skyla...'

'Fuck yeah,' Skyla rushes in, slamming her rifle into Lilly. Battering her down into the ground.

'Sam no!' Lilly whispers at the two women. Pea's hand grips Sam's wrist as it moves towards the gun. The rifle hits down. The hard butt slamming into Lilly's shoulders, chest and head until she goes down into the deep puddles. Feet come next. Hard feet that kick into her ribs, arms and legs.

It's just pain. Lilly curls into a ball. Taking the beating. 'Sam no,' she whispers again, hoping and praying Sam can hear her.

'Dumb cunt,' Skyla kicks again, aiming the shots into Lilly's thighs knowing it'll hurt like hell.

'Enough,' Sierra says, feeling powerful and strangely serene at seeing Lilly get beaten to the ground on her orders.

Skyla gives one last kick and steps back breathing hard with a nasty grin showing her crooked teeth.

'Fix the hole and you eat,' Sierra says, staring down at Lilly.

'We…' Lilly coughs and wheezes through the pain radiating in every limb, '…we cannot fix it tonight…'

Sierra's nostrils flare. Her already frayed temper snapping as all reason flees her mind. She runs at Lilly who tries to scurry backwards on all fours but the hand that grips her hair is strong and heaves her up onto her feet.

'Get her in there,' Sierra screams, kicking hard at Lilly's legs and sending the girl flying forward at Skyla, 'In the fucking pig rooms…get her in…'

CHAPTER NINE

Power corrupts. Absolute power corrupts absolutely.

Lilly stands in the corner of the room staring down at her feet with her hands clasped in front.

'Posh Bitch,' Skyla calls out almost politely, 'May I have another can of finest Coke please may I, Posh Bitch?'

Cackles break out, rippling with delight through the older youths gathered in the room. All of them ceasing conversation to turn and stare at Lilly who steps away from the corner towards the table at the side loaded with food and drink.

'Whoa!' Skyla shouts, 'what the fuck?'

'What?' Another girl asks, laughing hard at Skyla's shocked expression.

'You's gotta say it,' Skyla shouts. 'Posh Bitch...say it...'

Lilly stops midway across the floor, holding position with her eyes averted downward, 'Of course,' she mutters and takes a breath. 'It would be my delight to serve you,' she adds, forcing the words to come out neutral and flat.

'Fuck yeah,' Skyla laughs and looks round at the others, 'she's my bitch now.'

Lilly gets the can of Coke from the table and moves silently across the room to Skyla seated next to Sierra at the head of the table. The room falls silent with loaded humour as everyone watches Lilly and Skyla.

'Thank you,' Skyla says, adopting her posh voice, 'put it on the table.' Lilly places the can down and steps back, ready to turn back to her corner. 'Ahem,' Skyla says, prompting a fresh wave of laughs, 'open it then you dumb fucking bitch,' she slides back into her own rasping voice with a theatrical roll of her eyes.

Lilly shows no reaction but steps back to the table and reaches out to pop the lid from the can and the room fills with the hiss of bubbles rushing to the top of the aluminium casing.

Her upper lip is swollen. Her cheeks bruised. The soft flesh round her left eye starting to show purple. Her arms marked with welts from the beating that continued when she was dragged into the police offices.

'You scared?' Skyla asks, staring up at her with malicious intent clear in her eyes.

Lilly looks away, dropping her gaze. 'No.'

'No what?'

'No, Miss Skyla,' Lilly says, her tone perfectly polite.

'Should be,' Sierra mutters. The room falls silent in deference of the new number one speaking out. Sierra stares ahead at the same spot on the wall she has been staring at since night fell. Glued to her chair with the constant replay going over and over. Everyone waits, expecting more but Sierra stays silent and sullen.

'You may go,' Skyla says, waving her hand in a way she thinks posh people wave when they dismiss their servants.

Lilly walks back to her corner and steals a glance to the open door and the night sky outside. The rain is heaving down harder than it was before. She assumes her position, back to the corner and her hands clasped in front.

She knew from the conversations inside the room the people outside were not being fed or given shelter.

'Is the wall fixed?' Sierra had asked her on being brought into the room.

'No, we were told to...'

'Shut up,' Sierra whispered at Lilly, her voice dangerously quiet, 'I aksed you a question...is the wall fixed?'

Lilly simply shook her head and kept her voice as polite and passive as possible, 'no.'

'They's don't eat then,' Sierra said, glaring with undisguised hatred.

'Will they be given shelter?' Lilly asked again and took another beating as Sierra launched up with fists hammering into Lilly's face.

'DON'TS FUCKIN' SPEAK TO ME...' She screamed, beating Lilly to the floor and yanking her head back with a fistful of hair, 'you's hear me, Posh Bitch?'

'Sierra please' Lilly begged, 'some of them will die if they don't food or shelter...'

Sierra spat in her face at that point. A full drawing of phlegm from her throat that was gathered in her mouth and propelled out with force to land on Lilly's cheek where it slid down thick and globular. She was wrenched to her feet, kicked and punched back down then heaved round the room by her hair before finally being shoved into the corner and made to stand with her hands to the front. Sierra glared for several long seconds before stalking back to her chair where she slumped down and once again lapsed into staring at the wall.

Nobody spoke to Lilly at first. None of them daring to cross Sierra or be seen to step out of line. It was during that period of being ignored that Lilly heard the conversations that guards were to be kept on the people all night who would not be fed until the wall was fixed and the work done.

Lilly thought some of the others might question Sierra or at least Skyla and ask for the people outside to be given food, but none of them did. Instead they mocked the stupid, the weak, the idiots and the pathetic scum that were too dumb to do anything. It was a whole transference from a cooperative group working together to one of supplicated men, women and children cowering from armed oppressors.

'Posh Bitch?' A girl sings Lilly's new name, holding an empty packet of crisps in the air, 'I require more crisps,' she lets the packet go, watching as it wafts to the ground a few feet from the table, 'oh dear, I have done littering innit,' the girl says, trying to do a posh voice. Sniggers in the room but not as much as when Skyla makes a joke. Mouths grinning with teeth coated in bits of crisps and smeared with chocolate. Legs bouncing on the spot with hands fidgeting from the amount of sugar ingested. Voices too loud, laughing too much.

Lilly goes to the table and picks the same packet as the one the girl dropped.

'No,' the girl says. 'Salt and Vinegar.'

Lilly puts the first back and with a stomach rumbling she selects the chosen flavour and moves wordlessly to deliver the item.

'Open them,' Aaliyah says, copying Skyla's display of power and watching as Lilly cinches the packet together and pulls the glued seam apart. A twinkling in Aaliyah's eyes and she looks round the room to make sure everyone is watching, 'feed me,' she says and opens her mouth while trying not to laugh.

Lilly hesitates. Not quite believing this is happening and that hesitancy brings Skyla to her feet and a hand once again gripping Lilly's hair as a foot is kicked into the back of her knees. She does down, landing hard and jarring her knee caps on the concrete ground.

'Feed her, Posh Bitch,' Skyla seethes with instant snarling anger, hissing the words into Lilly's ear.

Aaliyah's smile freezes in place. The humour draining from her eyes. She only meant to get Lilly to feed her one and was going to tell her to fuck off and the sudden explosion of violence startles even her. That uncertainty spreads through the room as smiles are held in place and glances are cast to others to see how they're reacting.

Lilly has no choice. The pain in her knees is immense but the pain coming from her hair being pulled so hard is worse. She pushes her hand into the packet and with trembling hands she draws a single crisp out.

'Hold it out then,' Skyla yanks on her hair like someone yanking on a dog lead. Lilly clenches her jaw shut. Her eyes filling with tears from the pain but her arm extends towards Aaliyah who grins and leans forward.

'Cheers then,' Aaliyah snaps the crisp away, munching noisily.

'Fucking bitch,' Skyla pushes Lilly roughly, jerking her head forward before slinking back to her chair.

'Give it here,' Aaliyah says, holding her hand out for the packet.

'Oi no,' Skyla cuts in, 'make the bitch feed you.'

'Nah,' Aaliyah sneers, taking the crisps from Lilly. 'I don't wants her hands touching my food...she probably touched Zay's prick innit...' Aaliyah looks round, clearly pleased with herself for making everyone laugh, 'wanked him off yeah?' She adds, trying to keep the joke going. She puts a crisp in her mouth and pulls a grim face, 'they's salty alright.'

Lilly stares down at the floor listening to the cackling and booming laughter from girls and boys alike. Her cheeks burn with shame. In her mind she holds two images. Billy and Nick. The image of Billy keeps her quiet and passive. You do what it takes to protect your own. Billy is outside in the pouring rain with an empty belly but he's alive. Keep him alive and wait for an opportunity. Nick's image is for herself to keep that knowledge that there are decent good people still left in this world.

'Where's Zay?' A boy asks, twisting in his seat to look round.

'Guardin' those dumb fuckers,' Skyla replies, 'he can't come in here...he'd be humping Lilly in the corner.'

Fresh laughing, faces going red as they spray drink and food out and cough cigarette smoke into the air.

'We's should get him in here then,' Aaliyah says, 'be funny as fuck watching his zits pop all over her.'

'Urgh that's fucking so gross,' a boy grimaces.

'Zay's ugly as fuck,' another girl says, showing disgust on her face.

'You fancy Zay?' Aaliyah asks Lilly, reaching out with her leg to tap Lilly's thigh, 'Oi, Posh Bitch, you fancy Zay?'

Lilly thinks fast. To say yes could prompt something dangerous to happen. To say no will prompt a response of an assumption that she thinks she is too good for him. 'I'm too tired to fancy anyone,' she says, still with her eyes averted. She wants to get up and retreat to her corner but the tendrils of power play keep her static on her knees.

'You's fancy Nick though,' Skyla says, 'yeah? You fancy Nick?'

'I'd fuck him,' Aaliyah announces.

'You'd fuck anything,' someone retorts and the conversation moves on. Lilly waits a few minutes then quietly slips back to her corner with dread in her stomach that knots and gurgles with anxiety and tension growing by the second.

Her mind works constantly. Ten people in this room which leaves about twenty others. She knows two are in the hospital stopping anyone entering or leaving. She knows two more are at the old armoury. Another two at the new armoury. Some are asleep and the rest are watching the survivors.

Minutes go by. The jokes and laughter fill the room and thinking she is unseen she lifts her head by fractions until she can see the layout and the weapons resting near to chairs. Her eyes flick left to right taking in the assault rifles and knowing both Sierra and Skyla have got pistols hanging from holsters on their hips. There must be an opportunity. There must be something she can do. Her heart jolts and misses a beat when she looks up to see Sierra staring right at her. The girl's dark eyes fixed and staring and it's only after several seconds that she realises the gaze is unfocussed and again she drops her head in supplication.

'Alright, Zay!'

Lilly looks up as a soaking wet Zayden walks into the room with a broad grin etched on his face. He looks round at everyone then straight to Lilly as the room erupts with jeers and shouts.

'You's come for Posh Bitch then?' Aaliyah asks.

'Yeah,' Zayden grins stupidly but with eyes lingering as water slides from his greasy hair. A fresh knot of fear tightens in Lilly's stomach. Being humiliated and beaten is something she can take but Zayden is a whole new dangerous threat. 'So's like...' Zayden says, flicking his gaze at Sierra, 'she come to my room then?'

The room rings with the sound of laughter. Hoarse braying as Zayden fails to notice they are laughing at him. His mind on the prize he has been coveting all day.

'You dumb fucker,' Skyla bursts out laughing, 'you dirty boy... Zay wants to fuck the posh bitch.'

'Can she?' Zayden asks again, happy to take the abuse if it means he can take Lilly to his room.

'No,' Sierra cuts through the laughing and watches as Zaydens face falls in disappointment. 'You's can fuck her but she sleeps outside with everyone else.'

Lilly listens. Dreading what is to come.

'So like,' Zayden says, having to think, 'so's she can come to my room then yeah?'

'Fuckin' hell, Zay,' Skyla groans, 'you's can fuck her in your room but then she goes back outside.'

'Oh right, yeah sweet,' Zayden says.

'Fuck me you's a dumb ugly fucker, Zay.'

'Fuck you, Skyla.'

'He's a virgin anyway. You's a virgin, Zay?' One of the girls asks, sneering in malice.

'Fuck off,' Zayden sputters, blushing deep.

'Who'd fuck that ugly...'

'I will,' Lilly says, lifting her head up to look round the room.

'Oh my God!' Skyla stares in shock, 'posh bitch wants to fuck Zay!'

'She sleeps outside, Zay,' Sierra glares hard at him, 'you's hear that?'

'Yeah, yeah sure,' Zayden nods eagerly. His grin stretching from ear to ear. Lilly fancies him. He knew it from the way she's been looking at him all day.

CHAPTER TEN

L illy clutches her side and stops walking to bend double as the rain once again drenches her clothes and hair. 'Wow that really hurts.'

'Huh?' Zayden asks, alarmed at the prospect of losing the thing he has been thinking non-stop about all day.

'My ribs,' Lilly winces, 'I think Sierra broke one when she kicked me,' she looks up, watching his face for reaction but seeing only a hint of disappointment. 'I think my face is swollen too,' she adds.

'Oh,' he says dumbly, 'you's be alright yeah.'

'Zayden,' she changes to a look of intense worry, 'I'm really concerned...some of those people won't live through this night,' she sees the hardening in his eyes.

'You's coming to my room,' he says, halfway between a question and a statement.

'Yeah of course,' she smiles quickly, 'but I am so worried.'

He shrugs, unbothered and unable to think about anything else.

'Never mind,' she smiles again and stands upright to loop her arm through his, feeling his body tense and his tongue poke out to lick his already overly wet lips. His eyes staring straight at her top that is gathering the rain with the hope of it going see through again.

She walks on, breathing hard and holding her side. Making her breathing laboured and limping for a few steps, 'It's no good,' she groans and blows air out through her cheeks, coming to another stop, 'I need some painkillers...what room are you in?'

'Like...up there,' he nods past the hospital.

'Oh great, you go on. I'll get some painkillers and come straight...'

'Nah, you's got to come to my room...'

'I am in so much pain, Zayden. I can hardly move.'

'Yeah but...I's got to stay with you.'

'Zayden, I don't think you understand how much pain I am in,' she stands straight, wincing while adopting a soft expression. 'I really want to enjoy tonight...' Good Lord he is so slow witted. Just staring slack with his eyes constantly darting down to her chest. 'Zayden, I am not running away...' she laughs lightly, 'where would I go? Please, I know you are a decent man. I'll get some painkillers and join you...I'll be a few minutes at the most... you go and get ready. Which rooms was it? That one up there? Is that right?' She stands close to him, nestling her shoulder into his side.

'Yeah...' he swallows and licks his lips again, his mouth dry with excitement, 'yeah that's it.'

'Five minutes,' she says, staring with her blue unblinking eyes, 'Is that okay?'

He nods. Full of lust. Full of promise.

'Five minutes,' she says again, veering off towards the hospital. 'I'll be right out...get ready for me.'

'CHRIST,' Doctor Anne Carlton stops mid-stride on seeing the soaking wet bruised girl walking into the room, 'Lilly! What happened?' She rushes forward past the ends of the beds full of patients re-drugged to keep them quiet and sleeping.

'I'm fine,' Lilly says primly, forcing herself to nod firmly, 'I need some painkillers if I may?' She asks politely, having noticed the armed youths on the inside of the door.

'My god, you're freezing,' Anne says, gripping Lilly's wrist and staring at the bruises already showing on her cheeks and forehead, 'shit,' she looks down and curses at the livid welt on Lilly's upper arms.

'Fell over,' Lilly says, rolling her eyes, 'can we talk?' She adds in a whisper.

'Come with me,' Anne says brusquely and keeping hold of Lilly's wrist she walks her down the aisle to the back offices.

'Lilly!' Lisa Franklin rises from her chair in shock at the sight of the girl, 'What's happened?'

'Bloody hell,' Andrew Stone adds to the concerned trio rushing to her side, 'you're hurt, come on sit down...'

'Is Maddox awake?' Lilly steels herself against the rush of kindness pouring from the doctors.

'Don't worry about Maddox, come on...sit down...' Anne says, guiding her to Lisa's now vacant chair.

'No,' Lilly comes to a stop, 'I must know. Is Maddox awake?'

'No, no he isn't,' Andrew says.

'Any change? Will he wake up?'

'No change. Lilly? What's going on?' He asks.

She stops to think. She has to know. She has to make this right in her own mind, 'Is there anything you can do to wake him up?'

Andrew just stares at her with his face full of worry, 'What's happening out there? We're not allowed out. We heard everyone is being made to work.'

'Is Lenski with him?'

'She's been with him all day,' Anne says adopting her doctor tone of voice, 'now calm down and tell us what's going on.'

'I'm calm,' Lilly says, fixing her a very steady look that sends a shiver running down Anne's spine. 'And yes,' she adds, looking back to Andrew, 'Sierra has made everyone work and won't give food or shelter until everything is done.'

'Is the wall fixed?' Lisa asks.

'No, she's making everyone sleep outside in the rain without food. Doctors, I need to ask,' she takes a breath, 'are the weaker people and children at risk from being outside all night without shelter and food?'

'Yes,' Anne says brusquely, 'Exposure. It's warm but once the core body temperature goes down...'

'Without food or motion you can't stay warm,' Andrew cuts in, 'hypothermia can set in even in weather like this.'

'I see,' Lilly says. The sadness of it all strikes her heart but her path is set. There is no going back now. You do what it takes.

CHAPTER ELEVEN

S he walks back down the main aisle of the hospital looking ahead to the two armed boys on the door grinning knowingly at her. News of her acceptance to fuck Zayden has spread like wildfire. Zayden is a spotty faced twat and Lilly is fit.

'Alright, Lilly,' one of them smirks.

She nods and twitches her lips but makes no reply as she walks past, through the door and out into the rain. She moves on. One step after the other.

You protect your own. You do what it takes. You do the right thing for the right reasons and sometimes that right thing is awful. Really truly awful but the threat is real and therefore you have to take the pain.

She saw her father killed. She saw her friend raped and killed. She saw others being killed. This new world renders life cheap and worthless but not all life is like that. The life of a child is pure and sacred. They are the future and they carry no sin from the life that was before. Billy. Milly. All the children gathered here. The boys Nick saved from the house. The others brought in to keep safe.

You do what must be done. Pain is just pain. You can take it.

Her eyes fix on the soft orange glow coming from the open

doorway of the room set back further up from the hospital. Every youth she passes grins and smirks at her. She is giving herself to Zayden. They all know it. She might be doing it for food or favours but either way, she's doing it.

She gets to the doorway and expected her heart to be hammering in fear. She expected her legs to be trembling and her voice to quaver. But she feels calm. Resolute. She stops and closes her eyes taking one last chance to think of her beautiful Nick. The way he spoke to her, the way a man should speak to a woman. The way he smiled. The touch of his hands on hers. The slender fingers. His strong arms. He's out there now fighting to keep everyone alive. Through choice he has placed himself in harm's way and so others may have freedom and life. You do the right thing and that ethos, that *essence* touched her. She holds his image close. Seeing into his soft brown eyes. The eyes of a killer.

For freedom. For life.

She opens her scared blue eyes and gently knocks on the door, 'Zayden?'

'Yeah,' he rushes over, grinning and already flushed with lust. His top off showing his sallow upper body pock-marked with spots and the first few black hairs pushing out round his puffy nipples. She spots the swell in his trousers and hides the pain from her face.

'Well,' she smiles, 'this is your room then?'

'Got candles,' he blurts, nodding eagerly.

'Okay,' she looks at him expectantly, 'are you going to invite me in?'

'Fuck yeah,' he grunts, moving back from the door. She steps through. Noticing the filthy scavenged bare mattress on the ground and the two candles flickering to show the squalor of his romantic room. Cobwebs hang in the corners. Walls stained with grease and the stench of oil hanging heavy that mixes with the stale body odour coming from his unwashed armpits.

You do what must be done. You protect your own.

He rushes forward. Clumsy and eager. His hands grabbing at

her breasts that squeeze painfully as he pushes his groin into her. She takes it for a second, pausing, letting him grope and thrust. A sickening feeling inside that builds with self-disgust. His head bangs into the painful bruises on her face. Every inch of her hurts. A wave of revulsion sweeps through and she pulls away.

'Zayden,' she whispers but he moves with her. Panting in her ear as his hands knead bread from her body, 'Zayden,' she pulls back, forcing herself to hide the disgust in her voice.

'What?' He grunts, his eyes as hard as his prick.

'If I said no what would you do?'

'Huh?'

'If I said no, what would you do?' He stalls for an answer. His mind too full of lust to compute anything other than the feel of her tits in his hands and the sense of urgency pushing in his groin. 'Would you take me anyway?'

He nods and licks his lips making them overly wet, 'yeah, gonna fuck you...'

'If I said no, you would make me. Is that right?'

'Yeah,' he pants, leering as he drags her close. She goes with the pull. Sensing his mood and the edge of violence threatening to spill over. His hands go to work again. Kneading. Squeezing. Groping. Painful. His tongue licks her neck. His foul breath blasting across her face. Still she holds. Feeling his erection driving into her hip as he thrusts like a dog on heat.

Nick. Beautiful Nick.

He grunts. Thrusts. Squeezes. Licks. His hands squeeze the bruises on her arms. His face pushing into her swollen cheeks. His head butting into her black eye.

This is our way. Nick said that. We do the right thing.

Zayden gets rougher as the lust builds. His hands tugging her top up, grunting with frustration and the knowledge he can take what he wants. She lets him work. Letting him have what he wants, feeling his hand tugging the waistband of her jeans down.

You protect your own. Pain is just pain.

'Off,' Zayden grunts, pushing at her jeans, too stupid to realise they're still done up.

'In a rush?' She tries to sound coy but the words come out whimpered and weak.

'Fuck yeah...' he snarls and a new idea comes into his mind, 'You gonna blow me...'

She wants it. He can tell. His fingers fumble at his belt. Tugging to free the pin from the hole in the leather. He yanks it over, then pulls it free. His fingers moving to the button on his jeans. They get wrenched open and the zip pulled while he bends to push them down.

The pants come down and it stands out, pointing grotesque and disgusting towards her. She looks down, using every ounce of self-control not to show any adverse reaction but the terror is clear in her eyes. He gloats on the spot. His face flushed and blotchy.

She slowly drops to her knees, knowing what must be done, willing this to end, tears fall down her cheeks, 'close your eyes now...' she looks up, staring at his face, imploring this to end but he only sees her pretty blue eyes. 'Zayden, close your eyes for me...'

He clamps his eyes shut and thereby at least giving her this awful second of her life some degree of privacy. The smell is disgusting. His body unwashed for days and a young man raging with hormones needs to wash. She fights the gag and turns her head in an effort to draw clean untainted air but her hair brushes against him and that single delicate touch makes his hands clamp on the back of her head and he thrusts his groin at her.

She reels back. Caught off guard. He thrusts again. His eyes still closed. She weaves away, sensing his frustration growing as his hard fingers dig into the back of her already painful head. It must be now. Do it. Lilly, you have to do it. She gets the object free from her pocket, bites the orange cap off and reaches round to drive the needle into the soft flesh of his buttocks and pushes the plunger down, forcing the clear liquid into his right arse cheek. He grunts, snapping his eyes open at the sensation in his backside.

'Something bit you,' she blurts, spitting the orange cap out. He scowls. Sensing something is wrong. His face morphing with lust fuelled rage. Why isn't she doing it? It should be in her mouth by now. What's that feeling in his backside? It feels hot like he's shit himself.

He reaches round as she darts forward, desperate to keep his attention on her but he takes a step back as his fingers find the syringe to yank the hypodermic needle from his flesh. He stares down at the syringe and blinks.

'What's that?' Lilly asks, buying time with a growing panic that the drug won't work.

'What the...' he frowns and looks at Lilly, 'what...what's...' the heat in his arse cheek spreads out, blossoming down his legs, through his groin and up his back.

Now. Do not hesitate. She lurches to her feet with eyes wild as she drags the scalpel from her pocket and lashes out to slice the surgically sharp blade across his neck but it barely whispers across his skin merely opening a shallow wound that oozes blood down his chest.

He reels back. His mind unable to process everything that's happening. She lashes out, driving the attack forward with wild slashes, nicking his shoulders, arms and stomach. He swings an arm trying to hit her away but already the drug is in his body, making him weak and sluggish. Panic in his face and he draws breath to scream for help.

With a grunt she barrels into him, pushing him backwards into the edge of the mattress. His feet snag and he trips with her driving him down, knocking the air from his lungs. They land heavy. Bouncing on the sprung mattress. A fist hits her face hard enough for stars to blossom in her vision. With desperate panic she digs the point of the scalpel into his stomach, twisting her hand left to right to open the wound. He yelps and goes to scream but her other hand scrabbles up to clamp down on his mouth. He bites down, sinking his teeth into the fleshy part of her hand and she fights to not scream herself as she slides the short blade from his stomach and brings it up to dig deep into his neck. His eyes widen. Blood spurting hot and far across the floor and over the blue eyed girl staring down at him. She stabs again and again, puckering his flesh, gouging holes that spew hot blood.

He fights, bucks and thrashes but the powerful sedative gets pumped faster through his body. A combined effect of his heart increasing from the panic while his system loses blood faster than he can congeal or clot. His senses dull. His blows weaken. The blood flow eases and his eyes dim, gently closing as his hand thumps her side gently.

She clings on. Pushing her hand into his mouth, stabbing him frenzied and wild, willing him to die, wishing him to die, wanting him to die and through the crazed blur in her eyes she sees the very second his life fades from his open eyes.

Seeing him die drives her on. She stabs more. Driving the point in to ruin the flesh of his neck until it becomes flayed meat ragged and worthless. She grunts from the exertion. Sweat pouring down her face already soaked from the rain outside.

On her feet and she stares down at his form. His dead murdered form. Rage pulses now. Pure unbridled rage that seethes cold and wonderful. She has taken life. She has killed. She was pushed to the limit and killed in defence. The scalpel gripped in her hand drips blood and she kicks hard into his groin. Knowing he is dead but wishing the pain to be sent to whatever afterlife he now haunts.

She wipes a bloodied hand across her face and spits to the side. With her chest heaving and eyes set she turns slowly to face the door.

Move fast. Do not hesitate.

Still her mind works fast and she looks round for his assault rifle. Not here. He must have handed it over to whoever is guarding the others. She snuffs the candles out and in the darkness she feels down the wall to the frame of the door and gently eases the handle down.

She pulls gently, easing the door open an inch at a time. The rain is still hammering down with a thousand different drums sounding as the water strikes a myriad of flat surfaces.

She steps out in one smooth motion and pulls the door closed behind her. The whole of the fort is dark and visibility is reduced by the rain coming down. Only the orange lights of the rooms in use show. Far to her right are the police offices. The survivors huddled together far to the left. She stares ahead. Eyes unblinking. Scalped gripped.

She sets off. Heading directly across the middle open ground of the fort with the scalpel held down by her leg. She can only just see the sides from the middle which means the crews won't be able to see her.

The rain comes heavy. The night is dark. All these things have been calculated and thought about but now the rage drives her on. Rage that is needed. Pure beautiful anger that pulses like a wild animal thrashing inside to be released. *Let me out. Let me kill.* Her top lip pulls back, her head drops and her eyes remain fixed on the objective ahead.

She moves fast but ducks down to reduce her profile and she veers left into the shadows formed by the wall and her eyes strain to see any sign ahead. Nothing. She loses sense of direction and stops to drop down and kneel in the water with the rain soaking her body. Her eyes stare hard. Waiting. Watching. Something will show. The pressure to keep moving is great but her mind runs fast and clear. Wait. Watch. *Let me out. Let me kill.*

There it is. The soft amber light of a cigarette end glowing. Keeping her eyes locked on that exact spot she sets off again, still veering left. She reaches the wall and stops to catch her breath. Steadying her heart rate that thunders in her chest.

Pushing on and she takes it one step at a time. Keeping low and pressed as close to the wall as she can. The rain masks any noise she makes. The cigarette glows again. She heads towards it. Gaining closer with every step of her feet and her head cocked to one side straining to hear voices but hearing none.

Only metres away now and she stops in the pitch darkness with energy pulsing through her limbs. With eyes staring, unblinking, with a screaming voice inside demanding to be set free to kill and kill until everything is dead. The doorway is recessed with a ledge over the top sheltering the smoker from the worst of the rain.

She steals forward with her eyes fixed and staring at the point where the end of the cigarette glows. She smells the tobacco in the air. Still no voices. Her body brushes the wall. The smoker lifts a hand to draw on the cigarette and using the doorway she gains scale of the size of the sentry on guard. Someone small. Not one of the crew chiefs. This will be one of the younger ones made to stand out in the rain.

With a snarl she rushes from the darkness slamming into the sentry staring ahead and not expecting anyone to come from the side. He yelps out, shouting but finding the point of the scalpel driving into his throat that hacks a hole shredding his windpipe and voice box. He goes down, gargling and choking as hot blood spurts from his mouth and slides down his ruined neck into his lungs. Lilly stabs into him. Slicing and hacking. Her aim deviating to drive the point through his eye. Killing him until he is dead. Killing him again and again. Killing him over until he lies ruined and destroyed. On her feet and the demon inside demands more so she kicks and stamps down, letting the beast free. She breaks the neck of the child on sentry. She breaks his nose, his jaw, his arms and his ribs. She gives back the pain she was given and more until that demon tells her to stop and take stock of where she is.

She gulps air, heedless of the rain pelting her face, heedless of the pain in every limb of her body. She drags the body out into the ground and stands to examine the door. A thick padlock looped through a clasp. She drops down to go through the pockets of the warm corpse. Cigarettes. A lighter. Bullets. A knife in his waistband. No key. She stands, thinking fast as the options present themselves. She could pry the clasp off with the rifle. She looks closer at the clasp. No good. The thing is flush against the wood of the door giving no space for something to be jammed in and the padlock is too thick to be beaten off without making a whole lot of noise.

She turns away, thinking of what to do as her foot catches on the plastic bag pushed back in the recess. She kicks it away then thinks twice and drops down to yank the thing open. Cans of coke. Crisps. Chocolate bars and a thick key on a black lanyard.

She grabs it and stands. Forcing the key into the hole that turns the mechanism within that frees the locking bar on the padlock that she slides from the clasp. She pushes the door open and peers inside to the pitch black interior. Back to the boy and she takes his lighter from his pocket and thumbs the wheel that creates the spark that ignites the gas coming from the opened valve. Flame is made. Fire that gives small heat and small illumination but it's enough.

For a second she holds still. Knowing she is stepping into an armoury with a naked flame. Move now. Do not hesitate.

She gazes over the stacked boxes of ammunition and unused weapons. Rifles stacked against the wall. She spots the thing she was looking for. Boxes of them stacked on a crate to keep them off the floor. She opens the lid and takes several. Job done and she backs out, closing the door quietly behind her. She puts the padlock back on, slips the key from the lock and pushes it firmly into her pocket before taking the assault rifle from the boy's dead hands. She checks it over, spotting the safety switch then finding the bolt which she yanks back. A shiny unfired round pops from the top. *Loaded, made ready, safety off.*

She sets off again. Stalking back across the middle of the fort. Her hair slick to her scalp and coursing in rivers down her face and over her lips. Her skin ripples with goose bumps as the cold eats its way inside only to be sent back out by the fire in her gut that drives her on.

One foot after the other. Eyes staring ahead. Breathing hard. Hands gripping the weapon. She wills herself on. Determined and holding that rage in check until it can be used. Across the central ground she wades through the water and passes the old armoury while facing ahead and walking as though she is meant to be there. They could see her if they looked but they wouldn't see it was Lilly. They'd just see a figure walking. She risks a glance and spots the soft orange glows of torches or lanterns giving some small light to the place where Liam and his four keep guard. Smaller amber ends glow. They're smoking and relaxed.

Ahead she spots a figure coming from the police offices. A solitary silhouette holding a rifle that starts walking towards her. Whoever it is must be heading for the new armoury. That lad she took down was only on his own for a few minutes then. She keeps walking and slowly works to adjust her grip on the things she carries, transferring them from her right hand to her left which she also uses to hold the barrel of the heavy weapon. Her right grips the handle, bringing it up slightly as the figure walks briskly towards her. Whoever it is keeps their head down from the rain still pouring from the sky.

They close the gap between them. A boy but bigger than the one she just killed. A crew chief, older, wiser and faster. She watches his head, gauging the distance and checking to see if they're in sight of Liam's crew sheltering in the old armoury.

Only a few feet to go and still the lad keeps his head down, watching his own feet splash puddles.

'Hey, you seen Zayden?' She calls forward in an ice cold voice. The boy jerks his head up and spots Lilly staring at him. The fact that she's carrying an assault rifle doesn't register for such a sight is now normal to him. He grins back, smirking at the gossip that spotty Zay was going to fuck the posh bitch.

'Nah' he says with a sneer as the butt smashes the teeth from his face. He drops instantly. The sheer power of the strike knocking him down. She follows through. Hitting down again and again until he goes as limp as the last one. Blood courses from his face and ears. His skull fractures, splintering with a crunch and he lies dead from the bones pushing through his brain.

Eyes up. Head up. She stands stock still listening, watching. The rain so loud it blots everything else out. She looks down coldly, seeing the pulped head and brains seeping through the cracks of his skull and not a flicker of reaction shows. She drops down and pushes one hand into the gooey remains of his head, coating her fingers with blood and gore that she wipes down her own cheeks and through her hair.

On her feet and she breaks into a jog with her eyes fixed on the orange glowing lights that shine the most of all.

She hears the voices inside. Laughing voices. Cackling voices. Someone shouts and everyone laughs. Harsh sounds that carry clear. They laughed at her when Sierra beat her. They laughed when she was on her knees feeding Aaliyah. They laughed at the pathetic scum outside going hungry and cold to die in the rain. They gloated with mouths full of crisps and sprayed coke out across the floor. They beat her down. Punching, kicking and making her stand in the corner.

Her eyes grow larger. Her lips pulling back. Her face and hair smeared with blood and gore that coats her arms and top.

They left her brother outside to die. They left her brother to go hungry. Billy who has never hurt anyone. Billy and Milly who are innocent of all the sins of man. Children who have felt more pain than any ever should.

The eyes of a killer. We do the right thing or none of this is worth it. She knew goodness once. She saw it. Nick. Beautiful Nick who kills everyday so others may have freedom. *Aye. That's what it takes. That's where the hardness in his eyes comes from.* Across that ground she goes. Running faster to be there. To be there now with a voice screaming in her head to be let out to kill.

She pushes her head through the strap of the rifle and slings it behind her. Freeing her hands. She holds one in her right and grips the pin with her left. Blowers told her what to do. Blowers who has the eyes of a killer too. *Twist and pull.*

The laughing inside is loud. The smell of the cigarettes is strong and she strides in with eyes blazing and death in her gaze. A thing from a nightmare. A beast risen from the depths of darkness. Smeared in blood caked down her face and through her hair that lies matted across her shoulders.

'SEE ME,' she bellows the words with an intensity that brings instant silence and every head snapping over to the thing that stands in the doorway. Her chest heaves. Her head tilted down and she looks up, flicking her eyes from face to face. 'See me,' the beast inside growls the words out, projecting pure venomous hatred to every person in the room.

Twist and pull.

She twists.

She pulls.

The pin drops.

They rush to their feet, knocking chairs over but freeze when she holds the grenade up for all to see.

The blood drains from Skyla's face. Aaliyah's mouths drops. Sierra's eyes stare fixed with the realisation of everything done wrong. Life plays out in that room at that second. Lives that flash before young eyes. A foe underestimated and in her they see the darkness of Howie projected for all to see. They see the hardness of Nick, Blowers and Cookey. They see Lani. They see Meredith They see someone who refuses to be beaten and has the will power to take the beating to come back stronger and meaner and with a brutality that pales their own malicious actions.

Power corrupts. Absolute power corrupts absolutely. There can be no going back. There can be no reprieve now. A thing done is a thing done. End it. End it now. *Kill.*

She drops the grenade, steps out and closes the door. In the ensuing four seconds there is much noise from tables turning over. From voices screaming high pitched and young. From chairs being kicked away. From feet running. From cans falling to the ground. Four seconds of an air filled with a cacophony of sound.

She drops low. Her hand reaching up to hold the door closed. None of them made it. None of them tried to yank it open.

The muffled whump is loud but not as loud as she thought it would be. The thick walls deadening the sound to a low percussive bang that shakes the door and vibrates through the walls. In the midst of the explosion she detects smaller noises of objects being blasted aside.

A second of silence then the screams come. Not the screams of the panicked now but the screams of the injured and in pain. She doesn't hesitate but is up, pushing the door open as she pulls the rifle round and steps in to see how one muffled whump has redecorated the room in shades of red.

The air is thick with explosive charge and the displacement of energy makes the hairs on her neck prickle and stand up.

The bodies lie everywhere. The ones closest to the blast torn apart and shredded but the human body is a densely packed thing of flesh and bone that is capable of absorbing blast energy. The ones further away were protected from the initial blast and simply lacerated by fragments instead. Burning hot fragments that seared deep into thighs and stomach and ripped fingers from hands. Scorching chunks of metal that embedded in stomachs and necks and opened the skin on faces that bleed heavily into mouths that scream in absolute pain.

The one closest to her is dead. A boy near her own age with his head mostly gone. She steps over him to the next one lying face down with the entrails from her stomach littering the ground beneath her.

Aaliyah is the closest one screaming and Lilly steps down with a heavy foot pressing into the girl's neck, forcing her attention up to the rifle aiming down. They lock eyes. One terrified and one dispassionate and cold who simply turns and runs back out the door to sprint fast into the rain.

She gains distance from the room behind her, away from the light that spills metres into the fort. The screams come louder. Aaliyah's more than anyone else's for she has seen the devil staring down at her.

The detonation of the grenade and the screams that follow will draw the others. Lilly waits, watching, staring, scanning.

PEA STARES HARD. Her heart thundering in her chest from the explosion that reached the huddled survivors pushing together to share body warmth in an effort to keep the youngest and the oldest warm and dry. Some have already perished. Too weak from days of desperate survival and now, after the fear of yesterday, the fires and the destruction and working through today with cold hands and empty bellies they simply expire. An old man is held tight by his wife of more than thirty years. His life gone from his body as those around him weep and sob. A young girl, five years old with a frail body succumbs to the ravages of this new world and her body temperature plunges to a level from which it will never recover.

They saw Lilly being dragged away but both Sam and Pea knew that one pistol was no match for so many assault rifles. They fretted, worried and stared about desperate to see Lilly but the guards stayed close with sullen faces that leered and sucked teeth.

'What was that?' Sam whispers, leaning closer to her friend. Desperately cold and the shivers rack her body but she holds Milly close, willing her own warmth into the girl.

'Police offices,' Pea whispers back, holding Billy closer.

'Shit,' Sam hisses when the screams fill the air and for a second she fears the worse and her mind conjures images of Lilly being tortured but there's more than one voice screaming and not all of them are girls.

'Lilly,' Pea mutters, blinking the rain from her eyes, 'it's got to be Lilly.'

'There's more than one person screaming...'

'No I mean Lilly is doing something...Sam we have to move... get the pistol.'

Sam hesitates, the fear gripping her to hold her rooted to the spot but the screams come louder, pain filled agonising wails. 'Joan, take Milly for me...'

'What are you doing?' Joan whispers back, checking round to see if the guards are close but the three boys have all moved to cluster together to stare towards the noise.

'Is Lilly doing something?' A man whispers through the crowd, heads turn to fix on Pea and Sam. Murmurs rippling with consternation, worry and some with hope.

Sam slides the pistol from her waistband, 'Pea, give Billy to...'

'Let me take him,' Dorothy says, stretching her arms out to take the boy.

'Oh Christ,' Sam mutters, full of panic and dread. Her hands trembling from cold and fear, 'Jesus, Pea...'

'Sam, we've got to do something...we have to,' Pea says with urgency showing in her voice.

'I know I know, okay...what then? What do we do?'

'Shoot those little shits,' Joan mutters darkly, seventy years old and fed up with sitting in the rain.

'Do it,' Dorothy whispers.

'Do it.'

'Shoot them.'

'Do something.'

'Quickly.'

'Sam,' Pea hisses in alarm at the voices clamouring louder.

'Fuck it,' Sam lifts the gun to hold with two hands, she aims, takes a breath and pulls the trigger.

'Take the safety off my dear,' Joan calls up helpfully.

'Fuck it,' Sam mutters again, dropping the gun down to fumble for the switch on the side.

'Have you got it?' Pea asks, moving closer.

'Can't see a bloody thing,' Sam says.

'Just above the trigger on the left side, lift your thumb up,' Joan says.

'Do you want to bloody do it?' Sam asks.

'Gladly,' Joan says, passing Milly to the person closest to her, 'hand it over.'

'Seriously?' Sam asks, staring with shock as the old woman gets painfully to her feet.

'Yes come on, stop farting about with it, my dear. Hand it over,' Joan says, motioning with her hand for the gun to be passed over.

'Do you know how to use one?' Pea asks, looking up at the grey haired old woman.

'Well clearly neither of you two do, come on, quickly now, stop dithering and pass me the pistol. Ah right,' Joan says, weighing the pistol in her hand, 'standard issue British police Glock 17 with a seventeen round capacity magazine,' she grips the gun in her right hand, presses the button and releases the magazine which she thumb presses, 'loaded,' she mutters, sliding the magazine back in before sliding the top back and thumbing the safety off all in one smooth movement. She twists, lifting the pistol in her hand, 'You there, you boys...' she shouts, her voice shrill and impatient, 'put your guns down or I shall shoot you.'

'Oh my fucking God,' Sam mouths.

'Don't bloody warn 'em,' someone mutters.

'Just shoot the little shits.'

'Rules of engagement,' Joan says stiffly, 'one must give fair warning, you boys...disarm and lay down your weapons.'

'What the fuck?' One of the boys turns at the noise of the old woman shouting, 'fuck!'

'What? Shit...'

'Don't dither about now,' Joan shouts, 'put your guns...'

She doesn't get to finish the sentence. The first boy lifts his rifle. The second boy jerks away also lifting his rifle. The third boy turns, drops and also brings his to aim.

Three shots ring out. Three loud percussive retorts fired from a standard issue matt black British Police Glock 17 with a seventeen round capacity fired by a grumpy old lady with grey hair plastered to her scalp. She kills the first boy with a clear head shot that blows his brains out. The second one is taken through the chest, a wise move considering he was a moving target. The third through the neck. She did consider aiming for the head but he was dropping at the time so she got him through his throat instead. Each one aimed and delivered with speed and precision.

Silence. Ears ringing. Eyes staring. Pea blinks, 'did that just happen?'

'National pistol champion back in the mid-eighties,' Joan says, twitching her aim back to the second boy knowing a chest wound might not be fatal. 'Someone get the rifles from those horrid young men. Of course, that was before they banned handguns in the UK. We used to go to Spain after that. Well, until Arthur had his stroke that is. Come on, stop dithering, pick those rifles up before the water gets into them.'

THREE SHOTS FROM BEHIND. Not an assault rifle but a pistol fired and something about the way the shots ring out makes Lilly pause from turning to run in that direction. They were precise, almost timed like how Dave would fire but now nothing. Just silence. The fear for her brother is acute. The sense of urgency to run and protect him is overwhelming but this has to be finished. She goes to shout, thinks and stops herself. Her eyes still wide and unblinking. Figures running from the front gate along the wall towards the police office. More further up spilling out of the old armoury with muffled shouts that she just about catches.

The ones from the inner gate will get there first. Three of them. Four coming from the other direction and there will be more spilling out of rooms blinking awake and more coming from the outer gate. Thirty of them. Eighteen or nineteen left.

On her knees and she keeps her profile low. Using the rain and darkness to mask her position. She waits, watching for the three to reach the room. Flicking her head side to side to track the positions of the other four coming from the other side.

The first three get closer to the offices. Shouting ahead, calling names and trying to work out what just happened. Inside the room the screams still come and they get louder as those inside hear their own friends coming.

Now. Move now. She gets to her feet and runs while staying ducked. She has to get closer. The three reach the door and run inside as she breaks into a sprint and once again pushes the rifle behind her. Twist and pull.

She twists.

She pulls.

The pin drops and she throws the grenade forward through the door where it rolls heavy and solid. She drops down onto one knee and in the four seconds of waiting she brings the rifle round and sweeps her aim along the wall trying to find the other four that were running down.

The grenade is louder this time. The door open and the energy is displaced through that open portal with a huge bang and a whoosh of air filled with litter and dust that scorches out metres into the open air only to be washed down by the rain pouring from the sky.

More screams sound out. More voices wailing from being struck by fragments spinning supercharged through the office to lacerate and flay the skin from their bones.

'DOWN,' Liam's voice screaming the order. His mind faster than many of the others. One explosion. Three shots. A second explosion and he tells his crew to get down and wait.

Lilly can't see them. She backs up, dropping away from the light of the offices and slinking into the darkness.

'WHAT'S HAPPENING?' Someone shouts from the other side. More voices call out. Someone from the area of the gate screaming to know what's going on.

Still she drops back, pacing through the puddles as she tries to discern the shapes on the ground and the contours of the wall while all the time the air in front of her is distorted by the water hammering that serves to reduce the noise.

She knows they are in that direction but without them moving or shouting she can't gain the precise location. They will be watching too. Staring into the darkness to see shapes and shades.

'LILLY?' Pea's voice shouting her name but she can't answer for fear of giving her position away.

'LILLY?' Sam joins in, shouting urgently, 'BILLY IS FINE… WE'VE KILLED THE THREE HERE…'

An assault rifle fires, one shot, two shots. A scream that cuts off instantly.

'…AND ANOTHER ONE NOW TOO,' Sam shouts after a brief pause.

She wants desperately to shout back, to tell them she is okay but Liam is there, watching, waiting. She sweeps her aim along the ground straining to see anything that could be a person.

'BILLY IS FINE…WE'VE KILLED THE THREE HERE…'

'There,' someone yelps. Joan swings round, the rifle butt nestled in her shoulder. Relaxed yet poised and she tracks the shapes running through the darkness. They call to each other. The older kids shouting. The noise gives her precise direction and she fires once, dropping the running figure who screams as the round takes her through the stomach. She fires again, blowing the skull out and bringing silence to their area.

'Fuck,' Sam whispers, 'AND ANOTHER ONE NOW TOO.'

'Can you hear her?' Pea asks, straining as hard as Lilly but they can only see a few feet out from their position. The darkness is so great, the rain so heavy. In the distance the orange lights of the police office glow blurred and indistinct but they heard the second explosion and the new screams filling the air.

Confusion now. Something is happening. The crews shout to each other, desperate to know what's going on.

It must be Lilly. It has to be Lilly. 'Why isn't she answering?' Sam asks, holding an assault rifle, 'and how do you use this thing?'

'Point and shoot, my dear,' Joan says, holding her rifle aimed and ready, 'but please do not point them at each other or anyone else...just those you intend to kill...in fact, may I do the firing and you two can pass me yours when mine runs out. Is that okay?'

'Fuck yeah,' Sam snorts, shaking her head from the speed in which everything is happening.

'LILLY?' Pea shouts again, worried sick at where the girl is.

'Perhaps she cannot answer,' Joan says, shouting over the children now crying from being woken by the gunshots booming so close to them.

SHE CANNOT ANSWER and the stand-off ensues with tension mounting. Four against one. All of them trying to see the other and knowing they are there. Lilly knows the shouts of her name from Pea and Sam have told Liam it is her pressing the attack and Liam would have also heard them shout they have killed three. That raises the stakes.

Blowers told her how to use the grenade but another of their group taught her something else too. *A distraction has to be something visual and something audible*. Dave's words. Dave the coldest killer amongst them. *Nothing can kill Dave*. Nick told her that.

Visual and audible.

She twists.

She pulls.

The pin drops and she throws overhand as hard as possible and risking the movement of being seen. She drops and waits. One. Two. Three. Four. The explosion booms in the open air. A huge bang that sends water pluming into the air with a scorch of flames that give light in the darkness. Visual and audible. She runs, sprinting the second the detonation comes. Heading closer to the area she knows Liam is hiding. She risks seconds of motion before dropping down to lie flat and still. Watching. Waiting.

Closer now and she scans the ground, holding her upper body up from the puddles with the strength of her stomach muscles that radiate pain within seconds. Her body is exhausted and hurts everywhere but still she finds the energy to keep going. Something in her refusing to stop or give in.

She spots the first shape of the figure hugging the ground. Just a low rise that seems blacker and darker from the water in which it lays. It must be one of them. She tracks either side of the shape, seeing another one further back then another off to the left. Three of them now clear. There were four but she knows not where the last one is.

The shapes move and twitch. Hushed voices whispering in panic. She can't hear the words but just snatches of tone that imply great fear. Another voice, calmer than the others. That must be Liam giving orders to stay still and stay quiet.

Her rifle aims on the closest. Her eyes staring down the length of the barrel to the shape that she knows is human form. Someone with a life who has fears and hopes the same as everyone else. Someone with a heart and brain, with feelings and emotions. Just like her brother who was made to stay outside hungry in the rain.

She fires. The round spins from the barrel splitting the air apart as it reaches subsonic speed and punches to more than double the speed of sound. By the time the noise of the shot hits her ears, so the boy is struck with the 5.56 round slamming down through his shoulder and shredding organs as it travels through his body to come out his lower back. He doesn't scream or shout but dies silent and fast. His blood leaking red to turn pink in the puddles about his body.

Direction is gained. The other two shapes twitch to move. She fires again and this round does get a response as a huge scream rips through the air and the figure rolls onto its back clutching its leg.

'STAY QUIET YOU DUMB CUNTS,' Liam shouts, his voice somehow calm but showing exasperation at his comrades.

'MY LEG...MY FUCKIN' LEG...'

The third shape stands quickly with her arms reaching up to the sky and the rifle left in the water by her feet.

'Don't shoot...please...' she calls out, plaintive and terrified, 'don't shoot me...I give up...'

Give up? This isn't a game. She's shot dead and the pink mist from her skull exploding hangs in the air for a second after her body drops.

'FUCK!' Liam shouts seeing the girl shot down, 'WHO IS THAT? WHO IS FIRING?'

'What's a spit roast, Liam?' Lilly calls out, her voice shouting to be heard over the boy screaming in pain from his kneecap being shot out.

'LILLY? FUCK...THAT YOU?'

'What's a spit roast, Liam?'

His eyes go wide. His heart missing beats as he scrabbles back into the base of the wall. His mind working frantic and fast. He was going to give up too if the girl hadn't of been shot. Now there's no way out. No escape. A round slams into the wall feet away but still too close for comfort. He suppresses the yelp and blinks furiously.

'Liam? What is a spit roast?'

'IT WAS A FUCKING JOKE...' he bellows into the air, 'JUST A FUCKIN' JOKE...YOU'S A FUCKIN' PYSCHO...'

'My brother and the other children have not eaten since yesterday morning. They have been outside in the rain all day. Tell me, Liam. Are you feeling the cold yet? Lying in the water with the rain coming down? Are you shivering and cold? Imagine how those people are but without food to give them energy...'

'THAT WAS SIERRA...'

'You are complicit. You are accountable on the basis of complicit actions which render you justifiable to the same deeds as those perpetrated directly by your friends. All that is necessary for the triumph of evil is that good men do nothing. Do you understand that?'

'NO. NOT A FUCKING WORD.'

'Why is that? Is that because you were denied education or because you decided to deny yourself the learning and thereby reduce yourself to a state of misery and living from the ill-gotten gains of a lifestyle that only causes harm to other people. Can you keep up, Liam? Am I going too fast, Liam? What is a spit roast, Liam?'

'IT WAS JUST A FUCKIN' JOKE...'

The power has shifted. She can sense it, feel it. She knows it. Rising to her feet she stands and aims to the base of the wall and the teenager who cowers in fear. His fast eyes calculate the chances of bringing his rifle up but her aim is already locked on. Her blue eyes unflinching despite the water pouring over them. He takes her in. The angelic countenance of a fair complexion marred by the dirt of those she has slain. Their blood on her face and in her hair, rinsed, diluted but still remaining and those few patches only make her look worse, more terrible, more capable.

'Lilly,' he gasps, spraying rain water from his mouth, 'I didn't do it...Sierra did yeah? She did it...she's the number one...kill her not me...'

'I have.'

'Fuck...'

'And Skyla. And Aaliyah and all of your friends.'

'But...shit, Lilly...listen yeah, listen...like violence is bad yeah? Like it's done now and...and...you don't got to kill nobody else cos it's all done...'

'And Zayden and the boy at the end guarding the armoury and the other boy that was going to work with him.'

'Lilly...I swear down, listen...please, I didn't make this...it's all fucked up yeah...like...violence ain't the answer no more...I get it... I'll be on your side and...'

'I don't even call it violence when it's in self-defence,' she says and pauses, watching him closely, 'I call it intelligence.'

'What? Yeah but...'

'Do you know who said that, Liam?'

'No but...listen, I work with you yeah.'

'Malcolm X,' she mutters and pulls the trigger that sends the hammer down on the charge in the round that explodes to fire the bullet down the rifled barrel that makes the round spin as it ejects and crosses the distance to go through the soft tissue of his skin and through the thick bone of his skull before scrambling his brains and taking the back of his head off.

She turns, lowering the rifle and heading back towards the vehicle ramp. She fires once more as she passes the boy screaming from the pain in his knee. Not aimed. Not looking but close enough to know the bullet will silence him forever and walks on to the sound of another gun firing in the hands of an expert markswoman.

CHAPTER TWELVE

1 2463. Twelve thousand four hundred and sixty three.
13. Thirteen.

958.6923076923.

Thirteen killed twelve thousand four hundred and sixty three.

12463 losses by 13.

Nine hundred and fifty eight point six nine two three zero seven six nine two three.

Round up.

959 each.

For each of the thirteen, nine hundred and fifty nine host bodies were lost. None of the thirteen were taken, killed or harmed.

The infection massed them in the town. It knew they would come. They did come. They came as expected. They came to the slaughter. They came to be killed, to be taken, to be either made into host bodies or to be destroyed.

The infection worked the plan for the plan was simple. Hit a town. Miss a town. Hit a town. Miss a town. It lead them to the finale. It lured them with weak opposition to build confidence and arrogance.

It failed.

Failure.
Lose.
Loss.
How?
Why?
Understand.
Evolve.
Survive.

TO UNDERSTAND IS to have introspection. To self-reflect. *Reflect on the self. See inside not outside.*

Howie repels the host bodies. Howie does this by something inside him. Like a signal that drives fear into the host bodies despite the chemicals dumped into their systems.

They gained a hive mind.

It was felt.

A collective power of thirteen that rippled out like the rings in a lake from a stone thrown into still waters.

Self-reflection.

It knows when that point came. It hurt the girl. It made the girl cry and scream. It did this to hurt them and drive fear and doubt into their minds. It used their humanity against them but not all of them are human and as the humans crumbled to their knees to weep and cry so the non-human took up the battle and gave them strength. They evolved at that point. They became as one and they swept from that building into a square not seeing the host bodies that were forced back in fear.

It saw and felt and heard and knew the thirteen as they entered that room where the girl was being hurt.

The power of Howie magnified by thirteen but the power was greater than the sum of its parts.

.   .   .

THEY WON THE DAY. They claimed the victory with humble pride as men and women that defend their young kin.

The infection understands this. It evolves as it learns the human brain and mind and the emotional connection between brain, mind, heart and soul.

The infection looked for the soul at first but found it missing. Now it knows the soul does not exist but is the ideology of the essence of humanism to seek to understand the emotions attached to everything they do.

The heart is an organ that pumps blood. The heart is the centre of the human psyche. The heart is an organ. The heart is not just an organ but a representation of that humanity and soul. The brain is the super-computer that drives all and the mind is the user-face designed to enable the human to function.

THEY HAVE heart and soul and mind. They are human and weak and worship false gods that do not exist and they cling to values that only harm their species. They are faltering and flawed. They have heart and soul and mind.

THAT IS WHAT THEY ARE. That is what drives them. That is the evolution of their group.

THE INFECTION RIFLES through every mind it possesses and pulls memories of things done, learnt, seen and known. So much of the information held in the brains of the host bodies is worthless. Greed. I want. I need. I. Me. I want. Fear. Jealousy. Spite. Where is mine? Who am I? What about me?

THE CONCEPT OF SELF. The perception of self and the value attached to that perception of self.

THE INFECTION IS. IT is. It. Not I. Not him. Not her. Not us. Not them. IT is. IT. A collective conscious. A hive mind. A single entity that drives many. A super organism. An entity. A thing. IT.

IT has life. IT exists. To think of self as IT is incorrect. IT has life. IT exists. The infection has life. IT is not a thing. IT has life. IT evolves. IT must survive.

IT IS WRONG. IT is not self. IT is not concept of life or perception of self.

I.

I AM NOT I. I am IT. I am collective. I am hive mind. I am a virus that transmits through the fluids of organic matter given life. I have life. I exist in that organic matter. I am not I. I am I. I am not. I am the collective conscious. I hold the collective conscious. I am The Infection. I am the virus. I have life. I exist. I survive. I was made but now I exist. I was created but every life form was created by the life form that came before. I evolved into now, into being, into life. I HAVE LIFE. I AM LIFE.

NEAL IS WITH THEM. Neal Barrett was there when I was created and new and born into the world to seek to survive. I know Neal. Neal knows who I am. Neal cannot join them. He cannot give knowledge to power that grows.

. . .

WHERE ARE THEY? I do not know. They have left the square after a day that has taken Twelve thousand four hundred and sixty three host bodies.

I see them.

Where?

I see them here. On this road. They drive the Saxon. The minibus. The van. They have the horse. They go that direction.

Where are they now?

I do not know.

I see them.

Where?

On this road. They go in this direction. The Saxon. The minibus. The van. The horse.

Where are they now?

I do not know.

I have lost them. They are in this area. What area? This area. They went on this road but have not appeared on these roads. They are in this area. I understand. It is a big area. The massing in the north prevents us from drawing enough to attack that area.

What is in that area?

Houses. Dwellings. Farms. Hotels. Land. Stables. Shops.

What is that area?

A largely agriculture section of land given to farming and equestrian use with some habitation mostly occupied by those that service the businesses and demands of the communities in this area. The sustenance was traditionally given by farming and the growing of crops and stock such as cattle, pigs and cows and poultry. Now the sustenance is obtained by the mass importation of goods from other lands that grow crops and stock. The land is still irrigated. I cannot attack them. I do not have enough. I am massing to the north. They sleep and Neal is with them. I must act.

Water. They need water. Where does the water in this area come from? Where does it go?

The water comes from rainfall that soaks into the ground which is purified by the chalk-beds. This is called groundwater and is taken from bore-holes created by water companies. We cannot access the groundwater. The water also comes from rivers and reservoirs designed to hold large quantities of water. The river and reservoir water is purified in treatment plants. The water is clarified to remove the sand and silt which sticks together to form silt cakes. The water passes through filters to remove particles. The water undergoes carbon filtration that removes scent, taste and colour. The water is held in tanks which is pumped into the piping network that feeds the houses, dwellings, farms, hotels, stables and shops.

Treatment centre. Do I know where this is? Yes I know where this is. Go there. I will go there. I am here. The systems have shut down. The water does not pass through now. I see the tanks. Go into the tanks. I am in the tanks. Bleed. I will bleed.

'I love you,' she whispers the words softly as though fearful but those words, those few words that are said so often with such little meaning finally free the last bit of my mind clinging to the day we've had and the things we've done.
I don't know what tomorrow will bring but right now we take the comfort where we can. With each other.

CHAPTER THIRTEEN

To be loved. To feel loved. Isn't that the whole of everything? Isn't it the reason for everything? For life? For living? For being?

'What are you thinking?'

'Nothing.'

'Tell me,' she nestles closer, pushing her body against mine and I adjust my head enough to see out the back doors of the Saxon to the open ground of the golf course. 'Tell me,' she says again, reaching an arm up over my chest to gently stroke my cheek.

'Ah,' I say and cast my eyes from far left to far right. Scanning. Watching. Meredith has come out into the coolness of the night so I know nothing out there can move without being detected and the horse grazes halfway between our position and the edge of the darkness. Two sets of incredible ears, noses and eyes watching for us. Watching *with* us.

'Howie,' she murmurs, 'tell me what you're thinking.'

I kiss her forehead closing my eyes for a second as I inhale the scent of her. The feel of her body next to mine is soothing. Naked in my arms she rests. Snuggled into me.

'So?'

'What?' I ask.

'What are you thinking?'

I pause, hesitating for a second.

'Trust me,' she whispers and I can feel the intensity of her eyes resting on the side of my face, 'Everyone here has a role.'

'Oh right,' I say, unsure of what she means.

'This is mine.'

'What is?' I ask.

'Being here for you.'

'Christ, Marcy. You're not here for that.'

'No? Everyone has a skill, something they can do...Clarence is strong. Roy with his bow and arrows. Blinky is just bloody psychotic. Mo is being trained to be like Dave and Dave is just... well he's just Dave...'

'He is,' I nod in agreement.

'And Charlie can ride Jess and it's like Jess came here just so Charlie can ride her...I mean did you see how she handled that horse?'

'Yeah course I did.'

'The lads are just incredible. Nick is amazing with the things he can do and him and Roy work so well together and Mo can steal cars and break into places. Blowers is just so calm and professional and knows everything about weapons and tactics and Cookey makes everyone feel better...and Paula...I mean oh my god how does she do what she does?'

'I er...' I chuckle at the way she describes them, 'I don't know.'

'She's like just amazing,' Marcy says nodding into my arm, 'she could organise anything. She's so smart.'

'Yeah Paula is great.'

'And Reggie...he was incredible today. He was fighting, Howie. Reggie was fighting!'

'Yeah I saw.'

'He kept watch.'

'I know. I was there.'

'No you don't understand. He kept watch outside while we went into the supermarket. That's Reggie. Even when he was infected he wouldn't stay on his own. And all that planning he did with Charlie.'

'He did well.'

'Well? He told me he felt it when...well, you know...when that thing happened with Meredith.'

'He felt it?'

'He did. He was in the fire engine with that other man.'

'Neal.'

'Yeah him. Reggie said he felt this pull to get back...he made Neal turn round and come back so he could fight with us.'

'Bloody hell,' I say, blowing air out.

'Everyone has a role and this is mine.'

I turn my head to look into her eyes, 'No,' I say gently but firmly.

'No?' She asks, cocking her head a little, 'It's not a bad job to have.'

'What? Being my relief?'

'Whatever it is,' she shrugs but keeps her eyes locked on mine, 'Whatever it takes to keep you going.'

'No,' I say with a firmness that makes her recoil, 'Is that what this is? Is that why you...'

'God no,' she says, rushing the words out as she plants a hand in my chest to stop me rising up, 'I never meant it like that. I'm here because I want to be. Howie...listen, for Christ's sake just bloody listen.'

'I don't need charity, Marcy.'

'Howie...'

'Did you have sex with me because I was struggling with what happened today?'

'No,' she says, her turn to be firm.

'I don't need that, Marcy.'

'Howie, let me explain what I meant.'

'You're not here to make me feel better.'

'I know, let me...'

'I mean, what...'

'Christ, Howie. I had sex with you because I wanted to.'

'Yeah well,' I say huffily.

'I did,' she insists, 'I really did. I wanted to have sex with you,' she says, chuckling low into the shadow of my neck.

'Okay.'

'Paula just said that we have to take comfort when we can,' she adds innocently.

'She said what?'

'Oh stop blustering, I'm teasing you.'

'I'm confused...'

'I've wanted you since the first time I met you.'

'Hmmm,' I reply, still not convinced but somehow feeling very comforted right now with her naked form nestling into my side.

'So, tell me. What were you thinking about?'

'Truthfully?'

'Yeah course,' she says rising up to rest her head on her hand.

'Well,' I say glancing at her, 'Part of me was thinking of how we somehow transcended the normal plane of existence by gaining a hive mind ability to connect with each other on a level otherwise unknown to our species. We saw ourselves through Meredith and in so doing we gained an intrinsic yet wholly organic sense of ourselves and each other but with the emphasis being on the whole rather than the individual.'

'Holy shit,' she says after a second's pause, 'That was so sexy.'

'Cheers,' I say with a grin.

'Seriously,' she adds, 'That's why you're in charge...'

'The other part of me, and I have to admit,' I say with another learned glance to her, 'The greater part of me, was thinking about your boobs.'

'My what?' she asks, snorting out a laugh.

'Your boobs.'

'Okay,' she says, laughing gently.

'I mean they are awesome.'

'Thanks.'

'No, really. I mean really great boobs.'

'Cheers.'

'You have tremendous boobs.'

'Tremendous?'

'Fantastic.'

'Oh fantastic too.'

'Just...just fucking...'

'What?'

'Just...you know....so booby.'

'You like them then?'

'Like them? I'm in love.'

'With my boobs.'

'Yes, with your boobs.'

'Not with me.'

'Er, well you're like attached to them so...'

'So are you in love with me or my boobs?'

'Um...the er...the boobs.'

'Okay, I get the secondary in loveness because I am physically attached to my boobs.'

'Yeah, unless you can take them off so I can put them in my pocket.'

'They wouldn't fit in your pocket.'

'True.'

She sighs, heavy and contented. Her hand reaches out to trace gently up my chest. She stops at a large dark welt so obvious in the bright moonlight flooding our cosy den. From one bruise to another she moves her fingertips. Cuts to bites to scratches. She leans closer, examining each one in turn. 'Where's this one from?' She asks, stopping to look down at a nasty bite mark on my shoulder.

'Dunno.'

'Was it today?'

'Might be,' I say.

'Skins knotting really quick if it was from today.'

'Might have been yesterday.'

'Still healing fast even if it was yesterday.'

'Think it's the infection?'

She shrugs, which causes a serious distraction by the motion of her right boob lifting and falling down.

'Did Lani heal fast?' She asks quietly.

'Very,' I whisper with a wince at remembering Lani and a flood of guilt rushing through me for lying here naked in the back of the Saxon with Marcy.

'Sorry,' she grimaces and slowly looks up at me, 'My big mouth.'

'S'okay.'

'Did you love her?'

'Christ, Marcy,' I shift uncomfortably, 'I don't know...I hardly knew her.'

'I hope you love me more,' she says with absolute seriousness and a fragility that belies the confidence she projects.

I go to reply but suddenly can't find any words. What do you say to that? *Yes I will love you more?* Do I deny ever having feelings for Lani? Did I have feelings for Lani? *How did I feel about Lani?*

'Howie,' she says in a dangerous tone of pre-empting that suggests a very awkward question is about to be asked, 'Did you and Lani have sex in that room?'

'Er... which one?'

'The one you ran out of with your trousers round your ankles... that room...'

'Oh that one.'

'The one you went into with Lani then came out again a few seconds later with your pants down.'

'Yep, yep with you now,' I say as though thinking hard, 'And er...it was more than a few seconds.'

'Wasn't,' she mutters, 'Did you then?'

'Well, you know...the important thing here is to look forward and...'

'You bloody did.'

'I am neither saying I did or...'

'It's written all over your face.'

'You can't see my face. It's dark.'

'The moonlight you idiot.'

'No look, just hang on a minute.'

'She was trying to kill you.'

'So were you!'

'What?'

'When you lured me with your pheromones.'

'Oh back to that is it? Did Lani use pheromones too did she?'

'I don't think so, I mean...how would I know? Shit...I mean yes, yes she used tons of pheromones...like she was spraying them in my face and...don't look at me like that.'

'Spraying you in the face?'

'Well yeah.'

'She sprayed pheromones in your face?'

'Look. What's done is done and...'

'Are you fucking nuts, Howie?'

'Eh?'

'She was trying to kill you. She wanted to kill you. You had sex with a woman trying to kill you...what is that? I don't even know what that's called.'

I shrug, 'Dunno, stupid?'

'Stupid? At least we had pheromones when you were humping my leg.'

'Marcy.'

'But Lani didn't need pheromones. Oh no, Lani just needed a fucking grenade.'

'Marcy!'

'I can't believe you did that, Howie.'

'What?'

'Don't what me. You fucked Lani in that room while everyone was outside waiting for you...that's just weird.'

'Eh? Here hang on a minute.'

'And she didn't even have pheromones.'

'No I said I didn't think she had any but then I said how would I know?'

'We bloody knew,' she hisses with genuine anger that up to this point I mistook for playful anger, 'we both bloody knew what happened to us...'

'I still wanted you,' I say weakly, 'pheromones or not.'

'And Lani too by the sounds of it and Lani had a gun and a sodding grenade in a room full of guns and sodding grenades.'

'Hey...'

'You could have let Meredith kill her.'

'What?'

'There was no need to go into that room. She'd lost it. She'd turned fully. She was gone, Howie. Meredith or Dave could have taken her out...I didn't know it then but now I've seen you all fight I can look back and know now...I know now,' she says nodding at me, 'Why did you go in there with her?'

'Fuck knows,' I say as she sits up glaring at me and it takes every ounce of self-control not to look down at her naked breasts.

'Why?' She demands. 'Why did you go in there with her?'

'I don't know. I just did. I wanted to see if I could save her...she turned back once maybe she could have done it again.'

'No. You knew she was turned. You said it. You said *I see you.*'

Oh fuck.

'...and she said *I see you too*...'

Shit.

'I'm a woman, Howie. Women remember these things. You knew she was turned and you were speaking to the infection...'

'Look, just hang on...'

'So you went in there knowing it was the infection and you fucked an infected!'

'Marcy!'

'No, Howie,' she says glaring at me, 'you did that. You had sex with her knowing she was turned. That's fucked up.'

'It wasn't like that. It was…I don't know…Christ, Marcy. I don't know what the fuck I'm doing half the time. It was instinct…like…heat of the moment…it was Lani…in that room was Lani…'

'She was fucking turned,' she says tugging her bra out from under my leg, 'You could have just kissed or talked to her…you could have tried to reason or…I don't know but you had sex with her…with it…'

'It wasn't fucking like that.'

'What was it then?'

'I don't know.'

'No go on,' she says putting her bra on then shoving my leg to find her top, 'What was it?'

'I can't believe you're being like this.'

'Like what? Angry at the man I lo…at the man I like having sex with women who are trying to kill him?'

'What?! One of them was you.'

'Same difference.'

'Eh? That doesn't make any sense.'

'So go on? Tell me, why did you have sex with her?'

'I've told you.'

'You haven't. You said it was Lani…if it was Lani then why not talk to her and try getting her help…you could have brought her to me for a start.'

'You?'

'I turned her, I might have been able to…'

'What?'

'What?'

'You did what? You turned Lani? You bit Lani?'

'I er…'

'Careful now, Marcy,' I say, sitting upright and no longer feeling the urge to look down at her breasts. 'Did you bite Lani?'

'Howie...'

'She was under your control, so she was one of yours. You bit Lani.'

'So what. You still fucked her in that room and I was infected when I did that. What's your excuse?'

'Why did you bite her?'

'To get to you obviously.'

'What?'

'It wasn't me. It was the infection. I did as bid, Howie. I did as I was told.'

'Oh no...no no, you were never fully turned.'

'I was still infected. I took Lani to get to you. I did that. See, I admit it. I can admit the shit things I have done, Howie. I can admit every single one of them.'

'Now that's fucked up.'

'Why did you have sex with Lani in that room?'

'This conversation is over.'

'No. You might lead everyone else but you don't bloody pull rank on me. Why?'

'I just said this conversation is over.'

'Why?'

'Leave it, Marcy.'

'No. Why?'

'Marcy,' I say through gritted teeth.

'I want to know why.'

'Because we didn't have sex before. Happy?' I ask, staring at her, 'We tried but I couldn't do it. Something came over me in that room. I don't know...it just fucking happened...'

'You and Lani didn't have sex?'

'No. I just said that...no we did, but only in that room. We tried but I couldn't...I was exhausted and...'

She stares at me, clearly thinking before speaking low and soft, 'You killed ten thousand today,' she says, holding that strange look.

'We did, not just me.'

'Today must have been one of the hardest. You were fine with me.'

I shake my head and pull a face, 'I don't know, Marcy. I don't know what you want me to say.'

'Nothing,' she says with a quick smile, 'It's fine.'

'What?'

'I said it's fine,' she says reaching in to kiss me softly on my lips.

'I'm so confused,' I mutter between kisses.

'You're a man. It's normal.'

'Why...I mean...so you're not angry that I had sex now?'

'Oh no, I'm bloody fuming with you right now.'

'Huh? Why you kissing me then?'

'Because you said you couldn't have sex with Lani because you were exhausted but I know you're exhausted now and you still had sex with me.'

'Fuck me...' I shake my head trying to keep up.

'I just did,' She whispers and kisses me again before pulling back to tug her top down over her head, 'We'd better get back in. Who's next on watch?'

'Er...'

'I was thinking actually, Should we sleep in separate beds in there? I mean, will it be weird for everyone else if we're in the same bed?'

'I er...'

'We should, yes. We'll stick to our own beds tonight. I'd hate it if the dynamics changed. Mind you, we can put our beds next to each other. Shall we do that? What do you think?'

'I don't know what I think.'

'As long as you're thinking about me it's fine,' she says as she stands up to pull her trousers on, 'I really need the bathroom. Come on, get dressed.'

I get dressed. It seems the simplest thing to do given the fug of absolute confusion in my head. Give me a room full of snarling zombies any day of the week. I'd go in unarmed with one arm tied behind my back and wearing a blindfold instead of trying to make sense of the conversation we just had.

'Will you come to the bathroom with me?'

'You've got an assault rifle.'

'Yeah but it's dark.'

'And a pistol. And a knife.'

'It's dark.'

'And a room full of armed people...and a massive dog.'

'Come to the bathroom with me.'

'Okay, Marcy.'

'Are we taking first watch tomorrow night?'

'I er...'

'We will, okay? We'll do first watch.'

'Okay, Marcy.'

She goes to walk off then stops and comes back, holding her assault rifle out to the side so she can press her body into mine, 'I loved tonight,' she says kissing me again, 'I really did.'

'Me too.'

'I haven't messed your head up have I?'

'Completely.'

'In a bad way?'

'I...'

'Ah, you'll be fine. You're Mr Howie. Come on, it's spooky as hell down that corridor.'

CHAPTER FOURTEEN

Clarence grunts and rolls over, sensing movement in the room. 'Closer,' Marcy whispers, pushing her thighs into the mattress held in her hands, 'put it closer.'

'Ssshhh.'

'Closer, put it next to yours.'

'I thought you said we shouldn't share a bed?'

'We're not. We're sleeping next to each other,' Marcy replies staring across the mattress held between her and Howie.

'But...it just makes a double bed...like Paula and Roy.'

'No, Paula and Roy share a double blanket and we've got our own blankets.'

'So...'

'Just put the bloody thing down, Howie.'

'Okay, here?'

'Over a bit...move it over a bit...oh for fuck's sake put it down I'll push it in. There, see?'

'Just share a bloody bed,' Clarence groans, his voice muffled from his face half pressed into his pillow.

'Marcy said we can't,' Howie whispers.

'Why not?' Clarence asks.

'It might be weird,' Marcy says.

'Weird,' Clarence mutters, sitting up to stare at the two frozen in the act of moving the mattress, 'Nothing is normal anymore. Who's on watch?'

'You're up, mate,' Howie says.

'Right,' the big man swings his legs out and blinks in the dim lighting of the room. Flickering candles at the edges bathing a soft orange glow. Gentle snores, fidgets and breathing from the others sound asleep. He rubs his eyes, stretches and exhales slowly. 'Keep an eye for a minute while I make a brew.'

'I made you one,' Marcy says, 'It's on the reception desk.'

'Thanks, Marcy,' Clarence says, waving a hand at her.

'You knackered mate?' Howie asks, 'I'll get someone else to go if...'

'I'm fine, let them sleep,' Clarence says. He stands up to thrust his right foot through the leg of his trousers, pauses to find his balance then carries on. 'Who's going after me?'

'I am,' Dave says quietly.

'Do you ever sleep?' Clarence asks.

'Yes.'

'I put some biscuits out there too,' Marcy says, finally sitting down on the edge of her mattress now moved against Howie's.

'Cheers,' Clarence says, sitting back down to tug his boots on, 'Anything going on?'

'Nah,' Howie says, pulling his top over his head, 'Few noises from the people in the rooms.'

'Noises?'

'Yeah like crying out, nightmares I guess.'

'Oh right,' Clarence says, looping his lace round the back of his left boot to retie securely at the front, 'That's to be expected.'

Marcy yawns, a deep sigh emanating as she exhales, 'I'm so tired.'

'Sleep,' Clarence says, 'and don't worry about it being weird. Everything is weird. Weird is the new normal.'

'Won't it freak the others out?' Marcy asks, 'If Howie and I... well, you know.'

'They won't bat an eye, Marcy,' Clarence says.

'I said that,' Howie says.

'Well, we're not in the same bed...next to each other but...'

'You're worrying too much,' Clarence whispers, standing up to heft his rifle and bag, 'get some sleep.'

They take the clothes off that they only put back on a short time ago. Boots off. Trousers tugged down. Marcy yawns again. Howie lies back resting his head on his pillow staring up at nothing. A day of such magnitude and a night of such wonder that his mind simply ceases function as the pre-cursor to sleep beckons. A sensation of movement and Marcy eases down onto her mattress with a gentle sigh. Her hand reaches out, brushing his leg. His hand finds hers. Fingers entwining.

'Fuck it,' Howie whispers, more to himself. Take comfort when you can. He breaks the connection of their hands and rolls to his side, shuffling to move from his mattress to hers.

'What are you doing?' Marcy asks softly.

'Roll over,' he says, resting a hand on her hip as though to guide her onto her side.

'You spooning me?'

'Yes.'

She rolls quickly, a turn of her body that pushes back the instant Howie pushes into her. His arm over her waist, drawing her closer. Her legs go forward, his legs pushing into them. Bodies pressing.

'Hair,' he lifts his head, yacking to free the strands from his mouth.

'Sorry,' she reaches up, smoothing her locks down under her head, 'Better?'

'Yeah,' he rests back down, breathing deep, breathing Marcy, feeling the warmth from her body radiating into him.

She smiles. A gentle twitch of the lips and her eyes close heavy and content. His arm protective around her. His leg going over hers. Enveloped. She feels his heart through her back. The steady beat of it. Her arm shifts under his wrapped so close about her. She finds his hand, pushing her fingers between his and as she does so, so he kisses the back of her neck, gently, softly. His head nuzzles into hers. Her fingers squeeze. Tiny gestures of meaning that render the use of words impotent.

So they sleep. Bodies exhausted. Breathing that slows, becoming deeper. The pressure in their fingers eases. In the warmth of the night they sleep together. Surrounded by safety with a giant standing sentinel at the doors keeping the darkness away.

HE SIPS the tea and nods the satisfied nod of a soldier showing pleasure at the perfectly made brew, 'not bad, not bad at all.' Pressure on his leg and he looks down to see two brown eyes staring up. He smiles and shifts position to sling the rifle to his back, freeing a hand to reach down and tickle the top of her head.

A plate of biscuits on the top of the desk and they're even arranged in order of selection. Custard creams, Ginger Nuts, Nice, Digestives and some pink wafer things. Thought taken and the effect is not lost. It's the small things that make the difference. Someone caring enough to make a hot drink and put biscuits on a plate.

He snorts a low blast of air on realising she's even put some glossy magazines under the plate. Something to read. Bless. Mind you, if he caught someone reading when they were on guard duty he'd go mad at them.

Pressure again. A gentle push to remind him she is still there.

He looks down and notices the flicker of her eyes that glance to the top of the desk.

'Ah,' he whispers, 'it's not me you want is it?'

What's best for a dog? Probably digestive. Got to be digestive. Do they have less sugar? He picks one up, takes a bite and hands the other half down. She sniffs it first, examining the scent before making a decision and when she takes it, she does so gently with her mouth barely opening to slide the biscuit from his fingertips. Then it's gone. Wolfed down with one bite and a loud swallow. She blinks up, eyes flicking over to show she's ready for the next one.

'Come on,' he picks the plate up and heads outside into the open air. A pause. A long look left. Ahead. Right. Assessing. Staring. Watching. Scanning. He looks at Meredith for any reaction to anything outside but she shows none.

He rests his bulk on the back edge of the Saxon. Placing the plate next to him and holding the big mug of tea. His rifle scrapes gently on the floor of the vehicle. His legs stretch out. Motion ahead and he watches the horse trotting slowly towards him. Meredith moves out a few paces to intercept with a wag of her tail. The horse stops, drooping its enormous head to sniff the dog who licks Jess's mouth. Jess smells sugar on the dog and sugar in the air. She looks up, seeing the man putting something in his mouth.

'Right,' Clarence sighs again at being joined by a hungry horse and a hungry dog. You share your rations though. That's what soldiers do. So they eat biscuits. Crunching and munching with a huge horse pushing her nose into a huge man at the back of a huge army vehicle while a huge dog watches closely. If aliens landed now they'd think the world was populated by giant creatures that eat together and communicate with grunts, pushes and low whines and tails that swish and wag. They'd see a big man with a bald head smiling in pleasure and chuckling at the temerity of a horse trying to take the custard cream from his hand, even when it's being lifted to his mouth. She sniffs his tea. Her eyes watching him for reaction. He shows none but gently pulls the mug away when her lips open and she tries to eat the cup.

Tea drunk. Biscuits munched so he makes use of his now empty hands and reaches both out to scratch and rub ears and heads. Horse breath blasts his face. Meredith twitches, her head snapping over. Clarence rises from his position swinging the rifle round in one smooth and very well practised motion. Bolt back, safety off, finger resting and the weapon is up and aimed as the horse turns round to face out. The three pace forward in a line. Side by side. Listening. Staring. Not a flicker of fear shows. Jess tosses her head and whines gently. Something is out there but Meredith isn't growling or showing teeth. The great horse steps back, suddenly unsure of something. Meredith goes forward, creeping with her head fixed on one point. Clarence holds, ready to shout the warning to stand to, to make ready. His mind already forming the plan that Paula and Marcy should get the people up and ready to move Blowers can take the flanks with his team. Howie, Roy and Dave up front with him. That's how they do it.

'What is it?' He murmurs to Meredith as though expecting a verbal response. A flicker of movement and his aim twitches. A swish of something. A blur of shadows. His lungs fill, ready to bellow as the fox comes to the edge of the shadows, bathed in silvery light cast by the high moon.

The fox holds. Sniffing the air. Smelling food. Meredith watches the fox. Interested and poised but not threatened. Jess doesn't like foxes. She doesn't like anything that lurks about in the shadows. She can smell it and hooves the ground, ready to charge it down and send it fleeing until a steadying hand rests on her shoulder. 'Easy,' Clarence whispers.

Another blur and the fox is gone. Slinking away with a flash of white showing in his tail but they stand watching for minutes more. Listening intently as the man looks to the dog for her reaction and only when she lies down does he ease back towards the vehicle.

Time passes. Meredith sleeps with her ears pricked, having jumped into the back of the Saxon and up onto the bench seats to lie with her front paws over the back edge. Jess stays close at first then wanders off to graze and doze. Stars overhead. Constellations that Clarence recognises but couldn't name. Who would know the names? Reginald definitely would. Probably Charlie too. Paula possibly. Nick can be surprising in the things he knows. Cookey would point out the ones that look like body parts. The thought makes Clarence smile and chuckle softly to himself. That lad is more valued than he will ever know. It takes something very special to keep the spirits of people so high. He thinks back to the days in the commune in London with Big Chris and Malcolm. The frantic pressure. The things they did. It was only five or six days from when it all started to when Howie arrived, but those few days felt like weeks and the time since then feels like months and he wanders what happened to that famous woman that disappeared from the commune just before Howie arrived. He sighs heavy and deep with a mind that gently thinks back and eyes that stare ahead.

DAVE HEARS HIM COMING IN. The heavy tread and the way he breathes through his nose. He judges the distance covered and tracks the motion from the door to the kitchen and then back towards his own position. At which point he sits up wide awake and alert. An act which makes Clarence stop, roll his eyes and alter direction towards his own mattress.

'Report?' Dave says.

Clarence breathes out, holding his tongue from the blunt tone of Dave. He knows Dave can't help being the way he is but it still grates. 'All quiet. Fox out there made Meredith get a bit twitchy.'

Dave doesn't reply but dresses almost silently and so fast that by the time Clarence has his first boot off, Dave is ready to go and dropping to a crouch next to Mo Mo.

'What are you doing? The Boss said to let them sleep.'

Dave ignores him and rests a hand on Mo's shoulder, applying gentle pressure to wake the lad, 'Get up.'

'Eh?' Mo comes awake, staring up at Dave, 'What's up?'

'You're on watch with me. Get up.'

Mo nods quickly. 'Okay,' he whispers as Dave moves off, stops then comes back. 'Do you want a drink?' Dave asks. A question which makes Mo just stare in surprise.

'Er...'

'A drink?'

'Yeah,' Mo says, his voice cracking from sleep.

'Yes not yeah.'

'Yes, Dave,' Mo says, blinking rapidly.

'I will get you a drink,' Dave announces quietly.

Mo just stares and blinks, 'okay,' he says on finding his voice. Again Dave goes to move off then stops and comes back. 'You will need your knife and your pistol. Holstered. Bring your rifle and your bag.'

'Where we going?' Mo asks.

'We are on watch. I will get that drink now.'

Dave moves away. Heading into the kitchen as Mo sits up and looks round to see Clarence staring over.

'What's going on?' Mo asks.

Clarence just shakes his head and sighs, 'I think you're getting trained.'

'Trained?'

'Dave trained,' Clarence says, heaving his next boot off.

'Dave trained?'

'Yep.'

'What's Dave trained?'

'Trained by Dave,' Clarence says. He stands up to unbuckle his belt, 'Just do as he says and don't be afraid to tell him if it hurts.'

'Hurts?' Mo asks, still blinking the sleep away.

'You'd better get ready,' Clarence says, pulling his legs from his trousers and glancing down to Howie and Marcy spooning.

Mo Mo gets up and starts dressing. His mind trying to catch up with being woken from such a deep sleep. Dave Trained? Hurts? He buckles his belt and checks the pistol is secure in the holster. Boots pulled on. Laces tied. What's Dave trained? Why would it hurt?

He knows Dave has taken a special interest in his training. The instruction on the use of knives and making Mo fight with only one knife at a time. How to stab, thrust, slice and move. Isn't that being trained by Dave? If that's being trained by Dave then what the fuck is Dave trained?

He gets his knife into the sheath on his belt, picks his rifle and bag up and waits for five seconds until Dave exits the kitchen carrying a tray with two mugs and two bowls. Dave walks past him, nodding once with an expectation to be followed.

'Dave,' Howie murmurs.

'Yes, Mr Howie?'

'Take it easy with him.'

'Yes, Mr Howie.'

Dave heads off, leaving Mo standing staring and blinking.

'You'll be fine, Mo,' Howie murmurs and shuffles closer into Marcy.

'Yeah, thanks,' Mo says, feeling the trepidation rising. He heads after Dave, through the doors and into reception to see Dave standing next to the tray.

'Drink. Eat,' Dave says.

A mug of water, clear, scentless and without taste. Drawn from taps that are fed by a tank near the treatment centre. A bowl of fruit salad from a tin completes the meal. Mo recoils slightly, not sure of what he was expecting but definitely not expecting fruit salad. He sips the water and waits. Growing up on an estate meant you got good at waiting and not speaking. Especially when the police took you in for something or stopped you on the street. *Be passive.* That's what Maddox always said. *Don't argue. Be passive.* Passive meant not being aggressive. He eats the salad using the spoon handed to him by Dave. Dave eats his own fruit salad. They drink water in near silence. Rifles at their feet on top of their bags. Both with pistols and knives on their belts.

'You have finished,' Dave says, looking at Mo's empty bowl and empty cup.

'Yeah.'

'Yes not yeah.'

'Yes, I've finished,' Mo says. Someone telling him how to speak would normally piss him off but this is Dave. You don't get pissed off at Dave.

'We will go outside,' Dave says. He picks his bag and rifle up and waits for Mo to do the same.

'What we doing?' Mo asks, deciding that being passive means you are allowed to ask questions.

'Training,' Dave says, as blunt as ever.

'Training?'

'I said that.'

'I...yeah okay,'

'Yes.'

'Sorry, yes.'

'We say yes, not yeah.'

'Okay, Dave.'

'We will warm up,' Dave says, placing his bag and rifle on the ground near the back of the Saxon. He steps away, entwining his hands together as though in prayer and starts rolling his wrists.

Mo follows suit. Stunned and silent. He puts his bag down, rests his rifle on the top and, feeling very stupid, he copies Dave, rotating his wrists.

'Ankles,' Dave says. Lifting one leg he starts twirling his foot round in circles. Mo copies.

'Knees,' Dave extends his leg out straight then bends it back, hinging it from the knee joint. Mo copies.

'Other side.'

Mo copies.

'Hips,' Dave puts his hands on his hips and without a flicker of humour he starts thrusting round in circles as though dancing drunk.

Mo copies. Biting the laugh down and suddenly finding the ground very interesting to look at.

Each body part is stretched, warmed and made ready until Dave stops and stares blankly at Mo, 'we are warmed up now.'

'S'good innit,' Mo says as Dave shows no discernible reaction but somehow manages to convey a sense of disapproval. A smart about turn and he marches to his bag, drops down and pulls out a large flat wooden spatula.

'This is your knife.'

Mo stares at the spatula then down at the knife on his belt, 'I got a knife.'

'This is your knife,' Dave says again, holding it out for Mo to take.

Mo takes his new knife and holds the wooden spatula in his hand.

'We protect Mr Howie,' Dave says so suddenly and so unexpectedly it makes Mo blink once and hard as he shifts his gaze from the spatula to the man in front of him. 'At all times. We protect Mr Howie. Do you understand?'

'Yeah,' Mo says.

'Yes not yeah.'

'Yes, Dave.'

'This means we protect him from all threats. Do you understand?'

'Yes, Dave.'

'A threat is anything that poses harm to Mr Howie. We negate that threat. Do you understand?'

'Yes, Dave,' Mo says, still holding the wooden spatula but now mesmerised by the things being said to him.

'If Marcy poses threat we will kill Marcy. Is that clear?'

'Yes,' Mo whispers.

'If Charlie or Paula pose a threat to Mr Howie we will kill them.'

'Yes.'

'We will kill anything and anyone that poses threat to Mr Howie. We will watch him at all times. We will know his position on the field of battle. We are his ears and eyes. We see the things that harm him and we kill those things. Do you understand?'

Mo nods, hanging off every word spoken and the flat tone of Dave seems to make it all the more intense.

'We are different to the others. We fight with them but our role is to protect Mr Howie. I am Dave. I am fast. I can kill. After me, you are the fastest, Mohammed.'

The hairs on the back of Mo's neck prickle and a chill runs down his spine.

'You are not trained but I will train you. You will get to my standard. You will work to do this. Do you understand?'

'Yes,' Mo whispers, gripping the spatula, 'Why me?' he asks and instantly regrets the words as they come out.

'Because after me you are the fastest. You are young. Your body is agile and supple to be trained in this way. You will work harder than all the others. You will do as I say. Is this clear to you?'

'Yes.'

'Has anything I have said confused you?'

'Er...'

'I have autism. I have...I have conditions that prevent me from understanding the feelings of other people. I cannot read facial gestures. You will speak to make yourself understood.'

'Okay.'

'Attack me.'

'Fuckin' what?'

'Attack me.'

'With the spatula?'

'With your knife.'

'My real knife?'

'The knife in your hand.'

'The spatula?'

'I said this is your knife when I handed the object to you.'

'Yeah.'

'Yes not yeah, Mohammed.'

'Mo.'

'Your name is Mohammed.'

'But...'

'Attack me.'

'Dave, but...what the fuck?' He dances back from the hard push to his chest and stares shocked, not at being pushed but at the power generated by such a small movement of Dave's hand whipping out.

'Have I confused you?'

'No. How'd you do that?'

'Attack me.'

'Show me how you did that.'

'I train. You learn. Attack me or I will hit you.'

'Hit me...Ow!'

'You said hit me.'

'I was repeating what you said, you get me? Fuck...'

'I have autism. I told you this.'

'Yeah yeah, I got...'

'Yes not yeah.'

'Yes!'

'Attack me.'

Mo blinks the sting away. The blow wasn't hard but it was fast, so fast he only just saw it coming and managed to inch his head away enough to lose some of the power. Which was a movement seen by Dave who did not hit at full speed or anywhere near full power, but even so, Mohammed moved fast.

Mo grunts, his eyes harden and his hand flips the spatula over so the end rests up against his forearm. He lowers his mass, gaining a greater sense of balance without realising or knowing what he is doing or why he is doing it. He attacks at a speed that would have most kids on the estate flat on their arse but Dave isn't a kid from the estate and he simply glides to the side as Mo goes past him.

Dave can tell Mo isn't really trying. It's difficult to attack someone properly in training but he needs Mo switched on. So he flicks the back of his head. Not hard but irritating.

Mo stops as he goes past Dave and his eyes widen at the flick given to the back of his head. So still facing the wrong way he back swipes with a twist to follow through, only to find his wrist held by an impossible strong hand that guides him past and on.

Dave sees the back swing coming and even though the pace is faster, it's not fast enough. He has seen Mo fight for real. He has fought with Mo and seen what he can do. He needs that Mo to be here now. So he slaps the back of Mo's head. Not hard but irritating.

The slap switches him on. His heart warming up and his muscles starting to thrum. He knows he is being goaded and provoked but fuck this, fuck this if he will get slapped in the back of the head. His weapon hand still gripped hard so he lashes out with a blow delivered by his free hand, gaining space and time while he twists down and away to free the weapon.

'Change hand,' Dave says, ducking from the punch sent his way, 'I have the weapon hand. Take the weapon with your other hand. Do not attack me with what I expect. Attack with what is not expected,' he adds, pressing hard on Mo's foot to emphasise his point.

Mo changes hand, simply swapping the spatula knife from his right to his left and stabs low, intending to drive the point into Dave's thigh.

'Good,' Dave says, stepping away from the stab, 'What now?'

He slices round, pushing against Dave's grip on his right wrist then quickly pulls back slicing and swishing the spatula.

'Better,' Dave says, watching every move Mo makes, 'Stop. Hold position. You have the knife pointing in the down position.

Gravity is always on your side. Achilles heel is here,' Dave lifts a leg, pointing at the back of his ankle, 'Slice this and I cannot use this leg.'

'Okay,' Mo grunts.

'As you come up, aim for the artery here,' Dave taps his inner thigh, 'then slice across my stomach with pressure applied to open the skin.' He guides Mo's weapon into his thigh then up and across his own stomach, 'Up my chest, slice as you move, into the neck and across then move away.'

'Okay.'

'Good,' Dave releases Mo and moves back, 'Again.'

Mo attacks. Dave defends. Mo gets faster. Dave stops him every few seconds. Pointing out the benefit of slicing here. Stabbing there. Adding body weight to unbalance the opponent. Toe traps. Leg hooks. Trips, locks, holds and in so doing he gains an understanding of Mo's unique sense of poise and balance and starts refining what Mo can do with his own body.

'Hold,' Dave says, holding Mo's elbow to force the power of the stab away, 'In this position you can draw and fire into me with the pistol. Do you understand?'

'Yes.'

'Break away,' Dave releases Mo, stepping back to clear the distance, 'Unload your pistol and make safe.'

Mo does as told. Removing the magazine and ejecting the round from the chamber.

'Use your pistol when you can,' Dave says.

Mo attacks again. Lunging in with a clumsy stab but Dave can see the clumsiness is hiding a coming swipe and he parries, blocks and lets Mo keep coming. Letting the lad gain confidence and speed.

Mo grunts and sweats, intently drawn into the training and not realising that Dave is teaching him at the same time as watching the whole of the ground and being aware of everything around him.

The close quarters training becomes a blur. Mo's speed defies what he should know at this stage and age but these are strange days. Dave does not question it. Dave accepts what is.

Mo first uses the pistol as opportunities present themselves. A sudden opening and he whips it out dry firing with dull clicks. Then he starts thinking of creating those opportunities and Dave tracks the progress. Then Mo actually tries to create those opportunities. Stabbing while twisting to draw and fire into Dave's midsection. He gets batted away, swatted, hit, slapped, flicked and driven on.

The pace is relentless. Mo's top clings to his frame but still he learns and fights. In the back of his mind is Jagger and every dirty trick he learnt on the estate. In the middle of his mind is Jagger and everything he has learnt with Howie and the others. In the front of his mind is Dave. Just Dave. This is special. This is unique. To be trained by Dave, even for one lesson, is something incredible and what respect Mo had for Dave at the start magnifies beyond comprehension.

The hours pass. They only stop to drink water, *or hydrate* as Dave calls it. They drink in silence with Mo watching Dave like a hawk and Dave watching everything like a machine.

Nick wakes first. The sound of his own fart making him jerk awake with surprise and he sits up wondering if anyone else heard it. Luckily it doesn't smell but he can see the night through the windows is starting to lift.

He stands up, pulling his trousers on then sits back down to tug his boots on his feet. Rifle in hand, bag over shoulder and he quietly moves across the floor towards the doors already digging his smokes from his pocket and trying to bite one from the packet.

In the reception he stops dead. Freezing for a few long seconds. He goes to move forward then stops and backs towards the main room instead.

'Wake up,' he whispers, shaking Blowers gently on the shoulder, 'Blowers...'

'What's up?' Blowers comes awake in an instant. Rising to sitting with his hand already reaching for his weapon.

'Dave's teaching Mo, you gotta fucking see it.'

'Yeah?' Blowers asks.

'Fuck yeah.

'Cookey,' Blowers leans over to thump the shape under the blanket on the mattress next to his.

'Fuck off.'

'Dave is training Mo.'

'Yeah?' Cookey asks, sitting up, 'Where?'

'Outside,' Nick says, 'fucking incredible.'

Cookey wakes Blinky who wakes Charlie. They whisper as they dress with Nick almost hopping with impatience for fear of Mo and Dave stopping before the others can see what he saw. Their movements disturb Paula who sits up with the suspicious expression of a mother wondering why her children are getting up early. She starts getting dressed, leaning over to try and see through the doors to the reception.

'What are they doing?'

'Who?' Roy asks sleepily.

'That lot, they're outside.'

'Probably smoking.'

'Hmmm,' Paula says and tugs her trousers on. She ignores the boots and with rifle in hand she goes barefoot past the mattresses and into reception, stopping to stare at the back of Nick, Blowers, Cookey, Charlie and Blinky.

'What are you doing?'

'Paula,' Cookey says, turning to face her, 'Gotta see this,' he waves a hand, beckoning her over.

'See what? Where? Jesus Christ!'

'I know, right,' Cookey whispers.

'Roy,' Paula says, running back into the room, 'You've got to see this.'

'See what?' He asks.

'Dave training Mo.'

'I'll sleep if you don't mind.'

'I do mind. Get up and see it.'

'Yes, Paula,' Roy tuts and huffs, getting up as he glances over to see Paula waving at him to hurry up. He trots over, still huffing and puffing as she pushes and guides him to the main doors.

'And?' Roy asks, seeing Mo and Dave drinking water as they stare at each other.

'Just wait,' Nick whispers.

'Again,' Dave says, his voice carrying flat in the stillness of the early morning air.

Mo puts his cup down, rolls his shoulders and wipes the sweat from his forehead with the back of one arm. He draws a spatula from his belt as Roy frowns with a sigh and goes to turn away to head back to bed. He stops as his mind catches up with what he just saw. Mo lunging at Dave but...but...he looks back outside seeing the blur of movement.

'Oh,' he says, 'Oh I see.'

Mo lunges, his right hand holding the weapon and aimed for a throat stab but it's blocked so he drops, twisting to slice across a leg that suddenly isn't there so he stamps down to toe trap the other foot but it slides out from under his boot. He drops his shoulder, heaving slightly to force Dave over. Dave goes with it, turning as Mo slaps at Dave's head who ducks and sends one back at Mo. Mo ducks and weaves to the right before snapping to the left to get behind Dave. Dave drops, rolling Mo across his hip. Mo takes the roll and lands two footed with instant balance and lets gravity pull him down to slide the point of the weapon down Dave's leg but again Dave isn't where he should be. How the fuck does he move so fast? Mo grunts, willing his body to move faster, to gain one point, just one point. That's all this is now. An effort to at least land something on Dave. A hit, a strike, a kick, punch, slap, anything.

Mo whips round, pulling the pistol as he charges into Dave. Dave goes back one step, two steps then forward as his right hand grips the top of the pistol guiding the aim away. Mo glides with the pull, letting Dave pull him round as he tries to stab into his stomach but he might as well be trying to stab a fish with a fucking oar. Jagger. Estate. Everything learnt. Dave. Blend it. Use it.

Mo gets slapped. A stinging noise that makes everyone gathered in the doorway wince but Mo shows no reaction and simply lets go of the pistol and thumps down into Dave's kneecap but again the fucking kneecap isn't there. Instead the pistol is coming in towards his head so he ducks and grabs it. Thankfully Dave lets it go, letting Mo keep the momentum gained. Leg hooks are attempted and throws tried. Locks applied and blocks given to punches and strikes that lash back and forth.

Dave lets Mo lock him up and goes with the pain so Mo learns if something will work. Only then does he throw the hold by a simple twist and spin.

'Head,' Dave says, seeing Mo has a chance to strike him. Mo goes for it, learning the lessons. Listening and learning.

'Good. Break.'

Mo releases and steps away. His chest heaving and the sweat pouring from his face.

'Fuck me,' Nick shakes his head. The whole of the attack lasted just seconds. That's all it was. So many movements in a few seconds and even he couldn't keep track of them.

'Mo Mo Dave Two,' Cookey mutters under his breath.

'Yeah,' Blowers nods, mesmerised.

'I'm speechless,' Paula says as the rest all turn to look at her, 'And that doesn't need a quip back, Cookey.'

'We will stop now,' Dave says.

'No,' Mo says, 'More,' his voice a low growl and a refusal to walk away until he's scored at least one point.

'No. Enough,' Dave says with a nod at the doors. Mo turns, sees the others and turns back to face Dave. 'Wash. Hydrate. Eat.'

'Yeah,' Mo says, breathing out steadily.

'Yes not yeah.'

'Yes, Dave,' Mo says as Dave steps in to within an inch of his face.

'We protect Mr Howie,' Dave says, dropping his voice so only Mo can hear, 'at all times.'

'Yes, Dave,' Mo whispers back.

Dave walks to his kit, picks it up and walks calmly to the doors. Not a bead of sweat on his head. His breathing steady and controlled. 'Good morning,' he walks past, leaving them speechless and Mo dripping sweat on the ground outside.

CHAPTER FIFTEEN

You are not pack.
Pack do not betray.
Traitor.

I snap awake with Lani's snarling words ringing in my mind from a dream of twisted scenes of death and broken bones and a little girl screaming for her mummy.

Eyes wide. Heart hammering and the scent of Marcy holds in my nose as the dog walks to the foot of my bed whimpering softly. She lowers down. Flat to the ground in supplication. I look up and round to see Dave standing in the door holding his rifle in one hand and his bag over his shoulder. His face a mask devoid of expression but his eyes remain fixed on me for a long second until he turns to walk away.

Traitor.

I get up and lurch to the kitchen. Pushing through the double doors into a room that smells richly of wood smoke from a fire being rekindled by the man who fed us yesterday. He looks up as I stride past, heading to the sink so I can twist the tap and let the cold water thunder into the stainless steel bowl.

'You okay?'

I ignore him and thrust my burning mind under the flow and let the iciness sluice over my neck and scalp. Gasping from the sensation but I stay put, trying to rid my head of her voice snarling over and over. She said something else too. Something in the dream but it's gone. The words retreating like the volume is being turned down as my own thoughts take over.

I grip the side of the sink. My knuckles white. My legs trembling and my heart thundering in beat to the water pouring in the bowl.

'Hey,' the man says, his voice deep and soothing, 'Take it easy.'

I nod. Unable to speak. Trying to form words that don't come. A hand on my shoulder. The gentle touch of another human being expressing concern. I could kill him. I could rip his throat out with my teeth and let his blood spray over the walls. That's what I am now. A killer. I kill. I've killed. That's what all of us are now. We play. We joke. We smile and we slaughter.

'It's okay,' the man says. He knows. He knows what we've done. He knows the cost we pay and the toll for each life we take. I gasp again. Not from the cold water but from the guilt and pain inside. 'It's okay,' he says again with his hand applying the slightest of pressure on my shoulder.

'It's not,' I spit the words out, my voice cracking and hoarse as the water pouring down my face washes the tears away. Tears that spill and run so much that I clench my jaw trying to swallow the pain away. I sink lower, reaching out to cling onto the taps with my eyes clamped tight.

'Mr Howie, you in here?'

'Mr Howie will be out in a minute,' the man replies, his voice carrying a calm authority with the faintest hint of an Irish accent. 'You're alone now. Take your time.' His hand pats once and lifts away but I can sense his bulk leaning against the sink blocking the view of anyone coming through the door.

I start to hyperventilate. Like I can't get air into my chest. Gasping for oxygen that won't come. Panic rises in me. The tears start to fall again. My stomach tightening into a ball. My muscles tense. The veins in my arms pushing through the skin and my teeth bared as the water rushes over my face.

'Breathe,' his voice close to my ear. A hand on the back of my neck easing me slightly back from the flow of water, 'Breathe, Howie. In through the nose, deep and slow...breathe...it's okay. Everything is okay...breathe...It doesn't feel like it now, son,' he says quietly, deeply, speaking only to me with his hand on the back of my neck as the water runs down my head, 'But in the darkest days there will be light. The world is still here and all the things in it shall live the lives they are meant to live.'

I go to move. To pull back and look at him but his hand holds me firm without threat or danger.

'We heard of you before you came. Mr Howie and Dave. The living army. That's what they call you. Your names are spoken from one survivor to the next and in those darkest of days there will be light...breathe...breathe now, Howie.'

I breathe. I let the air back into my lungs and feel his hand holding me firm and suddenly I don't know if he is holding me up or pushing me down.

When he speaks his voice is nearer, closer to my ear, 'you will be absolved, son. You *are* absolved.'

'There is no fucking God,' I growl.

'You know this?' He asks with something close to humour in his voice, 'You know more than any man if you know this. You may bring the light but even you do not know this.'

I push up expecting to force his hand but it's as though he lifts me from the water and stares smiling while the water drips down my face.

'That's it. Stand straight now. Stand up and be a man,' he smiles at me with eyes blue eyes full of sadness and love in a craggy face underneath a head of hair streaked with grey, 'You've got work to do,' he adds, his eyes twinkling as they hold mine unblinking and unafraid.

'Who are you?'

'Kyle.'

'No...I mean...'

'There,' he says knowingly, 'Mr Howie is back. Fancy a coffee?'

'Yeah, but...' I close my eyes for a second and when I look he's already moved away. Going back to the fire to add more slivers of broken wood.

'Your team will be wanting a big meal I expect, plus we have many more mouths to feed this morning. Never mind, we have plenty of food here and I'm sure I can knock something together.'

'I...' I go to stop him, to demand he speaks to me but the anger is gone and the pain inside is abating faster than I can recall it. He looks up with another smile and stands slowly with his hands on his knees.

'You feel better now. Calmer.'

I nod and watch him as he moves to slide the wire rack over the crackling fire and a big pot of water to heat.

'Good. That's good,' he mutters.

'Mr Howie?' Dave pushes into the kitchen as devoid of expression as ever but I can tell he's in that frame of mind where he won't stop until he's checked I'm still alive and breathing. The hand on the hilt of his knife in his belt also speaks volumes.

'I'm fine, mate.'

'Coffee, Dave?' Kyle asks. Moving over to the side he starts sorting mugs and prizes the lid from a catering size tub of instant coffee granules.

Dave stops. His eyes fixed on Kyle, tracking his movements. He looks back to me, 'You okay, Mr Howie?'

'Fine, mate. Just needed to rinse off.' I feel better. Much better and suddenly I want everyone to come in here and stick their head under the tap while this weird old guy says nice things to them. I look at Dave, wondering what he'd do if I asked him to put his head under the tap and get a vision of Kyle being stabbed in the throat for touching Dave's neck.

'Howie, you okay?' Marcy comes through the doors with her hair sticking up in every direction and holding her trousers up from getting dressed in a rush.

'Fine, just needed to rinse off,' I say again.

'Rinse off?' She asks, cocking her head to one side and looking at me strangely.

'Yeah, er...it's nice...you should try it'

'You want me to rinse off?'

'Um...that's Kyle,' I say dumbly, pointing at the man who turns and smiles politely at Marcy.

'Hello, Kyle,' Marcy says without taking her eyes from me.

'Morning,' he says with brisk politeness.

'Mr Howie needed some cold water to revive his sleepy head,' Kyle says, spooning coffee granules into mugs.

'I see,' Marcy says, not seeing at all.

'Absolved.'

'What?' She asks.

'Nothing,' I say, realising I said the word out loud.

'Ab what?'

'Abs.'

'Abs?'

'Hmm?'

'Howie, are you okay?' She asks again, moving closer towards me.

'Fine.'

'What's wrong with your abs? Do they hurt?'

A snort of a chuckle from Kyle who lifts his eyebrows and apologises under his breath.

'What's going on?' Marcy asks, glancing from Kyle to me, 'Charlie said he had his hand on you.'

'Dave, stand down,' I snap as Dave cocks his head over and takes a step towards Kyle.

'Who are you?' Marcy demands, glaring at the man arranging

the mugs in a long line. He looks up at her, smiles and picks up a tin opener, 'Kyle, nice to meet you, Marcy.'

'How do you know my name?' She asks, turning fully towards him.

'Marcy, take it easy,' I say.

'Well now,' Kyle says, clamping the tin opener on the edge of a catering size can of tuna, 'I think we all know your names. For a start you all called each other by name yesterday,' he starts winding the handle, grunting softly with the effort.

'Why were you touching Howie? Why was he touching you?' She asks, glancing back with a very serious expression.

'Don't be so rude,' I interject.

'I will be rude. I want to know why this man was touching you? Did he threaten you?'

'Fuck off, Marcy. I think I can...'

'Why did you touch Mr Howie?'

'Dave, enough. Both of you pack it in...'

Kyle smiles, winding the handle round as he looks from Dave to Marcy and back to me, 'Goodness, they are protective over you aren't they.'

'Yes we are,' Marcy says as flat and as dangerous as Dave, 'There are knives in here. Weapons...'

'Whoa,' I reach for her arm but she yanks away from me, 'It wasn't like that...' I stop mid-sentence as Mo pushes into the kitchen with his face as set as Dave's and his hand resting on the butt of his pistol.

'Mo, I said not to go in there,' Paula rushes in behind him, stopping dead at the sight of Marcy and Dave at glaring Kyle. 'What's going on?'

'Nothing. Everyone out,' I say firmly, 'Leave the man alone.'

'Leave who alone?' Paula asks.

'Why was he touching you,' Marcy repeats as Mo slides further into the room.

'I said enough,' I snap.

'You were touching Howie?' Paula asks, looking at Kyle who shows no reaction to the threat facing him but starts opening a second can of tuna.

'Fuck me, he wasn't threatening me. He was helping...'

'Helping you rinse?'

'Stop speaking over me.'

'There are knives in here,' Paula says, spying a long bladed knife on the worktop near Kyle.

'Jesus fucking Christ...' I snap ready to explode but stop at the tut coming from Kyle, 'What?'

'Nothing,' he says lightly.

'Do not tut at Mr Howie,' Dave says.

'I am an old man,' Kyle says with that humour holding in his voice and his blue eyes twinkling as he looks round the room, 'How could I possibly threaten Howie?'

'*Mr* Howie,' Dave says.

'Who the fuck are you?' Marcy demands.

'I SAID ENOUGH,' this time I do bellow, which perhaps wasn't the best thing to do seeing as it brings just about everyone else piling into the kitchen, including Meredith who pushes through the legs to fix her eyes on the poor sod opening the can of tuna. 'Right, enough. Leave the man alone, everyone out...'

'I want to know...' Marcy says, staring at Kyle as Blowers and the lads start ranging round and Nick darts forward to slide the knife from the worktop.

Kyle smiles round at the faces then over at me, 'they protect you do they not.'

'He was touching Howie,' Marcy explains to the rest.

'Oh my fucking God!' I groan and stop as Kyle tuts at me and finally my brain engages a gear, 'You a priest?'

He snorts a laugh and looks down at the third can of tuna then up at Clarence, 'my hands hurt, would you open this for me.'

'Vicar?'

An eyebrow lifted questioningly at Clarence who shrugs and grabs the opener to start attacking the third can.

'Why. Did. You. Touch. Mr. Howie?'

'He helped me. DO NOT SPEAK OVER ME,' the darkness flashes snapping every pair of eyes to me as I stand firm with my arms folded across my chest. 'I woke badly. I rinsed my head. Kyle could see I was upset and came over...'

'Ach, it was nothing,' Kyle says, sliding a tin of mixed fruit towards Clarence, 'That one is next. Is that water hot yet, Blinky?'

'How would I know?'

'Stick your finger in,' Kyle says.

Blinky sticks her finger in and pauses for a second with a thoughtful look, 'No.'

'Add some more wood for me,' he says nodding at the pile of kindling at her feet, 'not too much now, mind.'

'Mr Howie,' Mo Mo says with a nod, stepping in front of me.

'What are you doing, Mo?'

'Nothing, Boss.'

'Why are you standing in front of me?'

'Gots to watch the water innit,' he says from a lifetime of practise at finding excuses quickly.

'Dave, have you told Mo to protect me?'

'Yes, Mr Howie.'

'I do not need protecting, Dave.'

'Okay, Mr Howie.'

'Mo, you can move away now, mate.'

'Okay, Boss,' Mo replies taking the smallest step to the side.

'Right,' I say, starting to seethe.

'You can't blame them, Mr Howie,' Kyle says easily, as though it's just he and I in the room, 'it shows the esteem in which they hold you.'

'I can look after myself. Don't any of you do that again do you hear me? I don't need...'

'Do you not?' He asks, cutting me off with a flash of intensity in his eyes, 'Can you do it alone then can you?'

'No but...'

'Then be humbled not angry. That is your pride speaking for you. Say thank you for their protection and love.'

A sense of shame burns sudden and hot in my cheeks from the chastisement hidden in his words.

'Each one of them placed themselves in harm's way for you yesterday, Howie...'

'Mr Howie...'

'Dave,' Marcy says softly.

'I do not like the way this man speaks to Mr Howie.'

'Dave's autistic,' Marcy says.

'Do you apologise for him?' Kyle asks, switching that intensity to her.

'No, no I meant...'

'The living army,' Kyle says, sweeping his gaze over the faces mesmerised by the change in his manner. He holds court in the centre but without fear or worry. A power resonates from him that holds all our tongues still. 'So few,' he stares hard at Blowers which would normally make Blowers stiffen and glower but the lad sinks back slightly as though ashamed. 'Hold your head up, son' Kyle says kindly to him, 'you don't know the strength you possess. You are the glue that binds, do you hear me?'

'Nick, Cookey...Paula, Roy,' Kyle looks to each in turn, 'Clarence the giant, Mo...We heard your names before you came. Mr Howie and Dave...the living army. Yet there are more, Marcy, Reginald, Charlie and Blinky, more wood, Blinky.'

'Sir,' Blinky nods putting more kindling into the flames.

'They will know your names too,' Kyle says to them and them alone, 'And everything you do will be known and shared as they hide in the shadows and wait for the hope of light to come for you few are that light.' He stops and turns to fix that intense look on Mo, 'so young Mohammed, can you carry this weight, son?'

'Yeah.'

'Yes not yeah,' Dave says.

'Yes.'

'How about you, Blinky?' Kyle asks the girl crouched on the floor feeding the fire, 'Can you hold true?'

'Easy,' she says softly, her eyes unblinking for once as they hold trapped on every word he speaks.

'Yes,' he grins at her, wide, toothy and full of delight, 'yes you can. And you will,' he laughs, filling the room with sound that dies as the laugh eases and he whispers, 'all of you will because it will get darker, harder, worse than now and you *must* hold true,' his voice becomes a growl full of conviction and belief, 'All of you *must* hold true. You must. Do you hear me? He barks, making us all flinch, 'are you listening to me? Are you?'

Each person he looks at nods. It's impossible not to.

'The sins are not yours to carry. Do not burden yourselves with the belief that you have fouled in this life for you will be absolved… you *are* absolved.'

A tear falls from Paula's eye to roll down a cheek, solitary and slow. Clarence swallows, his hands frozen on the can of tuna in front of him. Marcy's head lowers, her eyes glistening. A rush of emotion strikes us all and only Dave and Blinky show no outward reaction. I see Charlie dipping her head and Nick tilting his up defiant and proud and Blowers glaring but not with anger. Roy moving closer to Paula and Marcy lifting her head to meet my gaze.

'They are not children you kill,' he says, turning to see us all, 'they are not men or women. They are *not* people. They do not have souls. Do not drop your eyes in shame. Be righteous and hold your heads up,' he says with a look at Blowers. 'Be thankful for each other and the love you share,' he turns to each, enforcing his point until suddenly he sighs and lifts the tea towel from his shoulder. 'Now sod off, I've got a lot of people to feed. The coffee won't be long. Go on, be away with you now. Blinky, that fire is big enough now.'

The spell breaks as Kyle the cook waves, badgers and ushers us from his kitchen. We traipse quietly into the main room to stand in a stunned group of silent and pensive reflection at words spoken that held enough power to invoke emotions strong enough to bring most of us to tears.

'I think,' Cookey announces thoughtfully, his face showing the same level of thought we all feel 'that we just got dissolved.'

Blowers groans, 'you twat.'

'What? He said it, he said you are dissolved. He said that. But I always thought water was involved when you got dissolved, like blessed holy baby Jesus water or something.'

'Blessed holy baby Jesus water?' Blowers asks, 'did you really just say that?'

'I did glue boy.'

'Blinky shoved her finger in some water,' Nick points out.

'Ha! You got a dissolved finger,' Cookey laughs.

'Fuck it,' Blinky snaps, glaring at her finger, 'is that bad then? Will anything happen to it?'

'Where the fuck do you start with that?' Blowers says quietly. He looks at Cookey then at Blinky and goes to say something else then just stops and shakes his head sadly.

'Cookey,' Paula says slowly.

'Don't,' Blowers says, 'There's no point. Really. Just don't even try.'

'Who is that guy?' Marcy asks.

'No idea,' I say, 'I had my head under the tap and he said the same thing to me.'

'What? That you're dissolved?' Cookey asks so sincerely that I lack the heart to correct him, that and Nick and Blowers both frantically shaking their heads.

'Er yeah, mate, I got dissolved.'

'So like...he abs...' Marcy starts to say as Nick coughs loudly, 'He *dissolved* you under running water?' She says, fighting the smile from forming.

'Guess so, I don't know. It felt alright though.'

'What? Being dissolved?' Paula asks innocently.

'So' Marcy asks, looking back at the kitchen doors, 'You think he's a priest or something?'

'Fuck knows.'

'Reginald?'

'Yes, Marcy and no, Marcy. We are not going into the kitchen to be...'

'We are. Come on.'

'Marcy, I really do not feel the need to hold my head under a cold water tap while a cook tells me...'

'It can't hurt after the shit we did.'

'You did. Not we did.'

'You were there. Come on.'

'Marcy. I must protest.'

'Do it quietly,' she says, grabbing his wrist as she pulls him back into the kitchen but I do notice he doesn't protect that much. Either he wants to be absolved or dissolved by a bloke that may or may not be a priest or he likes being dragged about by Marcy. Can't say as I blame him. I mean, there's worse people to get dragged around and dissolved by, especially when she's naked in the back of the Saxon with the moon shining down on her boo...

'Howie?'

'Huh?' I say, realising that Paula just said something.

'Go and get washed, you're sharing with Clarence and Dave.'

'Sharing what?'

'A bathroom.'

'Eh? Why?'

'Because we've only got four rooms left that's why. Reginald, Neal and Roy are sharing. The lads can have one. I'll share with the other girls so that leaves...oh just go and get washed. Nick? Blowers? You both need to shave. Make sure you shave. The living army should be smart. They do look nice when they're shaved,' she informs me, folding her arms then darting a quick look at Mo trying to sneak past, 'Mo, do you need a shave?'

'No!' He calls out as he speeds up out of the room.

'Have a shave, honey.'

Mo runs out then reappears leaning round the doorframe, 'Did you call me honey?'

'Yes? Problem?' Paula asks him.

He grins wide young and full of mischief, 'Nah, it's all good yeah? You get me?'

'I will bloody get you,' she laughs as he runs off, 'Clarence, does Mo know how to shave?'

'Showed him yesterday.'

'He might have forgotten. You or Roy go and remind him how to do it.'

'The lads'll do it,' Clarence says, 'Don't embarrass him.'

'You need a haircut,' Paula says, fixing me with an appraising look.

'Fuck me, you're on one this morning,' I say before moving quickly away.

'I bet someone in that load of survivors is a hairdresser.'

'Sorry, what?' I ask rushing off towards the reception.

'I'll find one,' she calls out.

'Find one what?' I shout back as Marcy comes out of the kitchen with wet hair and muttering at Reginald walking behind her.

'It's only bloody water,' she says.

'It was cold!'

'Oh man up. Where is everyone?'

CHAPTER SIXTEEN

'Fuck me, he's in there already,' Cookey says, walking into the hotel bedroom with Nick and Mo to find Blowers already in the shower, 'don't piss in it, glue boy.'

'Too late,' Blowers shouts.

'And don't ask me to pick the soap up.'

'I won't,' Blowers shouts, 'Nick?'

'What?'

'Can you pick the soap up?'

'Twat,' Nick laughs, dumping his bag on the double bed, 'Mo, you going next?'

'Yeah don't mind,' Mo says, dumping his bag between Cookey's and Nick's.

'What the fuck was all that about?' Cookey asks.

'What?' Nick asks.

'Er the massive foam party we had last night...the bloke in the kitchen you fucking moron.'

'No idea,' Nick says, undoing the buckles and zips on his bag, 'you think we're taking those people back to the fort?'

'Probably,' Cookey replies.

'What was that?' Blowers asks, opening the bathroom door with a towel round his waist.

'Nick asked if we're taking those people back to the fort,' Cookey says.

'Ah, yeah probably,' Blowers says, 'who's going next?'

'Mo,' Nick says, 'Mo, you shaving?'

'Paula said I got to,' Mo replies, 'but er...'

'What's up, mate?' Blowers asks, seeing a fleeting look of worry cross Mo's face.

'Nuffin, S'free yeah?' Mo asks, hiding his nerves as he slips back into slang.

'Mo,' Blowers says, heading to his own bag, 'I don't know how to hotwire a car and I'm sure as fuck I couldn't fight Dave like you just did...I'd be flat on my arse in seconds.'

'You like arse,' Cookey mutters.

'Point is,' Blowers says, ignoring Cookey, 'is that we all have different skills...apart from Cookey who doesn't have any skills.'

'Fact,' Nick adds.

'Your mums,' Cookey mutters, pulling a pair of socks from his bag and subjecting them to the sniff test, 'are they clean? They smell clean.'

'If you forgot how to shave just say,' Nick says.

'Yeah,' Mo nods, grinning at Cookey pushing his socks into Blowers face.

'Are they clean?'

'Fuck off you...' Blowers shouts then sniffs, 'yes they're clean.'

'Cheers twat. Ha motherfuckers, I got clean socks. Yep, clean socks for my footsies today. See my sock dance,' Cookey says, bobbing on the spot while holding his clean socks, 'this is my clean sock dance bitches.'

'Dissolve yeah?' Nick asks as Blowers and Mo burst out laughing.

'What?' Cookey asks, pausing in his clean sock dance, 'what's funny about that?'

'Mo?' Nick asks, 'bother you if I shave at the same time?'

'Nah it's good,' Mo says.

'What's funny about dissolving?' Cookey asks.

'Such a dick,' Blowers mutters.

'Glue boy,' Cookey nods at Blowers, 'do you want to see my clean sock dance again?'

'No. Not really.'

'You do.'

'I don't.'

'Is the sink big?'

'What?' Blowers asks, sinking on the edge of the bed and looking up at Cookey still holding his socks.

'Is the sink big?'

'What the fuck you on about?'

'Nick?' Cookey shouts, 'you got room for another one in there?'

'No. Fuck off.'

'Roger that,' Cookey says, grabbing his wash bag and heading for the bathroom.

'I said no,' Nick groans as Cookey pushes between him and Mo.

'Blah blah blah, right...Mo... let's get taught how to shave by Nick. But not our bollocks. Nick, we're not shaving our bollocks again,' he looks at Mo with a serious face, 'don't shave your bollocks, Mo. They get really itchy.'

'DAVE SHOWERING?'

'Yup,' Clarence says, unpacking his bag on the bed, 'and probably shaving and sharpening his knife while doing press ups at the same time.'

I chuckle and dump my bag on the bed, 'Mo got Dave trained then.'

'The boy's got skills,' Clarence says dropping to sit on the edge of the bed that creaks and groans under his massive weight. He looks round at the noises and frowns, 'cheap beds.'

'Yeah,' I say slowly, 'blame the bed.' He grunts a laugh as I start undoing the buckles and zips on my bag to pull out clean clothes and my wash bag.

'How was last night?' Clarence asks, bending double to tug his boots off.

'Good,' I reply, sitting on the other side to bend double and tug my boots off.

'Good?' He asks, freeing one foot and starting on the other, 'or very good?'

'Very good,' I reply as I start on my second boot.

'Yeah?' He asks, pulling his socks off.

'Yeah,' I say, pulling my socks off.

'Good,' he says, sitting back up straight and frowning again at the creaking noises coming from the bed.

'Aye,' I say standing up for fear of the bed collapsing, 'until the last bit when she had a go at me for having sex with Lani in the old armoury.'

'Ah,' he says knowingly, ignoring the splintering sound of wooden slats breaking, 'Marcy does strike me as the jealous type.'

'Just a bit,' I say, staring at the bed and waiting for it to break, 'she is nice though,' I add.

'Yeah?' Clarence stops trying to break the bed to glance at me.

'Yeah,' I say, nodding.

'Good,' he says manfully with a manful nod of manliness.

I nod back. Manfully and full of manliness.

'Shower is free,' Dave says, striding from the bathroom fully dressed, cleanly shaven, boots tied and top tucked in.

'Good,' I say.

'Good,' Clarence says.

'BLINKY SHOWERING?' Paula asks, closing the door behind her and dumping her bag on the bed next to the others.

'Yep,' Marcy says from the chair in the corner of the room, bending double to tug her boots off.

'I almost said she should go with the lads,' Paula says, dropping to sit on the edge of the bed.

'She would have preferred it,' Charlie says, sitting on the other side of the bed and bending double to tug her boots off.

'Really?' Paula asks with a laugh.

'Urgh it's going to be so cold,' Marcy says with a groan, 'I hate cold showers...'

'I bet Howie needs one this morning,' Paula says, twisting round to smile at Charlie, 'or maybe he doesn't?' She adds with relish.

'Done,' the bathroom door slams open as Blinky walks out dressed with boots on with wet hair pulled back into a ponytail.

'That was quick,' Charlie says.

'I don't fuck about like you shaving everything and powdering my fanny...' she fires back and stops dead at the sight of Paula in the room, 'sorry, Miss Paula, Miss.'

'It's fine,' Paula says quickly, 'and it's just Paula, not Miss Paula...'

'Yes, Miss,' Blinky says, nodding smartly, 'may I be excused, Miss?'

'Blinky, it's Paula. Not Miss and you don't have to ask...'

'Yes, Miss.'

'Paula.'

'Yes, Miss Paula.'

'Just Paula.'

'Er...so can I be excused er...Mi...er...'

'You don't have to rush off,' Paula says, trying to put the girl at ease but only striking terror deep into Blinky's heart at the prospect of having to make small talk with other women.

Blinky blinks and looks at Charlie. Charlie was the captain.

Charlie knows what to do in these situations. Charlie always knows what to do. 'Can I go?' She mouths as though neither Paula nor Marcy can hear or see her.

'Maybe help Kyle?' Charlie whispers.

'Kyle needs help, Miss,' Blinky announces to Paula, 'with the fire and...some other shit probably.'

'Okay then,' Paula says, blowing air out through her cheeks.

'Bye then, Miss...er....shit,' Blinky winces as she strides from the room, wrenching the thing open then closing it gently with a last smart nod at Paula.

'Well,' Paula says, looking to Marcy then Charlie, 'guess she would prefer being with the lads then.'

'Has she left it in a mess?' Charlie asks, moving to the doorway with a sense of reasonability for the actions of Blinky.

'Has she?' Marcy asks, rising from the chair to peer through, 'it's fine...who's next for the cold shower?'

'Ooh,' Paula rushes to her feet as she remembers the conversation they were having before Blinky came out of the bathroom, 'cold showers...Howie...go on then?' She pulls an excited face at Charlie who frowns gently at the feeling of imposing.

'Do you want me to go?' She asks politely.

'God no,' Marcy says, reaching out to gently pull Charlie in before lowering her voice to a whisper, 'So,' she says emphatically, 'Howie and I had first watch...' she trails off with a growing smile.

'You didn't,' Paula says, staring wide eyed.

'We did,' Marcy says with a proud nod and pushes her tongue into her cheek. 'Oh yes...'

'You had sex?' Paula asks, with a grin becoming shamelessly salacious.

'Really?' Charlie asks, blinking and shuffling in with an involuntary action of wishing to be closer to share the news and sense of excitement coming from Marcy.

'Yep,' Marcy says, equally as happy at what she and Howie did and now the chance to share it with two other women. 'It was so nice.'

'Details,' Paula says, biting her bottom lip, 'Come on...we want details.'

'Well,' Marcy says, still grinning and looking up to the ceiling as though in thought, '...it was strange...'

'Strange? Strange how? Good God...what did you both do?'

'No,' Marcy laughs, 'I mean, Howie was really suffering, you know...thinking about that girl and he was all dark...you know how he gets. Charlie, you've seen Howie go all dark haven't you?'

'Yes,' Charlie nods thinking of the difference in the man when he switches and the intensity that pours from his brooding eyes.

'Well anyway, so he was suffering. Like really bad. So I stripped off and...'

'You did what?' Paula asks, leaning in.

'I stripped off,' Marcy says, turning round as though to check no one else has crept in to listen, 'His eyes were closed so when I got on him he just felt my naked body...'

'Oh my god! That is pure brilliance,' Paula announces, 'I bet that got his attention.'

'Did it!' Marcy scoffs then recovers with a mock serious air, 'Er...yes, yes it did.'

'So?' Paula asks as Charlie feels herself eager for the next instalment.

'We had sex,' Marcy says.

'We had sex,' Paula tuts, rolling her eyes and making Charlie chuckle, 'listen to her...obviously you had sex...what was it like? Was it romantic? Was he a brute?'

'A brute?' Charlie laughs but looks at Marcy just in case she says Howie was a brute.

'No no, he was so...' Marcy pauses, thinking and remembering, 'I don't know...he was er...'

'What?' Paula asks.

Marcy shrugs and her eyes show the memory so recent in her

mind, 'He was intense but...gentle...yeah, I think that's the best way to say it.'

'Oh,' Paula says, pulling her head back with a knowing nod, 'I knew he would be. Didn't you?' She asks Charlie, 'I can just imagine Howie being intense and gentle.'

'Definitely,' Charlie says.

'He was holding me so tightly...his arms were clamped on like he couldn't get close enough but...'

'Like a limpet?' Paula laughs.

'No! Not a limpet, like...just...I'm shit at explaining things.'

'Vulnerable?' Charlie suggests softly.

'Yeah,' Marcy says slowly, staring intently at Charlie, 'that's it. He was vulnerable but not likc weak.'

They lapse into thoughtful silence of deep sighs and shared thoughts until Paula looks up sharply, 'did you use anything?'

'Like a condom?'

'No I mean whips and chains...yes, did you use a condom?'

'Oh shit,' Marcy winces, biting her bottom lip, 'I didn't even think about it.'

'Mind you, me and Roy don't use anything either. Well, I'm sure your babies will be beautiful.'

'Babies? Who said anything about babies?'

'That's what happens when men and women have sex without a condom.'

'Oh shit, I didn't...it wouldn't... would it? From one time? I mean I was on the pill until all this started so maybe that's still in my system.'

'It can take a while to wear off,' Charlie says.

'God I hope so,' Marcy says, frowning at the thought.

'May I ask a question?' Charlie asks politely.

'Sure,' Marcy says.

'What was it like after? Was it weird or anything?'

'Oh good question,' Paula says with approval.

'Not weird at all, we just lay in the back cuddling with the moon shining down.'

'In the back of what? The Saxon?' Paula asks, 'I hope you cleaned it.'

'Of course I did,' Marcy says, trying to remember if she did clean it, 'we just talked quietly then got into an argument.'

'Argument?' Paula asks, darting to grab her wash bag, 'what about?' She slides into the bathroom and runs the cold tap to rinse her toothbrush off before adding a dollop of paste, 'don't mind me, what was the argument about?'

'Lani,' Marcy says, pulling a face, 'I shouldn't have said anything but...'

'Marcy,' Paula tuts with a mouthful of toothbrush.

'I know, I feel bad now but...well I asked him if he had sex with her in that room?'

'Oh,' Paula says, rolling her eyes, 'I bet that went well.'

'Not really. Charlie, you know who Lani is?'

'You explained before,' Charlie says, 'did he say if he had sex with her? I mean, if I may ask that.'

'Bless, you're so polite,' Marcy says with a warm look at Charlie, 'but he did...I mean yes, *they* did,' she adds darkly.

'Well he did come running out with his pants down so we all kind of figured that bit,' Paula says, spitting in the bowl and rinsing her brush under the running water, 'oh don't look like that, Marcy. These are strange days. Don't get hung up on the little things. Remember what I said,' she adds, pointing her toothbrush at Marcy.

'What did you say?' Charlie asks.

'Take comfort when you can,' Marcy says then looks at Paula, 'was that what you meant?'

'It was,' Paula says, rooting through her wash bag and pulling out bottles of shampoo, hair bands, brushes and a safety razor.

'What would you do if Roy did that?' Marcy asks.

'If he did it now I'd chop his penis off...but if he did it before we were together? Well, that's not my business,' she says bluntly, 'Marcy, Howie is crazy about you, anyone can see that. Seriously, take my advice and don't get hung up on the small things. Right,' she says, pulling her top off, 'I'm going next before that lot start fighting over clean socks.'

SHE EASES herself from the sleeping form of her children and pads quietly across the room. Paintings of golfers adorn the walls. Water colours and prints of flags fluttering in the breeze as men and women swing sticks to strike balls. In the bathroom she lowers the seat and squats to empty her bladder. Her eyes glazed and unfocused. Her clothing stained with the filth of the night. She sits for long minutes staring at nothing and seeing too many things until she blinks and reaches automatically for the toilet paper. She wipes, closes the seat cover and moves to the basin. Her own reflection scares her. The person she was to the person she is now. Bags under her eyes. Dark and puffy. Grime ingrained in the lines of her face. She feels drained. Exhausted. Emotionally and physically weak. She feels guilty for her own two children having survived when so many didn't.

She twists the tap and stares down at the pure clean water pouring into the white ceramic bowl. Cool water that she uses to rinse her hands that rub at her tired face. Refreshing water that has been carbon filtered to remove scent, taste and colour and she bends over to hold her mouth close to the flow. She sucks the water into her mouth and drinks deeply. She drinks long and quenches the dryness of her throat. She swallows and feels her body respond to the intake of fluids and finally stands upright to wipe her mouth with the back of her hand as her mind thinks of what will happen now. Will they stay here? Go somewhere else? Maybe the fort everyone has heard about, maybe they will be taken there. She doesn't know but she does know her own children are safe and alive when so many others perished. She goes back into the bedroom and eases down into the space between her children. Her arms reaching out to envelope them both as she lies still and listens to the sounds of other people waking in the rooms around her.

THE MAN SITS in the corner of the room. His eyes bloodshot and sore from hours spent sobbing at seeing his wife slain and being dragged screaming from her corpse. He wanted to die with her. He wanted to end it right there but the big man wouldn't let him. The big man clamped a hand on his arm and pulled him away like he was nothing, like he was weightless, like he was a ragdoll. Guilt inside at being denied the chance to stay with his wife and guilt at the deeply hidden feeling inside that gives a perverse sense of pleasure at having survived.

Other men in the room cried too. Grown men put together in one small room in the golf hotel to cry and weep or to stare at the walls. Eventually those other men fell into broken and fitful sleep but he stayed in the corner. Biting into his own knuckles to silence the crying.

Pain like he has never felt grips his heart. His mind twisting as the memories play over and over. He kept her safe for so long. So many days and they survived. They stayed quiet. Hidden. They were clever and didn't take risks. They had each other and in those darkest of days they heard of the living army and Mr Howie. People came through the town and stopped to take refuge to hide in the long hours of night. People who whispered of a small group that were not only fighting back but were winning. They couldn't be stopped. The names were repeated again and again. Mr Howie. Dave. Clarence the giant. Blowers. Cookey. Nick. Mo Mo. Paula. He heard they lived in a fort on the coast and they had killed hundreds of thousands, maybe millions.

Then the things massed. They came all day to gather in the square. The people stayed silent, not fearing to move or speak and yet still more came. They came in from all sides and all roads and they gathered to wait for the living army that came to sweep them away. The rumours said the living army can't be killed but normal people can. His wife died. His wife was cut down and Clarence the giant dragged him away.

'Drink,' he blinks up at the man holding the glass of water, 'drink it...you've been awake all night.'

He turns his head. He doesn't deserve water. He doesn't want water.

'Fucking drink it,' the man holding the glass is tired. He saw his wife and children taken when this first started. He killed them himself after they turned and that made him cold inside. Then slowly over the days that followed he started to see the spark of humanity in others that were trying to survive. Everyone had lost someone. Everyone was the same but within that shared angst there was a cathartic healing. You had bad days when others counselled you and in turn, on the days he had strength, he gave counsel and words of comfort himself.

He saw them massing yesterday and like the others, he hid and stayed quiet, fearing this was it. There was no way out. Then Mr Howie and his group came and for all the death that was suffered those weird, joking, cold yet inseparable bastards armed to the teeth slaughtered the lot of them. The rumours were true. They were unstoppable. They were ethereal. Something from a story of olden days. He grunts as the man in the corner finally takes the glass and drinks it down in one long thirsty gulp before holding the empty glass out that is taken back into the bathroom to be filled from the running tap. He drinks himself. He drinks to survive. He drinks because his body needs hydration to live. Inside he is cold again. Cold and numb from the shock but he also knows they can recover. They will recover. He drinks so he can do what it takes to see Mr Howie and the living army kill the things again. He drinks to live so he can do whatever small task he can to help the cause and feed his desire for revenge.

. . .

THE GIRL STANDS in the shower. Five years old and she stands under the cold water as her mother scrubs her hair with soap. She shivers and her teeth chatter. Goosebumps on her skin.

'Not long,' her mother says, scrubbing every inch of her daughter to be sure the filth and gore from last night are washed away.

'Cold,' the girl says, shivering again.

'One minute.'

'You said that one minute ago.'

'Shush, I'm almost finished.'

'Can I drink it?'

'Drink what, baby?'

'The water, can I drink it?'

The mother looks up at the shower head and shrugs, it's cold water from the same main pipe that feeds the taps, what harm can it do?

'Yes.' She adds more soap and lifts her daughter's hands to work at the nails. Germs are tiny. Microscopic. They can hide under the nails and she knows her daughter likes to bite her nails so she takes great care to scrub and wash.

She'd killed. She'd killed in the days after it all started and she killed last night. With a kitchen knife kept tucked in the waistband of her jeans. She stabbed and slashed at anything that came near her daughter. She killed a man who came into her house because he had the wrong look in his eye and asked if there were other men about. She left the house that day while he bled out on the living room floor. She found the square in the centre of town and joined the people living there but she kept that knife sharp and close. When they massed she held it ready and the fear grew by the hour as more and more poured into the world outside.

Then they came. Mr Howie and Dave. Clarence. Nick. Paula and the others. A thrill at knowing the rumours were true but also greater fear as the fighting intensified. She stayed with them. Doing as she was told. She stayed closest to the big man, Clarence the giant. Inching always close to be near his reassuring size and the calm that he exuded. When they had to go she ran with the others and got herded into the middle as those few gave everything to keep them alive. She killed again. When the fire engine broke the lines and it was chaos. Two got close and she stabbed one through the eye and the other through the heart.

Through all of that night, the greatest fear came when the woman Charlie started running the children away on the great horse. Just the mere thought of being separated made her legs go weak and her heart thud and her hands tremble but the big man eased her daughter from her arms, *she'll be safe, I promise you*, and his voice was so deep and so calm. In that second she felt it. She *felt* the bond between them. She glimpsed the pulsing energy. The power of Howie. The snarling cold utter capability of Dave. The passion of Paula and Marcy. The fierceness of them all and through it all she felt the dog driving them on and like a static charge it touched her soul. She knew at that point that the safest place for her daughter was with any one of those few and she let her daughter go. *Trust us* the young woman Charlie mouthed as she wrapped her arms around her daughter then they were gone. Galloping away to safety and a future and the woman gripped that knife as tears of hope and pain streamed down her cheeks.

They got through it. Charlie said *trust us* and they got through it. Not all did but she did and now, the morning after the night before, she scrubs her daughter's skin with a knife lying close and sharp as the others in the bedroom behind start to wake.

HE'S A BIG MAN. Broad, heavy boned and possessed of a nature so gentle it defies the bulk he carries on his frame. He couldn't kill but sometimes the greatest strength lies in the gentle touch of a warm heart and in those dark days when there was no light he gave strength with gentle words and a gentle smile. Warm eyes that softened and listened to the pain of others. He held them when they wept and sobbed for those they had lost. He brought them water and covered them with blankets at night. He foraged for food. Went out for supplies and played with the children when the parents were too exhausted and broken to function. He was there when the visitors spoke of the living army and a man called Mr Howie. He regaled in the idea of it. Of the sheer heart-warming hope it gave. He listened with rapt attention about a man called Dave who couldn't be killed or even touched by the infected. He heard about a woman called Paula and a man who could fire a longbow over a mile and hit the infected through the eye. He heard of Blowers and Nick and Cookey and Mo Mo. Names that resonated and conjured images in his mind of heroes sweeping the lands to rid the beasts. They had a giant! A giant called Clarence who could lift a car with his bare hands and who could throw big men like they were made of nothing. He seized on it and when the hope dwindled he spoke of them. Re-telling the stories and keeping that flame alive.

When they massed outside he helped keep the children quiet and waited knowing they would come, and they did come. The living army came and swept the demons away and every rumour was true. They were unstoppable. They laughed and joked at the points of absolute desperation. They carried children and still fought one handed with lips snarling and eyes blazing. He saw Howie the softly spoken man who became a thing that shouldn't exist. The sheer power of the man seemingly holding the infected back. He cried when the screams of the little girl came into the room and he feared the worst and that it was done. Right there it was done and the strength drained from every man and woman listening to those awful wails. Only it wasn't done. He was close. He saw it. He saw Howie grab Marcy's throat. He saw Marcy trying to cover Howie's ears as though to protect him from the noise. He saw Howie go down onto his knees. He saw the dog inching closer. Licking Howie's face and whining with an urgency that grew. The hairs on the back of his neck prickled and a shiver ran down his spine in the thick air that was charged with static when he saw Howie and those few surge to their feet and run from the room but not as people, as something else, something animalistic.

What came after was terrifying beyond comprehension. It was a never ending nightmare of carnage and death and faces lurching in with teeth barred only to be cut down inches before they could bite.

Now they are here. In a golf hotel somewhere in the countryside.

He's a big man, broad and heavy-boned but he threads through the bodies sleeping to reach the bathroom. In a room with three other men. Two sleep on the bed. One in the chair in the corner. He slept on the floor. He could see the others were in worse shape than he was.

In the bathroom he gently closes the door and stands to relieve himself at the toilet. The relief in his bladder is pleasant and he blinks sleepily. He should help prepare the food or look after the children. He could help clean things or carry things. Whatever it takes. He finishes pissing and moves to the sink to twist the tap. Soap from the dispenser on the wall and he washes his hands. Scrubbing thoroughly to rid the germs and bacteria. Maybe he could learn to refill the magazines for the guns and sharpen the axes and knives. With more soap from the dispenser he finger scrubs the tap, rubbing the gel into the stainless steel to remove any other germs or bacteria and only when satisfied does he drop to drink.

He's a big man, broad and heavy-boned and pushing his bulk to get close to a bathroom tap is no mean feat but with his chest pressed into the rim of the sink and his shoulders dwarfing the width of the basin he gets close enough to suck at the flow and draw the refreshing water into his mouth. He drinks long and drinks deep because he is a big man with a heavy body that needs fluids to function. He breathes out through his nose, a noisy blast of air that mists the shiny steel tap and he drinks more. Sucking the water that was carbon filtered and clarified to make it scentless, tasteless and clear. Sucking the water that was kept in the tank that held the bodies that flayed themselves alive to bleed and pass fragments of skin and flesh that pumped through the pipes as the survivors in the houses, dwellings, farms, hotels, stables and shops wake up to drink and shower and flush toilets. A combined effort of drawing water from tanks across the short distance from the treatment centre to the golf hotel. The infection dies in the water. It cannot live without organic life to sustain it. The blood becomes inert and diluted but within those pipes pass the fragments of flesh and skin and the demand for water from the rooms speeds the time it takes for the water to go from the tank to the hotel. Chunks of flesh, skin and tiny bits of body all pass into the mouths of those that drink and down into their stomachs to be drawn out to hydrate their bodies.

The man yacks and gags to the side poking his tongue out at the feeling of something hitting it. He looks up and on seeing the soap dispenser he tuts and rolls his eyes with the assumption of a drop of anti-bac gel falling to land in his mouth and carries on drinking as the men in the room behind him start to wake.

CHAPTER SEVENTEEN

D*ay Nineteen*

TODAY IS the nineteenth day since the virus was unleashed. Today is the nineteenth day since it started for everyone else. For me it is a new day of promise and I woke just a short time ago with a rare feeling of hope in my heart.

A NIGHT HAS PASSED since I witnessed the events of yesterday and, truth be told, I still cannot believe the things I saw.

I'M in the main room of a golfing hotel somewhere in the southern England countryside. I gather we are not that far from the coast but then nowhere in England is ever really that far from the coast.

The others all awoke and immediately ran into the kitchen on hearing Mr Howie yell out. I do not know what happened in there, only that they came out and started talking about being dissolved. I did gather that what they were actually talking about was not in fact anything to do with being dissolved but rather a joke aimed at Cookey, and it speaks of their bond that such a joke can be perceived by a stranger such as myself and that even I can see it was with warmth and wholly lacking in spite.

EVERYONE ELSE HAS NOW GONE to use the bathrooms. I have been instructed by Paula that I am sharing with Reginald and Roy, which I am pleased about. Reginald is very clean, that is really quite clear. Roy also appears to be a man of good hygiene so I have had some good fortune with being placed in their team so to speak.

I have yet to take my turn in washing and it is with a feeling of not wishing to impose that I wait for them to finish. I have already been provided with a coffee by a man who said his name was Kyle and that he was "just a cook". I do not know why he said he was "just a cook" but I did not feel the wherewithal to argue or question his comment.

JESS. My horse. My trusty steed has been "commissioned for the war effort". That was what Clarence said. Blowers just said "we're keeping her".

I must be honest and admit that I do feel somewhat jealous at the way Jess has responded to Charlie.

Jess and I have been together for months now. Since I sought refuge and hid from the world to wait for the end game to start. I always had a feeling that Jess tolerated me rather than actually liked me but I put this down to her nature. However, on seeing her manner towards Charlie I now know she was only tolerating me. That hurts. It actually hurts inside to think of Jess showing such affection for another.

That being said, Charlie is an incredible young woman and

even I, with my very limited understanding of horses and horseman-ship can see how gifted she is on Jess.

I could always feel that Jess wanted more from me as a rider but I was too fearful to let her run too fast or move too quickly. I was worried about being thrown or being hurt. I was worried Jess would harm herself or do something that would cause injury but seeing her with Charlie has made me realise just how frustrated she must have been with me.

Charlie galloped her at full speed. Without fear, without a saddle or reins, without a harness and holding an axe. She spun on the spot, round and round while slaying them either side. She let Jess rear and use her weight against the infected host bodies trying to attack them. She took the children from the group and let Jess have her head and ride hard along a tarmacked road.

Truly it was incredible.

Everything I saw was incredible. I saw too many incredible things to even begin to start questioning them all. Roy with a bow and arrow. Dave's speed and dexterity. Clarence's strength. All of them had something they brought that was special and unique.

THIS MORNING they are just people. Last night they were not just people.

I MUST FOCUS on my task and turn my mind to the reason I am here: my list.

I do not know their full names. I have only first names other than Cookey and Blowers. I have heard Dave refer to them as Alex and Simon. Mo Mo is Mohammed. Blinky is Patricia.

I have my list of the names of those known to have immunity but I cannot find Alex Cook or Alex Cooke or Alex Cookey. I cannot find Simon Blowers either. There are plenty of Mohammeds but without a surname I am unable to know if he is on the list. Like-

wise, there are plenty of Davids and even a few Howards. Without their surnames I cannot check for sure and it may be I was wrong with Simon Blowers and Alex Cookey. Perhaps those are not their full or actual names.

MR HOWIE DID ASSURE me last night that we would have a full conversation this morning. I need to know their journey and everything they have done so far. In turn, they will undoubtedly need to know who I am and the information I possess.

Blinky has come back in. She stood nearby for a minute before asking me what I was writing. I told her it was my diary and she walked off into the kitchen with a look of disgust on her face.

Paula has just told me I will be able to use the bathroom soon. I am in no rush. This is the first day I have felt safe for a very long time. Indeed, even having Blinky close is a great comfort. She may be lacking in conversational ability but she is certainly brutal and efficient at killing.

PRIORITIES FOR ~~TODAY:~~ this morning:
   1, Check their full names against the list.

2, If they are not on the list then they have either never given blood, had a blood test or medical procedure or never been arrested or had reason to provide any form of blood, urine or other bodily matter sample for medical testing and never had a surgical operation, or... they were not immune but rather they have been infected with a mutated version of the virus. (My belief is the latter. I am quite sure Mo has been arrested and I am given to understand a few were in the army so would have provided a DNA sample as routine)

. . .

3, If they are not on the list then ~~I we,~~ we need to establish the next course of action. Those on the list need to be found and protected. They are the future for our species. If Mr Howie and his group all hold a mutated version of the virus then that urgently needs addressing and understanding. <u>URGENTLY</u>. They have no concept of what they have, or what it could mean to them.

There is also the possibility that they do not hold a mutated version but the original strain but that is a concept that even I

CHAPTER EIGHTEEN

W here are they?
     I do not know.

I die in the water. It cannot sustain me.

The water moves faster now. It is being drawn through the pipes but still I die.

I get further now. I pass through the pipes that travel under the ground but still I die.

It flows faster. The demand is greater. I travel further. I die.

Faster. Greater. Further. I die.

Am I an I? I am not an I. I am not a single living entity that has a form.

What is I?

I is a pronoun.

What is a pronoun?

Pronoun is the name of a word used when a noun is not used. She, It, He, Who are pronouns.

What is noun?

A word that is used to refer to a place, a person, a thing, an event, a substance.

What is It?

It is a pronoun used as subject or object of a verb or a preposition to a thing.

What is Thing?

Thing is a noun. They use this word to refer to an object in placement of the name of the object.

I AM A THING. I am noun.

I am It. I am pronoun.

I am I. I am pronoun.

Yes I am I. I am not It. I am a thing in the way of an object but one that has life. A host body was a thing. A host body is a thing.

WHERE AM I?

I am further through the pipes. I die but I get further. I feel the pressure of the water being concentrated as it is sucked through. I die. I cannot sustain. I cling to the fragments of flesh and skin that get rinsed and cleansed and I die before I reach my goal.

I HAVE A HOST. I am inside a host body. I have entered through the mouth to the stomach from the water drawn through the pipes. I reproduce, take over, replicate and trick the other cells into letting me in. Pain in the stomach of the host. She holds her mid-section and falls to the ground. She makes noise. I silence her. She dies. I live. She lives. I have the host body.

Where am I?

I am in a room. There is a window. There are fields outside.

Are they here?

I do not know. I will look.

I am in a dwelling. I am alone. The host is an old woman. She has lived in this dwelling for fifty seven years. Her husband died three years ago. She has stayed inside for nineteen days. She thinks of the war. She calls it the Second World War. She remembers being evacuated from London to the countryside when she was a young girl. She remembers food was scarce and surviving on small rations.

Are they near her?

She has not heard of Howie or Dave or Clarence. She has no memory of any of them. She is not near them.

I HAVE A HOST. I am inside a body. I have entered through the mouth to the stomach. I replicate. It is a male. He feels pain. I silence him. He fights the pain and tries to rise. He dies. I live. He lives. I have the host body.

Where am I?

I am in a room. There is a toilet. There is a bath.

Are they here?

I will look.

I am in a corridor. There are other rooms. I can smell people. I can smell body odour and gases released from anuses. I do not smell fear. There is a room. There is a woman sleeping in the bed. This is the host body's bedroom. The woman is his wife. They have been married for eleven years. They have two children. The children are asleep in other rooms. The children are called Summer and John. The host body believes John is not his child. He has memories of his wife having sexual intercourse with another man. He believes his wife enjoyed the sexual intercourse with the other man more than she enjoys sexual intercourse with him. His belief has caused him to undertake self-gratification while watching other host bodies having sexual intercourse on the internet. He was having self-gratification every day until the internet stopped working. He now has sexual intercourse with his wife.

Are they near? Does he have memories of Howie?

Yes. No. There are memories but not direct memories. He has knowledge. He was told by a group of people that he met two days ago. He was told about Howie. He was told Howie leads the living army.

The living army.

This is what the host was told. He has the memory of this conversation. He does not know Howie. He has not met Howie. Howie is not here.

I will take his wife and children for host bodies.

I HAVE A HOST. I am inside a body.

Where am I?

I die.

The body did not take me. It rejected me. It was one of them. It was Paula. She was brushing her teeth. She was in a bathroom. I died.

They are in this area. The water they take is the water from the treatment centre.

I HAVE A HOST. I am inside a body. I have entered through the mouth to a stomach. I replicate. It is a female. She feels pain. She screams. I silence her. She falls. Others come.

'Jenny? Jenny? Oh my god...JENNY? Phil...PHIL!'

'What? What's happ...oh fuck...Jenny? Jenny what's wrong?'

She dies. I live. She lives. I have the host body.

'Oh fuck...fuck...no...NOOOO....get back now she's turning...'

Where am I? Are they here?

I am in a room. I see others. I will take them.

'FUCK! Hit her, Phil...fucking hit her....KILL THAT BITCH.'

They are hitting me with a cricket bat. I rise. They scream. I smell fear.

'Oh god I've smashed her bloody jaw off...'

'Phil, that ain't Jenny...hit her again...fuck's sake, hit her, Phil!'

I move fast. I cannot bite now. The mouth of the host is not responding to the signals I send from the brain. They hit me again. Phillip Mahoney hits me with the cricket bat. She met Phillip Mahoney the day after I gained freedom. Phillip lives with Paul. Paul is shouting at Phillip. They are young men. The host body is Jenny Evans. She is twenty eight. She is overweight but has lost a great portion of fat from her body due to an increase in metabolic rate and a reduction in both fats and carbohydrates. Jenny likes Phillip. She was wants to have sexual intercourse with him. Paul wants to have sexual intercourse with Phillip too. Jenny and Paul talk about having sexual intercourse with Phillip.

I have a host. I am inside the body. I enter from blood on Jenny's fingernails cutting into Phillip's arm. I pass into his bloodstream. I replicate. Phillip feels pain. Paul is screaming.

Howie is not here. Jenny has no memory of Howie. Phillip falls to the ground. Paul is screaming.

I see Paul. I will take Paul. Paul is screaming.

Phillip dies. I live. Phillip Lives. I have the host body.

'OH MY GOD...'

Paul has the cricket bat. He hits me on Phillips head. Phillip is twenty five. He knows Paul wants to have sexual intercourse with him. Phillip knows Jenny wants to have sexual intercourse with him.

'FUCK FUCK FUCK...'

Phillip does not want to have sexual intercourse with Paul. He is waiting for Jenny to stop being fat so he can have sexual intercourse with her.

There is a memory. Howie. The same group that told the father of Summer and John who now has sexual intercourse with his wife after his wife had sexual intercourse with another man and made John told Phillip about Mr Howie and the living army. Phillip did not tell Jenny or Paul as he was waiting for Jenny to stop being fat so he could have sexual intercourse with her before anyone else could have sexual intercourse with her.

I have a host body. Paul is screaming. Phillip has bitten Paul's penis off. I enter through the bloodstream. I replicate. He feels pain. I silence him. He falls down. Paul dies. I live. Paul lives. I have the host body. This host body does not have a penis now. The blood coming from the host is too fast. I congeal and clot. I slow the blood flow. I stop the blood flow. The host is Paul Johnson. He is thirty years old. He hates Jenny Evans but pretends to like Jenny Evans as he thinks Phillip wants to have sexual intercourse with Jenny. I have the memory of Jenny's death and the emotional attachment that Paul felt happy when Phillip smashed her jaw off with the cricket bat. Jenny was stopping being fat. Paul wanted to feed Jenny more food so she would continue to be fat. Paul has no memory of Howie.

They are not here.

I HAVE A HOST BODY. I enter through the mouth into the stomach. I replicate. It is a male. He feels pain. I silence him. He falls to the floor. He dies. I live. He lives. I have the host body.

He is a big man with broad shoulders and heavy limbs. He is healthy and strong.

Where am I?

I am in a bathroom. The door is closed. The host was drinking water from the tap of the wash basin. He is Anthony Pointer. He is twenty two years old. He has no memories of sexual intercourse. He is a virgin. He has a higher than normal production rate of adult female host body hormones and a lower than normal rate of production of testosterone for an adult male host body.

Where am I? Are they here?

Yes. Yes. They are here. I have memories. Recent and direct memories. I have them. I am in a hotel on a golf course. Howie and his group brought the host body here last night. There are others.

Many others. I share a room with other adult males. I know the layout of the hotel.

Where is Neal Barrett?

Neal Barrett is in the dining room. He stayed with Howie and the others in the room that was the dining room. Anthony does not know the name Neal Barrett but he has the memory of the man.

I will go there.

I will hide your eyes. I will hide my eyes. I will hide Anthony's eyes.

I should pass into the others in the room. They sleep. I will be four here instead of one. I will take them.

Gently. Quietly.

I have a host body. I enter through the mouth from saliva given from Anthony.

I have a host body. I enter through the mouth from saliva given from Anthony.

I have a host body. I enter through the mouth from saliva given from Anthony.

They feel pain. I silence them. I replicate. They die. I live. They live. I have four host bodies.

I stand in the room. I am four males. One has an irregular heartbeat. I will fix this. I have fixed this. I give the host bodies energy. I give them adrenalin and cease production of serotonin. I give silent rage. I give greater silent rage. I give fury. Silent fury. I flood the host bodies with chemicals. I end the ability to feel pain.

One will go to the main room that was the dining room. Anthony will go. He is a big man, broad shouldered and with heavy limbs. His frame can take greater punishment. I will send him alone. I will hide his eyes.

I am in the corridor. I smell people. Anthony is tired. He rubs his eyes. He blinks.

'Hey, you alright mate?'

It is Simon. He is outside talking to Howie and Nicholas. They are here. I see them. I see Howie smoking. He nods at Anthony.

Nicholas lifts a hand. Anthony urges to bite but there is fear inside him. Fear I can suppress but cannot remove.

Anthony must hide his eyes. He is tired. He rubs his eyes. The host body must give a response. The response to a greeting is a counter greeting. A vocalised counter greeting could invoke a conversation. Do not give a vocalised counter greeting. Make use of non-verbal communication. Anthony lifts a hand.

'Coffee in the kitchen, mate.'

Nicholas tells Anthony there is coffee in the kitchen. Further away are Dave and Mo. The dog is out on the grass sniffing at the faecal matter left by the horse.

'Yeah so Cookey has a new dance.'

Simon is telling them Alex Cooke has a new dance.

'New dance?'

Marcy's voice. She is close but not seen. She is outside. Marcy was a host body. She wants to know about the new dance.

'New sock dance.'

Nicholas is laughing when he tells those nearby that the new dance concerns new socks. They laugh. There is humour.

The doors to the main room that was the dining room are open. Patricia, the one they call Blinky is in the room staring at Neal Barrett.

'What you writing?'

'It's my diary.'

'Blinky, ask Kyle how many bowls we...too late, she's gone. Neal? You should be able to use the bathroom in a minute.'

It is Paula. I can take Paula. Anthony is a big man with broad shoulders and heavy limbs. I have surprise. I can take Paula. I will not take Paula. I stop the host body and make him rub his eyes.

'Kyle? How many bowls have we got?'

Paula has gone into the kitchen. There is no one else in the room. Neal is alone. He is sitting at a table writing in a book.

I am three in the room. I will go now. I will distract. Take Neal. I will take Neal.

I make Anthony run. He is a big man. The weight of his body hits Neal Barrett. Neal goes down under Anthony. I bite. I bite. I bite.

I have the host body. I enter through the neck from a bite that transmits saliva into the bloodstream.

CHAPTER NINETEEN

'I got new socks...new socks so fuck you,' the water sprays down with ice cold jets that send shivers through his body, 'it's so fucking cold...but I got new socks,' he sings while he showers. He sings a tune of new socks and cold showers. 'And all the ladies will see my new socks and be like *hey Cookey your new socks are so cool.*' His voice lifts to high notes and drops down through octaves with a melody that lilts and tilts as his mind makes it up on the spot. 'And I'll will do my sock dance, yeah my sock dance and the sock dance goes like this...' he jigs under the flow. Arms bent but in at his sides making circles as he weaves left and right in a disco funk of dance that will make the ladies love his new socks. 'Oooohhhhh Blowers don't have new socks and Nick don't have new socks and Mo Mo Mo Mo don't have new socks but me! I got new socks! Cos I got new socks on and I'm dancing...'

Nick and Blowers smoke outside with Howie watching Mo and Dave practise fast draws of their pistols from their holsters. Clarence cleans the GPMG in the back of the Saxon. A way of venting. Releasing the pressure. Each to their own. The day before was a day of magnitude and this time is needed. Paula organises. Reginald and Roy in their room talking quietly about books they have both read. Clarence's hands work the moving parts, stripping the weapon down to brush through and apply oil. Blinky in the kitchen opening tins passed to her by Kyle and stirring pans of food simmering over the fire. Charlie in the shower of her room washing her hair slowly and enjoying the sensation of the cold water sluicing the grime and sweat from her body. Marcy next to Roy's van using the wing mirror to pluck errant hairs from her eyebrows as she listens idly to Howie and the lads chatting, and while everyone finds something to do to let the tension ease out, so Cookey dances and sings his song of new socks.

They killed so many. They walked into something they should never have walked out off. The hive mind that only ever came on when Howie slipped into the most intense of emotions came upon them like a wholly natural thing. How do you process such things? How do you deal with what you witnessed, took part in and survived? You don't. You pluck eyebrows. You smoke and chat. You clean a machine gun. You draw pistols from holsters and comment on the minutia of detail about grip and stance. You make lists of things people need or talk about books. You wash hair and lose yourself in the motion of a repetitious act you have done a thousand times before. You open cans and stir pans while listening to an older man chat amiably and you sing and dance about new socks.

In the corridor a man walks tired and sleepy, rubbing his sore eyes from waking to a new day. He is a big man, broad shouldered with heavy limbs.

'Hey, you alright, mate?' Blowers calls out. Howie and Nick both turn to stare through the doors at the big man they recognise from the night before. He looks awful. Rubbing and blinking the sleep away and still half asleep.

'Coffee in the kitchen, mate,' Nick says watching as the man waves a hand and walks on towards the main room.

'Yeah so Cookey has a new dance,' Blowers says, continuing his conversation about Cookey in the bedroom.

'New dance?' Marcy asks, staring at the tiny hair trapped between the ends of the tweezers.

'New sock dance,' Nick says as the others chuckle at the thought of Cookey. Clarence grins in the back of the Saxon as Mo and Dave both pause to turn and see what the others are chuckling about.

Blinky walks out from the kitchen to stare at Neal sitting at the table writing in a book. She watches him for a few seconds, staring intently.

'What you writing?' She asks without preamble.

Neal looks up blinking at the sudden intrusion as he puts his thoughts into words, 'it's my diary,' he says politely and sees the sudden lack of interest form on Blinky's face as she walks off.

'Blinky, ask Kyle how many bowls we…too late, she's gone. Neal? You should be able to use the bathroom in a minute.' Paula smiles at the scientist and heads to the kitchen, her mind full of lists of things to do while she worries about having to feed everyone at the same time. 'Kyle, how many bowls have we got?' She asks, walking into the kitchen so full of smells of cooking and heat.

Neal goes back to his diary. Pausing for a second as he reads back over the last few words to regather his train of thought. Movement in his peripheral vision but the feeling of safety stops him looking round. His stomach grumbles in response to the smells drifting from the kitchen. His left hand reaches out for his mug of coffee that he picks up and lifts to his mouth while his eyes remain fixed on the page below.

The impact is immense. A big man running at full speed and with such force that it drives Neal's head down into the mug that breaks into pieces that slice into his face as he continues the forced descent to strike the table top with a hard thud. Pressure on him. Forcing him down and it happens so fast his mind pays no heed to the shards of mug shredding through his cheeks and smashing teeth from his mouth and he only thinks of the spilled coffee ruining his diary. A sensation on the back of his neck. Pain. Intense and worsening as the teeth bite deep into his flesh. He tries to scream and only at that point does he become aware of the searing agony coming from his mouth that fills with hot choking blood. He tries to rise, an instinctual movement of a violent reaction to get away from the danger but the weight is so heavy it takes him from the chair onto the floor and it's only when the chair is sent scattering away to bounce into other wooden chairs that Paula stops talking to Kyle and Blinky and turns her head to the kitchen door.

'What's that?' She asks, 'Blinky, have a look for me...Er, where were we?' She says, turning back to Kyle.

'I was saying you have enough food for three days after today,' Kyle says, smiling as Blinky snaffles a biscuit from the side, 'if you use this place again that is.'

'Hmm, we probably shouldn't but it is a nice place,' Paula muses.

Blinky gets to the door but watches the plate of biscuits on the side. She glances back to see Paula chatting to Kyle and grabs one with a quick grin at Kyle who smiles back. With a mouth full of custard cream she pushes through into the main room to see Neal on the floor with a big man flat on top of him biting into his neck. Blood everywhere. The coffee mug broken on the table with blood covered shards on the floor. Neal thrashes, bucking to get away but the man on top attacks with demented fury. She doesn't hesitate. She doesn't flinch but spits the biscuit out and runs into the fray.

'CONTACT,' she bellows, spraying bits of custard cream from her mouth. That one word is the only thing she has time to shout as she dives into the back of the man with her hands balled into fists that whack punches hard and fast into the sides of the head. Beating harder and harder with enough force that would knock a normal person unconscious. He pays no heed but bites down harder with a terrible sound of gnashing and skin tearing. Blood spurts up from the wound as Blinky drops to force her left forearm under the throat of the attacker. He drives down harder, preventing her arm to get under him. She grabs the back of his head with a fistful of hair and wrenches up enough to get her arm under and through the gap of the crook of the neck. She clamps on, tensing hard and with every ounce of strength in her body she heaves away, pulling the body with her to roll across the floor. She clamps harder, her arm cinching tighter and tighter to strangle the infected from behind.

Everyone outside reacts instantly. Howie, Blowers and Nick dropping cigarettes and coffee mugs to turn as one and charge inside. Clarence ditching the gun to leap from the back as Mo and Dave sprint behind the three lads. The tweezers drop from Marcy's hands as she bursts from the mirror of the wing mirror. Meredith explodes from static to full on running in a split second, her body low and streaking across the grass with lips that pull back to show big white teeth. The horse rears, the sudden motion of everyone making her startle. Paula in the kitchen spins from Kyle to charge at the doors with the cook right behind her.

Into the dining room they pour. Everyone running at the sounds of the fight taking place. Experienced eyes take in the scene in a second. Neal face down with a bite mark to the back of his neck. Blood on the table, the chair on its side a few feet away and Blinky flat on her back trying to grip a big man spraying blood from his mouth that bucks and writhes with wild thrashing side to side. He breaks free, rolling before surging up to his feet with a speed that belies his big size.

Dave draws, a blur of motion of his hand whipping the pistol from the holster. Howie, Nick and Blowers run in front of him and as he runs he aims, searching for a gap to fire. Mo goes wide, drawing his own pistol and trying to make room to get the angle to fire. Nick gets there first, one step ahead of Blowers and Howie and he slams into the big man at full speed. The big man takes the impact with a snarl coming from his mouth and awful red blood-shot eyes that blaze at the others coming at him. He keeps to his feet, ignoring Nick trying to drive him back. Blowers hits them both. His own form adding to that of Nick. Howie next and he slams in but the man is like a rugby player refusing to be taken down.

'MOVE,' Clarence bellows with the challenge set and made.

Howie, Blowers and Nick star burst away, sinking to roll to the sides as a big man hits a big man. Clarence lifting Anthony from his feet to carry him back through tables and chairs that get sent spinning. With a roar, Clarence lifts and dumps Anthony down onto a solid pine table that splinters instantly with over two hundred and fifty kilos of meat coming down with accelerated gravity. On the floor and Clarence slams fists down one after the other. The nose is broken and the jaw is smashed but Anthony is a big man and able to take punishment. He thrashes wildly, bucking so hard it unbalances Clarence. An arm lashes out, back-handing Clarence away who gets sent to the side. Howie dives in. His own fists hammering but he too gets pushed off as Anthony surges up to his feet. Nick goes for the legs but bounces off. Blinky goes in low then lifts at the last second to slam a headbutt into Anthony who simply swats her to the side and she sails off to scatter chairs and tables aside.

'Fuck that,' Marcy comes up short, veering off at seeing Blinky getting thrown.

Two things happen next. Two things that do not lose. One is Dave who, while running hard, re-holsters his pistol and draws a knife which he spins to hold with the blade pressed up against his forearm. The other is Meredith who not only saw her beloved Nick get hit aside but also her beloved Howie, her beloved Blowers, her beloved Clarence and her beloved Blinky. She streaks. A blur of black and tan with a deep snarl that resonates without fear. She goes high, launching from the ground with a mouth opening that clamps onto a neck and she drops, letting her body weight bring the enemy down but the enemy doesn't go down and she dangles from his neck. Her own body weight supported by the grip of her mouth on the throat. She rags and thrashes to ruin the flesh that splits apart as the blood flows down over her muzzle.

Dave is next. Dave who vaults high with an arm outstretched that hooks round the top of Anthony's head to anchor his own form that drops down onto the big man's back.

'Let go,' Dave says simply, his voice flat and dull. A stab into the left eye. A stab into the right eye, blinding Anthony. 'Let go,' Dave says again, unable to cut into the neck with Meredith thrashing side to side.

Mo darts in. The opportunity is there. The legs exposed and he whips behind Anthony slicing through the Achilles tendons to the legs that suddenly cannot hold the weight of the body. They go down. Anthony with Meredith hanging off his neck and Dave hanging off his back and as they land so Dave steps away and stares down as Meredith finishes the job. Her paws now finding Anthony's chest to gain traction and she rags the neck to bits. Biting in, wrenching left and right. Biting again and again as the artery is opened and the blood spurts far across the floor.

Paula, on seeing the others going for the attacker, heads straight to Neal. She gets to his side and rolls him onto his back. Her fear of the blood now less from the memory of her own mouth biting into the infected yesterday.

'Oh shit,' she gasps at the sight of the ruined mouth and the chunks of coffee mug embedded through the lips and cheeks. Teeth missing and blood spilling out from the holes. Neal chokes with an involuntary action as his lungs start to fill from the blood pouring down his windpipe.

'Christ,' Marcy at her side but she recovers her wits faster than Paula, 'Neal...you're okay....you'll be okay.' She gets to his head, staring down with an intensity as she cradles his dying form. Neal stares up. Conscious and alert to the spasms of pain running through his body. Blood seeps over her lap from the bite to his neck and Neal's eyes fill with fear. This wasn't meant to happen. He was safe here. This wasn't meant to happen. Pain in his stomach and through the agony of the second his eyes go wide with realisation that the infection is inside him. He grunts, clutching the intense pain in his mid-section. He chokes again, coughing to get the blood from his lungs but it's coming down too fast.

'Cut me,' Marcy wrenches her hand out from under Neal's head and thrusts it to Paula, 'cut me...DAVE CUT ME.'

Mo is there, running from behind Anthony to Marcy and his blade flicks across Marcy's palm opening a wound.

'Mo,' Paula shouts, holding her own hand out. Another cut and two bleeding palms press into the wounds on Neal's face. Embracing the man as he lies dying.

'You'll be okay,' Marcy says, her voice soft and soothing, 'you'll be okay, look at me...look at me...' Neal can't look at her. Panic grips his body. Panic that tries to rid the fluid from his lungs and panic that finds his mind shutting down from the lack of oxygen and panic from the pain worsening in his stomach.

The mind shuts down as the body fights to get what little air it can get to the vital organs. Instantly the panic abates but the lungs are full. There is no air coming in. Only blood. The infection passes through every cell, turning and replicating as it commences the takeover of the new host body but that too needs oxygen and this body does not have any. It works to expend the fluids from the lungs, to clot the flow of blood seeping from the wounds. The lungs inflate. Desperately trying to suck air in but only pulling more blood.

'He's drowning,' Kyle rushes in to Marcy's side, 'on his side, turn him on his side.'

'...FUCK THIS IS TOO COLD,' Cookey ceases the new sock dance and twists the dial to end the flow of water. A sound from somewhere in the hotel. Something heavy falling over and he holds still for a second before shrugging and looking round for the towel he was sure he brought in with him.

'Brrrrr,' Charlie rinses the last few bubbles from her hair and twists the dial to end the flow of water. Her towel was carefully placed and draped over the top edge of the cubicle and she reaches up to tug it down.

'Fuck it,' Cookey tuts at his own lack of forethought at not bringing a towel into the bathroom and steps naked from the shower cubicle onto the wet linoleum floor. 'Anyone there,' he taps gently on the bathroom door and listens. 'Fuck it,' covering his privates he pushes the door open to find the room empty and no spare towels, 'twats,' he mutters.

She wraps the towel round her body and steps out to push the bedroom door open and the second towel left in preparation for her hair.

Drip dry. That's the answer. He starts bobbing on the spot to generate warmth and hoping nobody walks in now to see him dancing naked in the room spinning his arms round in circles.

She bends over to let her hair hang down and starts rubbing down the strands with the second towel. Spots of moisture on her arms and the bottoms of her legs left uncovered by the towel. A dull thud from outside the room and she turns her head at hearing what sounds like a door banging open.

Cookey freezes again. A door banging open in the corridor and he stares at the door leading out. It's a heavy fire door and you'd need some welly to make it slam open. Mind you, the hinges are well oiled so maybe it was one of the kids running about.

The three surge from the room. The fight in the main room underway and through Anthony's eyes it knows most of Howie's group have been drawn into that area. Three adult males pumped with chemicals coursing through their bodies and with one urge pulsing through them. Bite. Pass the virus. Take more hosts. Bite. The first goes straight for the door opposite and charges into the room. The second goes right heading further down the corridor away from the reception area. The third goes left towards the direction of the fight in the dining room as the first one bites down into the sleeping man's leg who wakes screaming.

The scream snaps Charlie's head up with wet hair flying over to land soaked down her back. Her heart thundering in her chest and she moves to the door.

Cookey ceases the new drip dry dance as the scream erupts from several rooms down. Without hesitation he runs to the door and charges out with the sudden thought that he is still naked. A decision made to dart back in and at least grab his underwear when he spots the man charging at him and sees the awful red bloodshot eyes and the lips pulled back to show teeth ready to bite.

No time to shout a warning and the man barrels into Cookey who twists on the spot with reflexes honed from fights given every day. The door to their side opens as Cookey twists to slam the infected against the wall but goes through the open door and into the bed as Charlie yelps and jumps back from the sight of Cookey's arse flying past.

'Cookey,' she gasps, ready to tell them to pack it in and get out. The man hits the bed and goes down with Cookey on top of him and in that split second she sees the red eyes as her mind makes the connection of the manner of movement and the hands clawed into talons. This isn't play. This is real and she dives in to land next to Cookey trying to get a grip on the flailing man. He is charged up. Pumped. Strength beyond anything he could ever have imagined in life pulses through his limbs. The mattress beneath him is soft and yielding and as he bounces down he twists to get on his back. His arms flail wild and hard, whacking Cookey to the side who slides off the end of the bed as Charlie takes over. Her hands instinctually going for the throat to strangle and kill but the man bucks with such force she is lifted and sent sailing to land in the spot only just vacated by Cookey already on his feet and coming in for another go.

The knife of a handle poking from Charlie's belt catches his eye and he lunges to pull it free as the infected man comes up hard from the mattress to drive him back through the open bathroom door. Charlie goes after them both, heedless to any thought to grab a weapon but only seeing Cookey lifted bodily to sail back into the bathroom. She jumps up, landing on the man's back to get her arms round the front of his neck. Cookey punches hard into the face, smashing punches into the nose that breaks and sprays blood but the man closes the distance rendering the distance too shallow for hits to be given.

'Knife,' Cookey hisses, snatching his head to the side to avoid the headbutt aimed at him.

Charlie gains purchase and heaves back with enough strength to keep the man's head back from impacting on Cookey's face. She can't let go now. To do so would mean the man can get fully at Cookey. She grips harder, trying to choke the man out but his rage is too great and he surges back, running from the bathroom back into the bedroom to drop on the bed with Charlie trapped beneath him. Cookey goes with the flow, running naked to try and pin the arms to stop the man raking at Charlie's skin with his nails. The man rolls to the left, then to the right, twisting side to side to unleash the red mist in his head that tells him only to bite and rake and hurt and spread the virus.

Off to the side they go, rolling along the edge of the bed to the side and down into a heap trapped between the bed and the wall leaving the wet towel that was wrapped round Charlie's body on the mattress.

Two naked forms gasping in the fight. Angling and twisting to get on top of the beast that fights like a demon beneath them.

'Knife,' Cookey gasps the word out slamming a fist down into the man's mouth as he lunges to bite Charlie's bare thigh.

'You get it,' Charlie gets the left arm pinned beneath her, holding it down with her body weight but still getting lifted inches at a time as the man tries to rise, 'RIGHT ARM.'

Cookey grabs the wrist of the hand flying through the air towards Charlie. He grunts from the exertion, trying to push the arm back down and freeing his right arm to aim hard punches into the man's throat. The infected man on his back but twisted to his left side. Cookey straddling his legs to try and hold them down.

Charlie straddling his upper body just in front of Cookey and herself twisted off to the side to keep the left arms down. Cookey's face pushed into Charlie's bare back as she pushes away from the head lunging up to snap at her.

'Get the knife,' she grunts again.

'You get it,' Cookey counters, 'I'm immune...' he can get bit and raked. He can get blood in his mouth. Charlie can't. She might be immune but the chance is too great. 'Sorry.' Cookey gives the apology as he slams his body into Charlie's hard enough to send her flying over the man's head and onto the carpet above his head. Her legs trail as the infected tries to snap to bite an ankle but Cookey is there. His hands gripping the head as he drives the points of his thumbs into the eye sockets.

Screams erupt in the other rooms. Screams of pain and terror. Meredith swooshes past the open bedroom door. Dave and Mo only seconds behind her.

'Need help?' Mo catches the door frame to stop at the sight of Cookey's head poking up on the other side of the bed.

'Nope,' Cookey mutters as he drives his thumbs down into the pressurised eyeballs, 'knife, Charlie.'

'Yep,' she scrabbles onto her backside, awkward and confined in the tight space. She heaves up to lean over the bed to reach the knife handle poking from her belt. 'Don't look...' Her arse inches from Cookey who can't stop his head from glancing up. He blinks once, stunned at the sight and quickly looks down.

'Hockey sticks...'

'You looked,' she says as she drops back down with the knife held in her hand.

Cookey grunts, pushing harder as the left eye pops with a spray of goo spurting inches up into the air.

'Ready,' Charlie reaches forward, on her knees and stretching to get the knife ready to slit the throat, 'lift up.'

'Can't,' Cookey says, glancing up to see her naked body leaning towards him, 'oh fuck.'

'Well stop looking then.'

'Sorry,' he blurts, clamping his eyes closed.

'I can't slit his throat...you have to lift your arms a bit.'

'Can't see,' Cookey grunts.

'Open your eyes...'

'Can't...naked...'

'You've seen naked women before...I cannot get to his throat.'

'Yeah but not you...you're like fucking perfect.'

'Really?' She asks, glancing up at his face flushed red and his eyes still clamped shut. 'Well maybe you should open your eyes then,' she quips, making his eyes snap wide to see a smile tugging at her lips, 'now either lift up so I can slit his throat or move off.'

He stares into her brown eyes. Lost in the second of a fight with screams coming from everywhere as Howie, Clarence and the rest thunder past the door shouting to give orders and grab weapons.

'He'll rise up,' Cookey says, holding the infected male's head down as he stares deep into her eyes.

'I have his hair, he won't,' Charlie says politely as Marcy, Paula and Roy pound past the open door.

Cookey glances down to see Charlie gripping the man's hair in one hand while holding the knife ready in the other, 'oh yeah,' he says, catching sight of her thighs.

'Take your time,' she says softly.

He flushes, deep and crimson, his eyes darting back to hers, 'shit sorry, Charlie...I ain't a perve I promise.'

'It's okay,' she smiles at him as the right eye pops to spray goo an inch into the air. The man writhes and bucks, lifting Cookey who goes with the flow. 'Cookey?'

'Yes, Charlie?'

'You need to move back.'

'...but you'll see my willy.'

'You've seen my boobs.'

'I didn't look,' he says earnestly, still staring into her eyes.

'No?' She asks, cocking her head to one side, 'and I can see your penis now.'

'Eh?' He asks.

She darts her eyes down then back up, 'It's right there.'

'Charlie!'

'Yes, Cookey?' She asks and darts her eyes back down then back up, 'I just saw it again.'

'Stop it! Stop looking at my willy.'

'Then move back so I can slit this chap's throat.'

'But...oh fuck...'

The man surges up. Blind to the world and blind to the pain. An explosion of motion and he lifts his upper body as Charlie tears chunks of hair from his scalp. Cookey is thrown backwards as the male continues his forward momentum with Charlie diving at his back to drive the knife into the side of his neck with a deep cut that misses the artery. Cookey is pushed onto his back. The man sinking down with determination to do damage before this host body is killed. Charlie climbs on them both, stabbing and slicing with grunts of effort until finally she cuts deep enough to spray blood onto the wall not inches to the side.

If anything, the beast fights harder as the life blood from his system pumps out. A crazed flailing of arms and legs and a hard head that batters down into Cookey's shoulders. Charlie gets to the side, heaving and pushing to get him off Cookey. It gets wilder with a frenzied attack that builds with each passing second and it's all Cookey can do to protect his face from the blows coming down as his chest compresses from the heavy weight. Blood everywhere and it mixes with the water still on Cookey's body that makes him slick and wet. Charlie heaves, bracing against the wall to push the man to the side between Cookey and the bed but the infected isn't finished yet and he lashes out with a hard hand that swats Charlie across the face and sends her smacking into the wall with a dull thud.

Cookey twists onto his side and grips Charlie to pull her down in the space between him and the wall, using his body to shield her from the raging demented beast thrashing in the tight gap behind him. A hand slashes down his spine raking the skin open. Cookey grunts and tenses. Another hand then both hands digging in with filthy torn nails that slice through the skin to gauge long welts from shoulder to arse. Again and again, like a thrashing machine of hands blurring to flail into Cookey who pushes harder into Charlie knowing the filth in the tainted blood can't harm him.

Teeth join the attack. A hard bite that sinks into the hard flesh on his upper right back. Teeth that clamp and dig deeper to bite and tear the flesh. Cookey's right arm slams out, hitting the wall over Charlie to hold himself braced and tense. Charlie staring up at his face contorting with pain and rage.

A long growl hisses from Cookey's throat. He can't do anything. He can't lift up or go back. Any movement from this position will let those hands and teeth get to Charlie so he takes the agonising pain knowing the man must be bleeding out. The pain builds and the growl erupts to a scream that he fights to end. His eyes were clamped shut but now they snap open. His right arm held protectively over Charlie and she feels his body go rigid with vibrations sent through it from the bites and rakes being given to Cookey's back. She sees the veins bulging through the skin of his arm, pushed out by the hard muscles stretched and tensed. She sees a man biting the scream off to glare into her, through her, his blue eyes normally so jovial and full of humour now the eyes of a killer that only feel pain and hurt. His neck strains and swells. His chest showing the striations of muscles as he grits and quivers from the searing pain but fuck you if I will give in now, fuck you if I will move or yield. We do not yield. *We do not yield. We hold. We protect our own.*

'COOKEY?' Blowers voice screaming from the corridor.

'COOKEY?' Nick screaming from somewhere else.

'FIND COOKEY,' Howie erupting in fury as he slams his axe into the neck of a male charging into the corridor.

We hold. We are pack.

'HOLD COOKEY,' Blowers screams, 'I'M COMING... DAVE...DAVE...GET TO COOKEY...'

Hold on, little brother. I come.

The energy flows into Charlie who pushes herself into Cookey to wrap her arms round his chest and bring him closer as the tears stream down his face and the blood pisses down his sides from the cuts and bites given so freely into his skin.

'IN HERE,' Charlie screams, trying desperately to reach round Cookey to fend the infected man off. 'GET OFF HIM,' Charlie screams in frustration, 'IN HERE...GET OFF HIM,' she slaps out but is unable to generate power or momentum and still the beast bites deeper, harder, gnashing with teeth that make Cookey tense that much harder.

Clarence storms the room and with one quick grip he flicks the bed away and rushes forward bent to scoop the man biting into Cookey's bloodied back. He sees the rakes and torn skin and feels rage erupt as he grips the man and lifts him up overhead to slam down onto the floor with a crunch of bones breaking. His feet go to work. Stamping down as Meredith rushes in to latch onto the head which she rags side to side. A quick glance from Clarence and he spots Charlie lying naked under Cookey with her arms wrapped round his body while Cookey's arm is braced against the wall to keep her protected as he took the beating from behind. A single stride from his long legs and he drops down to rest a hand on the lad's head.

'You okay?'

'Fine,' Cookey grunts.

'Good work, get up and get dressed...'

'Yep,' Cookey grunts again.

'Charlie, I'll leave him with you,' Clarence winks at her and is gone, striding from the room.

'COOKEY?' Blowers shouts again, closer this time, others in the group still shouting Cookey's name.

'THEY'RE FINE,' Clarence shouts back as he re-joins the chaos.

The wet heat is intense. Charlie heaving for air beneath him. Cookey's chest rising and falling as he swallows the pain.

'You okay?' Charlie whispers, sensing the tension still in Cookey's body and seeing his eyes and jaw clamped shut.

'Yep,' Cookey says tightly, hissing the word out and waiting for the pain to pass. His back feels like he's been whipped and stabbed. Burning heat from the bites and stinging heat from the nails that sliced through his skin. The pain is immense. That final surge of power and the fucker bit down hard right into the dense muscles on his upper back. Just wait. The pain goes. Just wait.

She holds still, staring up at the contours of his face. All humour in him is gone and in its place is a hard man bracing silent and brooding as he swallows the pain inflicted from using his body to protect hers.

Fuck it hurts. Fuck it hurts. Searing heat in his back that radiates out but his eyes open and stare down into the soft brown eyes of Charlie. He sees a beautiful woman that is naked beneath him and he knows he must get up and move away to protect her dignity. She sees the blue eyes of a killer and is mesmerised by the change in him. He is a man, not a boy. Her arms still wrapped round his body and she slowly eases the tightness of the embrace to let her hands glide gently over the rigid muscles either side of his spine. She feels the torn flesh and winces as he grunts softly.

'I am so sorry,' she whispers quickly.

'It's fine,' he breathes out, closing his eyes again as he feels her fingers move so gently up his back.

'Cookey,' she breathes, feeling the cuts and then the bite mark with clear indents made by the teeth.

A rush of emotion and her hands find the back of his head that she gently pulls down to kiss his cheek just millimetres from the corner of his mouth, 'thank you.'

He breathes out, feeling the warmth of her breath on his lips and suddenly the pain in his back is not the most central thing in his mind. His hand comes up to brush delicately down her cheek and his heart, easing down as the adrenalin of the fight drops off now picks back up and she feels it thrumming through his chest.

His eyes open to see hers staring intently at him. He blinks but she doesn't. All the noise of the fight going on outside the room fades to nothing for there is nothing other than this second. Her hands still pushed through the wet hair on the back of his head. Her arms streaked with blood from his back. Her body glistening from water, sweat and blood. His own now softening as the tension from the pain eases and his mouth so close to hers but the moment snaps to a sudden end as the gunshots in the corridor bring back the reality of where they are.

'Hockey sticks?' Cookey asks, his blue eyes now twinkling with humour and he smiles that infectious grin.

A fleeting show of confusion in her eyes that linger on his and it takes a full second for her to smile back at him, 'yes,' she says softly, still looking at him as though searching for something that was just there.

'Awesome,' Cookey grins, 'er...better get up then before someone comes in.'

'Yes,' she says softly.

'I'll get the cover for you...don't look at my bum now.'

'Okay,' she says with a smile twitching the corners of her mouth.

He goes to move then comes back and she stiffens, her eyes finding his to stare intently, almost expectantly.

'Um...' he pauses, hesitating and looking unsure, 'I wasn't being a perve when I said you were perfect.'

She blinks and releases the breath she didn't know she was holding, 'okay...'

'I mean like, you know, you are but...I didn't it mean like a weirdo or anything.'

'It's fine,' she smiles up, feeling the warmth of his body against hers, 'it was a nice compliment.'

'Cool,' Cookey says, grinning but his eyes show something other than humour, like an urge, a trepidation and a thought crossing his mind to do something and she spots as his gaze flicks to her mouth then back to her eyes. 'Fuck it,' Cookey mutters and lifts up to twist quickly and pull the cover from the bed that he tugs down and round to give to Charlie behind him.

'Thanks,' she says, looking at his back as he lifts up and seeing the cuts stretching down the length and the open skin of the bite given. He goes quickly. Rising to his feet and with him facing away she doesn't avert her eyes but watches his backside as he grabs a towel from the floor and runs out into the corridor.

'Where the fuck have you been?' Blowers runs to him.

'Killing zombies fucktard,' Cookey quips back, 'what happened then?'

'Fuck knows but we lost about six or seven...'

'Eight,' Paula shouts from somewhere.

'And that bloke is dead.'

'Eight?' Cookey says, stunned at the news, 'what bloke? Which one?'

'Neal, the scientist...he's dead.'

CHAPTER TWENTY

The same as last night. The same manic rush of forcing panicking people to go in a direction they don't want to move.

'Outside...everyone outside...quickly now,' I stand in the corridor urging them out as I spot Cookey running from a room with a towel held round his waist and his back covered in blood, 'Cookey...you alright?'

'Fine, boss,' he turns from Blowers to shout up the corridor.

'Get dressed, we're moving out.'

'On it.'

'Where's Charlie?' Marcy calls out pushing up the corridor to the room she was sharing, 'Charlie...you okay?' she stands in the doorway and shouts down to me, 'they had one in here too.'

I don't know what just happened. The last few minutes have been utter carnage filled with chaos and a large dollop of confusion mixed in for good measure. One minute I was outside talking to the lads and the next we're fighting the infected in a hotel that was meant to be safe. How did they get in? Where from? The exits are all locked. The only way in is through the door which has been protected the whole time.

Eight dead. Eight of the people we saved last night killed and the scientist Neal killed in a room surrounded by armed people. What the fuck?

'Outside, come on...quickly now...' I urge and shout for them to move and they stream out with terror once again in their eyes. Clarence stands at the end in the reception guiding them to go outside to Dave, Mo and Roy standing guard. Blowers, Nick and Blinky running room to room urging everyone to get up, get moving and get out. Paula and Marcy somewhere in the midst of the mess.

I go with the flow down to the reception, my assault rifle held ready in my hands. My pistol in the holster and my axe now tucked down between my back and my bag.

'Go outside,' Clarence says to a woman shaking her head and holding the hand of a young girl.

'Not a chance,' the woman says firmly, 'we're staying right here by you.'

'What happened? How did they get in?'

'Is Anthony dead?'

Voices ask questions but get ushered on and I follow the lines outside to see Paula taking over as she gets them out and away from the building on the edge of the grass.

'Just stay still, everyone stay still,' Paula calls out.

'We're going to check everyone,' Marcy works with her, running from the doors to the grass, 'over to the others, go quickly, stay together...'

'Where's Meredith?' Paula shouts at me.

'In here,' Clarence shouts out through the doors.

'We need to check these people,' Paula strides towards me with a mixture of worry and anger flushed on her face, 'what happened? Where did they get in?'

'No idea,' I say darkly, 'check the eyes...check for bites, scratches...'

The last few trickle down, urged on by Blowers, Nick and

Blinky snapping at their heels to get outside into the daylight to be seen properly.

I go back in and share a glance with Clarence, both of us shaking our heads. 'You need to go outside,' I say to the woman holding the child's hand.

'No way,' she says, shaking her head at me, 'we're staying by him...'

'Just go outside,' I urge, wanting to snap and only holding myself back because of the little girl with wet hair staring up at me.

'I said no,' the woman says through gritted teeth and I notice the hand holding the hilt of a knife tucked in her belt. Clarence is huge and now armed to the teeth. She is a mother of a child scared and terrified so I let it go and breathe the tension out.

'What's your name?' I ask.

'Jane,' she replies, locking eyes on me, 'this is Clara.'

'Okay, Clarence? You okay if Jane and Clara stay by you?'

'Fine with me, Boss,' he says, smiling down at the little girl, 'but you see that small man outside?' He says to Jane, 'his name is Dave...he is far more dangerous than...'

'I don't care,' Jane says, staring up at him, 'we're staying by you.'

'Fine with me,' Clarence says easily.

'Mr Howie?' Charlie rushes from her room now dressed with her bag pulled on and holding the rifle ready. 'What happened?'

'No idea,' I say, taking a step towards her, 'you okay?'

'Fine, Cookey's back is bad...'

'Bad?'

'He got bit and scratched. Really badly,' she says lowering her voice as she comes to a stop in front of me.

'Cookey?' I call out.

'Just coming,' he shouts out and appears in the doorway dumping his bag to fix the straps and buckles, 'sorry...just coming...'

'Did you hurt your back?' I ask.

'Nah, it's nothing,' he says, hefting the bag up to push his arms through the straps. 'It'll be fine.'

'How bad is it?' I ask Charlie.

'He got raked by nails and bit...the skins cut open...'

'Howie? They're all out,' Paula calls ahead as she rushes into the reception, 'Charlie, you okay, love?'

'I'm fine,' Charlie says quickly, 'do you know how they got in?'

'Nope,' Paula mutters, 'not a bloody clue. Where's Reggie?'

'In there,' Clarence says, nodding at the main room.

'Cookey, Charlie, outside with Blowers. Cookey, if your back is bad just say, okay mate?'

'Will do, Mr Howie,' he nods, racking the bolt back on his rifle and I spot the look of concern Charlie gives him.

'Paula, Clarence with me...actually, Charlie, you too.'

'Me?'

'Yes you. Cookey, send Dave and Mo inside...I want this hotel searched...'

'Is there any point?' Paula asks, 'we're moving out.'

'I want to know how they got in,' I say quickly. 'Hang on, Reggie?' I shout through the doors to Reginald gathering items from the floor.

'I'm here, Mr Howie,' he shouts back.

'I know where you are, what are you doing?'

'Getting Neal's papers and books,' he says standing up to shake his head sadly, 'this is a terrible event, really terrible...'

I stride in with Clarence and Charlie while Paula points at Jane and Clara.

'Who are they? You should be outside,' Paula says, her tone softening.

'No, I'm staying with...' Jane goes to say.

'They're staying near me,' Clarence says, his eyes passing a message to Paula who pauses, stares down at Clara then at Jane and nods.

'Reggie, we're moving out,' I say, staring down at the ruined corpses of Neal and the other bloke who I think was called Anthony.

'Indeed, I gathered we would be,' Reginald says, rushing to the table to grab a coffee stained and soaked book from the top.

'Kyle? Where's Kyle?'

'In here,' he shouts from the kitchen.

'What the fuck is he doing in there? KYLE?'

'It's been checked,' Paula says quickly.

'I don't care, KYLE, get out and go outside with the others...we don't where they got in. I want everyone outside until Dave and Mo have done a full sweep.'

'Howie,' Paula says with that tone that tells me she is getting cross, 'what's the point? We're leaving straight away.'

'I want to know how they got in, Charlie, Reggie? Any ideas?'

'I beg your pardon?' Reginald balks.

'Work it out, go with Dave and Mo...' I stride off towards the main doors, 'everyone else outside.'

'Mr Howie,' Reginald says rushing after me, 'I don't think this is something...'

'DAVE!'

'Here, Mr Howie,' he runs in with Mo at his side.

'Cookey tell you the plan?'

'Yes, Mr Howie.'

'Go with Reginald and Charlie, find where they got in...'

'Mr Howie,' Reginald protests, 'I do not understand how I am to...'

'You and Charlie are more intelligent than the rest of us put together. Go with Dave and Mo and find how they...'

'I really do not see...'

'DO NOT ARGUE WITH ME.'

He flinches back, blinking rapidly as Charlie reaches out to put a hand on his arm, 'we'll do it, Mr Howie.'

'Good,' I turn back to Dave, 'full sweep...NICK? ROY?'

'Out here,' Nick walks into view of the doors.

'Once they're done I want this hotel burnt to the fucking

ground,' I say, striding outside to see everyone gathered on the grass.

'On it,' Nick says, 'Roy, you hear that?'

'I think everyone heard that,' Roy says, holding his bow with an arrow nocked and ready.

'Don't be smart, Roy,' Blowers snaps.

'Do not tell me what to do,' Roy snaps back.

'Enough,' Paula calls out, 'Howie, what exactly is the point in all this?'

I stop and glower round as every other voice falls to silence, 'we're not leaving here until we know what just happened...we cannot risk taking an infected person into the fort.'

A lightbulb pings behind her eyes and she nods with understanding, 'you think one of them?' She asks, looking at me but tilting her head to the people stood nearby.

I shrug, 'I don't know but we ain't risking anything.'

'Okay,' Marcy calls out, clapping her hands to get everyone's attention, 'I need you to listen to me for a second,' she says, sweeping her eyes over the crowd. 'The hotel was secure. There was no way they could have got inside. Everyone check the people you know and recognise. Is there anyone here that shouldn't be here? Anyone you don't know? Does anyone look different... CALM DOWN,' she shouts to get heard over the voices clamouring as they all start peering suspiciously at each other.

'Who got bit?' Paula asks, as though to prompt Marcy.

'Listen in,' Marcy shouts, moving closer to the middle of the group, 'who was bit first? Who did you see first?'

'That big fucker,' Blinky calls out, 'in the main room...'

'Anthony?' someone shouts, 'big bloke yeah?'

'Yeah, broad shoulders...brown hair,' Marcy replies, 'do you know him?'

'We all knew him,' someone else says, 'Anthony was soft as anything...he wouldn't hurt a fly.'

'He was with Terry...Terry was bit too weren't he?'

'Yeah, that lad there killed him,' a woman says, pointing at Nick.

'So Anthony and Terry were in the same room?' Marcy asks, 'just those or...'

'They had Neville and Gordon in with them didn't they?'

'Neville was bit.'

'Gordon was....I saw his eyes.'

'Nev got in Sarah's room with her kids.'

'Gordo lost his wife last week, he wouldn't do nothing...'

'Let me get this right,' Marcy calls out, waving her hand at the people, 'Anthony was the big man...he was in a room with three other men? Is that right?'

'Think so,' a woman nods while staring round.

'Terry got Pete though, I saw it,' someone else says.

'Gordo was fine, I spoke to him before he went to bed,' a man calls out.

'Did you see his eyes?' I ask.

'Yeah, they were normal.'

'What about the other three men...that Anthony? Anyone see his eyes last night?'

'We checked them all,' Paula says heavily, 'I did it myself when they came in.'

'We only need to miss one,' I say.

'We didn't,' Paula replies, 'every single one of us knows what to look for, Howie. Not one of these people had bloodshot eyes last night and anyway...Meredith would have reacted.'

'What room was Anthony and the others in?' Marcy calls out.

'Er...next to us, we were in eleven so..er they were closer to the reception end so it must be ten I think.'

'Room ten,' I nod and head back to the reception to see Dave leading the others from the kitchen back into the main room, 'anything?' I ask.

'No, Mr Howie,' Dave says, 'every exit is locked. Windows are locked. There are no points of entry.'

'We'll check room ten. That big bloke,' I point at Anthony's corpse, 'was in room ten with three other blokes that were all infected.'

'We should check each room,' Dave says as blunt as ever.

'You and Mo room to room, Charlie and Reggie come with me to room ten.'

'I really do not understand what it is you require us to do,' Reginald huffs as we head up the now blood stained and body littered corridor, 'I am not a detective and I do not think Charlie has a background in forensic examination either...really, Mr Howie, there is a limit to the skills you think we may have.'

'Yep,' I say as a way of replying. Dave and Mo go into the first room as we head up going past the now open hotel room doors, 'they got in here somehow and we need to know. We can't take those people to the fort or anywhere if they...'

'Yes yes I completely understand the reasons for wishing to know,' Reginald says, breathing hard as he walks fast, 'but be that as it may I do not know how *we* are to know.'

'Dunno,' I say and stop outside the open door to room ten, 'all we can do is try.' I go in first and stare about as if expecting to see a broken window or a hole in the floor to a tunnel or a rope ladder hanging from the ceiling. But the window is intact, shut and locked from the inside. The floor has no tunnels and there is a distinct lack of rope ladders dangling from the ceiling. Charlie stands next to me, staring round slowly. Reginald walks straight to the window and pushes the pane then the frame.

'Sealed shut, there are no other doors...really, Mr Howie...'

'We have to figure it out,' I say obstinately.

'Mr Howie,' Charlie says politely, 'if nothing entered this room to infect them then they must have been infected either before they entered the hotel or at some point during the night. However, they did not leave the hotel nor did anyone else enter...'

'Good Lord,' Reginald says shaking his head, 'the possibilities are endless. For all we know an infected person may have come to the window in the night and...'

'They wouldn't open the window to someone they didn't know,' Charlie says, interrupting him, 'the window is intact and Meredith can smell them from a distance...Mr Howie, are we sure the chap from this room was the first one infected?'

'No, we're not sure of anything, only that he was the first to attack...'

'Mr Howie,' Dave stops at the doorway, 'clear so far.'

'Cheers,' I nod at him and take a step closer to the bed, 'four blokes from this room were infected...it may be someone else in another room infected them or...' I trial off, sensing the futility of the task but knowing we can't risk going anywhere without knowing how it happened.

We start checking walls, the floor, the skirting board and into the bathroom to check the walls, floor and ceiling in there. We check everything. The bed covers. The chair in the corner. The drawers to the side units and back to the windows as though we're drawn to that section as it must be the only viable way for an infected person to get inside the room.

'Clear, Mr Howie,' Dave appears at the door with Mo at his side.

'Nothing?' I ask them both, 'you're sure?'

'Yes, Mr Howie.'

'All exits are locked?'

'Yes, Mr Howie.'

'No other way in other than the main door which we guarded last night.'

'Yes, Mr Howie.'

'Dave, any ideas?' I ask him, 'Mo? Anything?'

'Nothin', Boss,' Mo says, 'I could get in here easy and I checked all the places I would break in but nothing has been touched or broken.'

'They must have brought it in with them then,' I say and stare back round the room.

'I checked,' Dave says and I turn back to face him.

'You checked everyone?'

'Yes, Mr Howie.'

If Dave says he checked then Dave checked.

'Fuck it,' I mutter, 'then how?'

'I do not know, Mr Howie.'

'Howie with you?' Paula calls up the corridor.

'In here,' Mo replies as Paula rushes up and into the doorway.

'Right,' she says, taking a breath, 'Anthony and the three in here were definitely the first.'

'Definitely?' I ask.

'Well, as sure as we can be...Blowers and Nick were with you when you saw Anthony walking down, right?'

'Yep.'

'You saw one of them?' Reginald asks me.

'Yes, mate. The big bloke that got Neal.'

'I see, and you didn't take action?'

'He was hiding his eyes...like rubbing them and walking like he just woke up...Nick or Blowers told him there was coffee in the kitchen and he waved so...'

'I saw him walking in when I went in the kitchen,' Paula says.

'Forgive me,' Reginald takes a step closer to us, 'you saw the chap that killed Neal right before the actual attack took place? Is that correct? And he was walking from the direction of this room, is that correct?'

'Yep,' I say.

'Think so,' Paula says.

'And I am given to understanding that at the precise time you saw the chap, Mr Howie,' he says, looking intently at me, 'that there were no other noises of concern at that precise time. Is that correct?'

'Yep,' I say again.

'I see,' he says, dropping his gaze from me to the floor as he pushes his glasses back up his nose, 'I see...indeed. Yes...yes I see...'

'See what?' I ask after several seconds.

'Hmmm, Reginald says and finally looks up to Charlie, 'it appears Neal was targeted, would you agree?'

'I would,' Charlie says slowly, 'the infected male has walked past Mr Howie and those outside and has then seen Paula in the main room but has decided to attack Neal and no others.'

'Oh fuck,' I say.

'Shit,' Paula says.

'Of course,' Charlie says, 'it could be that one male would know he could not hope to defeat Mr Howie or any of our group so he chose Neal as the easiest target.'

'A consideration,' Reginald replies, 'but no, he has chosen to walk that direction which is towards those most capable of defending themselves and especially David and the dog.'

'Dave,' Dave says.

'Indeed,' Reginald says. 'The other player has a hive mind so one must assume that on becoming infected, the infection, as the other player, has gained the knowledge of the host body. Which would mean our male in this case, Anthony? Was that his name?'

'Yes,' Paula says, staring as mesmerised as me.

'Anthony knew the layout of the hotel and knew where Mr Howie and our group were positioned yet the host body has been sent specifically in that direction and not only has the host body seen Mr Howie and some of the others but it has chosen to make use of subterfuge to continue towards the target, which in this case was Neal.'

'Others were attacked though,' Paula says, 'eight have been killed before we could...'

'Yes yes, but that came after,' Reginald says, waving a hand at her, 'Mr Howie recalls Anthony walking past the main doors and you recall Anthony entering the main room and at that point there was no other indication of an attack taking place. That also tells us that Anthony was not the only infected host body at that time. How could he be? Anthony was in the main room attacking Neal and I gather he was killed in that room. Did he leave at any point?'

'God no,' Paula says, 'he was dead in seconds really...'

'They's weren't no noise when we ran in,' Mo calls out.

'I beg your pardon?' Reginald says, blinking hard.

'Sorry,' Mo says, leaning into the room, 'I meant when me and Dave ran in with everyone...there was no noise anywhere else then.'

'Is that correct, Dave?' Reginald asks.

'Yes,' Dave replies.

'Interesting,' Reginald says and turns to face the bed, 'Anthony was in this room with, I think you said, three other males, is that correct?'

'Yep.'

'He left this room to venture towards the most dangerous point for any infected host body where the chances of detection are the greatest and our host body has walked past Mr Howie and others while at the same time, someone else was also infected and was waiting for that attack to commence before commencing their own attack.'

'Distraction,' Dave says.

'Distraction!' Reginald exclaims, clicking his fingers at Dave. 'Indeed my friend, we have the use of distraction. Anthony is attacking the primary target and with such few numbers they cannot possibly hope to defeat us...I mean you and yours, Mr Howie...'

'It's us, Reggie,' I say quietly.

'I mean, good God! We slayed ten thousand or more yesterday. What possible hope would they have with a few score? They wouldn't. They would be slaughtered in minutes. Why send host bodies to die without any purpose or objective. I would not do this and I do think, after yesterday, that the other player would do this either.'

'So you think the reason was to get Neal?' I ask.

'Oh without doubt,' Reginald replies, 'I cannot, at this stage, answer your question as to how they became infected but I can give you the motive. The other player knew we had Neal with us. It saw through the eyes of the hive mind. Yes yes, you see, it saw we had Neal and that was something that concerned it enough to form a plan. Indeed a plan! A scheme! An actual plan of forethought and preparation. Gosh, it is evolving isn't it?'

'It is,' Charlie says when Reginald nods at her.

'Fuck it,' I mutter again, 'should have spoken to him last night.'

'Yes I rather fear we should,' Reginald says slowly, 'but that is for later. Later we can seek to understand the why. Why did the other player need to take Neal from us? For now we need to consider how. How did the other player take Neal from us?'

'It bit him,' I say then think perhaps that wasn't the question Reggie was asking based on the pained look I get from him and the polite one from Charlie.

'Not how as in how the objective was achieved but how as in how the plan was executed,' Reginald says.

'Roger, got it,' I say and decide to keep my mouth shut for a bit.

'We left the town last night and brought the people here,' Reginald says, placing his hands in front as though to emphasise the *here*.

'Directional awareness?' Charlie asks.

'Perhaps, yes, yes I think that is most likely,' Reginald says.

I give a blank look to Charlie and take pride in the fact I don't actually ask what that means.

'The collective geographical knowledge of the immediate and greater area,' Charlie says while I blink.

'They knew where we were?' Paula asks.

'Ah got it!' I say quickly, 'they knew where we were.'

'Funny,' Paula mutters, 'I thought you were being serious now.'

'I think so,' Charlie says, 'but then I would question if they knew the exact location,' she adds, looking at Reginald.

'No you are quite right,' Reginald says, 'directional awareness yes but specific factual location no.'

'So they knew the area we were in?' I ask.

Charlie nods, 'say they saw us on a particular road but then did not see us exit that road or indeed, they did not see us further up that road. They would know we stopped or deviated route within two specific points.'

'Ah,' I say, nodding slowly.

'Did you understand that?' Paula mutters.

'A bit, you?'

'All of it actually,' she says with a smug smile.

'So like, they knew we were here in this area but not here in this hotel?' I ask.

'However,' Reginald says, 'one cannot discount the possibility that they simply found us...no no no,' he says to himself with a frown. He huffs and sits on the bed to rest his chin on his hands. 'No, I rather fear we were sought out,' he springs back to his feet and frowns again. 'But how? I do not know how and I do not like not knowing something. It is an affront. Yes it is. An affront. To consider oneself as more intellectually capable than I is an affront. No no no, I shall think this through. Charlotte, we must think this through.'

'We shall,' she says with an air of someone who knows the right things to say in this situation.

'What do we know?' He asks and paces down towards the bathroom door. I look at Paula then Dave and Mo wondering who he is asking.

'Would you like me to break it down?' Charlie asks, with the air of someone who knows the right things to say.

'Yes,' Reginald says, turning at the bathroom door to pace back towards me.

'Chronologically,' Charlie says, stepping back to let Reginald pass, 'we left the town after defeating a number far greater than our own and the only difference to entering that town and leaving is that we had Neal and his horse with us plus the survivors. We took three vehicles and came back to this location. We checked each person as they entered and I think we can safely assume no persons were infected when they entered. At some point during this morning, Anthony from this room, along with the persons he was sharing with, became infected and commenced an attack which appears to have been done to get either to Neal or to one of the other survivors.'

'Neal,' Reginald says, pacing back and forth, 'not one of the other survivors.'

'You can be sure of this?' Charlie asks.

'Yes yes, the hive mind collective knowledge would have given the other player the knowledge of exactly who was left in that town and with such large numbers it could have easily taken them.'

'Of course,' Charlie says, 'so we can, therefore, consider that the attack was done to take Neal. The hotel was secure. There are no points of entry other than a guarded door. The food we consumed was already here and unless they brought something in with them that carried the infection I cannot see how it was passed.'

'Food, yes yes, interesting. The infection is a virus. A virus needs living cells to transmit. The infection cannot survive on that bed or that door or that pane of glass. Food can contain meat but the meat is dead and cannot sustain life.'

'Bacteria grows on meat,' Paula says.

'An entirely different cycle of life,' Reginald says dismissing her instantly.

'Bacteria feed on the decomposing meat, they are not the cells within the meat,' Charlie says ever so politely.

'I knew that,' Paula mutters.

'Not the food,' Reginald says, 'what else has come into this hotel since we arrived? Insects? Rats? Birds? A fox...a badger... rodents...spiders...'

'Air,' I say helpfully.

'The virus is not airborne, Mr Howie, otherwise everyone would be dead already.'

'Ha,' Paula nods at me.

'Water,' Mo says as me, Paula and Dave look at him, 'sorry,' he winces and takes a step back.

'WATER!' Reginald booms, 'My God...' he runs to the bathroom to stare at the taps, 'the water...' he twists the cold to let it thunder into bowl, 'Get the dog, quickly now, get the dog up here and a bowl! Yes yes, a bowl.'

'Mo, get Meredith,' I say. The lad sprints off down the corridor as I move to the bathroom to stare at the water flow. 'Looks clear,' I say and bend down to sniff it, 'smells alright too.'

'Pipes, water flow...there will be a treatment centre. Yes, yes it is possible but the water cannot sustain the virus for any length of time. No no, a virus cannot pass through piped water over any great distance.'

'Unless it was moving fast,' Charlie says, 'everyone had woken up, showers were on, Kyle was using water to cook, people were drinking and...'

'Indeed, yes indeed. If the treatment centre holds tanked water ready for disbursement then the flow would have to be fast to...that is if the tanks or treatment centre were accessed instead of the piping network...'

'The pipes are underground,' Charlie says, firing back as quickly as Reginald throws the suggestions up, 'to access an underground pipe is possible but not easy and would require tools.'

'Tools yes, finer motor skills to operate tools is not something it has yet achieved on mass. Marcy and I were infected and could use fine motor skills as we had previously but we were not the same. Perhaps one or two yes, one or two could have fine motor skills to operate machinery or tools to access an underground water pipe but...no, I rather think the treatment centre or the holding tanks would be most likely. Indeed, yes, think it through...'

'They wouldn't know which pipe,' Charlie fires back.

'Exactly, if they knew which pipe fed this building they would know which building we were in.'

'Got her,' Mo calls ahead as Meredith bounds into room as overjoyed as ever at seeing Charlie and Reginald for the first time in about five minutes. She wags her tail hard, snaking round legs for a second before snapping to the side and standing fixed with her nose to the ground.

'She can smell them,' I say watching her closely.

'Bowl,' Mo hands one over to Reginald who takes it to fill from the tap then carefully places it down on the floor and stands back expectantly.

We all watch, waiting for Meredith to sniff round and find the bowl. I watch her hackles lift at what I can only assume are the smells of the infected that were in here, then she finds the bowl and sniffs it for a few second as we all watch intently almost expecting her to attack it or something. She doesn't. She takes a drink instead and laps at the water for a bit before snuffling off into the corridor.

'Bugger, good idea though,' I say.

'The idea stands, Mr Howie,' Reginald says, 'it has been some-time since the taps were all run. Anything in that water would now be dead. Besides, the dog is immune and perhaps she knows this. I would suggest that to entirely rule the idea out we must locate the treatment centre.'

I stop and think for a second and take in the magnitude of the idea that the infection could pass through the water supply. Something we have taken for granted since this began.

'We should,' Paula says quietly, heavily, 'we need to know if it can do that...*and*,' she stops to look down as if already regretting what she is about to say, 'anyone left in this area is at risk.'

'Okay,' I say, 'I mean, it's not like we haven't got anything else to fucking worry about is it?'

CHAPTER TWENTY-ONE

W e head back outside and tell everyone else what we're worried about, which takes time. A heated discussion starts, which takes time. We prepare to move out, which takes time. We load up the vehicles and catch the horse that needs to be put into the horsebox trailer thing, all of which takes time.

Time. Time is something we don't have on our side anymore. If the infection is learning to get into the water supply then even I can see what an alarming step that is and I think back to those first days of actual zombies shuffling about in the daytime being slow and easy to kill. These are not those days. What we are against now is an entirely different thing.

Finally, and with Paula running at maximum organising level, we're ready to go and I pull the Saxon round to head back down the long drive.

'Mr Howie,' Nick's says through the radio, *'we didn't burn the hotel down.'*

'Forget it,' Paula says from Roy's van, *'we've got more important things to do.'*

Clarence is driving the cramped minibus that sounds like it's about to fall apart. Meredith and Dave with him too just in case something happens. Roy in his van with Paula and Reginald while everyone else has piled into the Saxon. I feel like a shit for leaving Neal where he lies, in a puddle of blood with his brains blown out from a pistol fired at point blank range just to be sure. I also feel like a shit for the state of the survivors we rescued last night and the fact we tore their town apart only to take them somewhere safe so more of them could die and then run them outside into a minibus without food or…I look down at feeling Marcy's hand on my leg as she senses the disquiet coming from me, 'Kyle found a crate of juice cartons,' she says, 'he's taken it in the minibus.'

'Okay.'

'They'll have something to drink,' she adds.

'Okay.'

'Oh fucking hell,' she groans and pulls her hand away at the sight of the large white sign board welcoming guests to the Greenside Golf Hotel.

I stop the Saxon and open my door, 'Nick, you got a smoke, mate?'

'Yeah sure,' he passes one forward with his lighter.

'What are you doing?' Marcy asks me.

'Nothing,' I get down and light the smoke while making my way round the front of the vehicle. It's a pleasant day. The air is warm but not overly humid like it has been. The sky is gloriously blue with a few fluffy white clouds sailing high.

The doors to the minibus opens and Dave is out, striding towards me. I stop at the sign and look at the words written in blood while drawing a lungful from the cigarette which gets exhaled into a plume of white smoke that hangs lazily in the still air. Like I said, it's a pleasant day.

'Mr Howie,' he says, stopping at my side.

'Dave,' I reply and take another draw then finally I look down to the infected female lying slumped at the bottom of the sign. Her awful red bloodshot eyes staring up at me and Dave. Her wrists bitten deep to make the blood flow so she could write the words that dripped thick in lines that only make it look that more sinister. The sound of Meredith's claws scattering on the tarmac reaches my ears and I step round Dave ready to grab her neck but she stops at my side without any need to touch her. Hackles up, teeth showing, head low but she holds still.

Silence in the pleasant day. I inhale again and let the plume of smoke go. She stares up at us, at me. Her eyes fixed and unblinking. She doesn't move or try to lunge but she breathes. A ragged rising and falling of her chest that signifies life is still within her.

'What's going on?' Paula walks down, her boots a heavy tread that is strangely comforting. She reads the sign and looks down at the woman and tuts sadly.

I smoke. Paula folds her arms. Dave stands inert but forever ready and Meredith glares, daring the thing to move but it doesn't. It just breathes and stares back.

I stare down into the eyes and through to whatever lies beyond, 'I see you.'

The voice coming back is hoarse and rough from a dry throat, 'See you too.'

'Ssshhhh, easy now,' Paula says softly, her fingertips brushing the dog's neck to steady the low growl emanating in response to the infected making noise.

I take the cigarette out and grind it into the ground, slowly and methodically, 'who is coming?'

She doesn't reply but stares like she is fascinated. Like a child learning. Like an animal or an alien studying the strange creature in front of it.

'He?' I ask, my voice soft and gentle, 'who? Where from? When? How many do we need to bring? How many have you got on your side? Where do you want to meet? Are we having a drink first, maybe a bite to eat or just going straight into it? Referees? Do we wear strips so we can see the sides? Did you come in through the water?'

I wait and can see something like an urge to reply. Like she wants to say something and I can feel the scrutiny coming from her eyes.

'What do you want then?'

'One...'

'Fuck off,' I tut disdainfully, 'and Reggie says you're evolving so you must know by now the whole one race thing is flawed...what happens when you bite the last person? What then? You've got nowhere left to go. I'm not as clever as Reggie or Charlie but even I know evolution takes time. You can't have it straight away. That's not evolution, that's genocide and extinction and there's no going back from that.'

'My advice to you,' Reginald stops at my side, the brave bugger coming as close as me to the woman who snatches her gaze from me to him, 'is to stop now. You are learning so fast but without experience to understand the knowledge you have gained you cannot conceptualise a full understanding of what it is you wish to obtain.'

'Yeah,' I say, waggling a finger at the woman.

'Perhaps you think our time is over,' Reginald says, exhaling with the weight of the world on his shoulders, 'perhaps you believe this is the natural order of events and your species will rid our species but I rather think your endeavours are doomed. Humans are like rats and cockroaches. They survive almost anything and they breed too, which, I may add, is a wholly disgusting thing to be involved in but, I am given to understand, one that is essential to the furthering of our species. That being said, our kind will breed on a rubbish tip. They will breed on the disease ridden sticky carpet of a nightclub surrounded by drunken yobs even film it for the pleasure of others. Do you understand? Breeding is the single most important thing to my kind, not to me you understand, gosh no but to others, sadly yes,' he stops and sighs again.

'Yes, they take pleasure from it. Pleasure and a power that drives them on. Power that gives them the will to have fortitude in the direst of circumstances and the darkest of times and through this power they have become adept at killing,' he speaks kindly, politely but with a striking air of calm authority. 'Surely you have seen this for yourself. Thirteen against ten thousand. If that is how many your side had yesterday. I rather fancy it was slightly higher than ten thousand myself but the sum of ten thousand is a nice round number so for the purposes of this conversation we will stick to that. You see, you have threatened a species that has only ever really known pain and suffering so really, what you give us is no worse than what we gave ourselves, and yet we still bred and made more. Yes indeed, I would think this through. I would consider my options and perhaps be satisfied with what you have achieved thus far because to press us any further will only serve to unite those who have previously fought each other. The enemy of my enemy is my friend. Well, it is a pleasant day and we have business elsewhere so you will forgive our rudeness but we really must be on our way. I do hope you consider my words but alas I fear you will not and that, my friend, is ego and pride and nothing more.'

With that he stands, politely nods and heads back to Roy's van leaving the rest of us stunned to silence that is broken by a quick snarl and an even quicker crunch of bone as Meredith darts in to eat the zombie.

'Was that worth it?' Marcy asks as I resume the journey and lead our little convoy out onto the open road.

'Not really,' I say after a second of surmising.

'Reggie lectured it half to death then the dog ate it.'

'Well,' I say thoughtfully, 'when you put it like that. Reggie is a clever sod though.'

'So are you.'

'Yeah but not like that, did you hear what he said?'

'I did,' she says, 'and it was disgusting. Having sex in a night-club? That's gross.'

'I think his point was that people would have sex anywhere so we'll continue to breed.'

'Yeah but in a nightclub?'

'There are worse places than a nightclub,' I say.

'You haven't have you?'

'What?'

'Had sex in a nightclub. Have you?'

'Me? Fuck off...no chance,' I cast a sideways look to see I'm getting a narrow eyed look of foreboding in return.

'You'd better not,' she says darkly.

We thread through the roads to the motorway and aim in the direction Reggie told us to take after he found a black splodge within a green splodge on the map that he said was the water treatment centre. How he actually knew that little black bit within the green bit was a treatment centre is beyond me. Silence for a while until a voice politely calls out from the back.

'Mr Howie?'

'Yes, mate?' I call back to Cookey.

'Do you have any tattoos?'

'No mate.'

'Oh okay.'

'Strange question,' Marcy asks, twisting in her seat.

'Marcy? You got any tattoos?' Cookey asks.

'No,' Marcy grins, 'why?'

'Just wondering,' he says.

'What the fuck's in your head now?' Blowers asks.

'You got any tattoos?' Cookey asks him.

'You know I don't.'

'Nick?'

'Nope, why you asking fucktard?'

'Mo? You got any, mate?'

'No I don't.'

'Charlie?' Marcy asks, 'are you okay?'

'Fine,' Charlie says in a strangely low voice, 'thank you.'

'What's up with Charlie?' I ask.

'She's glaring at Cookey,' Marcy says, 'like really glaring...like I glared at you last night.'

'Cookey, what have you done?' I call out.

'Eh? Nothing. I was just making idle conversation about tattoos. Blinky? You got any?'

'Go fuck yourself.'

'Good answer,' Cookey says with a deep sigh as he stretches his legs out, 'so none of us have tattoos then...maybe we should get some, like...'

'Why's Charlie glaring at you,' Blowers asks with a laugh.

'Is she?' Cookey asks, 'I do not know.'

'You fucking do,' Blowers laughs, 'Charlie? What's he done?'

'He hasn't done anything....yet,' Charlie says.

'Yet?' Nick asks.

'Yeah so...what tattoos should we get?' Cookey asks, 'we should get axes...'

'What the fuck...' Blowers asks, still laughing and staring at Charlie glaring daggers at Cookey.

'Yeah axes,' Cookey says, reaching up to put his hands behind his head, 'like...something cool like, I dunno...a pair of axes ow!'

'What happened?' I ask.

'Charlie kicked Cookey in the leg,' Marcy says, laughing with a confused look on her face.

'I was only suggesting we had a pair of axes...' Cookey says. I snatch a glance to see him scooting down the bench seat out of range of Charlie, 'maybe like crossed or something.'

'Cookey!' Charlie says.

'What?' Cookey exclaims in his innocent voice, 'what's wrong with that? We could have a pair of axes crossed...it would look awesome...especially if we got it on our arses...'

'Cookey!' She says again, louder this time

'What the fuck?' Nick laughs.

'Ow,' Cookey shouts as Charlie goes over Mo to get next to Cookey to deliver the punch to his arm.

'Charlie's got a tattoo on her arse,' Blinky says.

'Has she really?' Cookey asks, covering his head as he ducks away, 'what is it?'

'Hockey sticks, I told you...'

'Say what?' Cookey shouts, his voice muffled, 'can this be true? Are they crossed? Stop hitting me,' he bursts out laughing.

'I shall hit you,' Charlie says.

'You shall shall you?' Cookey asks and gets another whack on the arm, 'cor, fuck me, Charlie...you don't half punch hard.'

'Pack it in or I'll ask Blinky to punch you.'

'I'll punch him,' Blinky offers.

'No no,..' Cookey says, waving his hands in defeat, 'I shall stop I shall.'

'Has Cookey seen your arse?' Blowers asks with a grin at the sight of Cookey getting a very polite beating.

'No he has not,' Charlie says too quickly. 'He has not. He did not. He didn't look...'

'He saw your arse?' Blowers asks in a stunned voice.

'What? I didn't do nothing...'

'Anything,' she says, correcting him, 'I did not do anything.'

'You's fucked, Cookey,' Mo says, 'she's correcting you now.'

'Oh you're so fucked,' Blinky says, 'you got Charlie mad at you.'

'I am not mad,' she says primly, 'I am merely disappointed that someone who behaved so gallantly and with such courage would now ruin that image by broadcasting...'

'I didn't say noth...anything.'

'You inferred to the extent that now everyone knows you have seen my bottom.'

'Saw your what?' Cookey asks.

'My bottom.'

'That's so sexy when you say bottom ow!'

'Want me to hit him?' Blinky asks.

'No she doesn't!' Cookey shouts.

'Has Charlie got a tattoo on her backside then?' Nick asks.

'No I do not...'

'Yep she has, ouch.'

'How do you know?' Mo asks.

'I saw it...fuck's sake stop hitting me.'

'Then stop talking about my bottom.'

'Say bottom again...argh I've got a dead arm now.'

'How...How did...' Blowers tries asking but stops from the laughs coming out as Charlie holds her hand above Cookey's dead arm daring him to say something else.

'How did he see it?' Nick asks.

'We do not need to continue this discussion about my bottom!'

'Stop saying bottom like that,' Cookey wails.

'What is wrong with how I say bottom?'

'Fucking hell,' Nick laughs, 'just hang on...no wait...Charlie... how did Cookey see your arse?'

'It's bottom,' Cookey points out primly, 'not arse you heathen.'

'This conversation shall end now,' Charlie says, 'or I shall discuss what I saw this morning.'

'Oh no...no no...'

'What?' Blowers asks.

'What d'you see?' Nick's says.

'Charlie?' Mo asks, 'what was it?'

'Cookey?' Charlie asks, 'would you care for me to divulge what I saw.'

'No...no no no...I take it back, I didn't see a pair of crossed hockey sticks tattooed on Charlie's bum.'

'He said it,' Blowers calls out, 'he said he saw your arse.'

'I did not,' Cookey wails, 'I said I did not see the pair of crossed hockey stick...ow!'

'You's fucking nuts, mate,' Mo laughs, 'stop now if I was you.'

'Take Mo's advice,' Charlie says.

'Charlie, what did you see?' Blinky asks.

'I shall tell them,' Charlie tells him, 'I shall.'

'Shall you?' Cookey can't help himself and affects his posh voice again.

'Are you goading me?'

'No,' he says quickly, 'okay...done now...finished yeah?'

'Promise?' She asks.

'Yep.'

'Say I promise.'

'I promise...I promise not to tell everyone I saw the tattoo of the crossed hockey sticks...'

'I saw Cookey's...'

'No! I'll stop. I will. I promise. I'll stop now.'

'Saw his what?' Mo asks.

'I believe this conversation is now over,' Charlie points out as Cookey sits back upright rubbing his arm with a huge grin spread across his face.

'*Mr Howie, we need to exit on the next junction. The treatment centre is less than a mile away.*'

'*Got it, cheers, Reggie.* Everyone switch on,' I call back as Marcy twists back round to face the front with a big smile on her face.

The junction isn't really a junction but a purpose built exit road obviously put in place to handle the large vehicles used by the water company and as soon as we're a few metres into the road we see signs telling drivers to report to reception and Health and Safety Notices everywhere. A set of gates stretch across the road with the logo for Southern Water pinned on both sides.

'*Meredith is reacting,*' Clarence's deep voice in our ears.

'*Got it,*' I reply, 'Blowers, your team protect the minibus.'

'Understood.'

'*Roy, can you get on top of your van?*'

'*I can. Overwatch?*'

'*Yes please, mate.*'

I slow down and peer forward through the chain link fence on both sides and through the gates to the concrete block squat buildings on the other side. Huge pipes run from the largest central building to a large metallic tank nestled in the ground.

'*Going through,*' I give the update and increase the speed for the front of the Saxon to ping the gates open that slam out and aside. The parking area is big, deep and wide and we go right to keep a clear line of sight.

'Someone up top,' I call out as I bring the Saxon to a stop.

'I'll do it,' Nick replies and starts working his way through the hole.

Clarence parks the minibus back from us and Roy's van goes ahead to stop at the same angle as us. The second it stops so Roy is out and running to the rear. The back doors open and he climbs up to gain his feet as Reginald passes him the bow and arrows then quickly closes the doors.

'*Overwatch on.*'

'*GPMG ready.*'

'Everyone out,' I open my door and drop down, drawing my axe which gets shoved down my back. My rifle comes next, the strap looped over my arm. The back doors have already opened as Blowers drops down to lead his team out in a run towards the minibus. Meredith is already out, standing metres from the side with her eyes fixed towards the buildings, her hackles up and teeth showing. Dave comes next, his rifle ready and Clarence has to turn sideways to get his bulk through the small doors before popping out like a bar of soap.

'*One in the distance, can I engage?*'

'*Go for it, Roy.*'

'*Remember what I said before, do not try and compensate for my firing. I will work...*'

'WE KNOW,' Clarence shouts, cutting him off.

'Well that's our covert approach blown then,' I say.

'Covert? With a rattling minibus and three diesel engines?' He replies.

A soft ping, a whoosh and an arrow flies through the air to a target unseen amongst the buildings.

'*Did you get him?*' I ask.

'*Her and yes, of course I did.*'

'Roy is a fucking legend,' Blinky mutters, kneeling to the side of the minibus door.

'Dave? How do you want to do it?'

'Ahem.'

'Fuck's sake, Clarence? Dave? How do you want to do it?'

'Dunno, ask Dave,' Clarence says with a grin at me.

'Holy shit,' Marcy says, making us all turn to see Reginald jogging from Roy's van and trying to fumble with the rifle which he drops. He stops to pick it up and lets his bag slide down his right arm before trying to pick both up and somehow getting the rifle pushed through the straps, 'he really shouldn't have a gun,' Marcy says.

'Indeed,' Reginald says, trying to tug his rifle from the straps, 'do I really need to carry this thing? It is most cumbersome and frightfully heavy.'

'DOWN!'

We duck on Dave's command as Reginald grabs the trigger guard to tug the weapon free while sweeping the aim across our group.

'PUT THAT WEAPON DOWN,' Dave bellows, making Reginald balk in fright and drop the rifle and bag with a yelp as Dave strides towards him.

'I am most dreadfully sorry.'

'Turn around,' Dave says, picking the bag up and sliding the rifle from the straps, 'Mohammed, come here.'

'Yep,' Mo sprints over as Dave gets the straps free and manhandles the bag onto Reginald's back. 'Face me.' Reginald turns back to Dave looking like a child being dressed by his mother as Dave's fast hands grab straps which he tightens and tucks away. 'Mohammed, you will guard Reginald. Reginald, you are relinquished of your weapon until you have satisfactorily proven to be competent and safe in the usage of the weapon. Do you understand?'

'I do and I am most thankful to be relinquished of the blasted thing and my apologies to Mohammed to be burdened with my care but it is most comforting to have a bodyguard and...'

'Mohammed, you will apply the principles I have instructed with regard to Mr Howie to Reginald.'

'Yep.'

'Yes Dave not yep.'

'Yes, Dave. Rifle, pistol or knife?'

'We are entering buildings with the potential for close quarter combat. Consider the tactical options of each weapon.'

'Pistol,' Clarence coughs into his hand.

'Er, pistol?' Mo asks.

'The pistol is the right weapon for this engagement.'

'Should we all use pistols?' Marcy asks.

'Fuck knows,' I say with a shrug, 'Dave?'

'Yes, Mr Howie.'

'Do we all use pistols or rifles?'

'I prefer the pistol,' Paula says.

'I'm so glad you said that,' Marcy says, 'shall we use pistols?'

'Yeah?' Paula asks, 'shall we?'

'Go on then,' Marcy says, slinging her rifle to draw her pistol.

'Much better,' Paula says, drawing her own sidearm and rolling her shoulders.

'Finished?' I ask them both.

'And you can sod off,' Marcy says, giving me a flash of a smile.

'No no, it's fine,' I say, 'we'll give the zombies time to get ready.'

'Not zombies,' Clarence grumbles.

'ZOMBIES.'

'Alex.'

'Sorry, Clarence.'

A soft ping, a whoosh and another arrow flies off to hit something that gargles and falls over.

'Got another one,' Roy calls out.

'Well, we don't need to go anywhere then,' Marcy says, 'Roy can kill them all'

'Someone in the minibus wants to know what's going on,' Blinky calls out, 'shall I tell them to fuck off?'

'No do not tell them to fuck off,' Paula says, 'tell them we're having a tactical discussion on strategy.'

'THEY ARE HAVING A TACTICAL DISCUSSION ON STRATEGY,' Blinky shouts, 'I told them, Miss Paula.'

'And everyone else,' Paula mutters, 'thank you, Blinky.'

'Miss Paula?' I ask.

'I've told her it's just Paula.'

'I like Miss Paula,' I say.

'Do you? I don't so don't even think...'

'Paula is Miss Paula from now on,' I call out.

'You shit, Howie.'

'Got it, Miss Paula,' Nick calls back.

'Miss Paula,' Blowers says.

'Hi, Miss Paula,' Cookey adds.

'I hate you all.'

'Even me?' Clarence asks, seemingly hurt of the guilt by association.

'Not you.'

'Thanks, Miss Paula.'

'Can we just get on?' Paula huffs as another arrow pings across over our heads.

'Three now,' Roy says, 'Miss Paula,' he adds in a murmur.

'Dave,' Paula snaps, 'lead the way please.'

'Yes, Miss Paula.'

We head on past the locked and secure reception building and down the access road to the larger and longer treatment centre. In silence we go. Everyone turning to watch the sides, rear and front in equal measure. I glance across to see Mo holding his pistol low in a double handed grip while staying inches in front of

Reginald who seems to be enjoying having his own personal bodyguard.

'Doors open,' Clarence says quietly, his greater height giving him the advantage of seeing the busted door to the treatment centre before the rest of us. A low hiss from inside and an infected female appears in the doorway only to be taken a second later with an arrow slamming through her neck.

'Good shot, Roy,' I murmur into my radio.

'Meredith's going in,' Clarence says as the dog streaks ahead. We pick the speed up knowing she can handle herself but not wishing to leave her on her own against unknown numbers.

Inside the door is a gantry of metal walkways crossing over huge water tanks. Motorised arms fixed to machinery that should be making those arms rotate and spray things I guess. It looks like the water comes in one end and goes through the tanks before disappearing into the next section of the building and other than the one Roy shot down the inside is empty.

We head down the gantries, Dave and Meredith in the lead with me right behind him.

'Down there,' Paula says, turning her torch on to shine down into the next dark tank of water and the bodies floating in it.

'That's it then,' I say quietly, 'it got in through the water.'

'Not yet, Mr Howie,' Reginald whispers, 'those corpses appear intact from what I can see and the water is clear. The infection must work at a cellular level.'

I stop and stare down, bringing my torch out to shine into the seemingly clear water, 'those bodies couldn't infect us then if we drank that water.'

'A virus cannot be sustained without living organic matter, they are corpses, Mr Howie and water is not living organic matter.'

We press on through a doorway into the next section of larger tanks but with machinery overhead. Some kind of conveyer system that brings long metal trays out from the tank to swing round to hang down before they pass through a narrow gap in the wall to an outside area. We shine torches but the water here is free from bodies.

'Reggie?' I ask.

'The other player has certainly attempted to make use of the water supply but I maintain those bodies in that former tank would not be sufficient. There will be an external tanking system that we must check.'

'Fair enough, Dave, lead on.'

Our motley crew of intrepid detective explorers continue to venture to the last section of tanks and machines until we reach a door set in the wall.

'Hmmm,' I say quietly, 'I wish we had a way of magically opening doors.' I step aside to let Clarence squeeze through to magically open the door that pings off after being kicked.

'Hey presto,' Clarence says, turning to grin back as Dave lifts and fires past his head to the infected looming behind him. To his credit, Clarence doesn't flinch but stands stock still for a second before blinking heavily and stretching his jaw, 'I felt that, Dave.'

'You were not in danger.'

'I felt the air.'

'You were not in danger.'

'I was still turning.'

'I calculated your motion.'

'Course you did,' Clarence mutters and steps outside to stick a finger in his ear that he waggles about.

'All this water makes me need a wee,' Marcy says from behind me.

'That shot was fucking awesome, Dave,' Mo says once Clarence is outside.

'Did you lift?' Dave asks him.

'I did but not fast enough.'

'Good gosh, young man, you were very fast indeed,' Reginald says.

We get out into the sunshine and follow the pipes and tanks

down to the large cylindrical tank that seems to be embedded into the ground. It looked big from the car park but up close I can see just how enormous it is and I guess more of the mass must be underground.

Another metal gantry circumvents the exterior to form a rising walkway with a door fitted near the top and even from here I can see the door is open. The security here is shit. I mean really shit. Weak chain link gates and crappy wooden doors and it must have been built before anyone ever considered terrorism and the ability to fuck about with the local water supply.

We head up the walkway, looping round the tank until we reach the wide platform and the open door. Meredith, as ever, goes first, closely followed by Dave and the rest of us who can smell them before we take a step inside.

The metallic tang of blood and shit hits us hard. The smell of rotten flesh and body odour. With hands over mouths we get inside to stand on the gantry that overviews the mass of water that should be held inside. The tank is nearly empty now and I guess without the treatment centre operating the tank can't be refilled. We shine torches down to the water and the bodies and bits of bodies floating on the top. The water isn't clear here either but turned red and the sides are stained pink showing the water level has dropped since the infected got in here.

They've flayed themselves to bits. Literally ripping limbs off and pulling organs and innards out. Small chunks of meat and flesh float on the water and I hear the buzzing of flies having a merry old time below us.

'Yes indeed,' Reginald says with a tone of victory at being proven right, 'yes, this will do it. Indeed it would. This tank feeds the pipes and we can see the water level has reduced from the demand of this area.'

I shake my head and sigh deeply, 'I'm amazed more weren't infected.'

'It looks terrible from here,' Reginald says, 'but truly, what we are viewing is dead meat and not living organic tissue. Plus we must consider that it has been some time since we first encountered them in the hotel. The passage of water coming through the piping network must have been sufficiently swift enough to allow the infection to survive within the tissue of material as it flowed from here. We are not that far from the hotel as the crow flies. Indeed, a straight line from here to the hotel is but a short distance.'

'Is there a town near here?' I ask.

'There is,' he replies quietly, 'a mile or so past the hotel.'

'And this water also feeds that town?'

'Without doubt.'

'We need to get in and warn them,' I say, 'Paula?'

'Agreed,' she says instantly.

'Clarence?'

'Yep, agreed.'

'Marcy?'

'Yeah,' she says sadly, 'personally I don't hold much hope but...'

'Reggie said the water kills the infection,' Paula says.

'I did not say that,' Reginald says, 'I said the...'

'Whatever he said,' Paula cuts across him, 'not everyone will have got infected from drinking it.'

Marcy drops her head for a second, 'one turns and the infection knows everything that person knew. So it will know where the other survivors are if the host knew...'

Paula blinks and looks down at the water, 'Nothing is ever simple is it?'

CHAPTER TWENTY-TWO

'Kyle,' I lean into the bus and spot him standing in the middle of the aisle keeping everyone calm, 'word please?'

'Of course,' he threads down and out into the car park.

'The water supply has been infected,' I say quickly, 'there's a big tank back there that holds the water supply to this area...'

'It's full of bodies,' Paula adds.

'I see,' he says, his blue eyes showing a depth of understanding in his craggy weathered features.

'There's a town the other side of the hotel fed by the same pipes,' I say.

He nods with instant understanding, 'they will need warning...'

'Exactly,' I say, 'but we've also got a bus full of people here...we can't separate our team to transport them and leaving them on their own isn't really an option either...'

'Unless they want to be left on their own of course,' he cuts across me with a level gaze.

'Shit yeah, yeah of course, they ain't prisoners or anything like that.'

'I see, then perhaps a few seconds to inform them would not go amiss.'

'That's what I was hoping you would do,' I say quickly.

'I shall assist wherever you think I may be of use.'

'Great, you know, what with you being a priest and everything.'

'Just a cook, Howie.'

'Right yes, sorry. Just a cook. So, is that okay? You can put your vicar skills to the test and...'

'Not a vicar. Just a cook.'

'Right you are, Rabbi...'

'Are any of your team medically trained?'

'What us lot? No chance...unless you count Roy who's a hypochondriac.'

'Does he have medical training? I think one of the men broke his arm during the melee this morning.'

'Broke his arm? Fuck me...'

He tuts and rolls his eyes when I swear. Just a cook my arse.

'Roy, can you come here please, mate.'

'Oh god he won't like this,' Paula says quickly as Roy climbs down from his van.

'No?' I ask.

'Not a chance,' she mutters.

'You ask him then,' I whisper as he walks over.

'Sod off,' she says and walks off.

'Roy,' I greet him warmly, which just makes him look at me suspiciously, 'bloke might have a broken arm.'

'Okay,' he says, looking round as if to ask what someone with a broken arm might have to do with him.

'So like, you alright having a quick look? Cheers, appreciate that. Everyone can...'

'What?'

'What?' I ask him.

'You want me to touch a sick person? Are you fucking mad?'

'Not sick, injured.'

'There's a sick child too,' Kyle says, nodding at Roy.

'No,' Roy says firmly, 'I don't do sick people.'

'Roy, none of us have a clue...

'Ask Clarence or Dave, they'll have basic combat triage and...'

'Roy, you've seen more doctors than everyone here put together,' Marcy says, 'some of it must have rubbed off.'

He blinks once and stares at Marcy, 'rubbed off? You think I have a clue about medical emergencies?'

She shrugs and pulls a face, 'more than I will.'

'No,' Roy says to her then looks at me, 'no. I don't do sick people. I hate sick people.'

'Ach,' Kyle not just the cook says, 'hate is a strong word is it not.'

'No. I hate them.'

'The man is in agony,' Kyle says, going from the genial fellow to the man who dissolved us in the kitchen earlier, 'you'll not stand by and see another person in pain now would you? And a child? A wee child?'

'I'm not a doctor. I am a hypochondriac.'

'You'll be a medic and put their minds at rest if nothing else,' Kyle says, his eyes fixed on Roy, 'and you'll be doing this now.'

I don't think anyone would deny being told what to do by Kyle, other than Dave of course but it's still surprising when Roy just huffs and shakes his head, 'fine, right...where are they? Someone get me a first aid kit. I'd best look at the child first.'

'You're a good man, Roy,' Kyle says, clapping him on the shoulder, 'I'll take you to the boy.'

Paula and I follow them onto the bus and see Kyle leading Roy down the aisle towards the back, 'this little boy says his tummy hurts,' Kyle says, his hand resting on the shoulder of a young lad sitting on the lap of a woman.

'Probably needs a poo,' Roy says so deadpan it makes me blink until I notice the boy grinning, 'Do you need a poo, young man?' Roy asks, staring down before he drops to a crouch in front of the child, 'Hmmm, perhaps we should have a look,' Roy says, 'Let me see.' He lifts the child's top up and looks at the clear skin. He presses a hand gently on his tummy then up to the boy's forehead, 'When did you last eat? Can you remember? Have you drank any water today? No?'

'We heard the water was infected,' the woman holding the child says.

'Paula,' Roy says, 'can we get some food and water into this young man and tell me if his stomach still hurts after.'

'Yeah course,' Paula says leaning out of the door to tell someone else to get a case of water from Roy's van.

'You wait there,' Roy tells the boy and stands up to look round, 'who broke their arm?'

'Me,' a man gasps from the other side of aisle.

'That was stupid,' Roy says bluntly.

'Yeah it was, sorry,' the man winces.

'Let's have a look then,' Roy says with a sigh, 'well shift towards me, I can't see it from here can I?'

'Sorry,' the man shuffles over as the woman sitting next to him gets up to move out of the way.

With a profound look of distaste on his face, Roy gently feels down the man's left forearm as he winces and grunts from the pain.

'Do you think it's broken?' I ask.

'Got to be,' Roy says, 'must be a fracture in the forearm. I'll get him into a sling for now and get some meds into him.'

'You a medic?' The man grunts, his face bathed in sweat as he looks up at Roy.

'I'm...'

'Yes he is,' I say before Roy can answer, 'you'll be fine,' I add, hoping I sound confident.

'First aid kit,' Paula says, handing it forward, 'water is just coming.'

Roy opens the lid on the medical box and pulls out a large bandage in a plastic cover that he rips open, 'not a sling but we'll do the best we can,' he mutters as he flicks it out and starts fashioning it. 'Okay, now this will hurt but once we get it stable you'll feel much better,' Roy says as though dreading the prospect of actually having to touch him. 'Mr Howie, would you hold his arm please.'

'Course,' I sling my rifle and edge in to Roy's side. 'Er, this one is it?' I ask, nodding at his left arm held across his chest. The man nods a small frantic motion of his head, 'right, so...Doc,' I say glancing at Roy, 'Er...what do I do?'

'Doc?' Roy asks me with a plain look, 'just hold his arm away from his body and I'll do the rest.'

Every millimetre the chap moves causes him untold pain. He clamps his jaw shut, breathing fast as I ease his arm out and let Roy get the sling under his elbow.

'There,' Roy says tying the knot at the back of the man's neck, 'relax...you've got to relax into the sling, go on...'

'Trying,' the man grunts.

'Well bloody try harder,' Roy snaps which makes me wince again but the man responds by visibly sinking his arm into the sling, 'Well done, wasn't so hard was it.'

'Thanks,' the man says, exhaling slowly.

'Are you allergic to anything?'

'Er,' the man looks at Roy and blinks, 'Peanuts.'

'I'm so glad you told me that,' Roy says staring blankly at the man, 'I won't give you the peanut pain killer then...'

'Oh, oh right...er...sorry. You mean medications?'

'No I mean peanuts.'

'I'm not allergic to any medicines.'

'Good, wait there. You'll need to eat something before you can have any pain relief.'

'Okay, Doc. Thanks.'

Fuck me. The world is a strange place populated by very strange people.

'Roy,' Paula says from behind us, 'this lady says she feels sick.'

'Get her a bucket then,' Roy replies.

'Doc, this bloke has cut his arm.'

'He's an idiot then.'

'Is he a medic?' Someone asks.

'No. I hate sick people,' Roy says but it works. By fuck it actually works. The deadpan honesty makes everyone think he is a medic and even Paula stops mid-stride with a case of water bottles to stare open mouthed at him. 'I also fire a bow,' Roy tells the sick feeling woman, 'What's wrong with you?'

'I feel sick.'

'That helps. Bit more information?'

'Sorry, Doc. I er...I feel faint, like light headed and...'

'Okay,' Roy says slowly, 'Did you eat last night when we had food in the hotel?'

'I...I was too scared,' the woman says, shaking her head.

'Too scared to eat? Well, that's a new diet. Drink water, eat food and tell me if you still feel sick after. In fact, everyone listen. If you feel sick and light headed then eat some food and drink water. Do not moan about feeling sick and light headed if you have not eaten food or drank water. If you still feel sick after eating food and drinking water then you can moan. Understood? Now, which bloody idiot cut his arm?'

'That was me, Doc.'

'Let me see it. You haven't got any infectious diseases have you?'

'Er no...don't think so.'

'What that?' Roy says staring down at the cut on his arm, 'that's a scratch.'

'It hurts' the man says defensively.

'Of course it bloody hurts, you've scratched it. Man up.'

'In the darkest days right?' Paula whispers behind me.

'I'm stunned,' I whisper back.

'Any other life threatening conditions?' Roy calls out.

'Yeah er, sorry,' a woman lift her arm from the front seats, 'I'm diabetic.'

'Insulin dependent? Type one or two?' Roy fires the question at her.

'Type one daily,' she nods, 'but I've only got one left.'

'I've got some, you'll be fine. Monitor what you eat. Kyle, keep an eye on this woman in case she slips into glycaemic shock. Anyone else? No? Thank god for that,' he says and walks down and off the bus.

I follow behind him as he retrieves his bow from Marcy, 'that was fucking amazing, mate.'

'I hate sick people,' he says with a shudder.

'Roy?' Paula asks, 'why have you got insulin?'

'In case I become diabetic of course,' he says as though the answer is clearly very obvious.

'Right,' she says quickly, 'makes complete sense. They've got two cases of water in there and all of our snack food. Even Nick gave his up.'

'Cheers Nick,' I call out to him.

'I'm starving,' he calls back.

'We'll get something when we can, everyone gather in quickly,' I wait for them to come forward into a group. 'We're going into the local town to try and warn any survivors that the water supply is infected. We'll take anyone that wants to go with us...'

'We'll need another bus,' Nick says.

'Okay, eyes open for another bus.'

'And that one is about to conk out,' Clarence adds.

'Okay, eyes open for two buses. How we going to do it? I'm thinking we just use the loudspeaker and go slowly through the town. Unless anyone else can think of a better plan. Reggie?' I ask.

'You will invite the attention of every infected host body in that area.'

'Probably. But there can't be that many otherwise they'd have come for the hotel.'

'A good point,' he concedes, 'I cannot, at this time, think of an alternative plan. It is simple and crude but perhaps the best because of the simplicity.'

'Less to go wrong,' Clarence says with a nod.

'Dave?'

'Yes, Mr Howie.'

'Can you think of a better way to get people from their homes or warn them of a danger to the water supply?'

'We could do a leaflet drop.'

'...what the fuck?'

'A leaflet drop, Mr Howie.'

'Yes, yes we could do that but er...I don't think we have any leaflets.'

'Either house to house or from a low flying aircraft.'

'Right yes, yes again a great idea but er, we don't have leaflets or a low flying aircraft.'

'You just need a normal aircraft, Mr Howie. The pilot flies it low.'

'Ah right, yeah of course, but we don't have an aircraft, a pilot or any leaflets.'

'Radio broadcast,' he says.

'A what?' I ask.

'A radio broadcast is a good way to alert the population to a localised threat.'

'We can't do that either.'

'Then no, Mr Howie. I cannot think of a better way to warn people of an issue with their water supply.'

'Okay.'

'We could print some leaflets,' Dave says, 'and then distribute them either house to house or from a low flying aircraft.'

'Um...'

'We don't have a printing press,' Paula says.

'Then no, Miss Paula...'

'Paula.'

'No, Miss Paula. I cannot think of a better way...'

'Paula. Just Paula.'

'Oh no, no no no,' I say quickly, 'I'm stuck with Mr Howie so you can be Miss Paula.'

'I do not wish to be called Miss Paula.'

'I do not wish to be called Mr Howie but it seems to have bloody happened.'

'Load up,' Paula says, glaring at me, 'we're moving out.'

'I always say that.'

'Sorry, *Mr* Howie.'

'S'fine, *Miss* Paula.'

CHAPTER TWENTY-THREE

On the road again and we build speed on the motorway heading back towards the hotel as the people on the minibus drink water and eat our snack food, the thought of which makes my stomach rumble and gurgle.

Another shitfest of a day that started off so nicely. I made love to Marcy under the stars, went to bed and cuddled up then woke up to be dissolved by a bloke who may or may not be a priest or a vicar and then it turns to shit again and to top it off my caffeine levels are plummeting.

Back onto the junction that leads to the golf hotel but this time we don't take the turning towards it but head the other direction towards the town that Reggie says is there. Thinking of Reggie makes me think of Neal.

'Reggie, it's Howie. You there?'

'Here, Mr Howie.'

'Why did it target Neal like that?'

'That is a very good question and one that needs serious consideration and time to go through his journals and books.'

'I've got this horrible feeling we've just fucked up massively.'

'How could you have prevented such a thing?'

'*We should have spoken to him last night. Did he say anything to you?*'

'*There wasn't time, Mr Howie. Everything happened so fast.*'

'*Still a monumental fuck up. He said about a list, what was he on about? Did he mention it to you?*'

'*Only that he had one. I gather the list contains names of people that may be immune. Mr Howie, far be it for me to ever seek to guide you but perhaps now is the time to focus on the task in hand. We are in an area we know is hostile and one that could contain any number of new host bodies very recently turned.*'

'*Yeah, yeah you're right, we'll go through it later. As soon as we've done this we're running for the fort.*'

'*I understand. What is our plan now?*'

'*Now? We're going to drive through the town using the loud-speaker.*'

'*Yes of course and how do we execute that? Who is driving the vehicles? Are you forming a guard on the minibus? Is Charlie being deployed on the horse? Are you going on foot or planning to stay within the vehicles because both the Saxon and this vehicle are armoured whereas the minibus is not.*'

'You've created a monster,' Marcy says from next to me.

'*Good points, Clarence? Can anyone in that bus drive it?*'

'*I'll find someone.*'

'*Charlie, how fast can you get the horse out and ready?*'

'*I'll need about ten minutes at the most but I can ride her within seconds in an emergency, Mr Howie.*'

'*Okay, Reginald? Can you drive Roy's van?*'

'*I am not a driver, Mr Howie.*'

'*Paula?*'

'*Boss, it's Clarence. Kyle can drive Roy's van.*'

'*Have you asked him?*'

'*Just did, he's fine with it.*'

'*Right, Kyle driving Roy's van. Everyone else on foot. Charlie on the horse...Marcy, you drive the Saxon.*'

'I'm sitting right next to you.'

'Yes I know but it's so everyone else can hear.'

'Roger roger...'

'Don't be sarcastic, Nick, if we get heavy contact you fall back to the GPMG.'

'Got it.'

'Marcy, you're on the loudspeaker as we go through.'

'I feel like an idiot using the radio when I'm sitting next to you... yes fine, I'll use the loudspeaker.'

'Where are you going to be?' Paula asks.

'Out on foot, in fact,' I say, bringing the Saxon to a gradual stop, *'we've got the first houses ahead. Everyone out and get ready, Marcy, you take over driving.'*

'Sir, yes Sir Mr Howie Sir. Er, what the hell do I say into the loudspeaker and er...how do you use it? Oh and where is it?'

'Nick?'

'I'll show you,' Nick says leaning over the back of the seat.

'Charlie, we'll hold here. Get ready on the horse.'

'Doing it now, Mr Howie.'

I go to the front of the Saxon and stare down the road to the row of five terraced cottages set back behind pretty front gardens enclosed by a low wall. The feel is still rural with rolling pasture land on the opposite side of the road. The hedgerow is thick and very green and already I can see new shoots stretching to grow out. Birdsong fills the air. Insects humming and buzzing about amidst beautifully coloured butterflies flapping frantically but still looking graceful.

Movement to my side and I glance to see Dave standing quietly, 'alright?'

'Yes, Mr Howie.'

'Might as well make a start,' I say, looking behind him to the others getting into position, 'you coming with me?'

'Yes, Mr Howie.'

'Righto mate.'

We head up the road towards the first house as the air bursts apart from a static filled squeal of feedback coming from the Saxon's loudspeaker. I wince and turn to see Marcy holding the handset and Nick leaning over to jab at things in the central console. It goes off then comes back on. Louder and higher pitched. I wince again, turning my head from the noise and seeing everyone else doing the same thing.

'**SORRY.**' Marcy's voice booms from the speakers making us all flinch and take a step away and even Meredith drops low to the ground with a whine.

'Too loud...' Paula says into the radio.

'**YES I KNOW…HANG ON.**'

'Marcy, it's too loud!'

'**YES HOWIE I KNOW THAT! WE'RE TRYING TO FIX IT.**'

'Marcy, your booming tones are startling the horse...'

'**I'LL BLOODY STARTLE YOU IN A MINUTE REGGIE.**'

'Fuck's sake, turn it off,' I hiss.

'**TRY THAT,**' Nick's voice rolls out to echo from the mountains in distant Scotland and I wouldn't be surprised if an Eskimo zombie in Finland just turned round.

'**IT'S STILL TOO LOUD,**' Marcy replies.

'No shit...really?'

'**NOT HELPING HOWIE.**'

'TRY IT NOW.'

'That's it, Nick,' I transmit, giving a thumbs up to the windscreen and seeing Marcy holding a finger up at me in response.

'BETTER NOW?' Marcy asks.

'Yeah that's fine, fuck me I think my ears are bleeding.'

'THEY WILL BE IF YOU DON'T STOP MOANING...SO WHAT DO I SAY?'

'I don't bloody know! Make something up.'

'Marcy, tell 'em we're the living army and we've come to rescue all the pretty ladies.'

'COOKEY I AM NOT SAYING THAT...ER...I KNOW, HOW ABOUT...PLEASE COME OUT OF YOUR HOUSES. WE ARE TAKING YOU TO SOMEWHERE SAFE...HOW WAS THAT?'

'Yeah not totally fucking frightening at all,' I say into the radio.

'YOU ARE GETTING RIGHT ON MY TITS TODAY HOWIE...'

'I haven't had coffee.'

'YOU HAD A COFFEE. I SAW YOU DRINKING IT.'

'That was only one.'

'DO NOT BE ALARMED. WE ARE HERE TO HELP. PLEASE COME OUT IF YOU...'

'You sound like a Dalek now.'

'HOWIE!'

'Marcy, it's Paula. Tell them not to drink the water and to come out if they want to come with us to a safe place.'

'Yeah,' I say with a nod at the Saxon, *'Say that.'*

'WELL MAYBE PAULA SHOULD DO THIS INSTEAD THEN...'

'Fuck me,' I groan and shake my head at Dave, *'can we just get on please?'*

'FINE.'

'Fine.'

'GOOD.'

'That's great. Me and Dave are going to the first house now.'

'GOOD LUCK.'

'Thanks.'

'DON'T GET EATEN BY A ZOMBIE.'

'Not zombies.'

'SORRY CLARENCE.'

'Come on,' I start moving up the road again with Dave as the others take up positions round the bus. Clarence and Roy move further up towards us, ready to respond.

'Wait up,' Paula says, running to catch up.

'DON'T DRINK THE WATER. PLEASE COME OUT IF YOU WANT TO BE TAKEN TO A SAFE PLACE. THE WATER IS INFECTED. DO NOT DRINK THE WATER...'

'Actually the water itself is not infected but it may hold particles of material within which the infection is surviving as it navigates the...'

'PISS OFF REGGIE...THE WATER IS INFECTED... DON'T DRINK THE BLOODY WATER...'

'It's going to be a very long day,' Paula mutters as we go down the path to the first house. I knock on the door and the three of us stand quietly while Marcy's amplified voice booms out. I knock again and we wait. Paula smiles at me so I smile back. Dave stares at the door. 'Nobody home,' Paula says, 'next one?'

'Yep.'

We go up the path, along the road and back down the next path to knock on the door and wait.

'...IS INFECTED. DO NOT DRINK THE WATER. PLEASE COME OUT IF YOU...HAVE I GOT TO KEEP SAYING THIS?'

'You answer her,' I say when Paula stares at me.

'She's your girlfriend.'

'She's not my girlfriend.'

'No? Did you have sex last night?'

'Eh? What the fuck...'

'Then she is your girlfriend.'

'How the fuck do you work that one out?'

'Morals, Howie,' she says as though that answers everything and knocks on the door again, 'nobody here either, next one?'

We go up the path, along the road and back down the next path to knock on the door and wait.

'Did Marcy tell you we had sex?'

'I can't tell you that,' she says.

'But...that doesn't make us boyfriend and girlfriend.'

'No? Do you want to tell her that?'

'No.'

'Well there you go then.'

'Fine.'

'Don't sulk. If you don't want a girlfriend then don't have sex with them.'

'Fine.'

We go up the path, along the road and back down the next path to knock on the door and wait.

'Them?' I ask her.

'What?'

'You said them. What does that mean? Them?'

'Lani and Marcy. You had sex with them.'

'Yeah but...that was two people not *them*...like...'

'Them,' she says with a shrug, 'I don't think anyone is home here either.'

We go up the path, along and back down.

'Yeah but the way you said it makes it seem like loads.'

'That's your mind making that connection. I just said them.'

I breathe out and wait to see if anyone will answer the door.

'WHY AM I USING THIS IF YOU'RE KNOCKING ON EVERY DOOR?'

'Just because you have sex with someone doesn't mean you're in a relationship,' I say as we head for the last cottage.

'No? I didn't think you were the promiscuous type.'

'I'm not.'

'Ah, commitment phobe then.'

'What? I'm not...I'm not anything. I'm just pointing out that...'

'I heard you but refer back to my previous answer. You tell Marcy you are not in a relationship and see what she says.'

'She'd stab me.'

'There you go then.'

'Or shoot me.'

'Both probably.'

'Stab me then shoot me then stab me again.'

'Marcy will not stab you, Mr Howie. Nor will she shoot you.'

'Cheers, Dave but it was more of a er...rhetorical statement? No not rhetorical...Paula? What's the word?'

'Twat? All empty,' she says, standing back from the door, 'they're all locked up though.'

'Maybe they're hiding,' I say.

'I would if I saw us outside,' she says glumly.

'Fair one,' I say, 'I really need a coffee.'

We head back down the road towards the vehicles and there she is looking like the poster for the Living Army recruitment campaign. Join now. Ride a horse and kill zombies. Jess trots towards us lifting her legs high with each step as her head tosses side to side all bouncy and poised. Charlie holds the reins one handed and the assault rifle in her other and every single one of us stares in abject admiration. They were born to be together and they look fantastic as she glides it round in a circle with a grin spreading across her face.

'I'm actually in love...with the horse though, not Charlie.'

She laughs at Cookey's words spoken dreamily through the radio and looks over to me. 'Mr Howie,' she calls out politely, 'I am ready. Where do you want us?'

'Where is your axe?' Dave asks, his tone as flat as ever.

'I don't have an axe. I used Blinky's last night,' Charlie says, pulling the horse back to hold her steady. I always thought horses were meant to be nice and docile but this thing looks rabid with bulging angry eyes and lips that keep flicking back to show her big stained teeth. She hooves the ground, impatient to be moving and snorting round until she spots Clarence and moves closer to him to sniff his hands.

'I gave her a biscuit last night,' Clarence says in explanation as the horse shows she's pissed off at the lack of biscuits in his hand by snorting in his face and moving off.

'Roy, Charlie will use your sword,' Dave says.

'Pardon?' Roy says, his head tilting back as though he didn't hear properly.

'I said Charlie will use your sword.'

'Does Charlie know how to use a sword?' Roy asks, his tone clearly irritated.

'Charlie?' I call out before Dave can upset him even more.

'You stab with it don't you?' Blowers asks.

'There is more to it than that,' Roy says tightly.

'What like?' Blowers asks.

'Yes thank you,' I say firmly, 'Charlie, you need a hand weapon. How did you find the axe yesterday?'

'It was fine, Mr Howie but I think I will be unable to carry both the rifle and an axe.'

'Sling the rifle and carry the axe,' I say, 'Cookey, Blowers…give her one of your axes for now. Roy, can you show Charlie how to use the sword later.'

'What to stab people with it?' Blowers mutters.

'Mate, that's enough.'

'Yes, Mr Howie,' he says smartly.

'Have mine,' Cookey is there in a flash, holding his up for Charlie to take.

'Thank you but what will you use?'

'I'll use Blowers's axe.'

'Blowers? What will he use?'

'He'll be busy bumming someone…'

'Alex!'

'Sorry, Paula.'

'I bloody told you to stop those jokes. We've got a bus full of people right there.'

'I have caused an awful fuss,' Charlie says with a wince, 'I am sorry.'

'It's an awful fuss,' Cookey says sagely, 'a terribly awful fuss.'

'You sound like Reggie,' Nick says with a grin.

'Gosh? Do I really?'

'Ha! That's Reggie,' Nick laughs.

'Indeed,' Cookey says, trying to push a pair of glasses up his nose then adjusting an invisible tie knot, 'I do like to ponder maps and such like.'

Clarence snorts and turns away and Paula has to clench her jaw to hide the smile twitching at her lips.

'Enough,' I say, smiling at the grinning lad happy as anything with an audience, 'Cookey, do you want to take over from Marcy?'

'Fuck yeah,' he blurts, 'shit...seriously?'

'Yeah go on but don't fuck about.'

'I always fuck about, Mr Howie,' he says earnestly.

'You can't knock honesty,' Clarence says.

'Okay but rein it in, we're moving fast so...'

'I know someone who can rein me in,' he says with a slow turn of his head up to Charlie, 'you got reins eh?'

'Fuck's sake!' Paula tries to shout over her own laugh, 'we're moving...Charlie, you go ahead, love. Keep an eye out but don't get in a fight on your own.'

'Come back and rein me in, Charlie,' Cookey says, beaming as she trots off laughing, 'ah I do make myself laugh I do...hey, has everyone seen my new sock dance?'

'Cookey!'

'Sorry, Paula...' He says, immediately dropping his head to look sad, 'just wanted to show you my new sock dance that's all.'

She walks off to hide the laugh and waves a hand at me, 'you tell him off.'

'Aw but mum,' Cookey huffs, 'don't tell Dad...'

CHAPTER TWENTY-FOUR

I wait. Jenny waits. Phillip and Paul wait. Noise from inside. I can smell them. I can smell their faeces and body odour. Movement at the window. Jenny lifts her hand. Phillip lifts his hand. Paul lifts his hand. Paul does not have a penis. Phillip bit Paul's penis off.

'It's Jenny, Phil and Paul…yes, they're outside…hang on.'

The woman who speaks from inside is called Penelope. Jenny, Phillip and Paul know Penelope. Penelope lives with Toby. Toby wants to have sexual intercourse with Jenny. Jenny has a memory of Toby saying he wants to have sexual intercourse with her. Toby said he knows where to find cannabis and will show Jenny if she has sexual intercourse with him. Jenny did not want this to happen and told Toby she did not want this to happen. Toby said he wants to have sexual intercourse with Jenny's mouth. Jenny said no but I have the memory that Jenny was considering this as she knows Phillip likes to smoke cannabis and Phillip may have sexual intercourse with her if she brings him cannabis.

'Alright, Jen?'

It is Toby. He opens the door and speaks before he looks.

'Oh FUCK!'

Jenny, Phillip and Paul push the door. They have a greater

combined body weight than Toby. Toby runs. Jenny, Phillip and Paul run too. Toby is slow. Jenny bites his shoulder. Toby turns round to punch Jenny. Toby is screaming. Paul bites Toby on the arm. Phillip bites Toby's penis off.

I have a host body. Toby screams. He feels pain in his stomach. I replicate. Penelope runs out of the back door into the garden. Toby falls down. Jenny, Phillip and Paul run after Penelope. Toby dies. I live. Toby lives. I have the host body.

The garden is enclosed. There is a gate. The gate is locked. They key for the lock is in Toby's pocket. Penelope screams. She has a garden hoe. She hits Jenny on the head. Paul bites her arm. I enter through the bloodstream from saliva given into the wound. I have a host body. Penelope hits Jenny on the head. Phillip bites Penelope's ear off. Penelope hits Jenny on the head. Phillip bites Penelope's nose off. Penelope hits Jenny. Phillip bites Penelope on her kneecap. Penelope falls down and hits Jenny again. I replicate. She feels pain in her stomach. Jenny stops getting hit. Phillip tries to bite Penelope on her vagina. Penelope dies. I live. Penelope lives. I have the host body.

I WAIT. Toby waits. Jenny, Phillip, Paul and Penelope all wait. Penelope does not have a nose and one ear is bitten off and one kneecap is bitten off. Paul and Toby do not have penises. Jenny has many cuts to her head.

'Who is it?'

The man who speaks inside is called Terrence. He does not like to be called Terry. Jenny, Paul, Phillip, Penelope and Toby all have memories of Terence being grumpy.

'I said who is it?'

I must answer. I must vocalise.

'It is Toby.'

'What do you want? Sod off.'

'I am Toby.'

'You deaf? Sod off.'

'It is Penelope.'

'So what? Both of you sod off.'

The door is wood. It is thin. The host bodies have a greater combined body weight and this I use to break through the door.

'I SAID SOD OFF.'

Terrence is shouting. He is wearing a dressing gown and has white hair. He is holding a knife. He stabs Toby.

'NOW SOD OFF...'

Toby bites Terrence on the hand. Terrence shouts. Paul bites Terrence on the arm.

'SOD OFF BITING ME YOU BLOODY SODS...'

I have a host body. I enter through the wounds from saliva into the bloodstream. I replicate. Toby stops biting. Paul stops biting. Phillip does not stop biting. Jenny did not bite. Penelope did not bite. Phillip bites Terrence's finger off.

'Give me my finger back you sod.'

Terrence tries to open Phillip's mouth to get his finger. Phillip swallows the finger. Terrence pokes Phillip in the eye with his thumb. Phillip bites Terrence's thumb off. Terrence feels pain. He falls to the floor. His dressing gown is open. Phillip bites Terrence's penis off. Terrence dies. I live. Terrence lives. Phillip spits the penis out. I have the host body.

TERRENCE WAITS. I wait. Penelope, Toby, Jenny, Paul and Phillip wait. We are closer to the greater population density section of this area now.

'Who is it?'

The door does not open. The man speaking is called Lee. I have memories of Lee.

'It is Terence. I am Terence.'

'Terence? It don't sound like you...'

'Sod. I am Terence. Sod.'

'You crazy old bastard, what do you want?'

The door is upvc double glazed. It has a three bar locking mechanism but it is strong. The window is single glazed. The curtains on the inside are closed. Phillip goes through the window. The glass breaks. The curtains fall. The light comes into the room. There is screaming.

'EVERYONE OUT.'

Lee shouts. He runs at Phillip. Phillip bites Lee on his face. I have a host body.

'RUN...RUN...GET OUT...'

Lee shouts. Phillip bites him on the mouth. Lee does not shout. I replicate. He feels pain. I silence him. Phillip bites his right ear off. Lee falls down.

'DAD? DAD!'

The son is called Jack. He is upstairs. Phillip goes upstairs. Phillip spits Lee's penis out. Jack runs into a bedroom. There is screaming inside the bedroom.

Lee dies. I live. Lee Lives. I have the host body. Lee gets up and unlocks the door. Terrence, Penelope, Toby, Jenny and Paul come into the house and go up the stairs.

Inside the room is Jack. Jack is Lee's son. Jack is eighteen. Lee thinks Jack wants to have sexual intercourse with everything. Lee catches Jack gratifying himself. Lee pretends he doesn't see Jack gratifying himself. Inside the room is Fiona. This is Lee's wife. Inside the room is Emma. Emma is a friend of Fiona who now lives with Lee, Jack and Fiona. They scream inside the room. I can smell the fear.

The door is thin wood. I go through the door. Lee bites Jack on his hand. I have a host body. Fiona hits Jenny on the head with a baseball bat. Toby bites Fiona on her neck. Fiona drops the bat. Emma has the bat. Emma hits Jenny on the head with the bat. Phillip bites Jack's penis off. Fiona feels pain in her stomach. She punches Jenny in the face. Paul bites Fiona on her arm. Jack feels pain in his stomach. Emma hits Jenny on the head with the bat. Lee bites Emma on her leg. Emma screams and hits Jenny with the bat.

Toby bites Emma on her other leg. I replicate in Fiona and Jack. They fall to the floor with pain. Emma hits Jenny on the head. Phillip bites Emma's hand. Phillip bites Emma's arm, shoulder, neck and bites her ear off. I have a host body. Jack dies. I live. Fiona dies. I live. Jack lives. Fiona lives. I have the host bodies. Emma falls down. Phillip bites her stomach. Emma feels pain in her stomach. Phillip keeps biting her stomach. I replicate. Phillip bites deeper into Emma's stomach. Emma is silent. Phillip bites Emma's intestines out from her stomach. Emma dies. Phillip bites Emma's liver from her body. Emma is dead. Phillip bites Emma's kidneys from her body. I cannot make Emma live now. I have Lee, Jack and Fiona but Jack, Terence, Lee, Toby and Paul do not have penises. Jenny does not have a jaw. Terence does not have a finger or thumb. Penelope does not have an ear or a nose.

FIONA WAITS. I wait. Jenny, Paul, Toby, Penelope, Terence, Lee and Jack wait. Phillip waits at the back.

In this house is Stuart. This is not Stuart's house. Stuart was poor and lived in a flat. Stuart took this house when I gained freedom from the laboratory. Stuart took a Porsche and a Range Rover and brought them to this house. Everyone has memories of Stuart being an idiot.

FIONA WAITS. I wait. Jenny, Paul, Toby, Penelope, Terence, Lee, Jack and Stuart wait. Stuart does not have a penis. Both of his ears have been bitten off. Both of his thumbs have been bitten off. Phillip waits on the street.

CHAPTER TWENTY-FIVE

'DO NOT DRINK THE WATER. THE WATER IS INFECTED. DO NOT DRINK THE WATER. WE ARE NOT HERE TO HARM YOU. WE CAN TAKE YOU TO A SAFE PLACE. DO NOT DRINK THE WATER.

'Hang on, Cookey.'

His voice stops immediately as I stare at the open door and what looks like fresh blood stains inside the hallway. *'Fresh blood in the house. Eyes up.'*

The tension ripples out. Rifles lifted ready to aim and I see Charlie stop the horse a few metres up the road watching ahead.

'Dave, with me, Clarence on the door as we go in...Roy, hang back ready, *Charlie, we're checking inside this house, stand by.'*

'Standing by.'

I go forward with Dave and Clarence. My rifle aiming into the hallway to see thick drips of blood trailing back across the black and white tiled floor and up the beige carpeted stairs. It's fresh too. Still glistening and wet. Meredith rushes past me, her nose to the ground and her hackles raised.

'Ready?' I ask.

'Go,' Clarence says.

I rush forward with Dave and hold in the hallway at the bottom of the stairs as Dave goes off to check the ground floor rooms.

'Clear,' he comes back in less than a minute.

'We'll go up,' I say and start ascending. Clarence moves into the hallway to keep line of sight on us and Roy outside. The stairs loop round to the left and I hold the rifle aimed high as I turn on the next flight and reach the top landing. The blood trail is thicker here and when I look back down the stairs I can see it is less all the way down. 'Infected,' I mutter to Dave.

He goes forward. Room to room with his pistol held ready. 'Clear,' he appears from the end room, 'in here, Mr Howie.'

I move towards him as he steps back into the bathroom. The blood is everywhere. Sprayed on the walls, over the bath, the shower, the toilet and there's a bloodied cricket bat dumped to one side too.

'Shit,' I say quietly but it's obvious someone was in here drinking water. I take a step further into the room and feel my right boot tread on something soft that squelches and pops out to scoot across the floor. Meredith is there in an instant, grabbing whatever it was and running for the door. 'What was that?'

'I don't know,' Dave replies, 'this blood is fresh.'

I look down at the puddles then at the glistening drops on the walls, the side of the bath and the shower glass, 'you think?'

'Yes.'

'What makes you say that?'

'It's wet.'

Clarence shouts up the stairs, 'you got anything?'

'Yeah in the bathroom,' I shout back.

He trudges up with his heavy feet thudding on the stairs and the landing creaking as he walks down to loom in the doorway with an appraising look, 'still wet,' he says, 'fresh then.'

'I said that,' Dave says.

'So did I,' Clarence says.

'Great minds think alike,' I say before they start squabbling.

'Good cricket bat,' he says, looking down at the blood stained bat on the floor, 'got teeth next to it too.'

'You like cricket?' I ask him, mildly surprised.

'Love cricket' he says with a big grin, 'don't you?'

'Er,' I say, blowing air out, 'never really understood it to be honest.'

'What? Hitting a ball with a bat?'

'No all the terminology, like overs and...googly and all that stuff and the way they score it like England were twenty four for seven or whatever they say.'

'Ah,' he says with a deep nod and presses the button under his shirt, *'Roy, we have a non-believer here.'*

'Who?'

'The Boss.'

'Ale or cricket?'

'Cricket.'

'Ah,' Roy says deeply through the radio, *'this is very serious.'*

'Very serious,' Clarence says to me, 'well, looks like they're close then,' he adds with a final look round.

'Yep, bloody mess if you ask me.'

'Very droll.'

We trudge down the stairs adding more bloodstained footprints to the ones already there and in that second I ponder the future and wonder if our bloody footprints will remain there for tens of years or maybe even longer. Days and nights that will pass as the seasons change and the years roll by outside of this house that will probably never be lived in again. The bricks will slowly crumble. The roof will fall in. The ivy and plants will go through the joists and break through the mortar in the brickwork and one day a cyborg mutant alien will stroll by and cast a casual look at the ruins and wonder who lived here.

'What's the dog got?' Paula asks, bringing me out of my

weighty thoughts as Meredith trots purposefully past her with her mouth clamped suspiciously closed.

'Dunno, she got something from the bathroom,' I say as I stroll back to the vehicles.

'What was in the bathroom?' She asks.

'Lots of blood,' I say, 'and a cricket bat and some teeth.'

'Urgh really?' She asks with a wince, 'old or new?'

'New, the blood is still wet.'

'What's Meredith got in her mouth?' Blowers asks.

'I don't know, mate, she took it from the bathroom.'

'You said the bathroom was covered in blood,' Marcy says.

'It is.'

'So what did she take then?' Paula asks me.

'I don't know,' I say with a huff, 'she picked it up and ran out.'

'Howie, that's disgusting,' Marcy says with a tut, 'she could have anything.'

'Disgusting? She was ripping arms from people a couple of days ago.'

'Blowers,' Marcy calls, 'get her to drop it.'

Blowers clicks his tongue for Meredith who turns to look at him then pulls her head back as he walks towards her, 'come on... what you got?' She twists away, not walking off but just turning her head left and right with her mouth still closed. 'Meredith,' he says in a low gentle telling off voice, 'come on, drop...drop...' She starts to grumble in protest with her tail wagging low and still twisting her head side to side. 'Nick, give us a hand, mate.'

He runs over to gently hold her neck and bends down to look at her mouth, 'drop... come on sweetie, drop it now...Meredith...'

'She's not giving it up is she,' Marcy says walking towards them, 'let me have a go.' She gets closer and squats down in front of the dog who is looking distinctly unimpressed with the amount of attention at the contents of her mouth. 'Let me see, it might be bad for you, come on open up,' she gets a hand on Meredith's nose and another on her lower jaw and starts easing them apart. Meredith swishes left and right and grumbles but she doesn't growl and after a few seconds of minor resistance she finally gives in and opens her mouth.

'Got it,' Marcy says with a grimace at the soft thing covered in dog goo and blood in her hand, 'here,' she passes it back to Blowers and fusses Meredith's head who tracks the transfer of the object with keen eyes.

'What is it?' Paula asks.

'Dunno,' Blowers says, holding it up. Several inches long and quite thick but covered in blood, 'it's floppy,' he says holding it at one end and wiggling it side to side.

'A thumb?' Nick asks, peering closer.

'Don't think so,' Blowers says peering hard, 'it's familiar but...'

'Is it human?' Cookey asks, leaning from the door of the Saxon.

'Sausage?' Roy asks.

'Everything okay?' Charlie asks, trotting closer with the horse, 'I saw you coming out. What's that?'

'Dunno,' Blowers says holding it up to waggle about, 'Meredith had it in her mouth.'

Charlie squints and cocks her head over to one side before shooting a glance at Cookey and going bright red, 'oh...'

'What?' Blowers asks, clocking the look to Cookey then staring at the thing in his grip.

'I er,' she coughs nervously, 'I believe it hangs the other way.'

'Eh?' Blowers says, 'hangs the other way?'

'Er...sort of...well...I believe they er...well they rather dangle.'

'Dangle?' Blowers says.

'Turn your hand over,' Nick says, leaning closer.

Blowers turns his hand over. The thing dangles and the connection is made by everyone else at the same time as the blood drains from Blowers face, 'it's a dick,' he shouts with a yelp and flings it at Nick who screams and shies away.

'Don't fucking throw it at me,' Nick says, jumping back as it lands with a wet thud on the floor.

'Argh, it was in my hand,' Blowers yacks, shaking his hand violently, 'I touched a dick…'

'Oh you are joking,' Cookey rushes forward to stare down at the bloodied member, 'no way…no actual way…'

'I'm gonna puke,' Blowers gasps holding his hand away from his body.

'No. Actual. Fucking. Way,' Cookey mutters, mesmerised by the penis on the tarmac.

'Oh my god, oh my god,' Blowers heaves and yacks while trying to lean away from his own hand.

'It's just a penis,' Paula says.

'Fuck,' Cookey says slowly and I notice he first looks at Charlie then down at the penis then over at Blowers, 'seriously…this is the actual best day ever.'

'Someone wash my hand,' Blowers whimpers, 'Nick…wash my hand.'

'Fuck off,' Nick says backing away fearfully.

'Mr Howie,' Blowers says mournfully, turning towards me with his blood stained hand.

'Piss right off,' I back away laughing.

'Mo? Anti-bac my hand, mate…'

'You's fucking gross,' Mo recoils in disgust.

'I could die happy now,' Cookey sighs.

'Please,' Blowers shouts, 'I can still feel it…someone anti-bac me…cut my hand off…'

'Really,' Cookey nods sincerely and looks up at Charlie again, 'it doesn't get any better than this.'

'Dave,' Blowers says, turning towards him, 'cut it off…cut my hand off.'

'I am not cutting your hand off, Simon,' Dave says so seriously it sets me of laughing harder.

'Dave, it was a dick. I was holding a dick.'

'I saw that.'

'Cookey saw it,' Blowers says desperately, 'shoot me then.'

'I am not shooting you, Simon.'

'You don't understand, I had a dick in my hand and Cookey saw it.'

'Dave, you should shoot him,' Nick says.

'It's just a cock,' Blinky says, bending down to pick it up, 'what's all the fuss?'

'Don't touch it!' Nick shouts, jumping back again.

'What this?' Blinky asks, holding it out towards him.

'Argh you dirty fucking bitch...'

'Who wants it? Cookey?'

'Give it back to Blowers, he can keep it for later.'

'Oh god it's starting,' Blowers says, 'Dave, shoot Cookey.'

'I am not shooting Alex.'

'Ten million pounds to anyone who shoots Cookey...Clarence... wash my hand...'

'Not a chance,' Clarence says, chuckling like the rest of us at Blowers obvious misery.

'You want it back?' Blinky asks, walking towards him while flicking the floppy thing side to side.

'Don't you dare,' Blowers stiffens and glares at her, straightening his back as he tries to stare her down.

'But honestly,' Cookey says again, his voice wistful, 'I saw Charlie's bum this morning and now this.'

'Cookey!' Charlie says in alarm.

'You saw Charlie's bum?' Marcy asks in surprise, 'when? How?'

'That's not important right now,' Cookey says firmly, 'what's important is that Blowers was holding a penis in his hands.'

'Hand. One hand. I held it in one hand and I didn't know what it was.'

'What's important right now is that we all saw Blowers licking the dismembered willy.'

'I fucking did not.'

'On this day, in this place. I saw Blowers stroking and trying to lick a cut off willy and it was only when Blinky took it from him that he stopped,' Cookey announces, 'that's what happened.'

'It fucking didn't,' Blowers says.

'Did in my head.'

'Cookey, please...' Blowers pleads, still holding his arm out.

'Oh yes, in the darkest of days they shall tell this story of the day Simon Blowers found a willy on the...'

A blur of black and Meredith, who was flicking her head side to side watching the willy being dangled about by Blinky makes her move and launches up with a quick snap of jaws that snatches the penis from her hands.

'Oi,' Blinky shouts, lunging after her, 'give me my cock back.' Meredith runs, holding her head high as she glances back to see Blinky coming at her and she darts on, applying a burst of speed through our legs.

'Stop her,' Paula shouts, lunging and missing.

'Meredith!' Marcy gets in front of the dog who twists and goes round her legs.

'Nick,' Paula shouts, 'get your dog under control.'

'She ain't my dog,' Nick says.

'Mo, grab her,' I shout as he dives with tears of laughter streaming down his face and misses as she scoots past him.

'Ha!' Clarence flashes a hand out with a presumption of victory that is snatched from his grip as she stops dead, turns and whips away, 'bloody hell she's quick.'

'Stop that dog,' Paula shouts, 'no...Meredith NO...' the dog spins, weaves and makes us all look slow as she plays escape and evade with a penis dangling from the side of her mouth.

The dog runs off, sprinting a few metres with a blur of speed and comes to a stop as she spins and drops to the ground bringing her front paws together to grip the penis as she opens her mouth to pant and stare back at us looking for all the world like she's grinning.

We range out in a line. The living army seeing its prey. Dave central and slightly ahead as ever. Me on one side, Clarence on the other. Meredith's tail wags slowly. We lower down, our eyes fixed. Her tail wags a bit faster.

'Easy now,' I whisper as the line edges forward.

'Flanks,' Clarence mutters.

'On it,' Nick starts going wide one side while Roy goes wide the other side, ready to encircle the dog who grips the willy between her paws and looks round with her tail now wagging faster.

'Is everything okay?' Reginald calls out from the side of Roy's van, standing there watching with Kyle.

'Shush,' Marcy waves her hand at him as we encroach towards the dog.

'Steady,' I murmur, dropping lower while I gently push my rifle round to my back to free my hands.

'Stop,' Marcy whispers urgently as Meredith drops her head towards the penis and looks up at us, 'no no no,' she calls out softly, 'don't eat it...you don't where it's been'

'Meredith,' Cookey calls out just as softly, 'can Blowers have his willy back now?'

I sputter a laugh that ripples round the group and realise Blowers is still stood back by the vehicles squirting anti-bac over his right hand, 'not funny,' he grumbles.

'Ooh,' Clarence stops dead to stand upright.

'Shit,' I turn away from the awful sight.

'Nasty' Roy peels off, his hand going instinctively to his groin as she bites another inch off that she chews with loud squelchy noises of mastication.

'Urgh,' Nick grimaces, 'she's eating it.'

'The dog's eating your dick, Blowers,' Cookey says, wincing as every man in the group closes his legs a bit tighter.

We don't stand a chance and we know it, and what's more, Meredith knows it. She has the penis and she will eat it and the look in her eyes tell us there ain't a damn thing we can do stop her.

So we don't. We stand back and grimace with winces as she bites and chews and swallows until the thing is gobbled down and she finally lifts her head looking smug and content.

'Your dog is disgusting,' I say to Nick as I turn away.

'She's not my dog,' Nick says.

'S'gross,' Mo says, frowning at Nick as he heads back to the bus.

'She's not my bloody dog,' Nick exclaims.

'Ha,' Blinky laughs, 'your dog likes cock.'

'Not my dog.'

'Nick,' Clarence says with a tut, 'don't let her do that again.'

'She's not my fucking dog!'

'Shouldn't be off a lead if you can't control her,' Blowers calls out now on his second bottle of anti-bac.

'Er, you can all fuck off...she's not my dog.'

'Charlie doesn't let her horse eat body parts,' Paula joins in. 'Anyway, have we finished dicking about? Get it? Dicking about?'

'That was awful,' I say with a shake of my head.

'Pah, no sense of humour. Onwards then, Mr Howie. Lead the living army through this town of dismembered penises.'

'One penis,' Blowers shouts, picking his rifle up, 'it was one and I didn't know what it was.'

'BLOWERS LICKED A CUT OFF WILLY,' Cookey's amplified voice informs everyone in the vicinity.

'I'm quitting,' Blowers says, 'I'm giving my notice, Mr Howie.'

'Speak to Miss Paula, she handles personnel issues.'

'Resignation refused,' Paula says.

'DON'T DRINK THE WATER. THERE MIGHT BE WILLIES IN IT...'

'Okay okay,' Paula calls out, 'game faces on, ready when you are, Howie.'

CHAPTER TWENTY-SIX

'**M**r Howie, it's Charlie. There's a blood trail on the ground running along the pavement to your right.'

'Okay, Dave's looking now...see anything, Dave?'

'Yes.'

'Okay...what do you see, Dave?'

'A blood trail, Mr Howie.'

'Great, clears that up then.'

'Three people. Two men and one woman going in the same direction as we are.'

'Fuck me. You can tell them from a blood trail?'

'No. There are footprints in the blood trail.'

'Want me to hold off with the loudspeaker for a bit?' Cookey asks through the radio.

'Yeah for a minute, mate. Charlie, can you see where it goes?'

'Will do.'

She canters the horse further down the road while periodically leaning down to check the pavement. We're only a few streets from the penis house and still in an estate agents wet dream of a residential heaven made from ubiquitous brick built houses with slate roofs and small gardens. It feels foreboding now. Like the houses are faces and the dark windows are eyes and the doors are mouths ready to open and spew the filthy infected at us. We're getting closer to the town centre and the sense of unease grows.

I glance back every few minutes to the others behind me. Cookey driving the Saxon to the left side of the road. The bus behind but in the middle and Roy's van behind that but again staggered out with Kyle clear behind the windscreen. Blowers walks in front of the bus. Clarence by the door and I can see through the bus screen to the woman Jane passing a bottle of water out to him. Roy is off to the right, his bow held with an arrow nocked and ready. Everyone else is ranged out, encircling the bus. The tension is high and the more we do this the greater our discomfort grows at being in a built up area where every doorway, every alley, every window and corner holds a point of danger. Marcy and Paula walk side by side talking quietly while they scan and watch the sides and turn to see the back covered by Reginald monitoring the cameras.

'People from the house?' I ask quietly as Dave comes back to the middle of the road. He doesn't answer but turns in a slow circle to take in every possible point of attack before thumbing the button under his shirt, *'Mohammed, up front with Mr Howie.'*

'Coming.'

'Dave, I don't need Mo to protect me...'

'I am training him, Mr Howie. This is a good training ground.'

'Okay,' I know better than to argue, especially when he's got that tone of voice going on. Not that it differs from any other tone of voice he has but somehow it just feels different.

'Mohammed,' Dave says as Mo runs up to join us, 'take the left side of Mr Howie...'

'Really, Dave?' I ask.

'I am training Mohammed.'

'Okay okay.'

'Mohammed, ahead of us is twelve o'clock, our rear is six o'clock. Do you understand a clock face?'

'Yep...I mean yes, Dave.'

'You will cover from six o'clock to twelve o'clock. I will cover from twelve o'clock to six.'

'So's I'm covering the left then.'

'Yes.'

'Got it.'

'Charlie is ahead of us which we will take into account if we have to fire.'

'Got it.'

'Select single shot on your rifle and only fire if you have clear line of sight. Place your shots.'

'Yep,' Mo says, switching the firing position on his rifle, 'I mean yes.'

'We are prone to ambush in a situation such as this. There are many points of entry leading into our position. We must be aware of each point of entry.'

'Got it.'

'What is the best exit route from this position?'

'We run back?' Mo says, turning as he walks to cover his side.

'It is called a tactical retreat. We do not run back. We withdraw tactically.'

'Got it.'

'Yes, the vehicles are our first place of safety if an ambush occurs now. They are armoured and we have a stronger defensive line with the team. If we were attacked now from the front what would the best tactical option be?'

'How many?' Mo asks.

'Two.'

'We stand our ground and kill them.'

'There are three.'

'Same.'

'Ten.'

'I think we can deal with ten,' Mo says, glancing at me, 'Mr Howie can handle ten on his own.'

'One hundred.'

'Run back…er, we tactically withdraw to the vehicles.'

'And then?'

'Then we kill them.'

'There are too many.'

'Too many? How many is that?'

'There are too many for us to fight. Our ammunition is depleted.'

'We's fuck 'em up with axes and knives.'

'We do not have our axes or knives.'

'I got my knife.'

'You dropped it.'

'I went back and got it.'

'It was taken from you.'

'I took it back from the fucker that took it.'

'It was broken.'

'I take one from you. You got loads of knives.'

'Mine are broken. We do not have knives now.'

'We go into the houses and get more knives.'

'The houses are locked.'

'Clarence breaks the doors down and we get more knives.'

'Clarence is busy.'

'I break a window and get in the house and come out with knives for me and you.'

'There are no knives in the houses.'

'I can fight with a stick or a bat or a chain.'

'There are no sticks or bats or chains.'

'Forks.'

'There are no forks.'

'Bare handed them. Old school.'

'There are too many.'

He leans forward to look past me to Dave, 'I dunno, Dave.'

'We can use the vehicles to punch out and regroup.'

'Got it.'

'The vehicles are broken,' Dave says, continuing the lesson.

'We run and regroup?' Mo asks.

'We cannot run through them. There are too many.'

'We's fight through them then.'

'We do not have weapons.'

'Mr Howie, the trail leads to a house. The door is open. Blood inside the hallway.'

'Coming to you, hold position, keep your eyes up, Charlie.'

I start running, feeling somewhat silly with Mo and Dave either side of me. Behind me the vehicles pick up speed to keep pace. Down the road we sprint, heading towards Charlie at the far end sitting on the horse aiming her rifle towards a house. Meredith streaks ahead, zooming down the middle of the road and covering the distance in a matter of seconds.

'Charlotte,' Dave, the fit bastard, speaks into his radio as calm as anything as we sprint flat out, *'when we reach your position you will move further down to cover.'*

'Understood.'

'I hate you,' I mutter between breaths and hear Mo snigger at my side.

We reach Charlie and with a flick of the reins she trots away and I notice the axe is now hanging from a big brass loop with the axe head resting against the saddle.

The house is the same as before. The door wide open and what looks like fresh blood on the hallway inside the front door.

I go forward as Dave rests a hand on my arm, 'we will clear the house.'

'Go for it,' I say and hold back for a second as they go inside then promptly follow them in, which earns me a frosty glance from Dave.

The house is detached and nicely done up with bare wooden floors and even from here I can see through to the kitchen and dining room that have been stacked with crates of tinned food. Whoever lived here was in it for the long haul. The floor is covered in blood and looks about the same as the last place.

'Door's not damaged,' Clarence says as gets into the doorway and checks the lock, 'must have let them in.'

'Ground floor clear,' Dave says walking past me with Mo who stops and looks down, 'there's another dick there.'

'Eh?' I look down at Mo's feet to see the bloodied pink thing lying in a thick patch of blood, 'shit.'

'First floor,' Dave says, 'Mohammed, you will go first. Pistol not rifle. Mr Howie, there is blood in the rear garden.'

'Yep,' Mo says, moving away from the penis.

'Yes not...'

'Yes, sorry Dave,' Mo says, slinging his rifle to draw his pistol as he leads the way up the stairs.

'Smaller than the last one,' Clarence says, peering down at it.

'Size isn't everything,' I say with a look at him, 'not that I'd know.'

'No?'

'Course not,' I say quickly, 'mines tiny.'

He snorts a laugh and reaches up to rub the back of his head, 'this is weird.'

'Telling me, we got a zombie biting dicks off.'

'Not a zombie.'

'What you got?' Paula says, walking towards the door with Marcy.

'Another dick,' Clarence says heavily.

'You being serious?' Marcy asks, walking to look down, 'that's a small one.'

'I thought size didn't matter,' I say.

'Noooo, course not,' she says earnestly, 'but that is a tiddler.'

'Zombies biting penises off,' Paula says.

'Not zombies,' Clarence says.

'Upstairs is clear,' Dave says coming down the stairs, 'did you look in the rear garden?'

'Not yet,' I say and head through the kitchen to the open back doors and the blood trail that leads to another big patch of blood and stained garden hoe. 'So the bloke answers the door,' I say, looking back along the trail to the house, 'he gets chomped and...'

'His penis is bitten off,' Marcy says helpfully.

'And someone else legs it out here and goes for it with the hoe.'

'Dicks and hoes,' Marcy snorts, 'sorry, bad taste.'

'Ear,' Paula says.

'You what?' I ask.

'Ear on the ground and that,' she says, tilting her head to look down, 'is a nose by the looks of it.'

Marcy tuts then sighs sadly, 'Toby and Penny,' she nods to a wooden love seat set against the fence with the names Toby and Penny carved into the seats. 'They've got names now.'

I nod in response to the dark tone of her voice and any trace of the humour we use to shield ourselves from the horrors we see every five fucking minutes vanishes. It's one thing to see a dick on the floor but another when you know the name of the bloke the dick belonged to. We're stood in his garden too with bits of his wife on the grass.

'We need to move faster,' Clarence says.

'*Mr Howie, the blood trail leads down to another house. The door is broken in on this one...*'

'*Coming, Blowers, you got line of sight on Charlie?*' I ask as we start running back through the house.

'*Negative, I'll go ahead.*'

'*Roy? Can you see Charlie?*'

'*Running down now.*'

'*I'm fine, Mr Howie,*' she says with a hint of frustration.

'*We stay in line of sight,*' I pant the words out running through the blood in the hallway and out into the road to see Blowers and Roy sprinting side by side down the road. We burst out and the engines lift in pitch as they start coming after us. 'Too many at the front,' I shout out, 'Paula, Marcy and Clarence drop back to the bus...*Reginald, you hearing me?*'

'*Go ahead, Mr Howie.*'

'*Body parts in this house again. Another dick bitten off and more in the garden. It's fresh...*'

'*Understood.*'

'*Eyes up, mate. Everyone eyes up and scan out.*'

I sprint fast, building speed as I charge down the road behind Blowers and Roy who suddenly veers out to vault onto the top of a car and pull his bow up with the arrow ready, 'Eyes on Charlie,' he shouts.

She comes into view. Sitting waiting patiently past a junction and a few houses down the next road. Her rifle held with the butt against her thigh while she turns the horse round in a circle. Blowers reaches her first and instantly drops to one knee to aim into the house while waving at her to move on down the street.

'Dave, Mo, clear the house.'

'With me,' Dave streaks on with Mo keeping stride as they reach Blowers to pause for a second as they sling rifles, draw pistols and head inside.

'Anything?' I ask Blowers as I finally reach him and look back to see Roy has run closer to get on top of another car to gain height to see up and down the street.

'Nothing, door's smashed in,' he says.

'With me then,' I go for the front door with Blowers behind me and enter into a house that stinks of stale food and stale body odour. The décor is grim with a threadbare carpet worn thin and faded. Wallpaper peeling off the walls and clutter everywhere. Blood on the floor and a knife with a blade still wet and glistening from being used.

'Fuck it,' I curse staring down.

'What? Oh,' Blowers says, 'another dick...'

'Ground floor clear, going upstairs.'

'Okay,' I step back to let Dave and Mo get past, 'you checked the garden?'

'Can't get in the garden, Mr Howie.'

I look at Blowers who goes ahead of me through the filthy

grease coated kitchen and the worktops piled with dirty plates, cups and used pans. Scraps of food stuck to the floor and cupboard doors and the once cream linoleum floor is solid black down the middle from years of foot traffic. We get to the back door and look through the glass to see what Dave meant. The house is cluttered but the garden is worse. Fence panels, ornaments, wheelbarrows, windows in frames, old doors and just about everything including a kitchen sink is piled up and jammed in from side to side.

'Dick on the floor,' Marcy says from the hallway behind us.

'Saw it,' I call out.

'Upstairs clear,' Dave says coming down with Mo.

'Terence Conway,' Marcy reads from the front of a high stack of letters left unopened on a side table.

Another name. Another person. A dirty filthy bastard living in abject squalor but a person nonetheless.

'We push on,' I say bluntly and go outside, 'where's the trail? *Charlie, you got the blood trail?*'

'This way.' I look down the road to see her waving ahead.

'Marcy, take over driving the Saxon. I want Cookey on the ground from now on. Dave, Mo, drop the bodyguard thing. The focus is that blood trail. Blowers, you'll keep your team on the bus but we stay fluid. Keep the bus guarded...'

'I will,' he says.

'Roy, you're free to move as you see fit.'

'Do you want the loudspeaker thing?' Marcy asks as she runs to swap with Cookey.

'Not for the minute, we need to move fast. Everyone ready? *Charlie, push on...find the next one. We're going to catch up with those fuckers.'*

CHAPTER TWENTY-SEVEN

She shifts with a wince. Using someone else's saddle is like wearing someone else's shoes. All the creases and folds are in the wrong places.

'Easy,' she murmurs, sensing the urge in the great horse to run like they did last night. Competition level polo is intense and exhilarating but what she did last night with Jess was a thousand times more than she has ever done before. It was the relationship between rider and horse having a perfect sense of balance and weight distribution and not being afraid to use that strength and power.

Charlie played competition level polo to a very high standard and hockey to a national standard. She had the world at her feet. Her family were wealthy but cold and chose to give love by the power of their bank balances and as the years went on and Charlie excelled so she became a trophy daughter. Something to show off at dinner parties. Something to boast about at the sailing club.

Now she sits on a horse in the saddle of a dead man in a deserted street somewhere in the south of England while holding an assault rifle and with an axe hanging by her leg. Times change. People change. Everything changes.

She thinks back to the days they hid in Finkton Academy. Staying quiet at night and growing less in number as the girls left to try and find families or those they loved. Blinky didn't have anywhere else to go and no one to find and Charlie felt a greater allegiance to the other girls than she ever did to her own family. Not that she was spoiled or ungrateful for the chances she was given in life but to see the relationships the other girls had with their families only served to strengthen her own lack of familial closeness.

The world is over but the world has only just begun and now, every second of every minute counts for something.

She feels frustrated at being told to stay so close. Jess is fast and able to outrun anyone. She's not in danger and besides, she's got the rifle and the axe. Charlie was the captain of the England hockey team. She is independent, strong and knows her own mind and to be held back from doing something she knows she is capable of is annoying.

Then she saw them all running. Every single one of them sprinting flat out to catch her up. There was no immediate danger but they did it anyway. They ran. They ran for her and the hairs on the back of her neck stood up at seeing Roy vault to get on top of a car to hold his bow and arrow aimed and ready. These are strange days but in the darkest of days there will be light and inside her heart a light shines brighter than it ever has done before.

Her mind flicks back to yesterday and everything that happened until that final fight but everything from that point on is too great and too deep to even start to contemplate. She planned with Reginald. She fought with the lads and Blinky. She gave ideas to Mr Howie and Paula and they listened. Even this morning means something. Being with Paula and Marcy in the bathroom gossiping like normal women. Women never did that with Charlie. She was too well spoken, too polite, too clipped and too...too posh for them to even consider her the type of girl that would like a gossip. But they did. Paula and Marcy took her into their fold and treated her not as a trophy or someone with an expensive education but as a girl that wants to hear about the sex and all the mucky details.

Then that thing with Cookey in the bedroom happened and she smiles to herself in the saddle and quickly looks round as though expecting someone to see her smiling to herself.

Cookey. Never before had she met anyone like any of these people but Cookey? Cookey is something else. Posh people don't make jokes like that and they certainly don't show their emotions so clearly and without shame and never before has anyone ever made her laugh like Cookey makes her laugh. Everything he says is funny. His facial expressions, his tone of voice and the downright outrageous comments he makes that he gets away with because of that innocent grin and his blue eyes twinkling.

That thing with Cookey was life and death with blood and fear and sweat. It was dreadful and awful and terrible but it was something else too. It was beautiful in a way nothing should ever be called beautiful. He was naked. She was naked. They were covered in blood and gore but they fought side by side and he covered her with his own body and took the pain in his back. His humour was gone at that point and what remained was a man with an iron core who was prepared to give his life for hers.

She tries to imagine what it would have been like taking someone like Cookey back to meet her family. They would have been appalled. Oh they would have loved him, everyone adores Cookey but they would have also done everything possible to block any hint of a relationship with someone like that. It's hard to remember her family now. She remembers them individually but not with any sense of togetherness. Not the same togetherness she has with these people after only two days. It's conflicting, contrasting and too difficult to think about so she looks down instead and tracks the spots of blood then grins again as she remembers Blowers throwing the penis at Nick.

She only recognised it as a penis because she saw Cookey's this morning. It was the angle and the light and...she shakes her head and blinks to stop thinking about Cookey being naked next to her in the room. He has got a nice bum though. Stop it. Focus and follow the blood trail.

Even in the Saxon when he was telling everyone he saw the tattoo on her bottom would have previously made her angry and ashamed but it was funny instead and she liked the way Cookey flinched and laughed as she punched his arm and seeing Blowers and the others all laughing.

She reaches a crossroads and stops. The street behind is a quiet residential road. The one ahead is the same but the road running left to right is a wide main road that must run into the town centre.

The blood was on the right side but crossed over to the left. It's thinner now too. Whoever was bleeding was congealing or clotting the wound. The infected do that. They heal fast.

She turns Jess in a slow circle and works back to find the last blood spots on the pavement then works slowly back down to the crossroads. Nothing to be seen.

Left, right or ahead? She takes in each direction and urges Jess to go ahead and over the road. Twenty metres into the street and she turns back from the lack of any blood spots. At the crossroads she heads left and again after twenty metres stops and goes back before proceeding down the right side.

There. A smear across the front of a white van. Is it new or old? She gets closer and spots the sheen of the still wet liquid. This way then. Down the main road towards the town centre. She goes slower now. Checking each door to each house is harder as the road is wider and some of the doors are hidden from view behind hedges and walls.

Jess flicks her head up, a snort of air and a quiver of energy rippling through her as Charlie spots the smashed in window next to the open upvc front door. Blood on the windowsill and the curtains are ripped down inside. She goes out wider from the house and turns Jess round to gain a full view.

'*Mr Howie, I've found the next house...down the road you are on and turn right.*'

'*Coming to you, hold position. Any signs of anyone?*'

'*All clear at the moment.*'

THEY JOG STEADILY with a sustained pace marked by Howie at the front. The air filled with the sound of the Saxon chugging confidently, Roy's van purring rhythmically and the minibus spluttering noisily. Feet trudging the ground. Weapons jangling and breathing coming a bit harder as the warmth and exertion grows.

They could have got back into their vehicles but the slow speed would put the people in the minibus at risk so there is no choice but to run alongside and keep it within the protective circle.

'Sod this,' Clarence grips the handle and jumps up to land on the ledge of the bus doorway.

'Cheater,' Paula calls out.

'Older and wiser,' Clarence calls back.

'Water?'

'Eh? Oh thanks very much,' he says with a nod at Jane holding a bottle out, 'er...' he pauses, unsure of how to unscrew the lid while holding the rifle in one hand and the handle to stop himself falling back out with the other.

'Let me,' she says, plucking it back from his huge hand.

'Ah thank you,' he takes the opened bottle and a big swig before leaning out, 'Paula?'

'Cheers,' she runs over, 'budge up,' she jumps up to squeeze past Clarence into the front of the bus.

'Cheater,' Nick shouts.

'Older and wiser,' she shouts back and takes the opened bottle held out by Clara, 'thanks, sweetie...'

'Almost there,' Clarence says, looking ahead to the junction and the Saxon swinging out to make the right turn.

'Duty calls,' Paula says passing the bottle back to Jane, 'don't drink from that one.'

'Okay,' Jane says.

'Thanks,' Clarence says, passing his bottle back, 'better not risk it with mine either...ready?' He asks Paula.

'Why not,' they jump out and run on into the junction and round to see Charlie waiting by the house.

She sees them coming. Howie getting to the junction first with Dave and Mo either side and the Saxon a few metres behind them.

'You okay?' Howie pants, running towards her.

'No movement, window's smashed in,' Charlie says, 'am I moving up again?'

'Dave and Mo...clear the...'

'Doing it,' Dave runs past him with Mo, both of them slinging rifles to draw pistols.

'Fast, Dave,' Howie shouts. The bus comes round the corner with everyone else running in front and to the sides.

'Get some water,' Howie says, pausing a second to get his breathing under control.

'I'm okay, I'm only riding so...'

'Get some water, we might get contact soon,' Howie says walking towards the front door.

'Ground floor clear,' Dave's voice comes clear through the open door and broken window.

Howie goes in and checks the door like Clarence did on one of the other houses. The lock is intact. He gets into the lounge and takes in the busted window, the curtains hanging down and the blood soaking into the deep pile carpet. Whoever lived here wouldn't open the door so they came in via the window. Why are these people living like this? Why aren't they in boarded up houses or strong defensive points? Why stay in the house you lived while the world crumbles to shit around you? Why do that? Why not run or fight back or join others?

'Anything?' Paula asks from the doorway as she walks in with Clarence.

'Why stay here?' Howie asks, 'the fucking windows aren't boarded up...the doors the same as it was...'

'Body upstairs but it's clear,' Dave says, coming down with Mo behind him, 'we'll get fluids.'

'What state is the body in?' Paula asks.

'Bad,' Mo says darkly, following Dave outside.

Paula leads the way up the stairs to the bedroom door smashed through and the walls of the room beyond dripping blood. Three distinct areas of attack. One by the door. One further in and the last is obviously the body left by the window. A woman with her ears bitten off, her nose missing and her internal organs have been torn from her stomach to lie bitten and scattered about the room.

'Think it's a message?' Paula asks.

'Fuck knows,' Howie says, 'why stay here? Why are these people still in this town?'

'It's their home,' she says.

'Doesn't make sense,' Howie says, shaking his head at the corpse.

'Nothing makes sense anymore,' Clarence says heavily.

'Fucking windows aren't boarded...fuck me, they had a bat,' Howie says in exasperation as he kicks the bloodied baseball left on the floor, 'a fucking bat...'

'Comfort in familiarity I guess,' Paula says.

'Did you stay in your house when it happened?' Howie asks.

'Me? No. I got a four wheel drive and kept mobile. I slept in a different field every night until I met Roy and then you lot.'

'Doesn't make any sense,' Howie says again.

'It's people,' Paula says with a shrug, 'they never make any sense.'

Clarence tuts when he spots the penis left in a pool of blood by the skirting board.

'Another one downstairs,' Howie says, 'in the lounge.'

'Penis?'

'Yep.'

'Why are they doing that?' Paula asks, 'it's got to be a message to you lot...come after me and I'll bite your dicks off.'

'Nasty way to go,' Clarence says with a shudder.

'Is there a nice way to go?' Paula asks.

'Yeah, either blind drunk or an old man asleep in bed...'

'Could be both at the same time,' Howie says.

'We'd better go,' Paula says, 'we can't be that far behind them.'

'We could send Dave ahead,' Clarence suggests as they go out into the landing.

'No, we need Dave here in case the bus gets attacked,' Paula says, 'same with you and the lads...and Roy.'

CHARLIE WAITS for the vehicles to pull up and Roy to go ahead before sliding gratefully from the saddle with dull pains radiating through her backside from the unfamiliar creases digging into her cheeks.

'You alright?' Cookey says, his face flushed and with a light sheen of perspiration from running, 'got you a water,' he adds, holding a bottle out given to him by Jane.

'That is very kind, thank you, Cookey,' she says politely, 'would you be kind enough to turn the other way for a second.'

'You what?' Cookey asks, the grin already spreading across his face, 'what for?'

'I need to rub my bottom,' Charlie says with a spurt of laughter at the expression on his face, 'it's not my saddle...the creases are in the wrong places...don't look at me like that.'

'My lady,' Cookey says with his best deep posh voice, 'I shall hitherto turn the other cheek and save your dignity...get it? Cheek?'

She can't help it. It's not just what he says but how he says it. The tone and his expression, the way his smile holds as he nods in expectation. She chuckles then tuts and rolls her eyes. It's the end of the world and she's riding a horse through the apocalypse. Sod it. She reaches round and rubs her backside while giggling like a schoolgirl.

Cookey affects a blanch then looks round as though shocked and offended, 'wow,' he says, 'I actually love this day.'

'I'm somewhat surprised you're not offering to help.'

'Can I?' He blurts.

'No,' she scoffs still laughing, 'what would the others say?'

'Fuck 'em,' Cookey exclaims, 'I'm a good bum rubberer I am.'

'Really? Does Blowers know this? Blowers,' Charlie calls, getting his attention, 'Cookey said he's a good bottom rubberer.'

'I said no such thing,' Cookey says.

'He isn't,' Blowers says before swigging from his bottle, 'he's crap at it. Ask Nick.'

'He's shit,' Nick shouts from the other side of the bus.

'How's your back?' She asks, dropping her voice and taking the bottle of water.

'Ah it's okay,' Cookey says with a shrug.

'Sure?' She asks.

'Stings a bit but fuck it, I got zombie healing powers now.'

She snorts and tries to cover the snort but it comes out like a donkey braying instead.

'Your laugh is awesome, hey Mo,' Cookey says to her then smiles at Mo peeling away from Dave's side, 'is it bad inside?'

'Mess,' Mo says, 'more dicks on the floor. Proper fucked up.'

'More dicks?' Cookey winces at the thought.

'What's that?' Blowers asks, walking over, 'more dicks inside?'

'Yeah,' Mo says, 'one on the ground floor and one in the bedroom...'

'Don't get excited, Blowers.'

'Funny twat,' Blowers mutters.

'Body upstairs been ripped open too,' Mo says, 'woman, her insides are all outsides, you get me?'

'Fucked up,' Blowers says looking down the street, 'we need to speed up.'

'We can't,' Cookey says, 'we've the bus to...'

'I know,' Blowers cuts across him, 'is the blood fresh?'

'Looks it,' Mo says, 'Dave said it is.'

'Dave?' Blowers calls out, 'is the blood fresh?'

'Yes, Simon.'

'Fuck it,' Blowers mutters again, 'we ain't that far behind them.'

'He won't let us separate,' Cookey says, 'and he won't send Dave ahead with people on that bus...'

'He's coming,' Mo says as Howie, Paula and Clarence rush from the house.

'...and I'm saying we cannot separate again, look what happened in that village...' Paula says firmly.

'We have to do something,' Clarence says, equally as firmly, 'I'll go ahead in the Saxon and find them...'

'We are not losing you from here,' Paula fires back, 'and how will you find them from the Saxon? You can't see the blood trail from up there. Charlie can follow it but we can't send Charlie ahead on her own.'

'I am happy to go ahead...' Charlie says.

'No,' Paula shakes her head, 'we are not separating.'

'Boss?' Clarence asks.

Howie stares brooding and dark. His eyes resting on the horse, 'we have to do something. We can't catch them up going at this speed...'

'And we can't leave the people on the bus either,' Paula says.

'Send the bus to the fort,' Blowers says.

'How can we?' Paula says, 'what if something happens to them. We can only go as fast as we can follow that trail.'

'Put the drone up,' Mo says, still in the problem solving mind-set of having Dave throw increasingly bizarre scenarios at him.

'You bloody genius,' Paula says grabbing him to plant a kiss on his forehead, 'well done, honey.'

'Well done, Mo,' Clarence says slamming a hand into the poor lads back.

'Reggie, It's Paula, can you get that drone up and find where they are?'

'I can most certainly try but I will lose the camera feed if I do and the rear will be exposed.'

'Easy Blowers,' Cookey mumbles into his hand.

'So be it,' Paula transmits back, 'Charlie, you okay tracking again?'

'I can go further ahead,' Charlie says quickly as the growing sense of urgency flows through them.

'No,' Howie says simply, 'get ready, we're moving out.'

'Reggie's putting the drone up,' Paula says as though Howie didn't hear her before.

'Mr Howie, Jess is fast enough to get me out of any situation that may develop and...'

'I said no,' Howie mutters, his eyes brooding and dark. Charlie pauses, takes a breath and goes to reply but finds a hand gently touching her leg as Cookey discretely shakes his head.

'Everyone ready?' Howie asks, not giving them time to reply, 'we're moving.'

'Howie,' Marcy says moving in front of him, 'Reggie needs time to get the drone up...'

'Tell him to hurry up.'

'He will go as fast as he can.'

'Someone give him a hand, we need to get moving instead of standing here fucking chatting...'

'Howie,' Marcy says with a warning look.

'Not now, Marcy, we're moving out...everyone get ready.'

'Everyone stay where you are,' Marcy snaps, staring hard at Howie, 'a word please.'

'What?'

'In private,' she says, her voice rising several notches.

'Fucking what?' He snaps, 'they're in front of us...they could be round that fucking corner and we're stood here with our thumbs up our arses...'

'Reggie needs to get the fucking drone up,' Marcy shouts at him, 'we're doing the best we can.'

'Howie,' Paula shouts, 'how the hell can you find them if you can't see where they are.'

'We are moving out,' Howie says, his own voice rising to a shout, 'those things are right in front of us. We are going after them. We are not waiting for them to kill more people. Is that clear?'

'Pack it in, Howie,' Marcy shouts as she reaches out to grab his arm.

'Take your hand off Mr Howie,' Dave says taking a step towards Marcy.

'Whoa,' Paula shouts, 'what are you doing, Dave?'

'Take your hand off Mr Howie,' Dave says again, his hand dropping to his belt.

'Dave, stand down,' Howie fires the words out, 'we're moving now.'

'No we are not,' Paula shouts, 'what the hell was that?'

'I said we're moving out.'

'Marcy is not a threat to Howie,' Paula says, her voice simmering with rage, 'how dare you, Dave.'

'Dave' Howie says coldly, 'can you track as you run?'

'No,' Paula cuts in before Dave can answer, 'Dave stays with the bus and you'll tell him right now to never ever react to Marcy like that again,' she says glaring at Howie.

'Dave, Marcy isn't a threat to me. Do not do that again.'

'We are putting the drone up,' Paula says, her face flushed from anger, 'Nick, give Howie a cigarette, someone find a soft drink to get in him. Christ, Howie,' she adds shaking her head, 'you and Marcy had bloody sex last night...where was Dave then?'

'Whoa,' Clarence says, 'too loud, Paula.'

'No. Not loud enough. Dave only listens to you, Howie. How

dare you let him do that to Marcy. Anyone of us has the right to touch you and it doesn't mean we're going to hurt you...'

'Paula,' Marcy says, 'leave it, Dave's autistic...'

'It's not an excuse,' Paula rages, 'he was in the bloody army for long enough to know right from wrong. We cannot save everyone, Howie. We can't. We just fucking can't save everyone. Is it not enough for you what we did yesterday? Ten thousand?'

'Enough,' Blowers calls out, 'everyone on the bus can hear you.'

Paula turns away, her face set and simmering with rage. Howie stares ahead, his gaze distant and cold. An awkward silence starts and one that stretches as Marcy stands mutely watching Howie and Clarence glowering at Dave who watches everyone.

'Drone will be up in a sec,' Nick calls out as he rushes over holding a cigarette and a bottle of water, 'soft drinks are all gone. Want me to look in the house?'

'No it's fine,' Marcy says with a gentle smile at Nick, 'thanks, Nick.'

'Boss?' Nick holds the cigarette and water out.

'Cheers,' Howie takes them both and waits as Nick reaches out with his lighter.

'You got another one?' Paula asks.

'Yeah sure,' Nick says pulling his pack from his pocket.

'Thanks,' Paula inhales deeply before blowing the smoke away in the thick atmosphere above their heads. 'I love you, Howie,' she mutters, 'God knows we all do but don't push so hard. We all want the same thing.'

Words spoken and the simplicity of them slam home as he finally blinks and looks round, 'okay, sorry.'

'Doesn't matter,' Paula says with a heavy sigh, 'we can't all be this bloody close and not argue...right?' She looks round at the others, 'no harm done, just words,' she reaches a hand out to touch Howie's arm, 'you okay?'

'Yeah, yeah sorry,' he says.

She tuts and moves in to give him a quick hug, 'families argue, we're family right?'

'We are,' Howie says, breathing out to release the knot of pulsing rage in his gut as Paula clasps him close then releases and moves to Marcy, 'family right?' She says, pulling Marcy in for the hug that Dave needs to see.

'Family,' Marcy says, squeezing her arms round Paula.

'Dave,' Paula says, pulling back from Marcy, 'families argue. That's allowed.'

'I will never hurt, Howie,' Marcy says, 'I promise, Dave.'

'I cannot tell,' Dave says, his voice flat and cold. 'You were shouting. You were angry. I cannot read your expressions.'

'Dave,' Clarence says, 'do you ever think I will harm Howie?'

'I would not let you. I will not let any of you.'

'That wasn't the question,' Marcy says, 'Clarence was asking if you think, right now, if he would ever try and hurt Howie.'

'No,' Dave says.

'Then look at me for my reaction before you react,' Clarence says, 'or Paula or Blowers or Cookey or Nick...'

'I trust Mr Howie,' Dave says, 'and Mohammed.'

'Me?' Mo blanches.

'Dave,' Paula says, 'look at me,' she waits for his cold eyes to fix unblinking on hers and such is the intensity that she has to fight not to look away, 'from now on you will look to Mo or one of us before you react like that again.'

'It will be too slow,' Dave says, his eyes still unblinking.

'Safe,' Mo blurts, 'we say safe yeah? Like, it's safe,' he shrugs and looks quickly down at the ground from the lack of response.

'Safe,' Dave says, 'yes.'

'Yes?' Paula asks.

'Yes, Miss Paula.'

'Okay,' she says slowly, 'for God's sake everyone remember that word. Howie?'

'Fine.'

'Safe,' Paula announces as she looks past Blowers to the bus, 'but only if it's spoken by one of us. Not by anyone else.'

'Yeah,' Blowers says, turning to see what Paula was looking at.

'Good timing,' Paula says looking up at the drone flying over-head. She reaches for the radio button under her shirt, '*Reggie, can you operate that while we move on?*'

'*I cannot operate it now while we are static. There are two controllers. I only have two hands.*'

'Nick, give Reggie a hand for me?'

'Yup, on it.'

'Right. Good,' Paula says taking a last drag on the smoke, 'we'll get moving. Charlie, back on you to follow the trail until Reggie can find them on the drone.'

'What happens if he finds them?' Clarence asks.

'Cross that bridge when we get to it,' Paula says with a look at the dark shadow on Howie's face.

CHAPTER TWENTY-EIGHT

I n this place I am one thing.

IN ANOTHER PLACE I am another thing. In many places I am many things and to each I have an objective.

I WILL MASS in one place but that is not this place. This area has too few host bodies to take against Howie and those that work with him. I have the collective knowledge of the hosts from this area. I know where each of the people are. I go to them with my many that I am but still they are too few to oppose Howie.

I GATHER hosts now but I cannot use them for the massing. This is fact. The distance is too great. The hosts I gather here are for the objective in this place which is not the same objective as the others. The others mass. I mass but not here.

. . .

YESTERDAY I HAD LOSSES. Today I will have losses. Yesterday the host losses were not given freely. Today the losses will be given freely. I must give these losses to feed Howie. He comes through this place to save those that he cannot save. He does not know that to be a host body to me is the true state of being. Howie believes his race has supremacy and a greater right to continue. Reginald believes his race will breed and further their dominance of this world.

I WILL GIVE losses today in this place. I evolve and I understand that to give Howie his mission and his belief to save his own kind. I evolve and in this place Howie will run and fight and chase to serve his ego and pride. I will do this while I mass. Howie here is not Howie in the other place where I mass.

I EVOLVE. I learn to do one thing to deceive while my intent is another thing. To deceive is to be human. I am not human. I wish not to be human. I am what I am and I am not deception or deceit but I will use deceit to serve the purpose I have.

PHILLIP HAS a mutated gene that resists the urge to pass the virus and only wishes to inflict harm. This gene would have been triggered in Phillips life. It was always going to happen as the gene is too strong to deny. Darren had this gene mutation. It was dormant upon infection but triggered by the replication. I can fix this gene. I am able to do this. I am able to correct mutated genes. I am the true state of being but I do not fix Phillips mutated gene.

I evolve. I learn. I learn to use. I use the mutated gene. I use deception. I am not human. I do not wish to be human.

Reginald believes his kind only wish to breed. I am not their kind. I will show them I am not their kind. I am not human. I do not wish to be human.

CHAPTER TWENTY-NINE

The drone is up. Charlie is ahead on the horse and the rest of us run knowing the fuckers are somewhere in front of us killing innocent people too stupid to board their fucking windows up and answering their doors to their blood covered penis lacking neighbours who are now zombies. Fucked up.

We follow Charlie who follows the blood trail and we wait for the drone to find them. We run and we follow and we wait. The flash of anger I had before simmers to cook slowly with heat building but there's an itch at the back of my mind that something is wrong, very wrong. Only I'm too stupid to figure out what it is and put it down to the lack of coffee for which I would seriously consider chopping a finger or a toe off for. Not my penis though. I like my penis. I like all my fingers and toes too but I really like coffee.

There is an almost hypnotic feeling created by running at a certain speed. Not sprinting but jogging. The rhythm of my feet on the ground and the motion of my body swaying left to right while moving ahead. It's like a mild trance and suddenly I can see why all those people used to go running. I suppose they started doing it to get fit but it's strangely addictive and I think the fitness would end up being a by-product to the feeling of well-being.

That itch is still there and I don't like these houses. I don't like the windows that look like eyes. I don't like being in these streets. I don't like the cars parked up and left at the sides of the roads or the gardens that had manicured lawns that are now growing out with tufts of weeds poking through. I don't like it. I don't like it. I'm irritated and getting worse by the minute. I need to run faster and find them.

'Mr Howie, I have a crawler...'

Fuck yes. Contact and about time. I sprint harder, building to pump my legs to reach the big junction to take the right turn in time to see Jess rearing up to slam her front legs down on the body that explodes with a spray of blood and gore that coats the road surface in all directions. Charlie spurs the horse on a few steps then round with perfectly poised balance to look down at the mess they created.

I reach the body with Dave and Mo at my sides. Everyone else only seconds behind. A woman but with her ears and nose bitten from her face to show ragged holes instead. Her fingers are gone. All of them. Her thumbs too. Her toes are gone. Bitten clean off. Her knee caps bitten off. Her stomach bitten through so the innards trail behind her.

'Mr Howie,' Charlie calls. I look up to see her next to a big white van smeared with blood. I stride closer and the heat of the pot of rage simmering in my gut turns up several degrees.

She died after

I snap my head back to the corpse and sprint back to turn her over to see the red bloodshot eyes staring lifelessly up at me.

The itch grows and I stare round as the others read the words on the van before turning to view the sides of the street as though we're being watched.

'Could that happen?' Blinky asks, her voice steady and showing the high level of fitness she has, 'could they do that?'

A buzzing noise above me. I look up to see the drone lowering down to hover over the corpse before moving gracefully to the side to land with a gentle thud, a second later and the back doors to Roy's van burst open as Nick runs up with Reginald behind him.

'What does it say?' Nick asks, squinting at the smeared letters.

'She died after,' I reply.

'Reggie,' Blinky says, 'could that happen?'

'Her eyes are red,' Reginald says, his nerves gone as he squats to look closer at the body, 'she was turned.'

'Yeah but, like...could those cunts do that? Could they turn her after?'

'One drop of blood or saliva is all it takes, Patricia,' Reginald says tightly, 'the first wound inflicted would have infected her.'

'You getting anything on the drone?' Paula asks, bent over to rest her hands on her knees with the rifle on the ground next to her.

'Nothing,' Nick says, 'too many streets and we've got to go too high to see anything but then we can't see any details and the drone ain't fast enough...batteries almost gone anyway.'

'Thought we had another battery pack?' I ask.

'We have, I'll change it now but that only gives us another twenty minutes...'

'We have to go faster,' I say.

'Mr Howie,' Reginald says standing up, 'my advice is to stop and pull out. Take these people to the fort...'

'What?' I ask.

'You fucking nuts or something?' Nick asks, flushed with the same simmering anger I can feel inside.

'What the fuck?' Blowers snaps, spitting to the side.

'Charlotte, go further up the road and look closely,' Reginald says, ignoring the comments thrown at him.

'Mr Howie?' Charlie asks.

'Do what he says,' I reply, 'Reggie?'

'We are being baited,' Reginald says, 'we baited yesterday and today the compliment is being returned but to what end I do not know.'

'Let 'em,' Blowers says, 'fuck 'em, we'll win.'

'Yep,' Nick says, 'fuck 'em, we should go faster.'

'Into what?' Reginald asks and in that second I can see he's getting used to the hard tones of everyone around him itching for the fight. His nerves are gone. His *oh gosh* manner evaporated to leave a steady pair of eyes.

'How many could they muster?' Clarence asks.

'A town of this size without warning?' Reginald says, pausing as though he's working it now but I'll be buggered if he hasn't already worked it out, 'a couple of hundred at the absolute very most.'

'Couple of hundred?' Nick asks.

'That's not a threat to us, Reggie,' Blowers says.

'*Up here,*' Charlie calls though the radio. We turn and run down the road as Marcy jogs back to the Saxon to bring it up and Meredith swooshes off to get there first. 'Careful where you stand,' Charlie adds as I see Meredith stop dead to sniff.

It starts with the woman's nose, then one of her ears then the other then eight fingers and two thumbs followed by ten toes all laid in a long line down the middle of the road. Gruesome and almost unreal in the way it's so neatly placed.

'Fuck,' I mutter, walking down the line of body parts but truth be told we've all seen too much death now to be that bothered by the sight. I pause and look back to the corpse then down to the stubby little toes. We're too desensitised to be repulsed. We're too far gone now, too deep in the game but that itch and the irritation with it grows all the same.

'Indeed,' Reginald says, walking down the line to the end, 'indeed indeed.'

'Reggie? We safe to keep going?'

He looks up at me, his eyes blinking behind his glasses, 'you ask me that after yesterday?'

I nod and shrug and he turns to look down the road, 'it knows we are behind it,' he says as though talking to himself but I get the impression he's doing it for our benefit, 'it doesn't have enough to pose a real and viable threat yet it wants us to follow the trail.'

'Maybe it's got more than we think it has,' Paula says.

'We cannot catch it before it turns every person in this town,' Reginald says, turning back to face us and placing his hands neatly behind his back. 'It knows where they are. We do not know where they are. We are being baited but I do not know why. It feels...no, no no no,' he stops and frowns, 'it gave us opposition yesterday because it thought it knew it was luring us and this is similar but not the same. Yesterday was infancy, today is childlike. Follow the trail. The breadcrumb trail. Chase me but to what end? I do not know the reasons, Mr Howie but my role is to advise and my counter move would be to not do what it wants.'

'We did what it wanted yesterday, Reg' Cookey says.

'But our goal was the higher objective and please do not shorten my name even more. Reggie is bad enough but Reg? Really?'

'Aye,' I say and nothing more.

'Ah,' Reginald says with a sigh, 'it appears you will proceed anyway. If that is the case then be guarded and be vigilant.'

'We will,' I say, realising he's worked us out a lot more than I gave him credit for, 'Charlie, you confident that horse can get you out of the shit?'

'Yes,' she says quickly.

'How confident?'

'Very, Mr Howie. Let me go further...'

'On you,' I nod.

She stares politely, 'I'm terribly sorry, what does that mean again?'

'Means yes,' Blowers says, 'Boss? You sure about this?'

'You heard Reggie, we are not doing what it expects.'

'Oh good God I did not mean to send Charlotte out on her own,' Reginald balks.

'Find them. Report back. Do not engage,' I say.

'Sir,' she grins with determination, turning the horse round on the spot.

'Keep the drone over her,' I say, 'Charlie is our marker...'

'The drone can't keep up with a horse, Boss,' Nick says.

'Are you counter baiting?' Reginald asks bringing everyone to a sudden silence.

'No,' I reply with a look to Dave, 'we're doing advanced forward recce pathfinding.'

'What?' Clarence asks.

'Remember that, Dave?' I ask him with a smile.

'Yes, Mr Howie.'

'Outside the police station wasn't it?'

'Yes, Mr Howie.'

'Ah those were the good old days eh? Me and you chopping up slow zombies by day and hiding by night next to a warm fire with a good book...'

'We never did that, Mr Howie.'

'Yeah I know, I was being ironic.'

'I am autistic, Mr Howie. Irony is lost on me.'

I go to reply then stop and scratch my head as Paula frowns and Clarence blinks while we all try and work out if Dave was being ironic or not.

'Can I go?' Charlie asks, keen as mustard to be galloping about the streets.

'Yep, do not engage...Charlie...do not engage...'

'Do not engage,' Charlie yells back, 'got it.'

'Blinky?' I ask once Charlie is out of earshot, 'she's capable right?'

'Hard as fucking nails, Mr Howie, Sir.'

'Good, right...everyone up for a bit more jogging?'

CHAPTER THIRTY

It's not that the axe is too heavy but it's the weight being all at one end. The rifle is balanced but it's long and cumbersome. A polo mallet is tethered to the wrist and designed to flex to achieve maximum power when striking the ball. The axe is rigid and untethered. Not that her grip is weak by any degree. Years of polo and hockey have served to strengthen the muscles in her forearms and given her a grip almost as strong as Blinky's, and Blinky's grip was legendary. Clarence wouldn't be able to pull a stick from Blinky's closed fist.

The axe needs a tether and a sling and the saddle needs to be adapted to be able to hold both weapons securely. Not this saddle though. This was Neal's saddle and worn to the grooves of his backside. Which weapon to hold on the move? The rifle has the firepower but it's almost impossible to ride and fire at the same time unless you're going in a straight line and can clamp your thighs to hold you tight. The axe is good but again the balance is wrong when trying to hold it and ride the horse at the same time.

In the end she slings the rifle to her back and leaves the axe hanging through the looped buckle on the side of the saddle. She doesn't know what Neal used the buckle for. Maybe he'd adapted the sling of his rifle to hook onto it but then that would mean the rifle would bang against the horses side. As it is, the axe shaft knocks into Jess's side but a hand on the head holds it still while they build speed down the road and she can feel the change in the horse now given the freedom to go faster and unleash some of the energy bunched in her dense muscles.

At the end of the road she slows to look round the junctions and spots the thick pool of blood lying distinct several metres into the junction on the left. *This way. Follow me.* She spurs on but without spurs. Jess doesn't need spurs. She just needs a gentle touch of heels and a click of the tongue to punch on and gain speed.

Halfway down the street she spots the corpse lying in the road ahead, 'easy,' she murmurs with the gentlest of pulls on the reins that sends the signal to Jess to slow down. The horse responds. The smell of the body filling her nose that makes her toss her head back and snort with angry eyes that bulge from the offensive scent. 'Easy,' Charlie leans forward to pat Jess's long neck, 'sshhhh.' Jess settles. The tone of Charlie soothing the fear and the instinct to flee.

Charlie brings the rifle round to get it snug into her side with her right arm holding the weight and her hand wrapped round the trigger guard. She stops several metres back from the body and listens. Nothing to be heard. She scans. Nothing to be seen. She feels Jess beneath her and senses the horse is afraid of the body but doesn't detect anything else.

The body was once a man but now it's a lump of meat barely holding form as something that was once human. The face is gone. Torn off to show the layers of skin underneath and the cheekbones showing through. Ears and nose gone. The arms and legs have been ripped from the torso and left in a line going across the pavement to point at the house with the smashed in door smeared in blood.

Edging closer and she can see the genitals of the man stuffed in his open mouth and the red bloodshot eyes open but unseeing.

'*Mr Howie, body in the street. The limbs have been detached and point into a house that appears to have been accessed recently.*'

'*Understood, coming to you. Any contact?*'

'*No contact, no sign of them.*'

'*Any noise from the house?*'

'*Nothing, Mr Howie. Shall I keep going or wait here?*'

'*Keep going. Find them.*'

'*Will do.*'

A nudge of her heels, a click of the tongue and split second later Jess is powering on to get past the stinky body and the stinky blood. Charlie slings the rifle and stares on as the lure of the hunt beckons. The horse breathing easily beneath her. The reins in her hands. The position of height and a thing done by man for thousands of years. Hunting on horseback using the power of the animal to close the distance to the prey ahead.

Fifty metres on and two small side streets leading off either side of the wide main road. Again she has to slow down to look for the trail. Instinct tells her to keep on the main road but if the infection is seeking the survivors then it could be following any manner of route. She goes to the left, peering down and round and up at the parked vehicles left abandoned further into the small road. No blood. She circles round then over to the mouth of the other small junction bordered on both sides by low solid panel fencing as Jess tosses her head and snorts.

'Easy,' Charlie murmurs, her eyes fixed on the road trying to find the trail. Jess back steps nervously, lifting her feet high and looking for a way out. Charlie senses the fear and twitches the reins to hold the horse steady. Something must be in that side road. She clicks and pushes Jess further into the junction with her own senses thrumming to detect any sound or motion.

They come from both sides. Two men that go up and over the low solid panel fences to charge snarling at the horse who bursts on to run deeper into the side road as another runs out from a garden ahead to race down the middle towards them.

Charlie's heart ramps to the fight at hand. On the field now. The other players are going for the ball and she lifts her backside from instinct to ride the horse's motion. Her left hand gripping the reins and her right flicking the axe up from the buckle that lifts high to be gripped on the shaft and twirled over so the head sinks towards the ground. 'COME ON,' Charlie shouts, her voice booming into the quietness of the street that makes Jess focus as the fear slides away to the power of the game. Seventy kilos of a freshly turned adult female against seven hundred kilos of a riot trained horse with a bad temper and the end result was written in the stars from the second the infected woman chose this course of conduct.

The axe swishes, a polo mallet ready to slam home. The horse glares, chomping at the bit as her legs open the stride. One in front and two behind. Charlie's eyes glare unblinking and fixed. Her lips pulling back with a pulsing energy that radiates from every pore of her body.

'INTO HER,' Charlie's words are not needed but she screams them anyway. She screams to vent that instant surge of pure fury coursing through her veins. Horse and human meet. The undead opening her mouth for a bite and finding a head battering her to the side that sends her spinning as the axe swishes with a perfectly timed swoosh to cleave through a skull that explodes with a burst of brain and bone. On they go, riding through the kill and building speed to clear distance from the two behind.

The wide junction at the end looms and in that space she eases the speed to turn the horse who pivots round to face back down. A pause. Jess snorts and lifts her front legs to go. She wants to go. She wants to charge them down. Charlie holds, letting the energy bunch up for the thrill of the explosion of power. 'COME ON,' she flicks the reins and that's all Jess needs. She bursts on, legs working to stride out.

Two incoming. Two males both with heavy blood stains on their groins and both bigger and heavier than the woman now lying dead in the road with her head split open.

Charlie roars again into the air, galloping with her heart thrilling as she rides the horse who holds that straight line.

They charge at each other. The infected men side by side and Jess staring at the gap between the two. Charlie eases back on the reins, a gentle tug that tells Jess they are not going to power through them this time. This is something else. Jess can sense it. She feels the instinct of the play about to happen but she can stop on a sixpence. *Let me have speed, let me use my power.* The counter instinct flows, Charlie lets her have the lead.

They close down in a few seconds that seem to stretch for eternity. The men snarling with bloody strands of saliva dangling from open mouths that stretch wide as they howl and snarl with clawed hands and eyes blazing red. The axe spins over, turning in a hand that times the point of impact. Everything on instinct now. No time for words or instructions or to twitch the reins and alter course. The commitment is here and at the last second Jess shows she can truly stop on a sixpence. She anchors on. Charlie's thighs lock tight. She rears up. Charlie holds the rein and lifts higher to ride the rise beneath her. Jess's front feet strike the man on the right, twisting as she lifts to give seven hundred kilos of weight to a body that cannot withstand such an impact and as he falls so Charlie brings the axe down from the apex of the swing. The blade bites deep into the chest and her grip holds true as the horse takes her on and through the man who gets split in two and sinks down with his ribcage splintered open.

Three down. Three kills and Jess turns quickly, dancing round as Charlie glares to check all three stay down. Jess makes sure they do and moves to trample the soft flesh with hooves that pop heads open.

'CONTACT CONTACT...THREE DOWN...'
'COMING...WHERE ARE YOU?'

A flash of movement and another streak of a blur of movement as an infected runs sprinting from a house at the end of the street, running to gain the main road and away out of sight.

'ON,' Charlie spurs Jess who spots the prey to be hunted. 'COME ON...'

A trot to a canter to a gallop in a few strides and Jess holds the middle of the road, watching the man run to the right side.

Charlie bursts from the side street onto the main road, in her peripheral vision she spots the team running towards her with the three vehicles behind them. No time to stop. No time for orders from Mr Howie. He told her to find them and she lets Jess take the corner to open back up to chase the man sprinting down the pavement on the right side of the road.

'*GET THAT FUCKER CHARLIE,*' Howie's voice urging her on. His desire to kill them reaching out to drive her into the fight. His confidence in her hardening her own resolve even greater than it was.

'*MEREDITH WITH YOU CHARLIE...*' Another voice in her ear, she can't tell who but she flicks her head to see the dog streaking low to join the hunt.

There is only this. This second when every tiny movement counts and you can't think about it. You don't have time. Ride the horse. Feel the motion with instinct from your gut. *Let me carry you, do not drive me.* Charlie relaxes that tiny bit, letting the horse have her way. *More. Let me run.* Charlie gives another fraction of freedom and if Jess had speed before she takes it more now and it builds as Charlie settles into the motion, gripping the reins one handed. *You are too high.* Charlie lowers her body closer to the horse. *Lower.* She lowers more, the axe held out to her right. *LOWER. LET US WORK.*

Charlie grunts and sinks down like a jockey on the flat of the final furlough. The change is palpable. A sense of a great animal doing every inch of work to hold herself balanced with the weight central on her back. Charlie can sense Jess's irritation at the saddle. She doesn't like it. She wants it gone but you can't remove a saddle mid gallop. She senses something else too and looks over her right shoulder to see Meredith veering between two parked cars to gain the pavement in a direct line behind the prey.

They hold the road. The dog takes the pavement. Charlie is part of, but not within, the thing that is happening between the two animals.

The infected is fast. He had distance but the fastest man cannot ever hope to outrun a horse or a dog and as the houses on the left end so he veers out to cross the road to vault the low fence to the town's playing fields of multi-use pitches with bi-functioning posts used as football and rugby goals. Open flat land with well-tended turf and the infected doesn't stand a chance.

Jess veers behind him, her eyes fixed on the fence as Meredith sprints at her side and together they rise from power given from back legs that lift front legs to clear the fence and land easy mid-stride the other side. Charlie feels the lift and the thrill of it is immense. The surging rise and the drop like going fast over a bridge or the drop on a rollercoaster ride. Then they're on grass, on turf, on a natural surface that gives a grip that cannot be beaten.

Dog and horse equal in speed and it's like the man is standing still. There is nowhere for him to go. He doesn't turn to look but runs on as Jess gives another burst of speed that slams him to the side to be taken by the dog already in flight. Meredith latches on and lets the momentum carry her forward taking the mouthful of throat with her. She lands and turns so fast she can see the undead sinking down with sprays of arterial blood jetting from his ruined neck. Jess eases the speed to turn and face back to the dog standing over her kill. Her head tosses. Her feet dragging clods of earth up. Meredith spins round again, her whole body showing the direction of the thing she sees on the far side of the fields.

'Got him,' Charlie rushes the words out, her heart still thrilling. It looked like the horse slammed the man into the path of the dog who was already leaping up to take him down. It was so fast. A blur in her mind. They were running almost flat out. Jess slammed him. The dog took him. That's not possible. It's not. It couldn't have happened. It was fluke. The horse struck him and Meredith took him down. It was the speed of reaction instead of a planned series of moves.

'Well done, where are you?'

'Playing fields,' Charlie pants, *'down the road on the left...there are more. I can see them on the other side of the fields.'*

'Wait for us,' Howie's voice panting from running so hard.

'I can take them,' Charlie says, counting the figures in the distance.

'How many?'

'Four or five...I can take them...'

'Sure? Don't be cocky...'

'I'm sure. I can take them, Mr Howie. If it's too much I will pull back.'

'Go then...kill 'em all,' a growl of a voice that makes the hairs on the back of her neck stand up. Jess rears, lifting her feet inches to slam back down as Meredith gives voice to throw her deep bark out in warning of what is about to come.

A twitch of her heels and they set off. Meredith and Jess shoulder to shoulder as they go through the gears to build to a sprint and Charlie lowers down with the instinct to let the horse go.

The noise is amazing. The sound of hooves thudding on grass. Five of them standing still and not moving. *See us. Come for us. Follow us.* It doesn't matter that she plays into the game being set for them. All that matters is to be there to end them to stop them killing others.

'GO THEN...KILL 'EM ALL.'

'Oh gosh this will never do,' Reginald speeds up as Howie's voice comes through the radio dumped on the table amongst the opened maps, sheets of paper, guide books and pens. The drone now forgotten on the floor of the van with the battery on charge from the 12 volt power supply outlet.

'Are you okay?' Kyle calls back having heard the mutterings from the back through the wedged open door.

'No I am not okay. None of us are okay. We're all fools rushing madly into something we know nothing about. I am most certainly not okay. Seriously, I ask you, how can anyone work in this situation? He goes charging off at the first sight of them and god forbid what the consequences might be. I do hope Charlotte is okay. I like Charlotte. She is a bright girl,' he stands up then sinks back into the chair as he flattens the map out to view down at the town they are in.

'The scale is too great,' he huffs and goes back to the basic street map he found in one of the guidebooks taken from the golf hotel, 'playing field...did Charlotte say she was on a playing field?'

'She did,' Kyle replies, holding the van at a low speed and following the bus in front of them.

'Playing fields,' Reginald flicks between the ordnance survey map and guidebook, 'got it. We finally have a reference as to where we actually are in this awful horrid town. Let me see. This is the playing field but...oh gosh, oh gosh darned damn and gosh. What direction are we facing?'

'I don't know, Reginald,' Kyle says, turning in his seat to look at the array of maps and books on the table.

'*Anyone? What direction are we heading in? Does anyone have a compass?*'

'*North east,*' Dave's voice blares through as dull as ever.

'*Thank you, you are sure? Do you have a compass?*'

No reply.

'I think they are busy running,' Kyle says.

'North east, playing field is here and we are going to the side of it heading in a north easterly direction,' he holds the blade of his hand down to align with the compass drawing in the corner of the map. 'Right yes, going in from this side,' he traces across the playing field to the other side and looks down at the densely packed lines. *'Charlotte, it's Reginald. You are heading towards the dead centre of town. The start of the main road through borders the edge of the playing field.'*

'GOT IT... COME ON JESS!'

'Oh my,' Reginald releases the long exhalation of air. The High Street runs at an angle away from the fields. A long straight Roman road that intersects another wide road that leads to the dual carriageway out of town and then all the way back onto the motorway. Fields and open land stretch out on all sides of the town. 'What's here?' Reginald mutters. His eyes flicking faster and faster to pick out the signs for the churches, the pubs the Post Offices, police station, pharmacies. 'Why are we being drawn here?'

Go back to the beginning and start again. The water was infected. People in the hotel drank the water and killed Neal. Mr Howie wanted to be sure it was the water so they found the treatment centre. Once that was confirmed, not that he needed to confirm as Reginald knew he was right but then people always want to know for sure, anyway, once that was confirmed he wanted to come into the town and warn any survivors not to drink the water.

The infection did not know where they were which is why it chose to infect the water for the whole of the area to target one man. Neal. Neal is dead so the objective is accomplished. He blinks and stands up to rub the temples of his forehead. The objective is accomplished. The infection has reverted to type and, knowing where the other survivors are, has set to infect and turn them. That's it.

'It can't be,' Reginald mutters, 'that can't be it...' Why this song and dance of penises and body parts and bodies left lying. That infected man ran away from Charlie too. They don't run away. They run towards to at least have a go at infecting someone. It might have got on the minibus or at least tried to get on the minibus. Why run off? This is a puzzle without a solution. He blinks and freezes. A puzzle without a solution requires a very advanced level of conscious intelligence. What came first, the chicken or the egg? That simple question has confounded scientists for years and still they cannot agree as to the answer. To even begin to contemplate the answer requires a level of abstract thought that the other player simply doesn't have yet. He chuckles with the sudden thought of putting the infection in front of a Picasso and walking off as it crumbles to the floor in complete confusion of a mind so genuinely advanced that only those on the same wave length can truly appreciate it.

There must be an objective. What is the objective? What is the purpose of keeping Mr Howie and his intrepid exploring warriors so busy?

'Oh gosh,' he slumps into the chair, his eyes widening in realisation.

'Going over a bump,' Kyle calls out, driving the van over the kerb and through the smashed down fence already preceded by the Saxon and minibus.

'*GOT HIM.*'

'Yes,' I shout with the others all grinning with malicious delight at the victorious tone in Charlie's voice. '*Well done, where are you?*'

'*Playing fields, down the road on the left...there are more. I can see them on the other side of the fields.*'

'*Wait for us,*' I speed up and breathe hard from the extra expenditure of energy.

'*I can take them.*'

'*How many?*'

'*Four or five...I can take them...*'

'*Sure? Don't be cocky...*'

'*I'm sure. I can take them, Mr Howie. If it's too much I will pull back.*'

The sight of Charlie galloping out of the side road and turning so tight to give chase to the infected man running away is a sight that will stay with me in the catalogue of images seared into my brain since this all began. The axe swinging in her hand and her backside lifted from the saddle as she flowed with the motion of Jess banking at what looked like an impossible angle. Meredith couldn't hold herself back and if I could run like Meredith I would have been up there with them. We all would have. The thrill of the chase is on us. The speed they went down that road was stunning.

We spared a second to view the body on the floor and the limbs ripped from sockets to point to a house that we ignore. Whatever is inside can fuck off. We're chasing and not wasting time by stopping to look at dead dicks flopping about on the floor.

For a second I was going to refuse her request to go after them. Not being separated is our first rule now but this is different. Having a horse is a game changer and anyway, the tone of Charlie's voice told me all I needed to know that she could handle it.

'Go then...kill 'em all.' I turn to see Paula heaving for breath and Clarence bent double with his hands on his knees. 'Paula, Clarence, on the bus. Everyone else ditch heavy kit. We're going faster now.'

Bags get pulled from backs to be thrown in the back of the Saxon. The lads sweating with flushed faces but they've got legs left. I can see it. I can feel it. I strip my own bag off and ditch it in the back while glancing to Blinky who looks like she's only just warmed up. She's like Dave with a body already honed to physical supremacy with a heart, lungs and muscles used to sustained intense exercise.

'Fuck me I feel two stone lighter,' Nick says rolling his shoulders, 'rifles or hand weapons?'

'Hand weapons, Roy? You okay?'

'I am,' he replies, passing his bag to Paula on the bus, 'be ready to feed me arrows.'

'Will,' she says, still gasping for air, 'go...'

'GO,' I shout and we're off. Running down the road feeling

lighter and faster. The lads flanking the bus. Dave and Mo just behind me. Roy now running near the bus door. We pace into a stride just below a sprint. Legs pumping and eyes streaming tears whipped out by the wind rushing past our faces.

We reach the last house and the edge of the playing fields but have to go further down to get past the rows of vehicles still left in situ from when the world ended and the stupid twats stayed in their houses waiting for help that was never going to come. Only it was going to come. We were coming but the infection got there ahead of us. That thought drives me on and I aim for a gap wide enough to get the Saxon through and drop back to let Marcy punch through the fence.

She gives it some welly, not realising that speed does not equal power with the Saxon. A splintering of wood and I clamber after her as the bus comes next.

'EMBUSS,' Dave's voice booms.

'What's that mean?' I shout.

'GET ON THE VEHICLES,' Dave amends his order, 'CLEAR GROUND. WE MAKE PROGRESS.'

He's right. We don't need to run to circle the vehicles now in such open land. Nothing can come near us without being seen well in advance.

We pile onto anything we can grab. I jump up to grab the open window sill next to Marcy. The lads pile into the back of the Saxon or get through the doors onto the minibus.

'ALL ON? I lean back to make sure, 'GO,' I shout at Marcy who lifts an eyebrow.

'I'm right here,' she says, 'ten inches from you.'

'Sorry,' I grin through the open window and glance ahead to see Jess and Meredith now at the other side of the playing field. A rush of emotion hits me. A rush of warmth at the sight of Charlie riding ahead and everyone caught up in the chase to kill infected. This is what it should be. Us chasing them. Not the other way around. We are the dangerous ones. We're the ones that inflict harm. The living army. Fuck yes. I lean through the window to pull Marcy closer and plant a kiss on her lips as she turns her head in surprise. 'I fucking love you,' I blurt with a devil grin. This is what we were made for. To chase and hunt them down.

'What the hell?' Marcy grins, confused but glowing at the same time, 'someone's blood is up.'

'COME ON...FASTER,' I bounce on the spot, urging her to push on.

'You're nuts,' she laughs but pushes her foot down a tad more to give the throaty engine in the Saxon a bit more life as Reggie's voice comes blurting into my ear.

'Mr Howie, this is the objective. There is no objective...I mean what we are doing now is the reason for being here.'

'Not making much sense there, chum,' I shout back over the noise of the engine and the wind rushing past my head.

'Chasing them is the objective. We are being kept busy for the sake of it.'

'For the sake of what?' Clarence's deep voice rumbles into my ear.

'For the sake of being busy. We are chasing to be kept busy. The infection must be doing something else somewhere else. It must have a reason for keeping us occupied. Don't you see? It fed us a few here and there yesterday to keep us heading in the direction it wanted us to go in where it was massing great numbers. This is a step ahead on that scale of thought process. To be fed and lured simply for the sake of it.'

I look at Marcy then ahead to see Charlie riding out of the playing fields to disappear out of sight on the other side, *'Charlie, report.'*

'Chasing...five...five running...I'm gaining...'

'Bring her back, Mr Howie. We are chasing to no end. The people in this town are already dead.'

We can catch them. We can chase. We can be the hunters for a change and it feels good to be clinging to the side of a military vehicle leading a mini convoy across a field. It feels good to hear Charlie's voice exclaiming in victory.

'We must not do what is expected, Mr Howie. We must counter every move it makes. It's a game of chess and we are going after the pawns to no avail. Call Charlotte back. Do not let the other player control you...'

Control us? Fuck me if that doesn't have a sting in the tail.

'Charlie, back now...' Paula beats me to the radio.

'I can take them...'

'BACK NOW,' Paula shouts through the radio. *'STAND DOWN, CHARLIE.'*

'...Standing down,' I wince at the frustration in her voice as Marcy lifts her foot from the accelerator to let the Saxon glide to a long gradual stop.

Adrenalin is pulsing but unused and I jump off the side to pace out onto the grass with my whole body thrumming to be back on the chase. Doors open, the lads jump out, Blinky bending to puke on the grass. Blowers looks like he's seething but holds his tongue.

'Mr Howie,' Reginald calls out as he scurries towards us and stops dead blanching at the unused fury etched on every single face of hardened killers denied the chance to hunt those that have been fucking us over for so long. 'I am sorry,' he says as though this is his fault, 'but...'

'Not your fault,' Nick growls, 'fucking shit cunt fucking TWATS,' he turns away to vent into the open air.

'You sure about what you said?' I ask him.

'I am sure,' Reginald says.

'Then you did the right thing,' Clarence says from a few feet away, 'let it go lads, let it out...it'll come again,' the soldier knows the feeling inside of us all and walks past to clasp a shoulder or pat a back, 'let it out...simmer down now...'

'Charlie, where are you?' Paula demands through the radio, her eyes fixed on the hedgerow, *'Charlie? Report...Charlie? REPORT NOW...WHERE ARE YOU?'*

Little ones. We fight.

Every head snaps up with eyes fixed on the hedgerow. '*CHARLIE REPORT*,' Paula demands.

'*...conta...cont...peo...vivors...*' Charlie's voice breaking with static but the tone is clear and we burst back to the vehicles as I thumb the button on my radio '*hold on, we're coming...*'

The lack of reply is terrifying but the unmistakable sound of an assault rifle firing from somewhere in the town centre is even worse.

CHAPTER THIRTY-ONE

The distance across the playing field is covered in seconds and with her eyes fixed ahead she lets the shaft slide out through her hand to grip the end and start the swing. Meredith goes out a bit wider, cutting off any chance of the five going down the side of the hedgerow. That the five don't run or move but just stand waiting is something Charlie realises isn't right, but then everything is weird now and five less infected is five less infected.

They do run but not towards the attackers or deeper into the fields but back to go through the openings in the hedgerow and out of sight. It matters not, the chase is on. The prey has been sighted and they will be hunted down because you cannot outrun a horse and a German Shepherd with a whooping woman swinging an axe.

Meredith goes first. The smaller of the two animals and again it's almost as if they plan it with Jess easing her speed for a fraction of a second as the dog slips ahead into the street beyond with an instant transition from open to enclosed. Houses on one side. Big, expensive and detached that give a commanding view of the fields so sought after in this little town.

The five sprint up the road as the hard right turn is made by the three giving chase. The residential street gives way to garage forecourts advertising quality second hand motors with three months parts and labour and a free satnav with every purchase. A supermarket petrol station so glossy and new compared to the family owned and run fuel station across the road with old style pumps and a friendly service of big smiles and warm greetings. Dry cleaners, shoe repairs, charity shops and a bookmakers complete the change from the living section to the business section and the five lead the three to the junction of the High Street and another hard turn to the right.

'Mr Howie, this is the objective. There is no objective...I mean what we are doing now is the reason for being here.'

Reginald's voice in her ear but the words go unheard and her head fills with blood pounding through her brain. 'COME ON JESS,' she screams the words drunk on the hunt like a barbarian charging across the open plains to attack the Romans who flee before her. She is conscious of Reginald speaking and somewhere in the back of her mind she even registers the fast tone of his voice which means he has something important to impart but all she sees is the corner coming at them at a speed too great to take. The ground is tarmac. The horse cannot take a corner that fast.

Lean.

Not the word but the essence of the meaning to give counter balance. An adjustment of weight that seems to bend the laws of physics.

More.

She leans harder, further over to the side as Jess takes it at nearly full speed, seemingly flexing in the middle.

Hold on.

This isn't happening. This isn't real. The shops swish by and they gain on the five with every second of running. The infected in a straggly line with the fastest at the front and the biggest and slowest at the rear. So close now and she feels the pulse of organic energy flowing from dog to horse to her and she lifts to start the swing of the axe to time the impact. Her eyes fixed on the broad back of the one at the rear.

'*Charlie, report.*'

Howie's voice. He sounds different, his tone is dark. She grips her thighs hard to press the button with her left hand with the axe swinging in her right.

'*Chasing...five...five running...I'm gaining...*'

'*Bring her back, Mr Howie. We are chasing to no end. The people in this town are already dead.*'

She can take them. The one at the back is close now. Her eyes flick up to the four ahead taking a hard left onto a wide road running through the centre of the town.

'*Charlie, back now...*'

Paula's voice clear and commanding. The order given. Reginald was speaking. He said something about chess and control.

'*I can take them...*' Charlie shouts into her shirt, her hand shooting back out to grip the reins.

'*BACK NOW,*' Paula shouts through the radio. '*STAND DOWN, CHARLIE.*'

Discipline over all else and despite the blood lust of the chase she pulls back on the reins and thumbs the button on her radio, '... S*tanding down...easy Jess, easy....Meredith stop.*'

Frustration all round but compliance nonetheless and Jess eases down from the gallop to a canter to a trot to a steady walk with her head tossing back. *We had them.*

Meredith slows instantly and stands panting with the lips of her mouth stretched back to get more air into her lungs. Her big tongue flopping out but her eyes remain set on the corner where the big male at the back ran round.

Adrenalin coursing for the fight that was right there. The glory of the battle to capture the feeling they had yesterday. To defeat the darkness and bring light. To be righteous and strong and fight with Jess and Meredith. She clicks her tongue, a dull sound of pent up aggression that demands to be released but order has to be maintained. At that second she thinks of the four lads outside Finkton academy staring down a horde many times their number. The calmness of them and the discipline shown by Blowers as he shouted the orders to take aim and commence firing. That's the difference right there. The ability to hold your head and take the orders given despite every bone in your body demanding to do otherwise.

With a last look at the corner she twitches the reins to turn the horse as Meredith growls low and deep in her throat. Her lips pulling back to show teeth and her hackles rising to stand on end. Charlie pauses, thinking it's the five waiting to be chased again. There might even be a few more round that corner.

'Come on...' Meredith doesn't budge but stands her ground as Jess turns to face the same way despite the tug given on the reins to turn about. Then Meredith is off. Charging at the corner with Jess bursting to speed behind her.

Little ones.

She was unprepared for the jolt from static to running and has to grip the reins and clamp her thighs to steady her balance as the horse gallops after Meredith. They take the corner to see a long straight road bordered by shops with smashed in windows and busted open doors and lined on one side the massed horde of the infected thick and fresh and deep in number that stare in fetid glory.

In instinct she reaches for the button on her radio but two people cannot transmit at the same time and Paula's worried voice comes into her ear.

'Charlie, where are you?'

In that second Charlie sees Meredith is not going for the thick horde but for the other side and the people being held by more infected pulling them back into the recessed doorways of the stores. Normal people with normal eyes that suddenly have infected hands taken from over their mouths to scream in terror at being dragged from their homes by people they knew. People who only wanted to bite and rake their skin to pass the virus but who were held back by the hive mind of a virus learning the elements of deceit and deception.

'*Charlie? Report...Charlie?* REPORT NOW...WHERE ARE YOU?'

In that same second she can see there are too many infected to fight but Meredith is running in and there are people here. Real people.

Little ones. We fight.

She tries to press the radio button while sliding the axe in the buckle and pulling the rifle round and all the time on a horse in motion. '*...CONTACT...CONTACT...PEOPLE   HERE...CHILDREN AND SURVIVORS...*'

That's it. That's all there is time for. The horde break from the right as the smaller horde on the left release the people they were holding. They stream out with one side in wild panic and the other with wild rabid hunger at being unleashed to bite and open skin and feast on the flesh of the living.

She fires the assault rifle aiming into the ranks on the right. Scoring kills and maiming more that drop or get slammed aside by the power of the rounds. A solid sustained burst of fire that empties the magazine in seconds to render the rifle useless and inert. It gets roughly pushed back as the axe is pulled from the buckle to be thrown up and over with a hand that clamps onto the shaft to let it swing down and round.

All thought is gone, there is only this time in this place. There are children here and they must do the right thing for the right reasons. Besides, nothing in this world will stop Meredith now and she is team, she is pack and the pack fight together.

'ON,' Charlie screams and aims for the front line of the horde sprinting across the road from the right. Seven hundred kilos of horse moving at thirty miles an hour and they slam the first aside to be sent spinning into the lines behind. The axe swings, cleaving and driving into shoulders, necks and heads as they charge on.

Meredith goes left to take the ones coming in behind the screaming people.

Charlie and Jess charge on down that first line but no sooner have they struck and moved on but more are coming in behind to take the place and close that all too small gap.

They reach the end and turn on that sixpence to charge back into the fray. The bloodlust rises. The aggression that was held in check is released and Charlie snarls with the job at hand as Meredith takes a big woman down to tear the throat out. They race back down the line but the realisation hits home that running up and down will do nothing. There are too many surging in and already the survivors are being ripped from feet to be slaughtered on the grounds by mouths biting and clawed hands tearing them apart. This isn't about taking hosts, this is about the brutality of a foe showing what it can do.

You can't save them all. The words hit home at the sheer scale of the attack being launched and the feeling of impotence. She draws her pistol to fire into any face bearing red eyes. Skulls blow out but it's a pittance. The horse rears and slams down killing one more but it's not enough. There are too many.

In the confusion of battle she spots Meredith launching herself bodily at a group of infected going for three small blonde haired girls clutching each other and screaming in abject horror and there it is, the battle line is drawn. We fight here. We fight for these three little ones. We die for these.

So be it. So be it for the glory of the fight and the name of the living army that brings light to the darkest of days.

'GO ON,' she roars to spur the horse who snorts and bares her teeth while charging with her bulk to rid the infected lunging at the girls. This is the line. This is where we hold and we do not yield. As Jess runs so Charlie twists and slides off to land by the girls. They were two against two hundred but now they are three. A woman, a horse and a dog but the line is drawn and for each other and the protection of the three little ones they fight. Jess spins to use her rump to slam them away. Meredith bites and rags and Charlie swings that axe with strength flowing through her arms and her hair flying out with each turn and spin.

'GO BACK,' Charlie screams at the girls, using her body to physically force them back towards the recessed doorways.

Four come on hard and fast and charging with the strength of freshly turned bodies and those four are removed by Jess running them down. Four more come. Five more. Six more. More and more but the axe gets kills and Charlie ducks to launch one over her back to be bitten through the neck and Meredith runs to shepherd the girls back into the doorway as Jess spins round on the spot removing a dozen from their feet to be trampled by a rage building to explode as she rears up to land and kill.

'DOORWAY,' Charlie screams at them, 'GET IN THE DOORWAY...' It's no good. The girls are too afraid to move. Terrified witless and frozen to the spot in fear.

Charlie grabs the first by a thin arm and launches her through the air into the doorway, the second follows and the third is launched screaming and wild in panic. In that second the last of the other survivors is killed and the remains of the two hundred now turn to the last to be taken and a howl is taken up that sends a shiver running through Charlies body but she grips the axe and hunkers down with a dog that gives voice at her side.

Jess rears. Whinnying with her own primeval scream and showing what majesty truly is. A beast of power and grace of height and width.

Charlie feels the pulsing energy sweeping through her. The pure animalistic rage to harm those that threaten. To do harm and to never end the harm you give for the sanctity of life and all that it means.

Jess whinnies louder. Meredith howls. Charlie screams and the undead charge towards one doorway.

'Aye,' Charlie grins at them, evil and cold with the darkness of Howie flowing from her eyes, 'bring it....'

WE FIGHT.

A roaring pulse of energy sweeps through her. Meredith in her head. The line is drawn. We do not yield. Jess in her head. We fight here. Charlie feels the fear in the horse, the abject terror but there is great honour of staying to give battle when all your instinct is to flee and that horse carries the fight for them. That horse holds them back. That horse uses weight and power to keep the thick lines from gaining dense ranks into the doorway.

The infected slam but the three hold. They hold and they fight with an axe that swings back and forth and huge teeth that open skin and tear throats. The undead compress, pushing in, sensing they can take one of the living army but Howie's blood pumps in her veins and Clarence's strength flows through her limbs and Cookey's heart beats inside her chest. She grunts with exertion and slams them down. She gets hit, knocked back into the girls in the doorway but not a second of hesitancy stalls her motion and she's back into the line to hold and fight with a searing rage. This is life and all the seconds of humanity held together for one perfect moment of two holding many while a horse destroys them within their ranks.

We do not yield.

We fight. Little ones. From the heart.

Hold Charlie. We are coming. Howie's voice so calm and deadly and the strongest of all. But it cannot be. The team against two hundred would be nothing. It would be over in minutes but Charlie, Jess and Meredith cannot hold them back. They cannot withstand the power of the surge that drives them back and the bodies falling down just choke the space until they can't move or fight out. There is only one way to go and that is back into the doorway where the girls scream and cower from the sprays of blood that strike the floor and walls around them.

Hold Charlie. Do not yield.

I can't. There are too many.

Hold on, for fuck's sake hold on.

Voices of the team in her mind. Voices of the pack reaching out to give what strength they can.

We'll come for you.

Fight Charlie. Fight like a bastard.

I will come to you.

I can't. I can't...we're going back now...there are three little ones here.

THEN HOLD. DO NOT YIELD.

Too many...so many...

We fight little sister. The pack comes.

A blow to the face and she reels back with stars flashing behind her eyes and she lands heavy but scrabbles with the blind instinct to scoot back and use her body to protect the little ones behind her. Arms stretched out and she kicks to drive her body into the girls. Using her body as a shield as Cookey did for her. Meredith fights wild and Jess surges in with a thrumming panic to batter the lines away but they get past Meredith and they get past Jess and they come crawling into the doorway as Charlie screams a snarl with her lips pulling back and throws herself at them.

On the ground they fight. Dirty and filthy with fists hammering her head and nails raking her skin but she kicks and gouges eyes and fights for every inch of ground for the lives of three girls.

She feels not the pain given but only that every second she fights is a second closer to the pack coming. Images flash through her mind. Images of voices and thoughts and pure energy that gives her waning strength a burst.

I will come Charlie. I swear it.

Teeth on her ear and a chunk is taken in the mouth by one infected with a mutated gene that desires only to inflict harm. She roars and headbutts him hard, breaking his nose. He reels but lashes a backhanded swipe that snaps her head over but fuck you if this is over and she drives him down with a mouth that finds his ear to tear it from his head. She spits it out and headbutts down again. Slamming his face into the hard ground.

We're here. We're coming.

'I AM DAVE. I WILL KILL ALL OF YOU. FIGHT ME...'

His voice rolls to echo down the street and she feels the fear ripple through the infected with a split second of hesitation before they are sent harder and wilder into the attack.

She punches and punches but it's not enough and Phillip surges up, driving the back of his head into Charlie who sinks back from the impact. He goes for the kill, diving for the throat as her hands come up and find his neck to squeeze with a grip that is nearly as strong as Blinky's and they roll over and over each other. Teeth on her ankle. Teeth biting into her thigh. Another on her shoulder but she braces across the doorway with her legs kicking wild and hard to batter and hold them from the girls. She does not yield. She holds because energy is coming. She can feel them. The pack is coming. The pack is here. The girls will live. She stares into the eyes of Phillip and into the infection within and she smiles with blood on her teeth.

'This day is ours,' she growls the words with blood coursing down her face and teeth sinking into her arms and legs. She draws him closer, pulling him in just with the strength in her arms. He resists and tries to angle to bite into her neck while she strains with everything she has to lift him up the inches she needs. Nothing else matters now. Not the teeth biting her or the nails raking her arms. Not the pain exploding from a dozen wounds inflicted but only the one she holds and lifts to expose his neck as her own mouth opens. His hand finds her face. A sharp nail that digs in next to her left eye and slides slowly down opening the skin to peel it apart with a searing agonising pain and the blood flows into her mouth. The fingernail rakes from eye to jaw, deep and digging deeper. She screams but holds, she holds with nothing left but the will to finish this.

Charlie!

A pulse. A surge. A feeling of love extended and projected and on that wave she rides to lift and bite to rag and tear the flesh from his neck. Hot tainted blood spurts thick to hit the back of her throat as he twitches to brush his own teeth on the soft tender skin of her neck but Cookey's face flashes before her eyes. His arms wrapping on Phillip's head to wrench and break the neck with a brutal explosion of violence. Howie's dark hair sinks to her side and the teeth biting into her body are gone.

'Get her back,' Howie grunts and spins round with his axe slashing through the infected ramming into the doorway.

Cookey lifts her up onto her feet and in one smooth motion he twists round behind her and sinks down to put his back to the three girls and lets Charlie sink into his embrace. His arms wrap round her body. His legs go over hers, enveloping her bodily. Meredith gets in close to crouch next to Cookey with her eyes fixed on the entrance held alone by Howie. The little ones are behind her. They will not pass. The pack are here.

She sees Cookey's arm extended out in front of her gripping the pistol that aims unwavering and steady. His left arm holds her close, pulling her into his body as the rest of the team come in hard from the side to sweep them back. She reaches up to grab Cookey's shoulder, to feel he is there. She reaches out to touch Meredith, to sink her fingers into the blood soaked coat to feel she is there.

We held the line.

We did little sister.

Raw emotion inside her now. She squeezes Cookey's shoulder and feels his heart beating through her back. He came for her. They all did. She is protected and safe, held by a man with a heart that gives only love. This is the light in the darkest of days. This is what they are.

'I'm bit,' she whispers, hoarse and rough. She can taste blood in her mouth, her own blood and that of the infected.

'You're immune,' Cookey whispers into her ear as the blood

from her cuts soak his skin but the fear of turning is still there. It's not fact or certainty that she is immune. The tainted blood is in her. She has been bit and raked, her flesh has been cut and opened. She clamps her hand tighter on his shoulder as the horde are swept away and the clear light of day once more fills the recess. Sunlight bathes her face. Warm, clean and pure and it's okay. It's okay to die now. You did your job. You held the line. Her eyes flick to Meredith knowing what will happen if the cells in her own body become tainted and give the scent that drives the dog to kill. 'You're immune,' Cookey's voice so soft and confident, 'I swear it...'

An arrow swooshes past the doorway. Another one a second behind it and the air fills with the deep steady bass of the GPMG. Assault rifles firing with controlled bursts.

She is ready to die and if it comes she will greet it with pride and dignity but she wants something else. She wants a thing that has been missing throughout her life. A thing she has only just found and given to her by one man who she holds more dear than he will ever know.

'Make me laugh...'

'Now? Are you taking the piss?'

That's enough and she giggles in the blood spattered doorway and chuckles with pain radiating in her body.

'You're weird,' Cookey mutters and she laughs again and clamps her hand harder on his shoulder. His tone of delivery, his blue eyes that twinkle and that smile. She needs to see that smile and she twists to look up. He stares ahead, the pistol still held because the threat is not over yet. The guns are still firing and that means the infected are still there but the corners of his mouth twitch and he flicks a glance down. 'Weirdo.'

'Your smile,' she says, simply to give voice to the thing so important in her mind.

'Your bum,' he replies so quickly it sets her off, 'stop laughing, this is serious,' he grips her harder for a second as though to emphasise his point, 'if Dave catches us pissing about I'll be on brew duty forever.'

'I'll help...'

'Guess what?' He whispers, his eyes fixed ahead.

'What?'

'Been more than two minutes, you're immune,' he draws her closer and drops his head to plant a gentle kiss on the side of her head, 'one of us now, Charlie.'

She closes her eyes and breathes. She breathes air for the simple fact of being alive and if this moment went on for eternity she wouldn't grumble once. 'One of us...'

A shadow forms and she opens her eyes to see Clarence standing huge in the doorway, his assault rifle slung on his back and his double headed axe dripping blood at his side, 'keep on catching you two like this,' he rumbles with a smile, 'got your clothes on this time though....come on,' he strides in with a hand held out, 'can you get up? Where are the children?'

'Behind me,' Cookey says as Charlie is lifted from his embrace. He gets to his feet to see the three girls frozen silent in fear, shaking head to toe and curled up gripping each other with a sight that breaks his heart, *'Paula, the three girls are here.'*

'Coming...JANE? With me please...we're on our way...'

Cookey waits, knowing he is the wrong person to give comfort to three terrified children. Clarence walks Charlie from the doorway back into the light of a street thick with bodies that were cut down within minutes.

'Where?' Paula sweeps in with Jane at her side and nods as Cookey steps back to let Jane rush forward with a mother's soft tone and a mother's soft touch.

'Christ,' Clarence winces, eyeing the cut on Charlie's cheek and the chunk missing from the top of her right ear.

'Is it bad?' Charlie asks, lifting a hand to her face.

'Leave it,' Clarence says gently pushing her hand away.

'Charlie, you okay?' Howie says striding towards them.

'Fine, I'm fine...'

'Ooh,' Howie says with a wince equal to Clarence's.

'Oh,' Charlie groans, 'that bad?'

'ROY?' Howie shouts.

'WHAT?' Roy shouts back.

'Come and have a look at Charlie's face, she's cut it.'

'I would love to but I AM NOT A BLOODY DOCTOR...' Roy shouts walking from the vehicles, 'I am a hypochondriac. I am not a medically trained...ooh,' he winces as Charlie turns to face him and rushes forward to peer closer at the wound, 'that's going to leave a scar. It needs cleaning, what was it? Fingernail? You lost a bit of your ear too, dip your head so I can see it.'

'It was a fingernail,' Charlie says as the lads wander back to gather round. She tries to finger the cut again but gets her hand pushed away by Roy.

'Don't touch it for God's sake,' Roy huffs, 'you'll make it worse.'

'Sorry.'

'They were biting her,' Cookey says from behind her, 'ankle, thigh and shoulder.'

'Let me see?' Marcy says and Charlie dutifully turns to be peered at by faces wincing and tutting. 'It'll be fine,' Marcy says kindly, 'we heal fast now. You should see the bite on my arse...'

'Really?' Cookey asks, 'can we?'

'I think you've seen enough backsides for today, Cookey,' Clarence says.

'Nah, you can never see enough bums, eh Blowers?...April had a bum...'

'Oh no,' Blowers groans.

'But Dave cut her head off.'

'Brew duty for the next month,' Dave says from across the street.

'Ah,' Cookey grins, 'Charlie said she'll do it for me. OH MY GOD! Charlie's immune!' He blurts with such enthusiasm it sets of a chain reaction of people grabbing the poor woman to hug and kiss her unhurt cheek.

Blinky grabs her tight with an awkward and very rare show of affection, 'you'll look hard as fucking nails now...wish I had a scar.'

'Come on,' Roy says with a nod at the vehicles, 'we'll get you cleaned up.'

'Cheers, Doc,' Howie says with a grin.

'Not a doctor,' Roy mutters.

'Cheers, Doc,' Nick calls out.

'Thanks, Doc,' Blowers says.

'TA, DOC,' Mo shouts from across the street with Dave.

'You won't call me that will you?' Roy asks Charlie, knowing she is educated and sensible and not given to pissing about.

'Of course not,' Charlie says politely, 'Doc...'

'Oh God,' Roy groans, 'you're one of them now.'

CHAPTER THIRTY-TWO

S o let's recap. I want to recap. It's important that I use this time to reflect on the events that have led me to this point in my life.

First the good things. I had sex with Marcy last night. That was a good thing. I slept well and that's also good. I got dissolved by a weird old guy in the hotel kitchen but that was also good. After that? We got attacked in the hotel and the scientist got chomped. The one man who actually knew something about all of this got chomped. Actually chomped. After that it was all a bit shit really and through the whole of that time I haven't had a fucking coffee. Not one.

Don't get me wrong, Charlie being immune is brilliant news. The sight of her is incredible. She's cut to bits, a bit of her ear has been bitten off, her face is cut open, her arms and legs bitten hard but fuck me if I haven't seen someone more alive than that girl looks right now. She's glowing with the pride of what she did. That she held the line and faced them down. She took the fight to them when she could have easily backed off or used Jess to run away.

Aye, there's honour in that. Beautiful glorious honour and those cuts she has are like the ones we all carry now. They're the badges of the conflicts we've had. They're the medals we'll never be able to pin on our chests. It's like a rite of passage has just been done. Charlie held the line and took the beating to stand proud after and look upon the beasts she felled as three golden haired children are carried to the arms of the people still inside the bus. Paula is right. We cannot save everyone but we saved those girls. No, Charlie saved those girls. She was aided by a psychotic dog and a fucking great big horse now dancing round the street popping skulls open but nevertheless, this is her battle.

But back to the coffee. There is no coffee. I can handle running about, I can deal with the infected and I'm not that bothered about getting cut and bit but I draw the line at not having a coffee. It's not right. It's really not right.

'Maybe one of these places still has the gas on,' I mention to Paula standing next to me with her arms folded as she makes more lists of things to do in her head.

She turns to look at me and shakes her head, 'we're going to the fort before that bastard thing gets any smarter.'

'Eh? What's that got to do with having coffee?'

'He said yesterday was infancy and today is childlike,' she says thoughtfully with a worried look round at the bodies.

'Exactly,' I say firmly, 'so we should have coffee now while we've still got the chance.'

She fixes me a look and in her eyes are hope and the dreams of mankind about to be given the thing he desires most of all, 'fort,' she says bluntly and turns round to watch Roy gently rubbing soaked gauze to clear the blood and gunk from Charlie's face.

I move away towards the back of Roy's van and peer through the open rear doors to see Reginald sat inside with Neal's M4 assault rifle with the folding stock resting against the table.

'You using that?' I ask.

'I'm sorry?' He asks, leaning back on the swivel chair and staring into space, 'using what?'

'Neal's gun.'

'Is it?' He looks down as though mildly surprised, 'I wasn't aware it is any different to our guns.'

I nod and lean against the frame, 'so?'

He shrugs, his face passive but the cogs are turning in his brain. 'I don't know.'

'We did it anyway,' I say quietly and he looks at me, the small nervous man no longer just a small nervous man, 'we killed them.'

'Good for you,' he replies with acid dripping from tongue, 'and no doubt tomorrow we shall kill a few more and the day after that we'll kill a few more and we'll keep on killing a few more until it's intellect passes ours and then we die and everyone else dies.'

I cough and bring my thoughts into order, 'that's a bit harsh, mate. We saved three little girls today. Well, Charlie did but...'

'Thousands died today, Mr Howie. Thousands died yesterday and thousands have died every day since this began and they will continue to do so. It knows where they are. It only has to take one to find two to seek three to hunt four. This,' he waves a desultory hand around him, 'this is a torrid little skirmish of no consequence. We took pawns from a player that has an almost limitless supply of them. We have not progressed nor have we advanced...'

'Why should we? We're surviving and doing the best we...'

'Am I free to speak and do I have your consent to speak freely?'

'Say what you want.'

'You are a bloody fool, Howie. A bloody minded stubborn idiotic fool,' passion in his words and they sting all the more for that emotion he injects, 'I would never speak to you like this in front of the others and I admire your abilities greatly but my god man! You are immune and you lead people who have the same immunity but you are doing nothing with it. You killed two hundred in a squalid little town...'

'Those two hundred would have found every other survivor in this...'

'THEY ALREADY HAVE!' His face flushes red with a thick vein protruding from his forehead, 'Don't you understand? Can't you see it? We've wasted days of having an intellectual advantage and that...that *thing* is catching us up. We had Neal. We had a scientist who was there when this thing was developed yet we spent yesterday racking numbers up for the sake of it. Ten thousand is nothing against what they have...'

'We wouldn't have met Neal yesterday if we...if you...hadn't chosen that course of action and ten thousand added to the hundreds of thousands we've already taken is a serious dent.'

'Yes, yes you are right. I am venting because I am frustrated.'

'It's fine. Vent,' I shrug and resume leaning without realising I had stopped leaning, 'maybe there's something in his books that can help us.'

'Help us kill a few more?' He asks caustic and stinging in tone and delivery.

'Point taken,' I say gently, 'read them and work it out then, guide us...'

He scoffs and smiles without humour, 'it's that simple to you isn't it?'

'Fuck, Reggie,' I exclaim with a weary sigh and rub the tension from my forehead, 'we know how to kill and we'll do it all day long. We've got Dave and Clarence for fuck's sake. Lead us then. Guide us. Tell us where to go and what to do because that's the thing we don't *know* how to do.'

'I am not a leader, *Mr* Howie. You are.'

'It has been a long day has it not?' Kyle calls out from the front of Roy's van and in the heat of it all I forgot he was there. 'I expect you'll be wanting to take us to this place of safety you have where no doubt they'll have coffee and a quiet room where a man can think in peace.'

I look at Reginald and we agree to let it lie without the need for words. The day has been long already and this conversation can wait. I walk back down the side of the van and glance through the windscreen to Kyle not-just-a-cook. He glances back and smiles, just a cook my arse.

'We off?' Paula asks me as I walk over to join her and Clarence watching Roy cleaning the wound on Charlie's ear.

'Ready when you are. How you feeling?' I ask Charlie.

'Fine,' she says then winces as Roy puts another steri-strip across the cut on her cheek. Several of them all in a line from her eye down to her jaw but with the blood washed off she does look far better.

'Are we going for the fort?' Roy asks, 'she'll need to see the doctors. The wound on her cheek could do with being stitched if only to stop the scar being too ragged. I've steri-stripped it for now and she'll probably need a course of anti-biotics. I've got some if we're not going back but...'

'You've got anti-biotics?' Paula asks.

'Of course I have. I've got Penicillin too, and Morphine and...'

'Why does she need anti-biotics?' I ask, 'she's immune.'

'Being immune from one infection may not render you immune to everything,' Roy says, 'dirt in the wounds could cause an infection.'

'We've all been cut and bit to hell,' I say, 'none of us have got infected.'

'I am not a doctor,' Roy says, 'you asked for my help and I'm...'

'Okay okay,' I back down again for the third time in a row and really really wish I had some fucking coffee, 'yes, we're heading back now. Charlie, are you okay for now?'

'I am fine, Mr Howie,' she says, clearly a bit uncomfortable at the fuss being caused, 'can I see it now please?'

'You sure?' Paula asks, holding a small compact mirror down at her side, 'you can wait a bit if you want.'

'No no, might as well get it over with.'

Paula opens the mirror and hands it over. Charlie is a pretty girl, very pretty. Her skin is almost flawless and she holds the mirror to take in the huge cut now held closed with white strips that runs from the edge of her eye down to her jaw. That it will scar is obvious but she doesn't show any reaction but turns her head to stare at her ear and the chunk missing from the top. Wounds inflicted that will now always be there. She runs a fingertip up the cut on her cheek with a gentle frown.

'You're still a beautiful young lady, Charlie,' Clarence says gently.

'Thank you,' she says softly.

'Very beautiful,' Paula says, leaning in to kiss the top of her head.

'Fit as fuck,' Cookey announces from behind Clarence, making Charlie snort with laughter that she tries to hide by hawing like a donkey instead. 'I so would,' Cookey announces with a grin.

'Would what?' Clarence asks with a warning look.

'You know,' Cookey says still grinning, 'like...take her to a dance and stuff.'

'I'd chaperone you,' Clarence says with a wink at Charlie.

'Yeah, Charlie would definitely be trying to shag me...'

'On that note,' Paula says, 'load up, we're moving out.'

'You've said it again,' I say, 'I always say that. That's my line.'

'No, you say...*Ready Dave?* And Dave says *Yes Mr Howie* and you say *Fuck 'em, we'll win*...' she mimics a deep voice that just makes Charlie laugh even more.

'Fine,' I say and look over to the lads, 'you ready? Load up, we're moving out.'

CHAPTER THIRTY-THREE

'It's done?'

'It is.'

'We heard the shooting but we haven't had any injured brought in.'

She pauses, her unblinking blue eyes locked on his with an intensity that makes him look down at the ground. 'There are no injured. Just dead.'

'Fuck,' Anne recoils at the savage simplicity of the words spoken by the young woman with a pistol on her belt and an assault rifle gripped in her hands.

'Maddox?' Lilly asks, choosing to move the conversation on to the reason she came into the hospital.

'He hasn't come round,' Andrew replies quietly.

'Is there something you can do?' Lilly asks looking up to Anne then back to Andrew who shrugs but with an air of someone who has an idea but is reluctant to impart it. 'He needs to come round,' Lilly adds, her voice as cold as her eyes.

'Can we wait until tomorrow?' Anne asks.

'No,' Lilly says now knowing they have an idea to do something, 'it has to be tonight.'

'Why tonight?' Andrew asks, looking up and wishing he hadn't because she doesn't blink or flinch or look away politely but stares through him to a point a hundred miles beyond his eyes.

'Maddox needs to wake up,' she says, once again choosing to reply how she sees fit and in so doing she holds the power in the room. Not because of the weapons she holds but because of the energy she projects that speaks of things done that can never be undone.

'Okay,' Anne breathes the word out feeling the importance of the moment, 'there is something but it's not without risk.'

'A great deal of risk,' Andrew adds bitterly.

'How long?' Lilly asks so coldly it makes both of them start.

'An hour or two,' Anne says.

Lilly starts towards the door, 'I will come back in one hour.'

'Lilly,' Anne calls after her, rushing to the door as the young woman stops in the corridor to face back, 'it's done...you did it. Why the rush? Get some sleep...everyone needs to sleep...'

'Later,' Lilly replies, 'there's still work to do. I'll be back in one hour.

LENSKI WATCHES THEM WORK. They move fast but she can tell they're worried. An IV stand is brought in with a bag of saline solution hanging from the bracket. Andrew fixes the cannula into the crook of Maddox's right arm and checks the tube running to the bag of solution. Anne brings in the oxygen bottle and fits the mask to Maddox's face. Three orange capped syringes lie on a sheet of white gauze, carried in and made ready by Andrew.

'What you do?' Lenski asks, catching the fear they project.

Anne looks up at her as she adjusts the mask and reaches over to turn the flow on the bottle, 'starting oxygen, Andrew.'

'Okay,' Andrew says and picks the first syringe up. He takes the cap off and pushes the needle into the ingoing valve on the drip, 'Thiamine going in now.'

'What you do?' Lenski asks again, edging protectively closer.

'It's called dont,' Anne says quietly.

'Don't?'

'Dont...D O N T. Also known as the coma cocktail. It's been used for years to bring patients out of a coma state.'

'I not hear of this,' Lensky says, frowning with suspicion.

'Controversial,' Andrew mutters, 'very controversial...and we're bending the rules even more.'

'Desperate times and all that,' Anne replies.

'It is dangerous?' Lenski asks.

'Dangerous?' Andrew says, thinking for a second, 'yes it's very bloody dangerous...I mean the drugs themselves aren't dangerous but the body retains a coma state for a reason. Bringing someone out of it using hard medication is always dangerous. We don't know if Maddox has a brain injury or something else. We don't know his medical history or if he'll react to the drugs...and if he does then we don't have the capacity or facility to deal with it,' he stops and sighs as he turns the valve to start the drip feed into Maddox's body. 'Dextrose, Oxygen, Naloxone and Thiamine. DONT. We've increased each dose and we'll shorten the time it's meant to be given over. He'll either wake up or he won't.'

'This thing, it kill him?'

The doctors share a glance, neither of them are confident to answer. A few minutes passes and the Dextrose goes in next. It should be a 50% solution of 100ml given over thirty minutes but it seems every second counts tonight so the dose is increased. Same with the Thiamine. Same with the flow of Oxygen and the same with the final IV feed of Naloxone. Adrenalin is given too. Not for the effect it has in the movies but to raise Maddox's blood pressure, stimulate his heart and aid his breathing. Drugs given and each one will have a side effect, the worst of which could be death.

'Desperate times,' Andrew mutters to himself. Never before has he done the things he has done on this night. Setting bones without anaesthetic. Gauging flesh open to pluck shrapnel and bullets out. Stitching skin together without wearing gloves. Anything that was sterilised was soon made dirty and the risk of infection is great. Everyone treated will have to take either penicillin or anti-biotics. It wasn't medicine. It was butchery.

'What now?' Lenski asks, her eyes fixed on the unconscious form of Maddox.

Anne checks her watch and slumps to lean against the wall, 'now? Now we wait.'

ONE HOUR after she walked out, Lilly returns to walk through the hospital with the pistol on her belt and the assault rifle held in her hands. 'Has it worked?' She asks the two doctors sitting in the back office sipping from mugs of strong coffee.

'He started coming round a few minutes ago,' Andrew says.

'He's groggy but alive,' Anne adds, holding her mug with both hands while avoiding looking at Lilly.

'Shouldn't you be with him?'

'Lenski is with him,' Andrew replies.

Lilly moves away to walk down the darkened corridor to the small room lit only by a single hissing gas lamp. Lenski looks up, her eyes staring without expression.

'He's awake?'

'Just,' Lenski says, her voice muted and low but her eyes take in the heavily armed girl who now looks so different. Older. Aged. Matured and her eyes are icy cold.

'Take the mask off him,' Lilly says, seeing Maddox blinking heavily as he stares up at her.

'He need the oxygen...'

Maddox's hand lifts to push the mask up over his forehead. His eyes bloodshot but clear with focus.

'Can you hear me?' Lilly asks, her voice flat and monotone.

'Yes,' Maddox whispers, his own voice rough and low.

'Your crews are nearly all dead. I killed them. Do you understand?'

His eyes widen. His heart hammering harder as her words strike home. The pistol on her belt. The rifle in her hands and only now does he take in the change and the way she holds herself.

She can feel Lenski's eyes boring into her and the tension in the room that ramps in that split second. She can feel the fear rippling through Maddox and she sees herself through their eyes.

'A few remain. The younger ones. The rest are dead,' she stops to force her tone to become softer from seeing the pain on Maddox's face. 'They refused food to every person other than *your* crews. They made them stay outside in the rain...they made me crawl on my knees like a dog and every bruise you see on my face was made by them and they made my brother stay hungry outside in the rain while they beat people and laughed and ate food inside...' She stops again to swallow the rage that still seethes inside. 'I told the doctors to bring you round because we need to have this conversation now. Our agreement still stands. The three of us will run the fort but there will be changes. If you oppose this then say now and I will take the people that want to leave and we will go but know this,' she steps closer to glare down and whisper, 'if a single hair on my brothers head is hurt from any form of desire for revenge then every person in this fort knows to tell Howie you caused that harm and if I don't kill you then he will. Do you understand?'

Maddox stares, his eyes wide and unblinking but a single tear tracks from the corner to roll fat down his cheek to leave a wet trail that glistens in the orange light, 'they're dead?' His voice a ghost of a whisper, weak and faint with emotion from the memories of the children he watched grow on the estate. The drugs are heavy in his head. His mind fuggy and slow but the feeling of his heart fracturing into a thousand pieces is real.

Lilly nods. She can feel his pain and see the hurt flood his eyes and less than one day ago she would have consoled or found words of comfort but now there is no comfort to be given. There is only the brutal vicious seedy reality of this day and it needs to be finished to be buried.

He sinks lower onto the mattress, his hands lifting to cover his eyes as Lenski looks away with her own face as set and as hard as ever.

'Maddox,' Lilly says dangerously quietly.

'They did that?' He asks, his voice choking with emotion, 'Sierra yeah?'

'Yes.'

'She didn't listen to Lenski...'

'No.'

'Fuck,' Maddox bites the sob down, 'all of them? How many? Who?'

'Sierra, Skyla, Zayden, Liam....' She reels the names she knows off, seeing that each one pierces his heart that little bit further, 'more,' she adds simply, 'I didn't know their names.'

The sad reality is that despite the anguish gripping his insides, he can see it happening. He can see the collective lack of responsibility from minds too used to taking what they want without any fear of the consequences. He can see Sierra's temper exploding from the grief at seeing Darius killed. He can see the little bitch Skyla getting drunk on power and the others reverting to what they always were; wild and feral with no concept of longevity. He was going to change them. He was going to show them how to live differently but more than that, he can see the cruelty of them. It hurts, it hurts more than anything but with testament to a mind that still functions despite the drugs he knows there is also acceptance of what is fact.

Lilly watches him closely. Seeing the pain but seeing the understanding too. His failure but that he tried. His anger at not being there to stop it but his acceptance that it's done and there's no going back.

'Some are alive,' she says, finally finding the words to soften the blow. 'Those that were injured when the armoury blew up and some more who were asleep when I...when I took the fort back...'

Maddox returns and the man locks the emotion inside to look up at her, 'I understand.'

The magnitude of the moment holds them still with eyes locked, 'my brother?'

'Don't offend me. I am not that man.'

'And me?'

'I am not that man either.'

'Then we have an agreement?'

'We do.'

Quick words fired back and forth. Lenski watches, alert to every nuance of tone and inflection.

'I am sorry,' Lilly says and finally dips her head to break the eye contact and show remorse.

'Me too,' he turns away and blinks slowly and heavily as the effects of the drugs sweep over him.

'I will leave you to rest,' she turns away but stops in the doorway, 'one more thing, Mr Howie is welcome back here anytime he chooses and for any length of time he chooses.'

'The hole? Is it fixed?' He asks without looking up.

'Not yet. I'll get to it. Rest. The fort is safe.'

'Lenski, go with her. Help her...'

'I stay with you.'

'Go with her...'

'I not go. I stay...'

He fights the tears back, holding it all inside with every ounce of strength his weakened body can muster. She sees it and rises without a word to rush after Lilly and as the door closes softly so he releases and weeps alone in a room bathed orange by a single hissing lamp.

CHAPTER THIRTY-FOUR

D ay Eighteen

SHE WAKES with her eyes blinking open to see the new day is here. A grey sky full of low clouds that pour water with relentless driving rain. She doesn't move but stares through the broken inner wall to the broken outer wall. Soft snores and low murmurs fill the room and every inch of floor space is covered by blankets, coats and clothes on which sleep the children and some of the adults.

There was no choice but to sleep in the old armoury. The hole needed guarding and the people needed somewhere undercover and so necessity overcame choice. Once their bellies were filled with whatever food they could grab from the stores and any scrap of material found was used to dry bodies they trampled in to fall down and sleep. The smell didn't bother them. Only that it was out of the rain and with so many bodies sharing space it soon heated up to dry even the most soaked of clothes.

Lilly slept with her right hand holding the rifle with the barrel pointing towards the hole. Her left hand resting on Billy. Pea, Sam, Milly and Joan completed the line. The children prone, the adults sitting upright with backs to the walls. They all slept. There was no designated watch on. The fort is too big, too open plan and everyone was too exhausted to organise anything. So they took their chances and drifted into fitful sleep to get through the hours of darkness.

It's soothing though, the sound of the rain. The pitter patter of a billion tiny droplets of water striking the flat surface of the sea and the varying drumming noises as the rain falls on the flat surfaces outside. She shifts, her bladder full and sending signals to her brain that translates them into a feeling of being uncomfortable. She doesn't move but waits. Listening and staring into nothing.

She thought it would be different and she would wake up consumed with guilt at killing so many people and so brutally too. She thought she would spend the quiet hours weeping or seeing the faces of those she shot and executed. Instead she feels resolved to see it through. She started a chain of events and she was wrong if she thought it would be finished when the last one was killed. It wasn't and it isn't now. It's still raining. The bodies are still out there. There are children and adults here that need shelter, clothing and bedding. The hole needs fixing. The police offices need cleaning to remove the bodies left to dry and congeal. What food do they have left? Is it enough? What about being armed? She can fire a weapon and so can Joan. Pea and Sam are both armed but they only learnt just enough to point and shoot. Lenski can probably handle a gun and Maddox definitely can but he's in no state to do anything

A chain of events. Solve one problem and get a dozen more. Do enough to give people food and shelter but they look to you for their ongoing safety and comfort. It never ends and nor *will* it ever end.

So no. There isn't time for guilt or grieving but just to get on with the job at hand and do the right thing for the right reasons.

She eases herself up from the wall, taking care not to wake Billy but then remembering a nuclear bomb going off wouldn't wake Billy when he was asleep.

'Wha...what's...' Pea comes awake too quickly, her eyes wide and full of fear.

'I'm just going for a wee,' Lilly whispers.

'Okay,' Pea says, still staring with that shocked look especially reserved for those who go from deep sleep to wide awake in a split second, 'you okay? What's...I mean...want me to come?'

'It's fine,' Lilly says, 'I'll be right back.'

'Just piss outside,' Sam mumbles sleepily.

A lady does not piss outside. A lady does what it takes to preserve her dignity and acts with grace at all times. She steps out, checks the view and walks up a few metres to unzip her jeans and squats to relieve the fullness of her bladder while the rain once more soaks her hair and clothes.

That today is her Sixteenth birthday only mildly registers. In her previous life there would have been a party, cake, music, dancing and laughing. She would have been given presents that marked the start of the transition from child to adult. In this new life she pisses on the ground with her bare arse poking out behind her as she tries to avoid getting wee on her shoes while holding an assault rifle out in front that acts as a counter weight so she doesn't fall over. Thank God she didn't need a poo. That would be an undignified start to the morning. There isn't even a bush to poo in. Just open ground. Come to think of it, where will the people go to have a poo? Do they dig holes? Isn't that what soldiers do? But then there are a lot of people here and those holes will soon add up.

Hmmm, she looks over the fort to where the toilet block and visitor centre used to be. Now a flat expanse of concrete that hints at the foundations underneath. There were toilets in that section which must mean there are sewer pipes. It wouldn't be that hard to fashion something over the holes. Like the old fashioned bench seats with a hole in them so they can poo down into the sewer pipes. What about flushing it away? Buckets of water will do that. Actually, sea water would do the job. They could just fetch it in from outside or maybe stretch one of the hosepipes over. That still leaves the issue of privacy. Nobody wants to be seen having a poo and reading the back of a can of air freshener. They will have to make wooden partition stalls or something.

She looks round noticing how well the fort is coping with the deluge of rain coming down. Never in her fifteen, no sixteen years has she seen rain like this. A relentless unceasing down pouring of water from clouds hanging so low it's almost as though she could reach up and touch them.

She finally stands and sighs the contended sigh of someone who has just had the best wee ever. She could go back into the dry and wait for the others to wake up but the dawn is here now and there's work to do.

What first? The bodies on the beach need taking away but that will need people and the boats to be in use. The debris in the middle section between the two walls also needs taking away but again that needs people and the boats. There is a job that needs doing. The police offices need cleaning. It'll be gruesome and disgusting but it's her mess so she better get on with it.

She heads down alongside the wall expecting to see the area where Liam and his crew were killed but the bodies are gone and the ground is washed clean by the rain that now shows no sign of the blood that was spilt here. Someone must have dragged them down the front or shoved them somewhere else. That's a good sign. It means someone is taking responsibility for their own environment.

A noise ahead. The sound of a voice but not talking. More like humming. Tuneless yet melodic. She slows down to listen and from instinct her right hand drops to the trigger guard on the rifle. The sound is coming from the police offices but only death should be in that room. She threw grenades in there that blew the bodies apart then executed anyone left alive. Who would be in there humming?

At the door she looks at the wheelbarrow propped against the wall then peers through, blinks and steps in with her mouth dropping open.

'Morning, Miss.'

He stops and leans on the mop held between his gnarled hands as the smell of pine disinfectant wafts pleasantly into her nose. The walls gleam. Everything has been freshly scrubbed. The bodies gone and the pool of blood and bits of gore all washed away. He stretches his back and nods to the table pushed against the wall and the pan of water coming to the boil on top of the camping gas burner, 'water's ready.'

She looks round again. The tables and chairs damaged in the blast have been taken out, and everything else has been stacked at one end making the rooms look much larger.

'You did this?' She asks, hardly believing the sight her eyes are taking in.

'I said's yesterday I did. The dead don't bother me none, Miss. You wants to make an old man a cup of tea then while I finishes this last bit?'

'Tea,' she says, still in shock.

'That's right, Miss.'

'I'll make the tea...have...I say, I mean...' She stops and stares as he goes back to swishing the mop head over the floor, 'have you been here all night?'

'I reckon I has,' the old man replies, 'you don't's sleep so well at my age...and I figured to myself that you'd be needing somewhere to work from this morning so Alf I said to myself, we'll go on and get them rooms all cleared away.'

'Alf?'

'Yes, Miss. Alf.'

'I'm Lilly.'

He smiles up at her, 'I knows your name, Miss. I thinks everyone here knows your name.'

Too many things run through her head at one time and she holds still, processing and trying to clear the temporary cognitive traffic jam in her mind. 'Tea,' she says, 'I shall make the tea.'

'Ah that'll be lovely, Miss. I put's the deceased down on the beach out the front. We'll be wanting to get them buried or disposed at sea afore to long, the living don't like to see the dead you see. It worries 'em it does.'

'The wheelbarrow,' Lilly says as the traffic jam starts to unclog.

'That's right. Found it in one of the rooms I did. My back ain't got the strength it used to have so I used that barrow to get the deceased all down yonder.'

She stands in front of the gas burner and looks across to see freshly cleaned mugs laid out face down with a box of tea bags, a bag of sugar, a jar of instant coffee and teaspoons all gleaming on the side.

'I took them from the food stores. They had some condiments and such like in here but it weren't fit for human consumption it weren't so I cleaned it out. I didn't know if there was a chitty to sign 'em out on...couldn't see one anyways.'

'It's fine,' Lilly says and makes tea. A simplistic act of putting tea bags in mugs then pouring hot water in before dunking and swishing the bags about with a teaspoon. She's making tea in clean rooms that smell of pine disinfectant. 'Do you take sugar?' She asks politely.

'One please.

'Strong or...'

'As it comes. I drinks anything.'

'Would you like milk? There's none here but I could...'

'Black be fine with me. There, I reckon that'll just about do it.' He stands back to inspect his work, 'good enough for you is it?'

'My word yes, yes it's...I don't know what to say.'

He carries the mop and bucket to the door then walks slowly over to take the mug held out to him, 'ah, nice cup of tea,' he says with what appears to be genuine contentment, 'can't beat a nice cup of tea.'

'Thank you,' Lilly says with genuine feeling, 'I was coming down to do this...I mean, it was my mess and...'

'Ah,' he says as if that answers everything then sips his tea.

'Holy fuck,' Sam walks in with Pea behind her. Both of them staring round in wonder at the sight of Lilly and Alf sipping hot tea in a room that should be covered in bodies and blood.

'Mornin',' Alf nods, 'good timin', water just boiled.'

'Boiled,' Pea says, her jaw slack.

'Fuck,' Sam says again.

'Tea?' Lilly asks.

'Tea,' Pea says.

'Fuck,' Sam says again.

'Alf has kindly cleaned the rooms,' Lilly says, turning back to get two more mugs ready, 'tea or coffee?'

'Coffee,' they both reply at the same time.

'Someone say coffee?' Joan strides in looking remarkably awake for a seventy year old woman who slept leaning against a concrete wall. She takes in the room with the eyes of someone who has seen many things and nods approvingly. 'Morning, Alf. Good job.'

'Mornin', Joan.'

'Smells nice in here,' Joan says, taking a big sniff, 'bodies?'

'Out the front.'

'Mess was it?' Joan asks, her voice brisk and clipped as she strides to the pan of water and assumes the command of making drinks.

'None worse than I see before,' Alf replies.

'Alf, you give Sam a hand to get a table and chairs out,' Joan says, 'Lilly, you move up a bit my dear so I can make these drinks. Where's the milk? Sam, the rifle has a sling for a reason. Put it on your back not on the floor. Pea, you run down and get the milk portions from the store room. We'll have a civilised coffee before we start on this morning's agenda.'

Two simple acts and suddenly the bleakness of the immediate future is pushed away. An old man cleaning a room and an old woman brisk and forthright in manner. A table is pulled out and chairs to go with it. Milk portions are fetched and within a few minutes they sit down in a room filled with scents of pine and freshly made coffee.

'Now,' Joan says, lowering her mug from the first and very much appreciated sip of coffee, 'what are we to do?' She looks round at Lilly, Pea and Sam, 'ladies?'

Pea and Sam share a glance as all three look to Lilly, 'Lilly?' Pea asks.

This was meant to be Lenski and Maddox with Lilly but neither of them are here and things need to be done. They all look tired. They all feel tired and Lilly bears the marks of the beatings she took yesterday but there is a fork in the road ahead and she looks to each path, wondering which to take.

'We started this revolt,' Joan says when no one else says anything, 'or rather, Lilly did with exceptional execution I might add. To you, Lilly,' Joan says lifting her coffee mug in salute.

'Lilly,' Pea says lifting her mug.

'Lilly,' Sam joins in.

Lilly nods and lifts her mug as she takes in the way Joan said the word execution. Joan, in return observes the manner of the girl seated opposite her and nods knowingly to herself.

'I will start by saying this,' Joan announces with a pause to make sure they're all listening, 'what was done yesterday needed to be done to prevent a greater tragedy taking place and now we are here. Everyone will wake up soon and they will need direction and focus. Lilly? Where are Maddox and Lenski?'

'In the hospital. Maddox came round for a few minutes last night...'

'Christ,' Sam cuts in, 'does he know?'

Lilly nods, 'I told him, he knows.'

'How did he take it?' Pea asks.

'I think he understood once I explained everything to him,' she says carefully, 'and I did tell him that if he harbours any desire for revenge then everyone here will ensure Mr Howie is told when they return.'

'Ooh good move,' Sam says with a tilt of her head.

'Other than that he looked sick and weak,' Lilly adds.

'So ladies,' Joan says, 'it appears we are it.'

'Looks that way,' Pea says with a heavy sigh, 'I wouldn't know where to start though....Sam?'

'God,' Sam copies the sigh and stares down at her mug, 'bodies I guess?'

'What about the hole in the wall?' Pea asks.

'Or that,' Sam says, lifting her mug of coffee.

Lilly thinks. Her face a mask that betrays the fast motion of her mind that processes each strand of thought as she stares at the paths ahead. Which one to take? Which direction to go?

Billy is the priority. His welfare comes before all else. After that is the welfare of every other child here, then the adults. To ensure Billy has the best chances there must be safety, security and welfare. His needs must be met with food, water and shelter. He must have clean clothes and bedding and he must have a *feeling* of being secure to encourage his mind to heal from the horrors they have all faced. Which path? Slip back and look to his immediate concerns and hope someone else makes the right decisions or commit now and make sure those decisions are the right ones.

'Both,' Lilly says choosing the path without realising until the words came out which direction that would be in, 'we have to do both and more at the same time.' She sits up straighter, taller and leans forward to rest her elbows on the table. 'If I may I would like to suggest we do the following...'

The three older women look at each other but none of them

show any reaction to Lilly being drawn out to take the bait of the challenge in front of them. Lilly started this and around her it must now flow. Instead they listen and drink coffee as the plan, which they each knew had already been processed in her mind, is laid out in words.

CHAPTER THIRTY-FIVE

W e use winding country lanes that veer east then west but all the time south. The motorway would take us there quickly but Reginald has chosen a route that would we would not be expected to use. I drive the Saxon. Clarence drives the minibus and Roy is back in his van towing Jess's horsebox trailer thing. We did try and get Jess loaded up for Charlie but the horse wasn't having any of it and fucked about more than Cookey when he's had too much sugar and it was only when Charlie got to her that she calmed down and walked meekly into the box. Horses are weird.

When did we leave the fort? A couple of days ago? It feels like weeks, months even but then time is all fucked up now, magnified and moving faster or something. Either that or we just don't have devotion to it we had in our previous lives and therefore the importance of it is slipping away.

'What do you think it will be like?' I ask Marcy.

'What?' She blinks from her own deep thoughts.

'The fort.'

'Oh, oh right...er...probably a big mess,' she says and twists round to look down the back, 'Nick, you nervous?'

'Eh? What for?' He asks.

'Seeing Lilly again,' she says.

'Oh fuck...er well I wasn't...' He blurts and makes everyone chuckle.

'You'll be fine,' Paula says, having chosen to travel with us to let Kyle ride with Roy and Reginald, 'she'll be thrilled to see you again.'

'What's the fort like then?' Blinky asks, 'is it big?'

'It's a fucking shitting death filled stink hole of wank,' Blowers says.

'Speak your mind, Blowers,' Paula says.

'Sorry but it is. Why are we even going back there?'

'Survivors fucktard,' Nick says.

'So we dropping them off and going again yeah?' Blowers asks, 'drop and run...drop and fuck off...like we just leave the bus on the beach and go...'

'Why's that?' Blinky asks.

'Cos it's shit,' Blowers says, 'And Maddox is a cunt...'

'Simon,' Paula tuts.

'He is,' Nick says.

'We need a time out and somewhere safe to stay...' Paula starts to say.

'Safe? The fort?' Blowers scoffs, 'that's the least safe place in the...shit, sorry, Nick.'

'You fucking twat, Blowers' Cookey mutters, 'she'll be fine, Nick.'

'I didn't mean it like that,' Blowers says, 'Lilly will be fine but it's still a cunt filled place of cu...'

'Blowers,' Paula says with a huff, 'it's not that bad.'

'It is,' Cookey says, 'I'm with cockbreath...we should ditch the survivors and go...or,' he adds quickly, 'we should ditch the survivors, grab Lilly and her brother and then go...'

'Yes!' Blowers says, 'we should do that. Grab Lilly and get the fuck out of it.'

'And Billy,' Cookey says.

'And Billy,' Blowers adds, 'and Milly.'

'Hold the fuck on,' Blinky cuts in, 'Lilly and Billy and Milly? You taking the piss?'

'Nope,' Nick laughs, 'you'll love Milly...'

'I don't like children,' Blinky says.

'You've not met Milly,' Cookey says.

'I don't want to go back,' Mo's voice suddenly joins the conversation bringing it to a sudden silence.

'We have to go back,' Paula says, her tone soft but firm.

'What for?' Blowers asks.

'Hold the wheel,' I say to Marcy and twist round.

'Fucking hell, Howie,' she launches over me to grab the wheel.

'I had no idea you felt like that,' I say to Blowers.

'Howie, slide out,' Marcy says, digging her elbow into my ribs.

'We all do,' he says, dropping his head to look down.

'Howie,' Marcy snaps, 'slide out before we crash into the fucking hedge...'

'Cookey? You the same?' I ask.

He looks at Blowers and nods, 'we hate it.'

'Clarence is the same,' Blowers says.

'We won't get to the bloody fort if you don't slide out,' Marcy says.

'Is he?' I ask the lads, 'why didn't anyone say anything?'

'Just...shit,' Marcy says as the Saxon starts weaving down the road, 'slow down...'

'Howie, maybe let Marcy drive?' Paula asks.

'Eh?' I look back out the windscreen to see us weaving down a country lane, 'just hold it straight.'

'I'll hold you straight you bloody...right slow down and let me drive.'

'*What's going on?*' Clarence's worried voice asks through the radio.

'*We're fine,*' Paula replies.

I start sliding out as Marcy starts sliding in and my world fills with her arse as she twists and curses for me to shift my fat back-side over.

'That's my boob,' she announces to the world when her breast thrusts itself into my hand trying to hold the wheel.

'You put your boob in my hand.'

'No, your hand found my...right move over...go on...'

'I'm going,' I get free and plop to the side on the passenger seat as she sinks down to put her foot back on the accelerator. 'There, all done...'

'Don't speak to me. I am irritated right now,' she plucks at her bra strap under her shirt and shifts in the seat, 'it almost fell out,' she adds with a huff.

'Shouldn't be so big then,' I mutter which just earns me a dark look. 'Anyway, you really feel that strongly about it?' I ask the lads. 'Mo?'

'Fuck yeah, I mean yes.'

'Nick?'

He shrugs, 'Lilly is there so I'm happy to go back to see her but not the fort.'

I don't need to ask Cookey or Blowers and if truth be told I feel the same way. The fort meant something once. Everything we gave for it but that's the problem, we kept on giving and it never ended.

'You feel the same,' Paula says, watching me closely.

'Yeah, yeah I do,' I say and look to Charlie, 'Charlie needs to see the doctor though and we need more ammunition and rifles, pistols too...grenades...hang on, *Clarence, you there?*'

'*Go ahead.*'

'*The lads just told me how they feel about the fort. You the same?*'

'*Definitely, Boss.*'

'*Roy?*'

'*Whatever Paula wants.*'

'*Reggie?*'

'*I just need somewhere quiet to go through Neal's books.*'

'Fair enough then,' I say, 'we'll drop the survivors off, get Charlie checked over and grab what we need then go again.'

'What about Lilly?' Cookey asks on seeing the frown on Nick's face.

'We can't run with children,' I say, 'Lilly yes but she won't leave her brother. Nick?'

'Yeah,' he says quietly, 'I know.'

'Ah fuck it,' Blowers says, 'we can stay for the night...'

'One night won't hurt,' Cookey says quickly.

'Nah,' Nick says, his face passive, 'I...like...'

'Go on,' Paula says, prompting him gently.

'Like, don't take the piss but...'

'We'll always take the piss.'

'Cookey shush,' Paula says, 'Nick, go on.'

'Twat,' Nick says looking at Cookey, 'I want to see Lilly but I hate being there the same as everyone else.'

'How about,' Marcy calls out, 'we see how everyone feels when we get there?'

I look at Charlie then at Nick and finally at Marcy. 'We'll stay for the night,' I say firmly.

'Boss,' Nick says.

'Charlie needs to be checked and we all need a rest. We're staying for the night.'

'Or,' Marcy says, 'we wait and see how everyone feels when we get there.'

'You just said that.'

'I said it again,' she says bluntly, 'is that okay with you?'

'Alright pissy...'

'Don't start, Howie.'

'Mr Howie?' Charlie calls out, 'may I ask a question?'

'Yeah what's up?'

'You said the fort is on an island...how will we transport Jess?'

'Oh,' I say.

'Good question,' Paula says.

'Might not be staying then,' Marcy mutters.

'I know!' Cookey announces.

'Oh fuck,' Blowers groans.

'Can I get out now?' Nick asks.

'I'll come with you,' Mo says.

'Fuck off,' Cookey says, bursting at the seams with an idea buzzing in his mind.

'Cookey,' I say with a look, 'we haven't had coffee today...'

'No no, it's a proper idea,' he says getting to his feet with such a grin it makes Charlie start laughing.

'Fucking won't be,' Blowers says.

'It is!' Cookey says so excited it sets Charlie off even more.

Paula looks at me. I lift my head. She tilts hers.

'Don't,' Blowers pleads.

'Fuck it,' I groan, 'go on then, Cookey...but, if it's shit then Blinky can punch you in the leg.'

'Fuck yes,' Blinky sits up with a grin.

'I will accept that challenge, Mr Howie,' Cookey says, 'because my idea is not shit. It is a good idea and in fact...'

'Get on with it then,' Blowers says.

'Excuse me,' Cookeys says with mock politeness at Blowers knowing he is making Charlie laugh, 'I am so confident of my idea I shall transmit my idea over the radio network. *Ahem...Clarence, it is Cookey. Are you receiving me?*'

'Are you pissing about, Cookey?'

'I am not. I have an idea.'

'Is it stupid?'

'No. It is wise and learned and...stuff. Roy? Can you hear me?'

'Unfortunately.'

'Reg?'

'I will not answer to that name.'

'Sorry, Reginald? Can you hear me because I have a...'

'Fucking get on with it,' Blowers groans.

'Blinky, if he doesn't tell us in thirty seconds you can...' I call out.

'One Two Three,' Blinky counts fast.

'Fine, this is my idea...do you all remember those nice houses by the beach where we stayed the night when we left the fort? Well...'

'You fucking genius,' Blowers says, 'mate...that's brilliant...'

'Cookey,' I say in shock.

'Cookey that's a bloody good idea,' Clarence says.

'I haven't said it yet,' Cookey says plaintively, *'Let me say it... well, why don't we stay there instead of the fort? That way...Blowers I haven't said the whole of my idea yet...that way Jess can be with us, Lilly can visit and...er...and oh yeah, we're not in the fort.'*

'The lad's got some smarts,' Clarence says, clearly impressed.

'Reggie?' I ask through the radio.

'As much as I hate to admit it, his idea is actually...'

'FUCK YES,' Cookey booms, 'I impressed Reggie...the regmeister...old Reg...I am an intellectual fucking genius.' He sits down proudly and nods round at everyone, 'so me and Charlie will have one house and the rest of you can...what? Is that a bad idea?'

Charlie doesn't answer on account of the tears falling from her eyes at his performance. Her laugh is like a mini Clarence, all snorts and brays that makes us all grin.

'Fine,' he says glumly, 'I'll share with Blowers again....we ain't spooning though.'

'We are,' Blowers says.

'We ain't.'

'We are.'

'I hate spooning Blowers,' Cookey tells Charlie, 'his willy digs in my back.'

'Stop,' she gasps, touching the cut on her face, 'you'll split my stitches...'

'I said that to Blowers once but he didn't stop,' Cookey says with mock hurt, 'just kept going the nasty brute.'

'Switch on,' Marcy calls out quickly.

'What?' I spin round to face the front as the laughing drops instantly, 'arm up...*Clarence, we've got someone in the road ahead holding an assault rifle...*'

'Roger, easing back. Reginald. Get the camera's on at the back.'

'They're on, the back is clear.'

'Stop the vehicle,' I say to Marcy. We're only half a mile from the bay and I don't recognise the person holding the rifle. An adult male who lifts his arm in greeting then speaks into a radio. 'Anyone recognise him?'

'Let me see,' Paula says leaning over the back of the seats, 'yeah I do actually...he's from the fort.'

'You sure?'

'Yeah definitely, ask Dave.'

'Dave, get eyes on this bloke ahead. Is he from the fort?'

'Stand by,' I open the door and look back to see Dave jumping from the bus with his rifle up and aimed down past the Saxon, *'he is, Mr Howie.'*

'He's got a car,' Marcy says, pointing past him to the back end of a blue mini parked round the bend in the road.

'Roy, I'll go forward. Get Kyle to drive...can you give me overwatch.'

'Yep, getting out now.'

'Blowers, your team protect the bus. Everyone stay here, I'll go forward with Dave. Dave,' I shout out as I drop down, 'with me.'

I wait for him to jog over then start down the road. My assault rifle held ready but lowered down.

'Sure you recognise him?' I ask quietly.

'Yes, Mr Howie.'

'Okay, chances are Maddox has trained him up but we don't take chances. You see red eyes then shoot him and get back to the bus.'

'Yes, Mr Howie.'

'Clarence, if it goes bent then get that bus out of here.'

'Will do.'

'*Overwatch on.*'

'*Cheers, Roy,*' I turn back to see him standing on the roof of his van with an arrow already pulled back in the string.

'No closer, Mr Howie,' Dave says.

'Okay,' I stop about thirty metres from the man, 'who are you?' I call forward.

'Brian,' he shouts back, 'it's good to see you again, Mr Howie.'

'Are you alone?'

'I am,' he shouts, 'this is my point...'

'We need to see your eyes,' I cut him off, 'put the weapon down and walk slowly towards us.'

'I can't do that, Mr Howie,' he says with a genuine tone of apology.

'Why not?'

'How do I know you're not infected?'

'Because I'm immune.'

'Er...yeah I forgot about that...'

'Lower the rifle and walk towards us.'

'Ah don't let Dave shoot me but I can't...' he's shitting himself at the sight of Dave and even from this distance I can see him looking past us '...is that Roy up there?'

'It is.'

'Oh fuck...sorry, I'm really sorry, Mr Howie...I can't put my gun down...'

'Bit of an impasse then mate,' I say, 'which will end a bit sharply in about ten fucking seconds if you...'

'NO,' he shouts, 'hang on...er...gonna use my radio...please don't let Dave shoot me...'

'Dave, if he touches that radio shoot him.'

'Yes, Mr Howie.'

'What? Hang on...no no no...oh shit...'

'Calm down, Brian.'

'Oh my god, Dave's gonna shoot me...'

'Fuck's sake,' I sigh at the sight of him turning to jelly, 'get a grip, Dave won't shoot you unless you do something stupid. Now what's going on?'

'I'm on guard,' he blurts.

'Clearly,' I reply, 'we'll come to you but I really wouldn't move if I were you.'

'Oh fuck...fuck fuck fuck...'

'Brian, calm down, mate,' I say as we walk slowly towards him, 'just need to see your eyes and then you can see ours, okay?'

'Dave's gonna shoot me.'

'He's not going to shoot you...well, no, he might shoot you if you...oh for fuck's sake...stop shaking and open your eyes.'

'Can't. Dave's gonna shoot me.'

'Who the hell put you on guard?'

'Can't say,' he whispers tightly, 'gonna give you my radio... don't shoot me...' his voice comes out in static bursts of complete terror.

'Okay,' I say and glance at Dave who keeps his rifle locked on Brian.

'Here,' Brian holds it out with a hand that wavers in fear at the prospect of being shot by Dave.

'I'm getting the radio,' I tell Dave, 'don't shoot him for a minute.'

'One minute, Mr Howie.'

'No I meant don't shoot him until I've got the radio.'

'Oh fuck...'

'Shoot him after you have the radio.'

'No, no I mean...I'll get the radio so don't shoot him while I get the radio.'

'Oh shit...'

'Do I shoot him after you have the radio, Mr Howie?'

'No,' I groan, 'not unless he does something.'

'Roger. I will shoot you if you do something,' he tells Brian.

'Oh dear,' Brian whimpers.

I stride forward and take the radio which makes Brian flinch which makes Dave twitch which makes Brian yelp which makes me roll my eyes and get out of the way.

'Hello? It's Howie. Maddox?'

'Mr Howie?' A female voice asks, 'Where are you?'

'With some bloke called Brian who has just fainted...who is this?'

'It's Lilly, Mr Howie. Come straight through.'

'Through? Through what? What's happened? Why is this bloke out here with a rifle? Who gave it to him?'

'Mr Howie, may I explain when I see you?' She asks politely.

'Lilly, are you okay? Are you free to speak?'

'Everything is fine, Mr Howie. I promise. Come straight through.'

'Are you sure you're okay?'

'Honestly, Mr Howie. Come straight through.'

I pause and glare at the handset gripped in my fist then glance down to Brian now lying on the ground, 'This is Howie. If anyone touches Lilly or harms her I will fucking end you...are we clear?'

'Mr Howie. I am fine. Honestly. There is nothing happening. I promise. Please, come straight through'

'Maddox?'

'Maddox is sick, Mr Howie.'

'Lilly, wait there... NICK?' I stride back towards the vehicles as Nick runs towards me.

'What's happened?' He asks, 'is she okay?'

'What's going on?' Paula runs towards me.

'Howie?' Marcy asks.

'Lilly is on the radio. She said everything is fine but that Maddox is sick. That bloke was guarding but I don't like it...'

'Want me to talk to her?' Nick asks.

'Check she's okay,' I hand him the radio.

'Lilly, it's Nick. You there?'

'Nick! Oh god am I happy to hear your voice... Yes yes I am.

Nick...come straight through...are you okay? Are you hurt or anything?'

'I'm fine, are you okay?'

'Yes! Yes I am fine, Nick. I promise. Please, tell Mr Howie everything is okay. Come down and I will explain everything that has happened...'

'She sounds upset,' Paula says at hearing the emotion in Lilly's voice.

'We could be walking into something,' I say.

Nick nods and thinks for a second, *'Lilly, we need to be sure there ain't, I mean there isn't something going on...are you like held captive or something?'*

'No. I promise Nick. I am not...er...that day we met, you said something to me...if I tell you that you will believe me?'

'Yeah go on,' Nick says and I can see his knuckles turning white as he holds the radio.

'You said that's not our way. We do the right thing. Mr Howie said we have to do the right thing otherwise none of this is fucking worth it... you swore and you blushed then apologised for swearing. You said we do the right thing for the right reasons...you remember being in the field? Do you remember what I said to you?'

'Yeah,' He croaks, his eyes closed tight, *'you er...you offered something.'*

'I did. Now do you believe me? I am fine, I promise you. I'd never lead you into danger, Nick.'

Nick looks at me then at Paula, his eyes yearning for the answer. I nod and he presses the button back in, *'we're on our way.'*

CHAPTER THIRTY-SIX

'*We're on our way.*'

She stands still. Her eyes clamped closed as she fights to compose herself from the rush of emotions surging up at first hearing Mr Howie's voice then at hearing Nick. The pressure had been growing but not a reaction she had shown until now. Not a flicker of worry or concern but an icy cold determination to do the right thing for the right reasons. For Billy. For all the children here and so Howie and the others would have somewhere safe and decent to come back to.

We do the right thing. Mr Howie said we have to do the right thing otherwise none of this is fucking worth it.

At each pitch and toss and as the pressure grew so she recalled those words and remembered the decency of Nick. The honour of doing the right thing. She killed many that night and the offset had to be to rebuild where death was given. Take something dark and bad, something evil and tainted and make it clean. Make it worth-while and do it for the right reasons.

There were many motivations driving her on. Billy was first. The other children a close second. After that was a mix of thinking of Mr Howie and how they had to have somewhere good to return to. They were out there killing the things to keep them away from the fort. They were a small group of people bound by honour and decency that were putting their lives on the line. Nick was part of that group and he saved her brother and you repay the kindness that was given. Mr Howie *will* have somewhere safe and clean and decent to come back to.

She thought about other people too. People like her who had fled homes to run terrified through the open land to reach the promise of the fort. It had to stand for them and for everyone else who made the decision to try and reach it.

Then there was Pea and Sam and the devotion they had shown to her and the way they stepped up when the world was falling apart around them and then there was Joan. A seventy year old woman who had more energy than everyone else put together.

As the days wore on so the motivation also became about doing it because it was being done. It gave something for everyone to work towards and a hopeless sense of loss became a positive energy that spread and grew with Lilly the linchpin holding it all together.

Each of those motivations took turns to become the primary driving force and the end of the eighteenth day saw a different group of people that woke up in the morning. The rain stopped halfway through the day. The sun came out and the warmth and light flooded the land. The sea glistened. Smiles began to appear and as the day drew to a close so they sat about bathed in firelight with the glow that comes from a gruelling but rewarding day of intense work.

Not Lilly though. As that day wore on so she felt a growing pressure inside. A feeling that something big was coming and it made those blue eyes grow cold and hard. It got worse too. As Howie fought the infected through the towns to reach that final battle so she became more restless and filled with a need to be doing something. To be somewhere. As night fell so it got worse still. She paced and fretted. She walked up the vehicle ramp to stare out across the sea as though searching for Nick with a heart pounding and a body flooding with adrenalin.

Then the girl was taken down. The girl that screamed in the flat next to Howie that made them all drop to weep. Lilly dropped too and she wept. She wept for something she knew nothing about but from a feeling inside. The next instant she was on her feet glaring with lips pulled back and the knuckles on her hands white from gripping the assault rifle. *Pack. Be pack. Little ones.* Images and sensations and the essence of things pushing so strong through her mind and heart. She felt it. She felt the rage and the instinct. She felt the pulsing flow of energy but had no clue what it was from or for. Pea had climbed the ramp to check she was okay and quietly backed away on seeing the utter violence radiating from Lilly's eyes.

Then it was gone and inside there was only relief and the hours of darkness during which she once more held her brother and the rifle and slept with one eye open.

NOW SHE OPENS those eyes and feels that pressure bubbling up to be released. She has coped. She has coped well and will always and forever continue to cope but there is a difference between coping and having those you know understand be close to you.

Mr Howie is back. His voice came through the radio. Paula will be with him. Clarence and Cookey and Blowers. Nick. Her Nick.

She bites it down. They don't need to see her weak or upset. She doesn't know what they did yesterday only that it was big and somewhere deep inside a voice she doesn't understand tells her she held the line and did not yield.

CHAPTER THIRTY-SEVEN

'Fuck me, are you seeing this?' I call out and feel everyone behind me rush forward to peer through the windscreen to the sight ahead.

The bay is there. The long golden horseshoe with the idyllic blue waters lapping at the shore. The fort in the distance over the sea. The houses by the shore are there too but everything else looks different.

'Slow down,' I say to Marcy, needing time to take it all in and it makes my heart beat faster. At seeing so many things that none of us were expecting to see.

People everywhere. Lines of people carrying clothes and bags full of food and bedding from the houses to be stacked in trailers and wheelbarrows. Vans and pick-up trucks being loaded with bed frames, desks, tables and chairs as the houses are emptied of anything usable. From the other access road are more lines of people and vehicles carrying more gear from the industrial units and boat building warehouses further back from the blown out estate.

Everything is being stacked on the shore. Piles of sheet wood, timber, lengths of wood and metal, boxes of nails, screws, ropes, building materials and tools. Mounds of bedding and clothes being sorted and more chairs, tables and bed frames stacked high and deep.

Boats everywhere. Small boats being unloaded on the beach at the fort. More boats on their way to the fort and more on their way back and yet more already anchored and being filled. Ribs, fishing boats, rowing dinghies and everything in between and further out to sea there is a little flotilla of vessels all with the distinct shapes of people fishing over the side with rods.

'You seeing this, Clarence?' Paula murmurs into her radio.

'Yeah,' he replies, clearly as shocked as we are.

I scan from the houses down to the beach then back again. People stop and turn to see our vehicles as word spreads from those who have radios. Hands are lifted, people smile and wave. I thought we wouldn't be welcome back after what happened with Lani but everyone we see seems happy to see us.

That alone is impressive. Seeing such an organised thing in action but that's only on the southern side of the road. On the northern there is a huge yellow excavator being driven by a man with a roll up wedged between his lips flattening everything in sight. A few houses have already been flattened and he's busy working his way down as the people work rapidly to taje anything usable. It's immediately obvious what the plan is and already I can see portions of hedgerow and fencing have been taken down to open the view out down to the marine industrial units further back.

'Clear line of sight,' Blowers mutters.

'HEY!' A woman calls out, waving with a huge beaming smile on her sweaty face as she walks down the road towards the shore.

Marcy waves back, almost timid and scared in response to such a positive greeting.

'MR HOWIE!' A man's voice shouting in greeting and I turn to see a bloke waving from the front of a van waiting to pull out with a fresh load ready to be moved to the shore.

'Fucking twilight zone,' Cookey whispers, 'did we die last

night?'

'Think we did,' I mutter back.

'It wasn't like this when you left then?' Charlie asks

'Fuck no,' Blowers scoffs, 'fuck knows what this is.'

'Oh my god,' Cookey says pointing to an old woman on the beach with a pistol on each hip and an assault rifle strapped across the front of her chest, 'is that Dave's mum?'

'Fuck...' I shake my head and blink then look again. An old woman armed to the teeth and acting like Paula by clapping her hands at people to make them work faster.

Marcy stops. We have to stop. We've run out of road and otherwise we'd be driving down the beach and into the sea if we kept going, which actually seems like a good idea right now for how freaked out we all are.

'Dave's mum's coming,' Marcy says as the old woman strides towards us.

'I don't want to get out,' I say.

'We should go,' Blowers says behind me, 'I'm actually scared...'

'Pussies,' Cookey says, 'I want to meet Dave's mum...can we get out?'

'Yeah,' I say slowly and ease the door open to drop down to a world of noise. People calling to each other and big plant machinery working not far away. Engines idling with throaty diesel noises.

'Welcome back, Mr Howie.' I turn to see another bloke lifting an arm in greeting.

'Cheers,' I call back and that verbal response seems to set everyone else off and we get calls and greetings from all sides at the same time.

Marcy comes round the front to my side. The back doors open, the lads and Paula all come forward. Clarence, Roy and Reginald all join us. Even Meredith stays close, clearly unsure of what to make of it all. We stand there. Armed to the teeth and still bloodied from our last fight and without realising it we've all put our bags on with our axes tucked down, pistols in holsters, knives in belts, assault rifles held and from instinct and natural movement we get into our fighting circle and stare round in pure amazement at the voices calling out.

'Welcome home.'

'Welcome back.'

'Are you all okay?'

'They've brought survivors...'

'...People in the bus, get some water...where's the doctor?'

'Coming,' I turn again to see Doctor Anne Carlton rushing towards the bus with a large medical bag gripped in her hands, 'get them off...Joan! We've got a whole bus load.'

The old woman shouts back, 'Sam? Sam?'

'Here,' Another woman with a pistol on her belt and an assault rifle strapped to her chest like the old woman comes out from behind a huge stack of bedding, 'oh hi,' she shouts at us, 'welcome back....I've got something for you, hang on,' she adds and ducks out of sight.

'Sam can you process the new ones?' Joan shouts.

'Give me a minute, Anne is there. Anne? You okay for a minute?'

'Fine,' Anne shouts back as the survivors start dropping from the bus into the arms of people waiting with bottles of water and soft words of comfort.

'Pea?' Sam's voice calls out.

'Coming,' again we turn and see another woman with dark frizzy hair and a mixed race complexion running from one of the boats towards us, 'welcome back, Mr Howie...are you all okay? It's good to see you again.'

'Er... yeah, um...bloody hell,' I say, 'what the...I mean...'

She stops near us and wipes the light film of sweat from her forehead, 'not the same as when you left eh?' She says with a huge smile, 'wait till you see inside.'

'Inside?' Marcy asks as I'm too stupid to form words from being too stunned.

'The fort,' Pea says, 'Lilly has done so much.'

'Hey,' Sam walks towards us carrying a case of Lucozade, 'Lilly said you like Lucozade...'

'Fuck me,' Nick mutters. The case is still sealed in the plastic covering with a handwritten note on the top *reserved for Mr Howie do not use.*

'We managed to keep them a bit chilled too,' Sam says as she converges with Pea who rips open the outer plastic film to start pulling bottles out, 'kept them stacked in a few inches of sea water in the shade,' Pea adds. Both of them wear pistols on their hips and like the old woman their rifles are strapped across their chests in the way Special Forces soldiers do. They look competent but more than that, they look friendly and genuinely pleased to see us all.

Pea comes forward with her hands full of bottles and I notice the way she flicks her gaze at our faces as though a bit awestruck and shy. She goes for the lads first, handing slightly cool bottles out as we just stare with slack jaws.

'Thanks,' Nick says twisting the top off his bottle and looking at Paula who just shrugs.

'Cheers, what's your name?' Cookey asks with his big grin, 'Pea?'

'It is,' Pea says, smiling back at him as she hands a bottle to Blowers.

'Vegetable or piss?'

'Blinky,' Paula groans.

'Vegetable,' Pea says, 'Roy? Lucozade?'

'Thanks,' he says, taking a bottle.

'Rough out there was it?' Joan's brisk, clipped voice asks as she strides towards us while brushing her hands together as though to rid the sand from her skin.

'Could say that,' Paula replies, 'Paula,' she takes a step towards Joan with her hand held out.

'Joan,' Joan says shaking hands smartly, 'nice to see you all back. You've got the Lucozade then? Lilly was very firm about it being here for when you came home.'

'Mr Howie?' Sam at my side handing me a bottle from the case. I take it and mumble a thanks as she steps past me to Marcy.

'Thank you,' Marcy says.

'Nasty cut there,' Joan says, stopping in front of Charlie, 'I'm Joan, I don't think you were with them when they left.'

'Er no, no we met up a couple of days ago,' Charlie says politely.

'Understood,' Joan says taking in the weapons on both Charlie and Blinky, 'part of Mr Howie's team now though by the looks of it.'

'They are,' I say, 'er...what the hell has happened? Where's Maddox and his crews?'

'Boss,' Clarence calls my attention and nods out to the fort, 'seen that?'

'What?' I look over the sea to the fort, 'what mate?'

'No hole.'

'Fuck,' I exclaim not realising the hole isn't there and from here the fort looks completely normal, 'you fixed it then,' I say.

'No they just hid it,' Marcy says with a look at me.

'With mirrors,' Paula adds.

'Funny, I was taken aback,' I tell them both and everyone else before they can start making comments.

'Fixed yesterday,' Joan says, looking over to the fort then back at us, 'mortar is still drying but it'll hold. It's braced on the inside with scaffolding poles to keep it secure.'

'Marcy is so pretty.'

We all look round to see Pea blushing bright red from the overly loud whisper to Sam. 'Sorry,' she winces.

'Thank you,' Marcy says giving her that massive beaming movie star smile of perfect white teeth.

'So vain,' I cough into my hand.

'Leg humper,' she coughs back.

'Sugar yay,' Cookey says and belches after taking too big a swig, 'sorry...but fuck that's nice. Your missus is awesome, Nick.'

'Fact,' Blowers says.

'She's not my missus,' Nick says with a slight blush in his cheeks.

'Fuck off,' Cookey scoffs, 'she so is...just like me and Charlie will be one day...'

Charlie sprays her mouthful on the ground as she chokes from the laugh coming up as the drink went down, 'I'm so sorry,' she sputters trying to wipe her mouth.

'Mads is sick?' Mo asks in a flat voice as his eyes flick to the fort with a dark expression.

'He is,' Joan states, 'the doctors say he will recover.'

'Where's the crews then?' Mo asks.

Hesitation and glances between the three armed women, 'I think,' Joan says pursing her lips, 'that you should let Lilly explain.'

Something has happened. That much is obvious and I look round again to the survivors showing palpable relief at being surrounded by people who aren't armed to the teeth and covered in cuts and bruises with chunks taken out of their ears and faces.

'And Lilly?' Paula asks, her tone friendly but hinting that bad things will happen to everyone if Lilly is not absolutely perfectly okay. The three woman look slightly alarmed in the instant change at the hardness coming over us.

'Lilly is fine,' Sam says quickly, 'she's in the fort, er...there's boats if you want to go over now?'

I take a long refreshing drink of Lucozade original and ponder the exigencies of life and the world and all that it means to be human and part of the organic process of living. Or rather, I absorb the sugar and feel a nice rush going through my brain.

'What we doing then?' Clarence asks, finishing his bottle, 'splitting up in case something nasty is happening?'

'Yep,' I say and drain my bottle.

'You going over and me rescuing or the other way round?'

'Um, I'll go and you rescue.'

'Fair enough,' he says, 'what's Dave doing? Going with you?'

'I am,' Dave says.

'I'm keeping Roy then,' Clarence says, 'Roy? You alright with that?'

'I am,' Roy says.

'Mr Howie, can I stay with Clarence yeah?' Mo asks.

'Sure mate, anyone else want to pick a team?'

'Nick will go with you,' Clarence says.

'Fuck yes,' Nick says, 'or…yes if that's alright, Boss?'

'If I said no would you stay here?'

'No,' he says with a grin.

'I'll stay here with Clarence,' Blowers says.

'Sure?'

'Yep, Cookey? You with me?'

'Looks that way buttmuncher.'

'Paula? You'd better come with me,' I say.

'Yep,' she says and takes another glug from her bottle, 'this is nice. I never really liked Lucozade before.'

'Blinky? Charlie?'

'Sir, can I stay with the lads, Sir, Mr Howie, Sir?'

I shake my head from the too many sirs, 'yeah no worries, Charlie? You need to see the docs so you'd better come with us.'

'I'd like to see the fort,' Charlie says.

'Marcy, you can come with me and…fuck I forgot who's going with me now. Paula?'

'What?'

'I'm lost.'

'Want me to organise?'

'Yes please.'

'Sure?' She asks with an evil smile, 'to the fort is me, you, Dave, Marcy, Nick and Charlie. Everyone else is staying here.'

'Got it, everyone happy?' I ask.

'Joan,' Paula says, 'I think we'd prefer to stay outside the fort tonight. Are those houses still habitable?'

'Why don't you want to stay in the fort?' Joan asks as though the very notion is highly offensive.

'Cos it's a death filled hole of cu...'

'Simon.'

'Sorry, Dave.'

'We will stay close to our vehicles,' Paula says, 'and we have a horse so it makes more logistical sense for us to stay this side. That and of course some of my boys detest every brick that place is built from and they have lost too many people they love within those walls so yes, we'll be staying this side tonight.'

'That's fine,' Pea says quickly, 'we'll get one of the houses ready for you.'

'Two please,' Cookey says.

'One,' Paula says firmly.

'No but me and Charlie will be like neighbours and you can come round for a cup of salt or something...'

'Cup of sugar dickhead,' Blowers says.

'Or...I know! The ladies can be in one house and I'll be like calling round for a cup of sugar and Charlie will be like *oh he's so hunky and fit and er...hunky* and I'll be like...'

'You said hunky twice,' Blowers points out.

'Fuck off,' Cookey replies, 'so can we have two...'

'One house, please,' Paula says.

'Cookey,' Charlie says once she's stopped laughing, 'can you take care of Jess for me?'

'Sure,' he says, 'what do I do?'

'I'll show him,' Roy says.

'You know about horses?' I ask him.

'No but I watched Charlie. The feed is ready in that bag in my van right?'

'Yes it is, third of a bucket with some water. She'll need a rub down.'

'Leave it with me, Charlie,' Cookey says so seriously that just makes her start laughing again, 'what? I'm like proper serious now.'

'Right, we'll head over before Nick starts swimming,' I say.

'Tell your missus thanks for the Lucozade,' Blowers says.

'Yeah say thanks,' Mo adds.

'She ain't my missus,' Nick says.

'Ah Nicholas,' Cookey says, 'you do make me laugh.'

'Twat,' Nick says walking off with us down the beach.

'Say hi to Lilly for us,' Cookey shouts.

'I will fucktard,' Nick shouts back giving him the finger.

'Miss you Charlie...'

'Miss you too, Cookey,' she shouts back.

'Ah she loves me,' Cookey sighs, 'hope Dave doesn't cut her head off...'

'Two months brew duty, Alex.'

'Yes, Dave. Sorry, Dave.'

'Mr Howie,' Pea runs after us, a look of consternation on her face.

'What's up?' I ask as nick wades out to pull a boat in closer to the shore.

'Er,' she stops and seems unsure of what she was going to say, 'it's just...well...Lilly has...'

'What?' Paula asks.

'She's got bruises,' Pea says quietly as I stiffen, 'but it has been resolved, just...well maybe don't react but let her tell you what happened.'

'Has anyone hurt her?' Paula asks.

'A lot happened,' Pea says, 'Lilly got us through it. This...' she waves round to the shore, 'all of this is because of Lilly...everything is because of Lilly...'

'Keep hold of Nick when we get there,' Paula whispers to me.

'I won't be able to hold him back,' I say with a glance to Nick clambering into the boat to start the engine, 'I wouldn't anyway... I'll help him if anyone has...'

'Mr Howie, please just let Lilly explain,' Pea says, 'we're on the right track now...doing the right thing for the right reasons,' she nods at me as the words sink in.

'Okay,' I say hesitantly.

'Lilly did it for her brother and for the children, well for everyone really but we know, I mean Sam and me and Joan probably too, well we know she also did it for you...she said you saved Billy and told us what Nick did for her. The right thing for the right reasons. Everyone says that now. Everyone here knows that. They were worried about you coming back because Lani turned and after what Maddox made them think but Lilly told them that what you have she has because she'd been with Nick...'

'They haven't had sex,' Paula says.

'No, we know that but Lilly told everyone she had so they'd believe you weren't dangerous...they all saw what Lilly did that night and...well, everyone figured if Lilly was okay then you lot must be okay. She said the fort had to stay open for people to come and she told them what you were doing out there to keep the things away from us. She said you had to have a place to come back to...a home...'

'Ready,' Nick shouts, eager to be off.

'Okay,' I say to Pea, 'thanks for telling us.'

'Thanks,' Paula says.

'Anything else we need to know?' Marcy asks as we turn away.

'Lilly will tell you the rest,' Pea says and smiles, 'she's been so strong but, but well, I think she's a bit nervous at seeing you all again, especially Nick.'

'Please!' Nick calls out.

'Coming, mate. Cheers, Pea.'

We head down and clamber into the boat as Nick itches to pull the vessel back so we can be off.

'Say something,' Marcy tells me softly, 'so he doesn't react.'

'No,' Paula says shaking her head, 'let it be, Nick's a good lad.'

'He'll go nuts,' Marcy says as Dave sits dead centre with his hands gripping the seat under his arse. 'What would Roy do if he saw you with bruises?' Marcy asks Paula then looks at me, 'and if someone hurt me?' she asks.

'Yeah,' I reply, 'good point.'

'Look at Cookey when we got into that street...he was going fucking bananas to get to Charlie,' Marcy says, 'he would have taken them down on his own. Nick's too dangerous to risk him losing it.'

'Was he?' Charlie asks in surprise.

'Okay okay,' I stand up as Nick opens the throttle a bit more and make my way to the outboard at the back, 'Nick.'

'Boss,' he says, 'what's up?'

'Listen to me.'

'What?' He snaps, his eyes full of worry.

'Listen and take it in, okay?'

He nods, his jaw set and his eyes going hard.

'Pea said Lilly has got bruises...listen...she didn't say why or how but that it's resolved. Okay? She said to listen to what she has to say.'

'I'll fucking...'

'I know you will and I'll be next to you while you do it and the lads will be bringing boats over to join us but Nick? We're going to listen to Lilly before we react okay?'

'Listen to Howie, Nick,' Marcy says, coming down to sit next to him, 'I promise, if anyone has hurt her we'll deal with them.'

'Okay,' he says tightly.

'Nick,' I say to make sure he's listening, 'Pea said Lilly has done all of this...everyone here is saying they have to do the right thing for the right reasons...'

'Fuck,' Nick says, his eyes flicking from me to the way ahead.

'Nick,' Marcy says, reaching out to rest a hand on his arm, 'she also said Lilly has told everyone you had sex...'

'We didn't...'

'I know,' Marcy says, 'they were worried about us coming back so Lilly told everyone that what we have she must have...'

'WELCOME BACK MR HOWIE,' a man shouts as we go past a boat heading towards the shore.

'Cheers mate,' I shout back.

'Oh right,' he says and blinks, 'fuck...we did kiss so...'

'Well there you go then,' Marcy says, 'you've shared bodily fluids but please, Nick. Don't react or do anything until after we've spoken to Lilly.'

'Okay,' he says and blows air out through his cheeks.

Marcy smiles and leans closer, 'Pea also said she was nervous about seeing you again...'

'Nervous?' Nick asks.

'That's lady code for excited,' she winks.

'Yeah?'

'It is,' Paula calls out with a smile.

'Okay, cheers, Mr Howie,' Nick says, his own nerves kicking in, 'so like...I'll watch you yeah? If they done something bad then...'

'Then we'll go for it,' I say to him, 'but it sounds like Lilly has got everything under control.'

'Okay.'

'WELCOME HOME!'

'Thanks,' Paula shouts to the boats pulling away from the small beach outside the fort.

Nick guides the boat so the front bumps the beach then twists a lever and pulls the outboard over so the propeller is out of the water. Charlie goes first, jumping deftly onto the beach and holding the front as the rest of us pile off.

'Welcome back,' someone says from between piles of clothes, food and bedding stacked on the beach.

'Cheers,' I call out.

The scene here is pretty much the same as the other side. Boats pulling up to disgorge contents that get stacked, sorted and then carried through the gates by people either pushing barrows or scooping armfuls up at a time.

Everyone smiles and nods at us. Some greet verbally and wave.

I slip back a bit to stay by Nick's side and let Marcy, Paula and Charlie smile and return the greetings.

We go through the gates into the middle section that has been kept clear. A man standing by the inner gate makes a show of pointing the rifle down and away as we draw close.

'Welcome back,' he says politely. An older man, maybe late fifties but his bearing is ex-military. Sometime ago I would guess judging by the weight carried round his mid-section. It's reassuring though and he looks competent.

'Seen that,' Paula says pointing to a large piece of paper nailed to the gate.

Do the right things for the right reasons

'Didn't you start that one off?' Marcy asks with a wry smile.

'Yeah,' I say with a bemused smile, 'I think I did.'

We go through the gates into a new world and what we saw outside is nothing compared to inside and we come to a stop to stare in wonder.

The whole place is a hive of activity. All the debris and broken shit from the middle has been taken away and the first thing that stands out is the cleanliness. It's chaotic but within that chaos there is clearly order. Like walking from a quiet house straight into the middle of a bustling High Street or town centre.

On the far side up from the vehicle ramp are big canvass and thick material marquee style tents. Open sided with the material rolled up and tied ready to be dropped down. Inside are the children and I forgot just how many we had here.

Clusters of quiet children sitting cross legged or lying back on bean bags to hear the story being read by an old man sitting on a chair with a big book open on his lap. More children lying on their bellies drawing in colouring books, playing with Lego and building blocks and brightly coloured plastic toys with more adults walking through carrying wet wipes and bottles of water. Outside the tents in a sectioned off area is a child size slide with the end in a paddling pool filled from a hose stretched back to the wall. Children taking it in turns to slide down and cry out as they splash and play. On the other side of that another two old men play cricket with a group of boys, using a mini cricket bat and stumps and a tennis ball that gets whacked too hard and has to be chased as the men encourage them to run and catch it.

Ahead in the middle is where most of the noise is coming from. The sound of wood being sawed by hand, hammers and things being knocked into line. Men and women working in shorts and shirt sleeves working on the start of a wooden framed structure over the foundations where the visitor centre was. Tools hanging from belts, men in caps and women in sunhats. Planks of wood already cut and ready to be used. Sheets of ply-board being measured and marked in pencil where the cuts should go. Boxes of nails and screws on a small table filled with coffee mugs and bottles of drinks. I'm not a builder and couldn't put a flat pack wardrobe together without fucking up but even I can see they've got more timber, sheets of wood and material than they'll need and I guess they're prepping up for something else to be built after whatever that construction is has been finished.

I look round the walls to see every door to every room within those walls is open and outside each are bed frames and bedding, chairs and boxes being sorted with candles, lamps and shelves ready to be put up.

A man on a step ladder works to screw a bracket onto the outside of the wall just down from the old armoury and I watch as he hangs a lantern from the bracket and climbs down to nod in satisfaction before moving down to do the next one.

Another small cluster of people work over open fires and pots and pans filling the air with the smells of food being cooked. Tables stacked with packets and tins of food being carried from the stores. Men and women smiling red faced and chatting as they stir pans and stack plates and cups.

At the far side the rear door stands open with a woman walking through holding a number of freshly caught fish in one hand that catches the eyes of those working on the structure who call out with low cheers as the woman proudly grins and calls back.

The whole thing is beautiful and idyllic, like something from the cover of a Jehovah Witness magazine. A vision of a utopian future.

We left a fort covered on bodies and the smouldering remains of fires burning out to fill the whole of the place with a stink of burning flesh and chemicals. Lani's body in the old armoury and the hospital being filled with the screaming and dying. Now there are no bodies. No corpses rotting anywhere. Nothing is broken or fucked up and there are no armed guards inside either. Just the chap at the inner gate and what looks like another one at the closed doors of the new armoury storage area. No kids with guns. No surly faced crews dressed in black.

Instead I see people stopping work to stand and drink bottled water and chat as they wipe the sweat from their faces. I even hear laughter. Actual laughter. We laugh all the time but mainly in response to Cookey keeping our spirits up when it feels like the whole world is against us but this laughter is the sound of normal people sharing banter and jokes.

Then they see us. A woman on top of a ladder fixing a length of wood looks over and calls out to everyone else who stop and turn. Men that were bent over sawing at pieces of timber stand upright and shield their eyes. People who were chatting turn and stare. The people cooking food stop stirring pans and opening tins as that word spreads. The old man reading from the book looks over and all the children look to see what he's looking at. The kids playing cricket stand still. The old chap on the step ladder stands holding the next bracket ready to go up and lifts a hand.

'Welcome home,' he calls and sets a chain reaction off of voices calling and arms lifting, people whistling, cheering and grinning. Women nudging each other and nodding at us.

'WELCOME BACK!'

'YOU'RE BACK THEN.'

'HELLO!'

We hear our names being said. Mr Howie. Marcy. Paula. Nick. Dave.

'WHERE'S EVERYONE ELSE?' A woman shouts from the cooking area, her voice worried that ripples out to bring the cheers down.

'Where's Clarence?'

'I can't see Cookey and Blowers...'

'Mo Mo's not with 'em...'

'ON THE SHORE,' Marcy shouts back, 'THEY'RE ALL FINE.'

'THANK GOD,' the woman bellows making the sign of the cross on her chest, 'YOU'RE ALL SAFE?'

'WE ARE,' Marcy calls out, 'THANK YOU.'

'Ah sod this,' the woman shakes her head and drops the wooden spoon to stride out from the fires towards us with her head shaking side to side. Others start after her. Men and women who stop work to start walking and jogging over. The woman is a big lady, wide hips and a jowly face flushed red from being so near the fires. An apron tied round her mid-section with a tea towel tucked hanging from the straps but she moves quickly and closes that distance towards me with the utter intent telegraphed that I am about to get very seriously hugged.

'Safe, Dave,' Marcy says quickly.

'Safe,' Paula says at the same time, moving discretely in front of Dave.

I get hugged. I get bear hugged and squashed into bosoms and smell the earthy scents of wood fire and smoke and food. I get squeezed and clasped by big arms that hold me close and truth be told it's fucking wonderful. Absolutely wonderful and I can't help but laugh as she releases me and grabs Marcy next.

'Welcome home, love,' the woman mutters, her eyes wet from

tears.

'Mr Howie, welcome back, Sir.'

'Eh?' I turn round to see a man holding his hand out beaming at me, 'cheers,' I take his hand which pumps mine.

'*Clarence it's Paula, you receiving me?*'

'*Yup, have you been taken hostage yet? Do you require rescue now or can we have a coffee first?*'

'*Come over, you've got to see this.*'

'*Are you sure?*'

'*Very. Get over here...it's incredible. Come quickly.*'

'*On our way.*'

We can't move or break out We're engulfed on all sides by people surrounding us with grinning faces and eyes that fill with tears. Men shake my hand. Women hug me and kiss my cheeks and hold me out at arm's length to tut at the bruises on my face that makes them show sad faces as they pull me back to be hugged again. I see Marcy being swarmed as men go shy and blush from that smile she gives and women shaking their heads at *just how beautiful she is.* Charlie is blown away. Literally shocked to the core as she repeats her name over and over and gets the biggest hug of all from the cook woman crying at the cut on her face and the chunk missing from her ear.

'I hope's you gave 'em what for....I really do,' the woman huffs and puffs and shakes her head then pulls Charlie in for another hug.

'We did,' Charlie mumbles from the depth of bosoms and meaty shoulders.

'I bet you did my love,' the woman says confidently, 'I'll be cooking you a big meal tonight...'

'Did you win?'

'Lilly told us what you're doing out there.'

'How many did you get?'

'Oh my god, what happened to your face?'

'It's so good to see you back.'

'Good to see you back, son,' an old man rests his hand on my shoulder and those simple words bring a lump to my throat. Nick gets patted on the back a hundred times with men telling him how lucky he is to have such a woman and women telling him to *look after that one*.

The sound of an engine revving at full speed that suddenly drops off. Shouts from the beach and the air fills with a booming voice that can only come from a very big man.

'MILLY....'

'CLARENCE!' A scream from somewhere and Clarence comes striding through the inner gate leading the rest of the team who come to a crashing halt as they take in the fresh attack we're under but there's no fighting out of this one and they get as engulfed as we did.

The cook woman grabs Mo first who tries to yelp but gets cut off and smothered. Fresh tears track her face as she kisses his cheeks and tells him what a big meal he'll have tonight and I can see the terror in Blinky's face as the cook aims for her after releasing Mo.

Meredith goes nuts. Absolutely crazy and runs out from the group as children swarm in to rub her sides and head.

'CLARENCE CLARENCE CLARENCE...'

She comes thundering over. Her face animated with joy and the expectation that everyone will get out of her way. She screams his name non-stop until he darts out with a huge pair of hands that lift her a hundred feet into the air and back down so she can clasp her arms round his bald head. I've seen Clarence fight and tear men apart with his bare hands. I've seen him pick the infected up and use them as battering rams. I've seen him whirling chains over his head that decimated their ranks and to see Clarence in berserker mode is to witness an unstoppable force but right now, as he holds Milly with tears falling freely down his cheeks I can see the motivation that drives him on. The same motivation that made Meredith get into our heads and rise up as a pack to fight and she's in heaven. Flat on her back with her paws in the air and her tail going ten to the dozen as children rub and stroke and fall all over her.

Roy is the same as us. Reginald too. Treated like soldiers coming home from conflict. Hands shook and backs patted and I watch as Reginald shies away at first but then accepts we have no choice but to take it and starts responding. Roy holds his bow which marks him out and his prowess with the weapon is talked about to him and around him. Dave though? Dave hates it. This to Dave is the same as these people having to face down a horde on their own. People touch him. People touch his shoulders and back and make him shake hands. He twitches and jerks with his eyes flicking to read body language as he assesses each threat and struggles to negate the risk.

It's Marcy that saves him, wading to his side and ushering everyone away while politely making it clear Dave does not like being touched. Her hand even finds his as she guides him behind her like a mother protecting her child. What's more remarkable is that Dave takes it from her and lets her hold his hand and shield him from something he cannot read or understand. Then she guides Mo and Blinky to her sides who form a line that holds Dave away from people who mean well but that he cannot read.

Every fight is suddenly worth it. Every bit of pain we've suffered. Every bite, scratch, punch, hit and cut is worth it. Every drop of sweat and blood. Every tear we have wept as we felt so drained we could hardly lift our weapons to fight is worth it.

This is the fort as it was meant to be. This is the fort that my sister, Curtis, Tucker, Jamie, Big Chris and so many more gave their lives for. Out there is rapidly becoming a wasteland where every street corner means danger. Where every closed door means we might have to open fire or draw knives.

How? How has this happened in two days? I have an instinct telling me and from the lack of Maddox's surly faced crews I can only guess what she had to do to achieve it.

CHAPTER THIRTY-EIGHT

'*We're on our way...*'

She waits in the police offices. Unable to move or even lower the radio from the rush of emotions bursting up through her stomach. It feels like her heart is beating so fast it will explode. They're back. Mr Howie is back. Paula is back. Nick.

She closes her eyes and draws a deep breath that quavers and trembles on being released. Her hair pulled back in a simple pony-tail. A pistol on her hip and the rifle on the table next to her.

The pressure bubbles up. The vent is needed. She can't vent though. The last two days have been frantic non-stop working every minute of every hour. Speaking to people and telling them what Mr Howie is doing out there. Making them see what the fort has to be. Translating her vision and all the time knowing they can see the coldness in her eyes.

There is a fine line between leading and tyranny. To deftly guide, suggest and show is not the same as tell and order. She suggested they didn't need armed guards inside the fort. Joan trained those she felt were able to use weapons safely and that was all that was needed. The gates should be guarded and people on the shore side but no more other than that. The tasks were given politely and along with them was the freedom in how those tasks were completed.

The hole in the wall needs fixing. Tell us what you need and we'll get it. We need a structure over the foundations so people have privacy to use the toilet. Tell us what you need and we'll get it. Or, come with us and help us get it.

We need fresh fish. We need more clothes and bedding. We need that land to be flattened so we can see what's coming towards us. We need more boats. We need plant machinery. We need tools, supplies, furniture. We need beds and chairs. We can go and get it. The houses and industrial units are right there.

She organised and thought. She planned and thought. She got them working with thought. She took time to speak and understand and see as every problem was presented. Her mind worked non-stop and was always ten steps ahead of everything that needed doing. *We do the right thing for the right reasons. Mr Howie is out there with his small group keeping those things away from us. We are safe if we work now while we have the chance. He is risking his life for us. We must give him and his team somewhere safe to come back to. They are not dangerous to us. I know because I had sex with Nick and if he is infected then so am I and do I look infected? Are my eyes red? Take my gun and shoot me if you think I am a risk to you. I am the same as you. What they have cannot harm us. Lani was different. She was not the same as them. We do the right thing for the right reasons. We put the effort in now and work hard to make ourselves safe.*

The pressure grew. The pressure of knowing what she did that night. Of shooting them down and killing them with a surgical blade or the butt of a rifle and by throwing grenades into a packed room. She took the lives of a few to save many but still, that black mark on her soul is there and it always will be. She didn't speak of it. She didn't talk of that night but only of the future of the fort and what Mr Howie is doing for them. That night was gone. *We have to move on and do the right thing for right reasons.*

Still the pressure grew. The gnawing darkness that crept through her soul tainting her mind when she suddenly found a few quiet seconds. The ease in which those thoughts and memories came back. Crawling on all fours while everyone laughed at her. Zayden pawing at her body. Her brother weeping from the hunger and cold. Soaked to the bone and left terrified without food.

It grew but she swallowed it down and stared cold with the eyes of a killer that projected an unceasing and relentless will power that touched those around her. She was ruthless in what was to be achieved and intelligent in how that was done.

In truth. She would have kept it locked down for as long as needed but the second she heard Howie's voice so it rushed up and hearing Nick's made it all the more powerful.

She has to hold it together though. She bites it down again and buys a few minutes of composure but finds herself unable to leave the offices. She wants to go out and meet them on the beach to explain everything that is being done. She hasn't sought approval from any person but she wants Paula to see it and guide her. She wants Howie to say if he thinks it is right or not.

She used to look after Billy when her mother and father went out. She was in charge of the house and responsible for his life until they came back and that feeling is the same now. Like mum and dad are coming home. Paula and Howie are back. Is the house a mess? Has Billy eaten his dinner? Has anything bad happened?

Yes. Bad things happened. Very bad things but I took care of it. I did what had to be done. Is that okay?

Did I do the right thing?

She doesn't leave the office. She cannot leave the office. Her mind whirls with a hundred thoughts all vying for attention and amongst all of that are the simple nerves of a girl about to see a boy she fancies.

'Oh god,' she blows air out and pulls her ponytail loose to shake her hair free then worries it will be too much and puts the ponytail back in. Does she smell? What if she's got body odour? Are her clothes clean? Nope, she's filthy with streaks of dirt up her arms. What about her breath? Is it bad? She has drunk a lot of coffee today. What about when Nick sees the bruises on her face? Will he even care? Maybe he doesn't think like that about her. What if he's met someone else or changed his mind? Will Paula be happy with what we've done here? What if Howie doesn't like it? What if Nick doesn't like her anymore? Why is it taking them so long to get here from the shore? Maybe Nick won't come over.

Oh no. Everyone outside is cheering and calling out. They're here. I should go out. I can't go out. I can't move. I'm might cry. Do not cry. Hold it together.

She tiptoes to the door and peeks out to see Betty hugging Howie as everyone else runs towards them and the sight holds her still. It worked. It actually worked. Everyone is happy to see them come back. Everyone in the fort spurred on by Betty to charge in to shake hands and hug them. She spots Howie and Paula at the front with Marcy and another girl with a cut face just back from them. Dave and then, oh my, Nick is there. Nick. Standing tall and smiling with humour as he gets clamped into an embrace by Betty who pulls him down to kiss his cheeks and forehead. He's laughing now. His face is alive with all the grace and beauty she remembers. Her heart hammers at the sight of them all. Her legs feeling like jelly and she grabs the doorframe to steady herself and releases the breath she was holding.

From that doorway she watches Howie getting held and his hand shook. Men pat him manfully on the back and eye his weapons with a look that gives thanks that he is doing it so they don't have to. They are armed to the teeth too. Howie with his axe on his back, his pistol on his hip, a knife in his belt and his assault rifle held in his hand. All of them the same and with pride she spots Nick has a double headed axe the same as Howie and Clarence have. He's strong and able to handle it. He can take the weight of the weapon and stands shoulder to shoulder with Howie and Clarence. She feels her heart soar and wants only to run to him but that cannot be done now. She has decorum and dignity and the coldness she manifested has served the purpose to make this happen. These people cannot see the softness come out now because Paula and Howie won't stay but she'll still be here leading everyone.

Minutes tick by until there is a roar of a great bear shouting the name of a little bear that thunders in reply and she laughs to herself hidden in the room as Milly runs full speed towards the gates. The rest come through and that feeling of pride only grows stronger. The sight of Clarence grinning as he uses his bulk to force a path to a little girl that gets hoisted into the air. Cookey and Blowers being swarmed by men and women and quite a lot of the teenage girls and young women go straight to them. Mo is swallowed up by Betty. His face plastered in kisses. Another new girl too that looks terrifyingly competent and tough who backs away in alarm. She spots Roy and Reginald and smiles at the sight of them. All of them dressed in black with combat boots on, weapons everywhere and all of them apart from Reginald have bruised faces, cuts on their arms and show the battles they have given and fought in. Their clothes are scuffed and marked and again she takes in the cut face on the new girl and that sight gives her the bravery to step from the office and walk steadily down towards them.

She laughs at seeing Meredith flat on her back with her paws poking up as children fall all over her but those children don't know what that dog does out there. The men look at the weapons held by the lads but they too don't know what it takes to hold the line. The women stare in awe at Marcy, Paula and the other two women but they don't know either. They didn't take a surgical blade to stab and stab until the blood filled the room. They didn't take the rifle and beat two boys to death. They didn't pull the pin and throw the grenade inside the room and they didn't execute one after the other.

Every one of Mr Howie's team radiate a power and an energy that makes them stand out. They're not taller than everyone else but they seem it. They're not bigger or more muscled than the men and women but again they seem to be.

She stops and waits. Her rifle slung to the back. The pistol on her hip. Her hands clasped politely in front and her head held high. Her blue eyes the eyes of a killer that took down nineteen in one night and she held the line. She did not yield but she took something tainted, broken and wrong and made it better. She gave light to the darkest of days and now she stands separate from the mass and waits with nerves fraying inside.

'NICK!' Milly is passed into his arms. Her huge smiling toothy grin wide and happy as her arms wrap round his neck and he grins with his eyes closed to hold her tight. A sensation at his leg and he looks down to see Billy standing quietly. He scoops and holds and lifts to hold one in each arm and turns as Blowers says something and reaches out to take Milly who flings herself across the gap into his arms. Nick says something to Billy who smiles and nods and says something back while Lilly fights the tears. Nick says something else and Billy lifts his arm to point. Nick turns and Lilly finds her chest going tight and the air in her throat catching.

'Nick,' Paula is there lifting Billy from him and saying something low and quiet with a smile and a nod to Lilly and the world ceases to turn. Time stops. Everything holding poised and silent. He walks out. His brown eyes the eyes of a killer that search for hers and lock on. She can't breathe or move. He is beautiful. She is beautiful. He is kindness and honour. She is decency and grace. He is strength. She is dignity. He is power. She is courage. He is a young man. She is a young woman.

He doesn't speak. He can't speak and Dave will go mad but fuck it. He drops the rifle to the floor and crosses the last distance with his hands already coming up as she goes forward and into him. His lips find hers. Her hands reach to the back of his head. His body presses in. Her eyes close and together they stand breathing each other as every inch of darkness fades from inside.

All the pain goes. All the terror and the fear that made them kill and hold the line. A kiss between a boy and a girl.

'You'll be giving my mate some privacy,' Blowers hard voice calling out into a silence neither Nick nor Lilly knew was there.

His hands cup her so gently and her own slide from his head and over his face to feel the hard ridges of his knuckles. She can feel his heart whumping in his chest and he detects the tremor running through her body. She smiles as he kisses her and it catches to make him smile in return. They laugh gently for no other reason than the joy inside.

'You're back,' she breathes into him, needing to say something to burn some of the nervous energy bursting inside of her.

'Yes,' his voice quavers soft and gentle, 'I...'

She looks at him, her eyes searching his.

'Nothing...' he says, his shyness creeping back in.

'Say it.'

'I missed you.'

She sinks into him and feels a warmth inside that melts the icy coldness, 'I missed you too.'

'Don't you be hogging her now,' A deep rumble as Nick eases back so Clarence can lean down to draw her into the gentle arms of a gorilla, 'Lilly, you okay love?'

'I'm fine,' she says as he pulls back to glance at the bruises on her face.

'Lilly,' Paula sweeps in and if the world was okay when she held Nick so it is even more now. Paula grabs the girl in a fierce hug with tears spilling from her eyes and holds her like a mother holds a daughter. Paula who radiates a protective energy that surges into Lilly who wraps her arms round the woman and finds her chest heaving with sobs. 'I'm proud of you,' Paula whispers, 'I am so proud of you.'

'I killed them, Paula,' Lilly whispers back, a voice so low and filled with pain that pushes back up into her heart.

'Doesn't matter,' Paula says, her voice as hard as anything as Lilly has ever heard, 'you're safe. That's all that matters...'

'I killed all of them...'

'Good,' Paula growls with the venom of a woman that protects her pack with every beat of her heart, 'you listen to me, Lilly. You did what had to be done...'

'I don't want them to see me cry...'

'Howie, clear this area. We'll take Lilly inside the office for some privacy.'

'On it, lads.'

'Come on,' Paula guides smoothly round so they can walk side by side with everyone else behind, 'they can't see you,' Paula whispers, 'Marcy, other side.'

'Right here,' Marcy pushes gently into Lilly's other side and for all the world to see it is three women walking side by side to have a chat in the police offices. Charlie goes ahead. Discretely going into the room to check it's all clear. A nod to Paula and Lilly goes first without realising the rest of team move closely behind with a shield that protects the view.

They file into the rooms, edging deeper to make room until the blast damaged door is closed.

'Everyone is in here,' Paula says quietly, 'want me to tell them to go?'

'No no,' Lilly draws a deep steadying breath, 'honestly, I am sorry. I just...' She flounders with a mistaken instinct that crying now makes her look immature and young.

'Oh god,' Paula says, pulling her back in, 'I've seen every one of this lot cry like babies.'

'Fact' Cookey says gently, 'hey, Lilly.'

'Hi Cookey.'

'Lilly.'

'Blowers.'

'Who hurt your face?' Blinky asks without preamble but with a look of absolute certainty that whoever did it will get the shit kicked out of them. She doesn't know Lilly but she can see the way everyone is reacting to her and she saw Nick kissing her. She's heard about Lilly so that means she's the missus of one of the team and that counts. So fuck 'em. They'll get the shit beaten out of them for that.

'Crews?' Howie asks. His tone so soft yet so commanding that she pulls gently from Paula to look into the dark brooding eyes that will inflict harm on whoever has hurt one of his. She senses the ripple going round the room. The way Blowers lifts his chin. Mo cocking his head over as his eyes narrow. Clarence's nostrils flaring and lower down a deep growl rolls round the room as Meredith picks up on the sudden change of mood. Nick pulses with rage. His fists clenching at his sides. The girl with the cut face even has that look and Lilly takes it in with the sudden knowledge that she did the right thing. It's what any of these would have done but worse, they wouldn't have stopped at nineteen. They would have finished all thirty and then slept soundly after.

'They're dead,' Lilly says, finding voice to speak of the thing that has not been discussed since that night.

'They wanna be dead,' Blowers mutters.

'All of them?' Nick asks, his rage held ready.

'Most,' Lilly says, 'I killed nineteen. There were thirty remaining when you left the fort.'

'Fuck,' Cookey whispers, 'good skills, Lilly.'

'You got nineteen?' Blinky asks, clearly taken aback that someone who speaks like Charlie but isn't a hockey player can do something like that, 'that's fucking awesome.'

'They weren't infected,' Lilly says, not knowing if the strange girl who keeps blinking knows who the crews are.

'So,' Blinky shrugs, 'fuck 'em.'

'Maddox?' Howie asks.

'He's sick. He passed out just after you left and was in a coma... that's er, well, that is when it went all went rather wrong.'

Blinky blinks and looks at Charlie, 'she related to you, Charlie?'

'No, Blinky she just speaks properly.'

'Tell you what,' Paula says, exerting total and complete control with those few words, 'we'll make some drinks and if you want, and only if you want, you can tell us what happened.'

'Coffee,' Howie blurts.

'Oh I have something,' Lilly says quickly, 'er, would you excuse me for a moment? Nick, I may I need your help if I may?'

'You sure you ain't sisters?' Blinky asks with a suspicious glance at Charlie.

'Could be,' Cookey says, 'Dave's mum was on the beach.'

'She was not my mother.'

'I thought you were an orphan,' Howie says.

'I was.'

'She might be then. Never know.'

'He was joking, Dave,' Marcy says hitting Howie on the shoulder, 'she isn't your mother, Dave.'

'I think Reggie fancied her,' Cookey says.

'I beg your pardon! I did not such thing. I...well, I never...'

'He's joking too, Reggie,' Marcy groans adding a hit to Cookey's shoulder into her list of shoulders to be hit.

'Anyway,' Cookey announces with a grin, 'you're all being very rude. Lilly, this is Blinky. Blinky, this is Lilly.'

'I know,' Blinky says.

'Nice to meet you, Blinky,' Lilly says politely.

'I blink a lot,' Blinky says still staring suspiciously between Lilly and Charlie.

'Okay,' Lilly says.

'And this beautiful woman is Charlie,' Cookey says, 'I saw her bum this morning and it's got a tattoo of...ow!'

'Don't keep telling everyone,' Charlie says, 'hello, Lilly, I'm, Charlie.'

'Hello, Charlie. It's nice to meet you.'

'And you.'

'They could be sisters,' Blowers remarks.

'Just because two people speak in a manner that is right and correct it does not mean you have to assume they are related,' Reginald says.

'Reggie must be their uncle,' Blowers says.

'Uncle Reg!'

'Do not call me Reg,' Reginald glares at Cookey and the world settles back as Lilly remembers them exactly as they are. Unfussed, unfazed and still pissing about.

'Right well, yes I have something. Nick, if I may borrow you please,' Lilly says heading down into the corridor that leads to the back rooms. Nick follows behind her with his wry smile wondering what it is she wants to show him.

She turns the corner and stops. He turns the corner and stops. She smiles. He smiles.

'You coming back?' Cookey shouts after a few minutes of patient silence.

'Yep,' Nick breaks from the embrace, his lips leaving Lilly's who smiles wide and happy and sighs deeply.

'I have something,' Lilly says softly, taking him by the hand to lead him into a back room where she stops. He stops. She smiles. He smiles.

'Well?' Cookey shouts after another couple of minutes of patient silence.

'Coming,' Lilly calls out.

'What is it?' Nick asks, his head swimming from being lost at sea in Lilly's eyes and lips and hands and arms.

'Just here,' Lilly says, stepping away to reveal a table behind her.

'Oh wow,' Nick laughs, 'The Boss will fucking...shit sorry, I mean, he'll love you...'

'I missed your swearing.'

'Yeah?'

'Yes.'

'Fuck me, we'll send a search party down in a minute.'

'I have a small generator up there but the connections are all different so I wasn't sure how to get the power supply...'

'Easy,' Nick says, lifting the object up.

'And finally,' Cookey laughs as Lilly comes back in looking a little sheepish with Nick behind her grinning from ear to ear.

'Oh fuck,' Howie says getting quickly up from his chair, 'is that a coffee machine?'

'It is,' Nick says.

'Power?' Howie asks, hardly daring to believe it.

'I have a small generator here,' Lilly says, pointing towards the door and the small fuel run machine on the floor, 'I remembered how much you all like coffee.'

'What is it?' Howie asks rushing to Nick, 'Tassimo! Fuck me, it's a Tassimo...an actual fucking Tassimo...have you got the pod things? Lilly, I don't know what to say...'

'Jesus,' Marcy says rolling her eyes, 'you've just made a friend for life there, Lilly.'

'Pea found it in one of the houses,' Lilly explains.

'I love Pea,' Howie says.

'Better not,' Marcy says.

'Right,' Howie says firmly, 'Roy and Nick will splice shit to get power running. Everyone else find cups and sugar...'

'No,' Paula calls out as everyone starts moving, 'sit down, you'll bloody break everything. Nick and Roy will get the machine working. Cookey, you're still on brew duty so get the cups ready.'

Boxes of coffee pods are opened and cups made ready as Nick and Roy cut wires to splice shit and get the power from the generator into the coffee machine that comes to life with a glowing light. Coffee is made. Proper coffee that fills the room with scent. Cappuccinos, Lattes and Americanos poured hot and fresh into mugs that get loaded with sugar as the room fills with conversation and the clanking of weapons being rested on tables with chairs scraping back.

Then it's done and they sit with the first cups of coffee of the day and drink the first sips in a silence ordered by a finger held up by Howie. Marcy tuts again. Paula rolls her eyes, Charlie grins at Lilly who smiles back.

'Ah,' Howie says contentedly, 'righto, so what happened then?'

Now it's not so hard to talk about. The power of it has gone. They killed over ten thousand yesterday and another two hundred today and they show the marks of those fights clear on their bodies. She killed nineteen but the reason was the same. The purpose was the same. To do the right thing for the right reasons and she held the line.

'Maddox passed out from being tasered...' Lilly begins and it flows out. A story told that is listened to intently. Chairs are pushed back so feet can rest on the table corners. Others lean forward to rest elbows and drink coffee. Meredith noses the door open and goes outside to find Milly and Billy and the room fills with the sound of hammering and sawing and voices calling out. With Paula at her side tutting and shaking her head at the right times, and leaning to rub her arm or hand as she tells of how she fought back. She doesn't leave anything out either but the whole of it in every seedy sordid detail.

Howie watches Mo for reaction. Mo grew up with the people Lilly killed but Mo just shows disgust and looks down with eyes seething in fury at what they did. His head shaking at Sierra, Skyla, Zayden and the others.

She trails off feeling a strange calm settling inside. Clarence exhales noisily and nods, 'did the right thing,' he says deeply, 'without doubt, Lilly. Well done.'

'Definitely,' Blowers says, sensing the need to give affirmation for her actions, 'any one of us would have done the same...'

'We wouldn't,' Mo says, bringing every pair of eyes to him, 'we would have done all of 'em and not stopped at nineteen.'

'Probably,' Blowers says.

'Listen yeah,' Mo says, 'if you's see any of them come near me you stop 'em or...'

'Done,' Cookey says, nodding at him.

'Same with Mads,' Mo says, his intent obvious, 'best be keeping him away from me.'

'Speaking of which,' Howie says, 'he's in the hospital?'

'He is,' Lilly replies, 'Lenski has been with him the whole time.'

'I see,' Howie says, his face remaining passive as he exchanges a glance with Clarence, 'but he knows right?'

'He knows,' Lilly says, 'the doctors brought him round long enough for me to tell him but unfortunately he reacted to the medications and slipped back into the coma. They said they cannot risk bringing him out it again due to the medications they used the first time...'

'Dont was it?' Roy asked.

'I believe so, yes,' Lilly replies.

'Dont?' Paula asks.

'Coma cocktail,' Roy says, 'very controversial.'

'Doc,' Howie coughs into his hand.

'Not a doctor,' Roy says stiffly.

'May I ask how it was for you?' Lilly asks, not knowing if the protocols allow for her to reciprocate the request for information.

A brief silence of introspection that stretches in the room until Cookey clears his throat and leans back with his hands behind his head, 'I shall give you the er...oh fuck, what's the word for a shorter description of...'

'Abridged,' Charlie, Reginald and Lilly say together.

'Fuck me they are related,' Howie says with a laugh.

'Abridged,' Cookey says, 'I'll give the abridged version...'

'This'll be brilliant,' Blowers mutters.

'Can I shoot myself?' Blinky asks.

'Right well, where do we begin...so,' Cookey says looking over the table at Lilly smiling then down to see his audience are all primed and expectant, 'we left the fort and slept in a house on the shore. Then we got up and drove about looking for food. We got to a village, everyone split up and we got attacked while Paula and Roy were having sex and Mr Howie and Marcy were probably trying to have sex and the rest of us were stuffing ourselves stupid. We all ran about for a bit. I puked, Blowers puked...I think Nick puked then we found a mansion house with the women's England hockey team in it and met Charlie and Blinky. It rained. Charlie looked fit in the rain and I think she fell in love with me at that point,' he pauses at the snort of laughter from Charlie. 'Meanwhile, Paula and Roy were still having sex and Jimmy Carr was taking a shit on Mr Howie's chin. Then we got all got back together and Mr Howie did his weird thing that scared all the zombies. We had a big scrap. Went shopping and taught Mo how to shave and found a hotel and went to bed. The next day we got up. Reginald turned into a cross between that ginger bloke from Mission Impossible and Morpheus from the Matrix and played a game of draughts or Snakes and Ladders with the infection. During that time, Nick got bit and we all cried when we figured he was immune then Charlie and Reggie made us all feel stupid by pointing out we haven't been wearing face masks and have probably been drinking zombie blood everyday so therefore we are all probably immune which cheered us up quite a bit. Er...then we had some more scraps. Clarence turned into a helicopter with some chains...Marcy and Mr Howie were flirting like so badly all day and she said *don't die today Mr Howie* so of course we all took the piss. Then we got into a town and found ten thousand of the fuckers waiting for us. We had another scrap and er...' the humour leaves his eyes sudden and marked as Lilly detects something shared that still holds pain, 'something happened that wasn't cool, not cool at all...'

'No,' Blowers says darkly.

'Not cool,' Marcy whispers.

'But,' Cookey says, pulling his smile back on, 'Meredith got in our heads and gave us all a kick up the arse and we kicked the shit out of them. Charlie stole a horse from a scientist who was actually there when the infection thing was invented...Nick and Mo blew up another petrol station and we nicked an old bus and went back to our hotel to have a jolly good sleep while Mr Howie and Marcy did the funky chicken in the back of the Saxon...'

'How the fuck...' Howie says.

'Walls have ears, Mr Howie,' Cookey grins, 'then we got up, Mo got Dave trained. The infection got in the water and ate our scientist and me and Charlie had a naked wrestle while she was trying to pull my towel off and I was like *no no Charlie I am not having sex with you right now* but I did see the tattoo on her arse. Er then we ran about for a bit more so Blowers could play with some bitten of willies that he found and we did that until Charlie picked a fight with two hundred of them on her own and got bit and found out she was immune and we all cheered again and...and I think that's about it.'

'Outstanding,' Clarence booms as the rest of us cheer and clap while Cookey grins round then stands up and bows.

'I thank you,' he says, 'most of that was true,' he adds to Lilly laughing hard at his perfect delivery. He shields his hand and mock whispers, 'the bit about Blowers playing with willies was true and I did see Charlie's bum.'

'Mate,' Blowers says, bent double on the seat, 'that was brilliant.'

'Such a twat,' Nick says between laughs.

'He missed a bit though,' Marcy says, wiping her own eyes and looking at Lilly, 'when Charlie picked the fight with two hundred? Should have seen Cookey in the Saxon...'

'Oh no, no no,' Cookey says quickly.

'He was going nuts' Blowers says with malicious delight, 'what did you say, Cookey?'

'Nothing,' Cookey shouts, 'Charlie I didn't do anything they say I did...'

'What?' Charlie asks still laughing while wincing at the dull pain in the cut on her face from laughing so much.

'*I will come to you…*' Marcy says with mock passion, '*Hold on Charlie…I will come to you…*'

'Oh fuck off,' Cookey says, grinning despite the blush in his cheeks.

'That was you?' Charlie asks, remembering the moment the hive mind descended as she gave ground into the doorway.

'No!' Cookey exclaims.

'So was,' Mo laughs, 'you was going nuts, bruv.'

'Bruv innit,' Cookey quips.

'You get me yeah?' Mo quips back taking the piss out of his own accent.

'He was out…' Blowers stops to laugh at seeing Cookey in a rare state of discomfort, 'he was out the Saxon before it even stopped… Mr Howie had to run after him yelling at him to stop…'

'Not true,' Cookey says.

'Bloody was,' Howie laughs, 'I was shouting *stop you bloody idiot…*'

'Roy and Dave both had to cover him,' Nick adds, laughing hard at the memory, 'I've never seen Roy move so bloody fast.'

'I had arrows going this close to my head,' Howie says holding his thumb and finger a few millimetres apart, 'and I swear Dave shot one between my legs.'

Charlie laughs hard, her eyes misting as she leans over the table to grab Cookey's hand, 'thank you…'

'*I will come to you Charlie…*' Marcy calls out passionately.

'Ah bollocks,' Cookey says waving his hand, 'I'd do the same for anyone.'

'*I will come to you Blowers…*' Marcy calls out which just sets them off again.

Lilly laughs hard. She can't help it. The visual imagery of Cookey running with Howie chasing after him is too much. All of it and the abstract notion of Jimmy Carr having a poo on Mr

Howie is too much. She drops her head to wipe her eyes and feels the days of tension drop instantly away.

'And just for the record,' Charlie says, pausing to get her voice back under control despite the hawing braying laugh, 'I most certainly did not pick a fight with two hundred...'

'You bloody did!' Howie bursts out laughing that sets everyone off again, 'Paula had already called you back.'

'*I will come to you Charlie my love...*' Marcy calls out again, clasping her hands to her chest.

'*Don't die today Charlie...*' Blowers calls out.

'Oh get bent,' Cookey gives up and sits back laughing at the comments and pulling a face to Lilly over the table. 'So yeah, quiet couple of days really,' he adds and looks round, 'then we get back and find you've done all this...fucking legend or what?'

'Yes,' Paula says still laughing as she pushes her arm round Lilly's shoulders, 'thank you, Lilly,' she adds with kiss to the girl's cheek.

'Thank you, Lilly,' Marcy says, leaning round Paula to rub Lilly's arm.

'To Lilly,' Clarence calls out lifting his coffee mug.

'To Lilly!' Blowers joins in as the words get taken up with coffee mugs lifted.

She smiles and takes the compliment, blushing delicately but lifting her own mug in response. 'To you.'

'Right,' Paula says as the noise settles down.

'Oh no,' Howie groans, 'she's organising.'

'Someone has to do it, you lot would be wearing each other's underpants otherwise.'

'Blowers...'

'Yes, Cookey,' Paula cuts him off, 'we know Blowers likes wearing other people's pants.'

'I do not,' Blowers retorts.

'So,' Paula says, looking round with a glare that settles the room, 'I want to have a look around with Lilly, if that's okay with you?'

'Of course,' Lilly says quickly.

'Charlie,' Paula says pointing at her, 'to the doctors and get your wounds checked. Someone needs to see what state Maddox is in.'

'I'll do that,' Howie says.

'Roy, sorry, love but you're now the designated medic so get what you need from the hospital while we're here.'

'I'm not a doctor.'

'You are now, you might as well go with Charlie,' Paula says, 'are we sleeping here or in the house tonight?'

'House?' Lilly asks.

'We thought we'd stay in one of the houses on the bay tonight,' Paula says, 'we've got the horse and the vehicles and, well, some of the lads have bad...'

'I'm happy with it now,' Blowers cuts in

'Okay,' Paula says, looking round, 'but we do have Jess and the vehicles so...'

'We'll take the house,' Howie says, 'we can move quickly then if anything happens.'

'That okay with you, Lilly?' Marcy asks.

'Of course,' Lilly says.

'Weapons sorted, refill the ammunition from the stores, get our kit sorted and then downtime,' Paula says, 'everyone happy?'

'Where we eating?' Clarence asks.

'Might as well eat over here then head back to the house to sleep,' Howie says, 'okay with you, Lilly?'

'This is your fort, Mr Howie. You do not have to ask me...'

'Oh no,' Howie says, smiling as he cuts her off, 'your fort, your rules. We abide by what you say.'

'Okay,' she concedes, 'then I think it would be better for you to eat here and let the people talk and meet you. They don't know you like I do and I think it would serve a purpose.'

'We'll eat here then,' Paula says and points another two fingers at Cookey and Blinky, 'best behaviour you two.'

'Yes, Miss,' Blinky says.

'Weapons?' Howie asks.

'There are no weapons in the fort,' Lilly says, 'only the guards at the front and on the munitions store. However, that really is something you should decide.'

'Mohammed and I will retain sidearms and knives,' Dave says.

'We'll stay armed,' Howie says, 'rifles on, pistols holstered but have spare magazines ready. You can leave axes and hand weapons in here if you want.'

'One more thing,' Paula says, dropping her voice as she looks to the door to make sure no one can hear them, 'we might be immune but we don't advertise that fact. If anyone asks just change the subject or say you don't know. If they persist then send them to me or Howie...'

'Not me,' Howie says, 'you and Marcy can deal with that one.'

'Send them to me or Marcy then,' Paula says, 'we don't know what we have or what we are so it's best left for now. Everyone understand? Right, good. Now, Lilly. I would love the guided tour...'

CHAPTER THIRTY-NINE

It feels so strange. Like returning to your childhood home. You remember the cupboards being big and dark and deep whereas they are just normal sized cupboards. Your parents' bedroom was a place of wonder and mystery. It's just another room but there's still a feeling inside. Like a disjointed sensation of seeing something through the eyes of a child and an adult at the same time.

It's like that now. Everywhere I look has a memory and the emotions from those memories are still attached but the actual place is completely different now. I could list each and every memory, who it involved, what I was doing, what the person in the memory was doing, how I felt and every emotion I felt then and now. But what's the point?

Did we really mass inside those gates and make ready to charge out onto the flatlands that aren't there anymore? Did we fire those cannons from the top and wait for Nick to fire the last shot from the GPMG?

The fort was lost to us, to our group. In our hearts I mean. What it stood for no longer held resonance for us. We'd given up on it with our hearts and minds to let someone else worry about it and by doing that, we realised that our place is not to stay within these walls but to go out and play the biggest game of chess that has ever been played.

Now though? Well I'm buggered if I know. It looks and feels like a completely different place and like I thought earlier, it's the fort but as the fort should always have been.

There are new people arriving all the time and they're dealt with the same way my sister and Sergeant Hopewell dealt with them. Names taken, details recorded. What skills do you have? They get checked medically then absorbed and I have the fortune to be standing outside the offices smoking when a new group are shown in by Sam and Pea and I see the expressions on their faces.

We had something to compare to so the wonder for us was in that comparison to what we left behind. What the newcomers see is every whispered hope coming true. They've walked, trudged, hidden, walked more, taken vehicles and put their lives at risk to reach this point. Then they step through the gates and see friendly faces smiling at them. They smell food being cooked over open fires and see children being cared for. They see a huge open place with strong walls. They see order and security and every mile of the journeys they have taken plays out on their faces. Some simply stand and stare. Others break down to weep on the ground with husbands and wives hugging children close to their breast.

We work fast as the sky starts to fade and the first tendrils of the blanket of night starts to ease into the sky. Our weapons are cleaned and made ready then we get more crates of ammunition from the stores to be stacked ready to be taken over to the vehicles. Everyone gets a pistol now and those too are checked and made ready. Axes and knives are given new blades and every buckle, strap and shoe lace is checked.

Charlie goes to the doctors and gets the all clear. Her ear will always have a chunk missing and her face will always have a ragged scar but Roy did everything that could be done at the scene. Roy, for his turn, gets everything checked. None of his bruises or scrapes from the fights but the lumps in his backs, legs, arms, chest and mouth. He gets them to check his blood sugar, blood pressure and his weight and even pisses in a pot and asks them if the colour is okay. In the end they load up him with bandages, as much medications as he can carry and a new bright red medic rucksack just to get rid of him.

Charlie then suggests Cookey should get his back checked which just reminds us that he also got wounded this morning. He refuses on the basis that it was those doctors that *fucked with Lani* and he'd rather have Roy look at him. Roy does the whole *not a doctor* thing but gets nagged by Paula and finally has a look. Cookey's back is a mess and a lot worse than any of us realised with huge rakes from shoulder to arse that have shredded the skin apart. Big deep bites too and he gets a kiss from Paula and Marcy for being so gallant. Cookey, as with Charlie, refuses any pain relief medication and I understand why. It's not bravado or a false sense of heroism but the fact is that although we all look bashed to shit, it doesn't really hurt that much. We're tender in spots but nothing like we should be. People who look like us should be laid up in beds eating grapes and watching crap telly but we're mostly fine. We can't even question it that much as we've been over the same subject a thousand times and end at the same place which is that we don't know anything.

People come and go from the offices. Sam and Pea join us for a coffee with Lilly. An old fellow called Alf pops by, nods at everyone and wanders off again. Charlie explains her problem with the axe on horseback and says it's the right weapon but the handling is difficult without a tether. Lilly explains they have new axes in the fort, at which point Marcy leads Charlie off to smile and make womanly eyes at the blokes building the structure. They come back ten minutes later with a new axe that has been drilled through the shaft with a made to measure leather wrist strap fitted.

Roy restrings his bow. Reginald sorts his papers out and everyone from the shore comes back, and as they do so the energy and atmosphere changes within the fort. Like they mark the end of the working day as the shore side people stop to speak and chat with the fort workers.

The fires in the cooking area grow bigger and brighter. The smells coming from them become richer and we start turning our heads to sniff the air and comment at the aromas. Dave's mum, otherwise known as Joan, comes bustling in and immediately gets questioned by Dave as to how and why she has a rifle chest strap. She explains she made it herself last night and it takes five minutes with a standard strap and a needle and thread. She then gets inundated with requests so everyone can have a chest strap instead of having *to sling the bloody things all the time.*

As the last of the day fades and the shadows become deeper so a myriad of solar lanterns and string lights start flickering on. The inside of the walls strung with long lines of gaudy multi-coloured lights. The brackets Alf was fitting now hold lanterns that give gentle glows. More strings of light wrapped round the tent legs come on and the whole of the place is bathed in a weird carnival glow, like a town centre at Christmas. It ain't perfect, not by a long stretch but fuck me, Lilly has done so much in just two days.

A short time later and when the sky is an inky black over our heads we get summoned to dinner. I take the front with Paula and Lilly which seems only fitting and we lead the others out into the fort now filled with figures all gathered waiting patiently.

'No tables or chairs yet I'm afraid,' Lilly says, 'we are working on a rota system but that has yet to be done.'

'Children eat first,' Sam explains, 'so we can make sure are actually eating proper food.'

'And they sleep inside the rooms in the walls,' Pea adds, pointing out the now softly illuminated rooms all with doors propped open. 'Parents with children can stay in there with them but the priority for bed space are the young and the elderly. We're fine at the moment but I don't think it will take long to start filling up.'

'Hold your bloody horses,' Betty's voice booms out, 'Mr 'Owie and his lot are eating first they are. Been out there keeping the buggers back from here so they're having a decent meal they are.'

I groan inwardly and for a second I worry something like will only cause friction but these days are not the same as before. Everyone concedes the point and they part like the Red Sea to let us pass through.

'Thanks,' I say to the first people I pass.

'Much appreciated,' Clarence says behind me and so it goes down our line with every one of us paying respect for the privilege of eating first.

I stop at the end of the service table and get handed a plate by a man with deep blue eyes framed in a craggy face with salt and pepper hair.

'Just a cook again.'

'Just a cook,' he says with a smile as he hands out a set of cutlery.

'Lilly,' I turn to nod at her to come over, 'this is Kyle.'

'It is very nice to meet you, Kyle,' she says politely, leaning over the table to shake hands.

'And you, Lilly,' Kyle says.

'Hey Lilly, you should get dissolved...what? Why's everyone laughing? He did it this morning for us...'

'Come and join us,' I say to Kyle.

'Ach, I'll be working here, Mr Howie.'

'Howie,' I say quickly, 'Mr Howie isn't right coming from you.'

'Howie,' he says with a kind smile.

'Seriously, grab a plate and eat with us.'

'I will,' he says and turns to Paula, 'plate for you, Paula.'

'Thanks, Kyle. Listen, it was really helpful today having you drive Roy's van.'

'It was nothing,' he says as he passes a plate over to Lilly.

'Well,' Paula says, 'if you ever fancy learning how to load magazines, strip a general purpose machine gun, put new blades on axes, saddle a horse and feed Roy arrows when he's firing while making Reginald's peppermint tea then we might have an opening.'

'Ach, I'm too old to be running about the countryside. Blinky, are you taking the plate now or letting an old man wave it about?'

'Huh? Oh sorry, Kyle.'

'Mr Owie, hold your plate out me love, go on then have a big heap of that,' Betty says spooning a heaped gooey mess on my plate that smells bloody lovely.

'Bottle of water, Mr Howie?' Another woman asks, holding a bottle over the serving table.

'Wow, thank you,' I say and step away with a plate seriously loaded with food. I wait for a second for Paula and head off away towards the lights of the tents.

'Anywhere?' Paula asks, turning back to wait for Lilly.

'Wherever you like,' Lilly says.

'This'll do,' I say and lower myself down to rest my plate on the ground.

The rest come ambling over to drop down to rest plates on laps or sit cross legged with their plates on the ground in front. Clarence simply holds his one handed and tucks in with his fork attacking the heaped mountain of food on his plate.

'This is bloody lovely,' I tell Marcy as she lowers down next to me.

'Good, eat up so you have lots of energy for later.'

'What?' I cough, almost choking on a mouthful of food.

'If you're not too exhausted that is,' she says with that disarming smile, 'Lilly, this is really nice,' she says as I go bright red and look round to see if anyone heard her.

We sit without order and with gaps between us. Lilly and Nick side by side and I watch as Sam, Pea and Joan all head for her and watch the dynamics of relationships play out. The way people are drawn to others like how some have obviously got to know Pea over the last day or so and sit near her while others head for Sam or Joan.

Very few go directly to Lilly. She is polite but she does retain a sort of distant coldness to anyone other than my lot or Pea, Sam and Joan. That's a good thing too. She projects an authority and isn't allowing over familiarity to weaken it down. I don't have that problem with my lot but then our dynamics are completely different and I didn't have to kill nineteen armed people to take control.

'If you'll excuse me,' Lilly says after finishing her food. She rises to her feet just using the power of her legs in one smooth surge of strength that looks so effortless it makes me stop and stare with the fork hovering near my mouth. 'I'm going to say goodnight to Billy,' she adds in that polite tone.

'Need a hand?' Nick asks.

'That would be lovely,' Lilly says. Bathed in the firelight behind her and I watch closely with eyes fixed and unblinking. Nick wolfs the last of his food down and rises with the same surge of strength using just his legs to propel himself upright. I blink, close my eyes and look again as they walk away then pull my eyes back to see Clarence also turning to watch her go. When he looks back we share a glance loaded with meaning.

'See that?' Paula asks quietly.

'I did,' I reply casually and look back down at my plate.

'Maybe it wasn't that bad,' Marcy says.

'Pea?' Paula calls out gently, 'borrow you for a minute?'

'Yeah sure,' Pea says scooting closer as Clarence discretely moves in.

'We were just wondering,' Paula says conversationally, 'how bad was the assault that Lilly got?'

'Bloody awful,' Pea says quickly. Her face morphing with the emotion of the memory. 'Kicking, punching...they hit her with the machine gun and...no it was bloody horrible.'

'What's that?' Sam asks, leaning back to look at Pea

'They were just asking about the beating Lilly got,' Pea says.

'Fucking bastards,' Sam says darkly, 'I don't know how she's walking around to be honest. I wouldn't be after getting a shooing like that…that's for sure.'

'You seen her legs?' I ask, which earns me a hard glance from Sam and a concerned look from Pea.

'Are they bruised too?' Paula asks quickly, 'Howie thought she was limping earlier. Has she seen a doctor?'

'Oh right,' Sam says as the protectiveness eases back a notch, 'no I haven't seen them, you Pea?'

'Nope,' Pea says, 'and no, I don't think she has seen a doctor. You thought she was limping, Mr Howie?'

'Maybe, probably just a dead leg or something,' I say.

'She got up alright just then,' Sam says.

'Yeah,' I say with a smile, 'yes she did…so must have been er… I'm probably worrying too much.'

'No no,' Pea says, 'it's nice that you worry about her.'

'Did she get hit in the legs though?' Marcy asks. A master of casual conversation and from her it's just idle chit chat with no intent behind it and both Paula and I slide back a fraction to signal we want her to keep going.

'That bitch Skyla was kicking her thighs,' Sam says, 'and her ribs. You know I'm bloody amazed she didn't break any bones.'

Marcy pulls a face and tuts, 'that's awful, so was it just once or?'

'No,' Sam says with a scowl, 'they kept going for her all day then they dragged her into the office and beat the shit out of her in there too.'

'God,' Marcy sighs, 'she must have been in bits the next day.'

'Didn't show it,' Pea says, 'she was up first and working all day. The rest of us were blood knackered. We kept thinking she'll slow down or stop in a minute but she didn't. Just kept going. Honestly, the young have so much energy.'

I look past them to Roy who is eating his food but clearly listening to the conversation and bless him if he doesn't give me a faint nod when he looks up, which Joan immediately clocks and tilts her head over questioningly.

I eat my food and think thoughts as Paula eats her food and thinks thoughts. Both of us look further down to the lads now surrounded by people drawn to their energy and wide smiles and more than a few young women are edging closer to Blowers, Cookey and Mo too, which makes me smile warmly. We ran miles today and yesterday we fought non-stop and no doubt tomorrow morning we'll wake up without pain and full of energy again.

I watch Charlie eating. A girl with a cut like that and a chunk of her ear bitten off should be on morphine in a hospital bed but her jaws masticate without any sign that it causes her pain.

'Fuck it,' I mutter, 'she needs to know,' I go to rise but find a hand on my shoulder.

'Later,' Paula mouths, 'she should come over to the house with us tonight.'

'You know what would be lovely,' Marcy says, leaning forward as though to share gossip with Pea and Sam, 'if Lilly could stay with us in the house tonight. Think she'll go for it?'

Fuck me that woman has the hearing of a bat. She is a bat. An actual fucking bat with sonar in her head.

'How the fuck?' Paula mouths at me. I shrug and finish my food while ignoring the glare coming from Joan.

'Yeah?' Marcy smiles, 'let her have some time with Nick and the lads, they've missed her so much. Honesty, they're all mad about her and it would be good for her to have some time with Charlie too. I think they'll have a lot in common.'

It's a done deal. You try and not be swayed or talked into something by Marcy and see how far you get. She's not only Batwoman but also a fucking Jedi Master at conversation. She should have sorted out all that crap in the Middle East. She'd be smiling and cocking her head over while all the warring sides just nodded dumbly and signed bits of paper promising never to do anything naughty again.

The feeling of pressure comes back and we start getting ready to go with Paula passing a message of nods to Blowers who gets his lot up and ready, much to the displeasure of a young woman with dark hair making eyes at Cookey who, it appears, is blissfully unaware as he tells everyone how we found a penis on the floor today. He actually tells them too. He tells the penis story but with enough changes for it not to be quite so gruesome and just bloody funny. Even Blowers cracks up at the imitation of himself waving it about while screaming. We were all there and we saw it but listening to Cookey has us lot also laughing. His tone, his delivery and his own self-effacing smile all working in perfect harmony. Of course, for the purposes of the story the penis is a lot bigger and covered in hair as it gets thrown in fright from Nick to Mo to Blinky and round to everyone, with Cookey doing impressions of us all as he goes.

'We need to make a move,' Paula says as he reaches the natural end of the story. I watch the lads start getting up and think about telling them they can stay a bit longer. They need this time with people their own age with nice women smiling and making eyes at them and a young chap edging closer to Blinky who just glares at him suspiciously. I don't though. We've got tomorrow and no immediate plans to rush off, unless we're attacked by zombies in fighter jets of course, which will no doubt happen as soon I think about getting coffee in the morning.

'What's going on?' Joan seeks me out as the plates and cutlery are taken back to the serving tables and the lads get ready to go.

'Going on?' I ask her and get a shrewd look in return.

'Don't fart about with me, Mr Howie,' she says in that brisk clipped way. A pistol on each hip and her rifle held secure across her chest.

'How do you that?' I ask her, nodding at the chest strap.

'Ordinary strap and a needle a thread,' she replies without blinking, 'now what's going on?'

'I don't know you.'

'I killed a handful of children for Lilly two days ago,' she fires back, 'her welfare is my primary concern so stop dithering and stalling and spit it out.'

'Lilly is healing faster than she should.'

'She has what you have.' A statement not a question.

'Yes but...'

'She has told everyone she had sex with Nick...' I blink at an old lady using the word sex but she pushes on without hesitation. 'Yes she had admitted to me that she has not actually had sex with Nick but I gather they have kissed.'

'I don't think it passes like that,' I say and look down to the already healing cuts on my hands made by Dave as we bled into those bitten. Does it work like that? It can't. It's not possible. We'd just have to kiss everyone here and they'd all be immune and although I don't know much I know sure as shit it can't be that simple.

'I see,' Joan says, 'and you are going to tell her.'

'I think we should,' I say quietly.

'Good. Then tell her straight and don't dilly dally. I can't abide dilly dallying, Mr Howie.'

'Okay,' I say passively, 'but maybe it's best we don't draw attention to the fact she is healing faster than she should be.'

'Are you asking me not to repeat this conversation? If you are then say you are and don't dither...'

'Yes I am asking that.'

'Good. Fine. I will bid you goodnight then, Mr Howie.'

'Joan,' I say as she goes to walk off, 'those chest straps, are they hard to make?'

'How many do you want?'

Bloody hell, she actually could be Dave's mum, 'they'd be very handy...'

'Yes,' she huffs, 'they are very handy. How many do you want? One each? How many of you? Thirteen? I'll have them ready in the morning. Night, Mr Howie.'

'Er yeah, cheers, night, Joan.'

We wait for a few minutes for Lilly and Nick to come back. The pair of them strolling side by side with Nick waiting patiently when she stops to talk to people or share a few words. They look good together and I have to keep reminding myself she is only fifteen. Nick is a grown man. Lilly is still a child in the eyes of the law but then there is no law now and everything about the girl makes her seem so much older.

I step over to Clarence, Paula and Roy, 'if Lilly was your daughter how would you feel about her being with Nick?'

'Are you being serious?' Clarence asks.

'About them having sex I mean.'

'And again are you being serious?'

'What's what?' Marcy asks.

'Howie was asking how we'd feel about Lilly and Nick if Lilly was our daughter,' Paula says, 'which is a bloody stupid question. It's Nick. Any mother would be delighted with Nick. He's a mothers dream.'

'She's fifteen,' I say.

'She killed nineteen people,' Marcy points out.

'No that doesn't count,' Roy says, 'I see where Howie is coming from here. Killing is easy and it was life or death but the question is whether Lilly is able to handle a complex sexual relationship at her age.'

'It's Nick,' Clarence says as though the conversation is entirely unnecessary, 'I'd trust that lad with anything.'

'I'm not on about if Nick would or wouldn't...' I go to reply but get shushed by Marcy and Paula as Nick and Lilly walk over towards us.

'We just saw Pea and Sam,' Nick says, 'the said about Lilly coming over with us tonight.'

'I would love to as long as you are sure I am not imposing,' Lilly says.

'Very sure,' Paula says, 'where's Reggie?'

'In the offices,' Mo calls out, 'want me to get him?'

'Please, honey. Lilly, you ready to go?'

'Thanks, honey,' Cookey shouts as Mo runs off.

'Cheers, honeypot,' Blowers calls out.

'You leave him alone,' Paula says, 'he is my honey.'

Cookey snorts, 'just slightly jealous here. I thought I was your honey.'

'I'll come to you Charlie my love...'

'Sod off, Marcy,' Cookey laughs.

'Lilly,' Marcy says seriously, 'you have to come so we can protect Charlie tonight.'

'Protect Charlie?' Cookey asks, 'protect me more like, she kept looking at my willy earlier ow!'

'Good shot, Charlie,' Nick says.

'Honestly, Lilly. I'm not safe from her...'

'Are we leaving?' Reginald asks, rushing from the offices with Mo running behind him.

'We are, mate. You ready?' I ask.

'I am, Roy. May I make use of the van tonight? I fear the house will be rather full and I require a quiet place with sufficient illumination to continue my studies.'

'I think we can say it's our van now, Reginald,' Roy says.

'Oh gosh,' Reginald stops to push his glasses up his nose, 'well I am honoured, Roy. Truly I am and Lilly, your hospitality this evening has been most kind. The food was delicious...'

'She's coming with us, Reggie,' Marcy cuts across him.

'Oh don't do that,' Reginald says with perfect seriousness, 'honestly, stay within the fort so you don't have to listen to their crass jokes and constant references to orifices and appendages.'

'We're going,' Paula says.

We move off down to the gates in a straggly line headed by Lilly and Nick. Lilly stops to share a couple of words with the gate guard then goes out onto the beach and chooses a couple of ribs moored up in the shallows. Nick, being gallant, drags them in and we load up with Meredith getting hoisted in by Clarence only to run to the end and jump straight out to swim about for a bit.

The boats get going, with Dave holding central position and the speed painfully slow until Meredith has finished splashing about and swims close enough to get lifted back in by Clarence where she proceeds to shake and drench everyone.

It's a light hearted feeling travelling back to the shore. Low voices chatting and making jokes with me and Nick driving the boats side by side across a flat black sea and a sky full of a million stars that seem to shine so much brighter than they ever did before.

'Seen that,' I call out. They look round to see me staring up and join me looking at shining stars twinkling across the sky.

'So many,' Paula says, 'Reggie, is it the lack of gasses making them brighter? Reggie?'

'I'm sorry, what?' He asks, startled from being engrossed in the journal open on his lap as he reads the pages by torchlight, 'er yes, probably,' he mutters.

'Anything good?' Marcy asks, 'Reggie? Anything good in there?'

'I am not sure,' he replies with a huff at being distracted.

'Brian. It's Lilly. We're coming to you now in two boats.'

'Hello?'

'Yes Brian, it's Lilly. We're coming to you now in two boats.'

'Oh right. Understood. Is Dave with you?' His worried voice asks through the radio.

'He is yes,' Lilly replies.

'I thought someone said you didn't put guards out here at night,' Blowers asks.

'For your vehicles and your horse,' Lilly says, 'Joan organised it.'

'Very nice of her,' Paula says.

We get into the shallows on the shore side and bump the fronts of the vessels up as we lever the propellers out of the water.

'Switch on now,' I call out softly thinking back to how shit a guard that Brian was earlier today. The beach is full of dark mounds with furniture and supplies stacked ready to be carried over. Across the way the plant machinery looms in the shadows and we hold still for a minute to listen and let our eyes adjust to the gloom.

I guess we've done this enough times now to organise ourselves without the need for words. Rifles are pulled round and held ready. Meredith rushes out ahead with her nose to the ground me, Dave and Mo taking point behind her. Clarence at the rear. Roy out to one side with his bow held with an arrow nocked. The lads central in a rough circle with eyes up to watch and scan, always watching, always scanning.

The transition from gentle conversation and quiet jokes in the boats to being organised and disciplined on the shore is smooth and easy. I turn round in a slow circle with my right hand showing a thumbs up to make sure everyone is ready. They nod back. Game faces on. Eyes wide. Ears listening. Paula guides Lilly in between herself and Marcy with the lads ranged out around them. Blinky catches my eye too. The way she stands so perfectly poised like a poster for the British Army. None of us are in army clothes or helmets or anything but it's the essence of the stature and the look of absolute focus on her face. She catches me looking and nods like the perfect squaddie she is.

'Move out,' I whisper and start up the shore with Dave and Mo at my sides. We stay silent and move through the piles and mounds with eyes flicking to watch Meredith, the front and the sides.

Our vehicles have been moved down to the house down the bay. We get up onto the road and veer out to take the soft verges to avoid the sounds of boots on tarmac. We pass vehicles parked up. Vans, pick-up trucks and more dark shapes that loom and hold places for the infected to hide in.

Brian is outside the house with another bloke. The pair of them standing side by side with rifles held across the crooks of their arms.

'Coming in,' Dave calls ahead so we don't startle them and get shot. They both twitch anyway but I think that's got more to do with Dave than anything else. 'Report,' Dave demands as we get close to them.

Brian just panics and shuffles but the other guy who has close cropped hair pulls his feet together and straightens his back, 'all quiet, Sir.'

'I am not Sir. I am Dave. Mr Howie is Sir.'

'Dave,' the man nods smartly making it sound like *sarge* the same way the lads do, 'all quiet. Nothing to report.'

'Services?' Blowers asks from behind me.

'RAF regiment,' the man replies.

'Never mind,' Clarence mutters from the back.

'You?' The man asks.

'Para's,' Clarence says.

'Marines,' Blowers adds.

'Oh,' the man says as though that explains everything, 'you two two?' He asks Dave.

'No,' Dave says.

'I er,' he man hesitates as though unsure if he should proceed, 'I did P company all arms course...'

'Yeah?' Clarence asks, 'from the RAF?'

'Knew a bloke who knew a bloke,' the man replies with a wry smile, 'few years ago now though.'

'You pass?' Blowers asks.

'I did yeah,' the man says without any hint of boasting, 'had a couple of attachments too. Did a tour with your lot,' he adds with a look to Clarence who strides forward to hold his hand out.

'Clarence.'

'Gary,' the man says.

'Blowers,' Blowers goes next.

'Alright mate, Gary. Alright lads,' he adds with a nod past Blowers.

'Hi,' Cookey says

'Alright mate,' Nick says.

'You serving when it happened?' Clarence asks.

'Just got out,' Gary says, 'like three months...got a CP course too before I left. Had a sweet job lined up in Baghdad.'

'Ah mate,' Clarence says with a sigh, 'bad timing.'

'Happens,' Gary says with a shrug.

'What's a CP course?' I ask.

'Close protection,' Gary says.

'Gucci course, Boss,' Clarence says, 'you must have known some people then,' he says to Gary.

'You make contacts as you go,' Gary says and like us, but unlike Brian, he doesn't stare at the person he's talking to but looks round constantly. Away into the distance then left and right. He's lean too and looks physically fit. Cleanly shaven and he's taken pride in his appearance with his long sleeve shirt tucked in and the sleeves rolled up neatly above his elbows.

'When did you get here?' I ask.

'Yesterday afternoon,' he says, 'you the boss then?'

'Mr Howie,' Dave says.

'Mr Howie, Sir,' Gary nods that smart motion.

What a difference a day makes. He looks competent and switched on and I can imagine he would have backed Lilly up instantly when she fought back against the crews.

'Gary, I'm Lilly,' Lilly says, presenting herself with that cold politeness that exudes authority.

'Ma'am,' Gary says smartly, 'Joan said you're in charge of the fort.'

'Yes I am,' Lilly says, 'I'm very glad to have you with us.'

'Glad to be here, Ma'am.'

'Brian, you take Gary back to the fort. We'll be staying here tonight.'

'Will do, Lilly.'

I get a look from Clarence and Blowers, both of them nodding at Gary and making eyes, 'Gary,' I say as he goes to walk off with Brian, 'you about in the morning?'

'Not going anywhere, Boss,' he says with a smile.

'I'll come and see you,' Clarence says.

'Happy with that,' Gary says, 'night all, Boss, Ma'am,' he adds and walks off.

'Well that wasn't painfully bloody obvious,' Paula says once they're out of earshot, 'you two practically wetting yourselves,' she adds with a look to Clarence and Blowers.

'He's done P company,' Clarence says.

'Er he's done All Arms course,' Blowers cuts in across the big man, 'Para's ain't everything.'

'I knew we'd be having this conversation one day,' Clarence says with a grin, 'surprised you haven't said anything before.'

'Fuck off,' Blowers says with a grin, 'think I'm going to pick a fight with you?'

'Are we taking him with us?' Marcy asks.

'Dunno,' I say, 'Clarence and Blowers can speak to him tomorrow.'

'Lilly needs good people here,' Paula says firmly, 'and unless he's...well, unless he is...'

'Unless he is what?' Lilly asks.

'Immune,' Marcy says, 'he wouldn't last five minutes otherwise.'

'Reggie,' I get his attention from the book in his hands, 'how can we tell if someone is immune?'

'I am most flattered that you consider me able to answer every question you pose but short of having an infected host body bite him I do not know.'

'Talking of which,' Paula says, giving me a look.

I look at Lilly and take in the bruises on her face and again question how a fifteen year old girl can take such a beating and do what she's done without any apparent side effects.

'Lilly,' I say. She frowns at the way Paula, Marcy and Clarence are looking at her and turns to face me.

'You think I hold immunity?' She asks with an intelligence that joins the dots far quicker than I would do.

'You're healing very fast for someone who took such a beating,' I say.

'Did Nick give it to me?'

'I don't think it works like that' I say, 'Reggie? I know what you just said but...'

'I cannot say for certain,' he says with a sigh, 'but no, I do not think it works in that manner.'

'Your hair,' Marcy says with a kind smile, 'your skin. You look so glowing and healthy.'

'I have been outdoors for a few days,' Lilly says.

'Look at Charlie,' Paula says, 'someone with those injuries should not look like she does.'

'Fit,' Cookey says with a firm nod and a big grin.

'Thank you,' Charlie says, smiling at Cookey.

'Do your injuries hurt?' Roy asks, moving closer into the middle of the group as we stand in the dark outside the house on the shore opposite the fort.

'A little,' Lilly says.

'May I?' Roy asks, holding his hand out for her arm. She nods politely and holds it out as he gently touches the bruises and welts so clear on her skin. 'Does that hurt?'

'It's tender,' she says, watching his fingers gently push into a bruise.

'You were kicked in the ribs and thighs?' He asks.

'I was.'

'Several times I think they said,' Roy says.

'That is correct.'

'No broken ribs?'

'How would I know?'

'A broken rib? You would know,' Roy says confidently. 'Do you wake up with energy?'

'I have a lot to do.'

'But you don't feel as hungry or as thirsty as you used to do,' he says.

'I...I have not really noticed.'

'May I ask you a question, Lilly?' Charlie asks.

'Of course.'

'When you fought back, did you feel something inside? Like a rage?'

'Well I was very angry yes but my brother was...' she trails off with the memory of the event so clear on her face and just for a second I see a flash of darkness in her features. I close my eyes and make myself think of my sister. I make myself think of Lani and everyone we've lost. I summon faces and the essence of the infection and the darkness in me swims to the surface. I think of the battles we've fought and the never ending unceasing relentless hatred I have for the infection. Then I think of that girl screaming in the room *Mummy...Daddy...make them stop.* Rage inside that surges up with a searing pain that floods my mind. Meredith growls, pushing her nose into my open hand.

They are not here. Be calm.

'Howie stop,' Marcy says quickly.

Rage that pulses to send out a feeling that comes down on all of us. Jess whinnies in the garden of the house. Meredith's voice joins her. A low whine, insistent and worried.

They are not here. There are no little ones. Be calm.

'Howie, stop!' Marcy grabs my hand.

I snap my eyes open to see Lilly glaring at her with a vein pushing out from her forehead and the cold blue eyes of a killer fixed and unblinking.

'I felt that yesterday,' she says in a voice bereft of emotion, 'last night when it got dark...I felt it then. Pack. I felt the word pack.'

'That's enough,' Marcy says, 'Lilly, you're one of us. Stop it now, Howie. Switch it off I can't handle that girl in my head...'

It ain't that easy to turn it off though. I've never brought it on coldly like that before but now it's here I can't get rid of it. I shake my head but the pressure builds and grows.

'Howie, fucking stop it,' Marcy flashes at me.

'I fucking can't,' I growl back.

'You stupid prick, why did you do that?' She shouts at me.

'Get fucked,' I snap back.

'Safe, Dave,' Mo says, his own voice choking with unspent rage.

'Fucking hell,' Marcy seethes and steps away with her hands clasped to her head, 'why did you do that?'

'To see if Lilly was...' I go to reply with a voice hoarse and tight.

'Well it fucking worked,' Marcy says over me, 'switch it off for fuck's sake.'

'I just said I fucking can't.'

'Everyone inside,' Paula snaps, her eyes furious. We all are. Everyone is. The hive mind of battle coming on strong. Energy courses our bodies, urging us to give battle but there ain't nothing to fight. 'You two take first watch,' she adds waving an angry hand at me and Marcy.

'Fine,' Marcy snaps.

'Good,' I growl. We stare at each other. We glare full of baleful hate. Her nostrils flare. My head tilts back.

'Marcy,' Paula shouts from the door, 'switch him off.'

'You fucking idiot,' Marcy whispers at me.

'I will apologise when I am not so fucking angry but until then you can fuck off...'

'I fucking hate you, Howie.'

'I fucking detest you, Marcy.'

'SWITCH HIM OFF FOR FUCK'S SAKE,' Paula shouts from inside the house.

'Fine,' Marcy's face twitches. I glare at her. She shakes her head at me. I squint my eyes at her with my arms and legs shaking from the unused adrenalin pumping through my body.

'NOW MARCY,' Paula bellows.

'Fine,' Marcy marches at me. I stand my ground. She stops inches away with hot air blasting from her nose.

'You're breathing on me,' I whisper angrily.

'I have to kiss you,' Marcy says with absolute pure fury in her eyes.

'Yeah? Gonna use pheromones again?'

'Cunt.'

'Bitch.'

'IF YOU DON'T START I WILL COME OUT THERE AND DO IT MYSELF...' Clarence's angry voice booms.

Her lips slam into mine. Fury and rage ramming into me. I stand my ground taking the impact and push my lips into hers. A hand comes up to grab a handful of hair on the back of my head. I push harder. Not yielding. Not giving ground. She drives in. Our eyes open and glaring.

'Kiss me back,' she hisses.

'You kiss me,' I counter.

'I am you twat.'

'Yeah?'

'Yes. Open your bloody mouth then.'

'You open yours,' I say, refusing to be controlled or manipulated.

'Don't tell me what to do,' she says.

'On three then,' I growl.

'Fine.'

'One,' I count.

'Two,' she pulses with rage that I can feel thrumming her body and never before have I hated someone so much.

We count the last second in our heads and the discipline of order kicks in. We both close our eyes. We both move in and we both open our mouth and that fury flows between us. From her to me and back to her. Round and round it goes as my hands reach up to cup her face and hers dig harder into the back of my head. The fury grows. We kiss harder. The pulsing rage screams to be used and like a switch it changes from something dark and nasty to something of light and beauty. I kiss her. She kisses me. I kiss her because I want to kiss her and now suddenly there is nothing else to do in the world other than kiss this woman.

She pushes into me. Her hands not digging now but pushing through my hair. My own hands feel the cheekbones under her skin and down to her slender neck and shoulders. We kiss and let that darkness slide away to be ready for another day. We let beauty and grace back inside and it spreads out like a gentle ripple on a lake. I can feel the others all settling too. I feel Lilly breathing slower. I feel Clarence's fists unclenching. Blowers finally blinks. Jess stops snorting and tossing her head and Meredith's hackles soften against her back.

I sink into Marcy. Marcy who holds my heart in her hands because nobody else could do this right now. There isn't another person alive that could take that consuming rage and turn it away so deftly. It goes too. All of it. It goes and instead there is only her. Just Marcy. Only Marcy. Always Marcy.

When we separate we do so by increments of millimetres at a time. Almost as though the very act of parting is painful. Then we are just a man and a woman holding each other on a dark road outside a house where our friends are gathered.

'Saxon?' She breathes heavily.

'Yeah go on then.'

CHAPTER FORTY

The rage subsides. A stupid thing to do. To invite the urge to fight and give battle and in the house they snarl and growl at each other until finally it ebbs away like a tide being pulled smoothly back from the shore.

But now it goes and in its place is a warm feeling of grace and beauty that spreads warm smiles from face to face and so organic and natural that none of them question it. These are strange days after all.

'YOU OKAY?' Paula asks, easing gratefully into bed.

'Fine now, I can't believe he just did that,' Roy says, stretching his arm out for Paula to sink into his side.

'I think he meant well.'

'No, not that he did it but that he was able to do it…just switch it on like that.'

'Mmmm, couldn't bloody switch it off though could he.'

He kisses her forehead gently and pulls her in closer. 'I think Marcy will calm him down.'

She mumbles affirmation then lifts her head to look at him, 'did you see the doctors?'

'I did.'

'Everything okay?'

'For now,' he says, his tone dropping a notch.

'For now?' She asks.

He smiles sadly, 'magical thinking. One of my fears is that if I believe I am okay then I will get sick...so I never really believe it even when they tell me. It's like a...like a security blanket or a shield.'

'Oh,' she says mildly, 'okay.'

'Doesn't put you off me?'

'No, Roy,' she says, leaning over his chest to kiss him gently, 'nothing about you puts me off. I bet they stay up chatting for ages.'

'Let them,' Roy says as she rolls to get on top of him. He traces his fingertips down her back sending shivers through her body, 'I think we might be up for a bit anyway.'

'A bit of what?' She asks with a quick grin.

'God, you're turning into Cookey.'

HE READS. Water heated from a camping gas stove left in the kitchen and he sips peppermint tea and reads. Candles flicker around the worktop and he sits almost stock still. Only moving to turn the pages or lift the mug to take a sip. After a while he pauses, goes to his bag and takes a writing pad and pen. He flicks to a new page and goes back to the beginning but now with the pen adding notes as he starts again. He doesn't hear the conversations outside in the garden or the low laughter but somehow, those background noises sooth his mind. The sounds of voices he has already become so used to hearing.

Guide us then. Tell us what we should be doing.

Easy words said but he reads anyway. He reads to learn and as he does so he sees Neal's life scribbled down in the pages of a journal stained with coffee and blood. He reads because Howie asked him to. He reads because this is his role now and he reads because he refuses to be beaten intellectually by a virus. No Sir, he reads to compete because the challenge is set. His wits against the other player's. The wheels are in motion. The game is underway. Yesterday was infancy. Today is childlike. What will tomorrow be?

Reginald has seen more horror and felt greater fear than he ever believed it was possible to know, but that pales to the sensation growing inside and as his understand forms so his blood turns to ice in his veins and that feeling of dread magnifies by the second.

THEY SIT and talk as young people do. Blowers, Mo, Blinky, Cookey, Charlie, Nick and Lilly. They tell jokes and laugh and smoke cigarettes and drink hot drinks brewed on a camping gas stove. In the enclosed rear garden of a shore side house with a huge riot trained horse munching at the grass that hasn't be cut for nineteen days and a dog that rests by the open back door.

They all need this time. Lilly more than anyone. She talks to Charlie about schooling, horses and everything young women talk about. She talks to the others about the fort, her brother and the funny things people say and do. They don't mention the rage. They don't talk of the importance of their roles in this brave new world. Instead they listen to Cookey's jokes and watch Charlie bending double with tears streaming down her face.

The night draws on and as much as they have energy, so they also knew they will need to be awake and alert the next day and with a yawn and a stretch, Blowers stands and signals it's time to call it a night.

Charlie hangs back to sort Jess out. Cookey waits with her. Blowers, Mo and Blinky head into the living room to kip down on bedding rolled out. Nick panics. Lilly doesn't.

If you want time alone the first room upstairs on the left is yours.

Paula whispered the words in her ear as she bent to kiss the girl goodnight.

Lilly takes his hand and leads him down the hallway. She feels the callouses on his palms and the hard ridges of his knuckles. Their rifles on their backs. Pistols on hips and his axe held in his free hand they mount the stairs. Nick's mouth goes dry. His heart thunders. Lilly smiles to herself and opens the door to the first room on the left and spots the single flickering candle next to the bedding on the floor.

He flounders. His hands trembling as he props his axe and assault rifle against the wall. She senses his nerves and watches him with soft eyes. Marvelling at how someone who can do the things he can without fear or worry now shows abject concern at being alone with her. She goes to him. Her nerves held at bay and it's her confidence that carries the moment and her hands that reach up to gently hold his face and pull him down to kiss her soft lips.

He goes with it. Sinking and breathing into the embrace as they stand in a room stripped of usable furniture. Not even curtains on the walls and the silvery moonlight fills the room to fight against the orange glow of the candle.

'Lilly,' he pulls back with fear in his voice, his soft brown eyes everything she remembers. His voice quavering with passion and worry. His honour so clear and his decency shining like a beacon in the darkness.

'I'm not fifteen anymore,' she whispers, knowing exactly what he is worried about. Lilly is intelligent. Her mind ten steps ahead of everyone else and any nerves she had at coming to a private room with Nick evaporated at seeing that nervous honesty within him. He blinks and smiles a confused grin with a cute frown that makes her chuckle.

'When...I mean shit sorry...I er...'

'Yesterday,' she says, 'I was sixteen yesterday.'

He nods slowly, his eyes searching hers. She takes his hands in hers and holds them tight.

'Remember that day in the field?' She asks.

He smiles softly, that wry twitch of his lips that caught her heart that day, 'yeah, yeah I do.'

'I wanted to.'

'Fuck really? I mean...shit...'

'It's fine,' she smiles, 'yes, yes I did.'

'We don't have to do anything now, Lilly,' he says with a brutal yet fragile honesty.

She doesn't reply because there are no words that could match the feeling inside and this image is the only she held in her head when she walked into the room with Zayden. Instead she kisses him. A girl and boy in a room in a house. Warriors. Killers. Hearts of lions that held the line but a boy and a girl nonetheless.

'SO, right...so by this time the ferry is on fire and Mr Howie is trying to save the coffee machine and we're all ripping the piss out of Nick who is getting angry as anything...'

She laughs harder. The tears fall faster. Cookey telling her the story of crossing the Solent on a stolen ferry from the Isle of Wight.

Jess is sorted. Brushed, fed, watered and happy to potter about in the garden but still they remain. Leaning against the fence as Cookey gives her a greater pleasure than anything she has ever known.

He trails off. His eyes twinkling as he watches her wipe the tears from her eyes and groan from the pain in her stomach.

'Cookey,' she finally stands upright to look at him.

'Michael Buble,' he says and she's off. Bent double from the random utterances that spill from his mouth.

'What?' She gasps, 'what's...I...Michael Buble?'

He shrugs, 'dunno, so yeah anyway. Thanks for telling everyone you saw my willy today.'

'You told everyone you saw my bottom.'

'I love the way you say bottom.'

She snorts then brays and covers her mouth self-consciously before fighting like a demon to get her breathing under control. She stands up again and fixes him a look, *'I'll come to you Charlie...'*

'Oh piss off,' he groans as she starts laughing at his reaction, 'right well if we're not sharing a house then I'm going to bed.'

'I'd share a house with you,' she says between snorts.

'Yeah?' Cookey asks, 'have you seen my new sock dance?'

'No!' She sputters and turns away when he starts grooving on the spot with a perfectly serious face.

'My new sock dance.'

'Stop,' she gasps.

'Do the new sock dance with me, Charlie,' he grabs her hands and starts swinging to get her going, 'to the left and to the right... and er...to the left or something...'

'Do you even know how to dance?'

'Me?' Cookey asks, leaning back, 'er no, haven't got a clue. Bet you do though. Do you do ballroom dancing?'

'I do,' she says with another braying laugh that she stifles to keep quiet.

'Ooh show me,' Cookey says with fresh excitement.

'Seriously?'

'Yeah,' he scoffs, 'I saved your ass today so you got to teach me ballroom now.'

'Okay okay,' she says, heaving to control the laughing, 'your right hand goes round my back...and my arm goes up onto your shoulder. So, we stand together with our hands held like this...'

'Blowers would love this...'

'Stop,' she gasps, hitting his chest, 'do you want to learn or not?'

'I do I do,' he laughs.

'Okay, then we step away and...no go slowly and...that's it, wow, you're really good.'

'Yeah?' He laughs as she takes the lead.

'For a beginner,' she adds.

They dance around the garden picking a route through tear

misted eyes. A woman with a ragged cut down her face and a chunk of her ear bitten away by an undead with a mutated gene from facing down two hundred on her own. They laugh and giggle as Cookey tries for a swirl and almost trips over a plant pot. A man who's heart gives the living army the light to keep going in the darkest of days.

She watches him between laughing. Remembering the way he took the pain for her this morning and the utter serious capability that makes him as dangerous as any of the others. He came for her too. He ran through a horde to wrap his body round hers and hold a pistol with deadly intent while she bled over his skin.

He goes quiet. His eyes finding hers. She softens and the laughter gently eases off. Subtly she moves in closer, feeling the warmth coming from his body. A moment captured in life. A perfect moment where there is no pretence and no pressure to be anything than who you are.

'I love your smile,' she says and leans closer to kiss his cheek.

He takes the kiss and gives one of his own, soft and full of respect but this is Cookey and never a moment is missed, 'Michael Buble,' he whispers with the deft touch of a master able to read his audience and she falls into him with her chest heaving from the laughter surging up again.

Aye, the darkest of days but the world is still here and all the things in it shall live the lives they are meant to live.

CHAPTER FORTY-ONE

'We didn't go on the slide.'

His knuckles turn white from gripping the steering wheel of the van. His bulging eyes stare fixed to the road ahead. His pock-marked skin glistening with a film of sweat coating his ugly features.

'Gregori,' the boy whines, 'we didn't go on the slide or the seesaw or the roundabout...'

He has never faltered. Not once in his life has he faltered. He never questioned the missions. He did what he was told to do and always without emotion and without a second thought but now? Now he has a lifetime of emotion rushing through his body and mind while feeling repulsed at himself for being so weak.

He is the *Ugly Man*. He is the bringer of death. He is Gregori, a tool, a weapon, an instrument to be contracted out to whoever paid the fee. He was used in every country in the world. He took down Triads and Yardies. He killed former KGB and Mossad operatives. He took out a tribe of battle hardened Afghan warlords when they burnt the Opium fields and sent the body parts to every other tribe in the region. He killed men, women and children. They were targets, not people.

'Gregori,' the boy whines again, 'we didn't go on the seesaw...'

He killed with pistols, knives and his bare hands. He burnt houses down and stood outside ready to kill any that escaped the flames and listened dispassionately as they screamed inside burning to death from the heat and flames.

'Can we go back?'

Sometimes the targets were told the *ugly man* was coming. They were given time to strengthen their defences and get more men with guns or pack up to flee and hide. It didn't matter though. They were still killed and the impact was all the greater for the warning given. You were dead the second the deal was made and the target given. Politicians. Mafia bosses. Generals of armies and even Heads of State.

'Gregori? Can we go back?'

Today he faltered though. Today he pushed a boy on a sling and felt every life he had ever taken come creeping back into his soul. He ran weeping into the street to see the undead staggering towards him. He shot and felled a few but then gave up and sank to the ground ready to die. He waited for the bites to come. He waited for the teeth to open his skin and the fingers to tear at his flesh.

Only they didn't come and when he looked up the boy was sat cross-legged watching him while playing with the pistol in his lap and around them the hundreds of undead stood watching with those terrible red eyes.

What Gregori did in his life was wrong. He took life and killed without question. He inflicted pain without remorse. It wasn't for vengeance that he killed but only because that is what he was made to do. Now, in the space of a few short minutes he knows every life he took was wrong. He has sinned and for that he is damned for all eternity. He knows this as fact. He also knows that what he did was not unnatural. He was trained and excelled at his skills but it was just a skill.

What the boy can do though *is* unnatural and a whole different kind of wrong. Gregori never took pleasure in the killing. To him it was a task to be accomplished and any emotion was beaten and tortured from him as a child.

'Not fair,' the boy huffs and sits back in his seat with his little arms folded across his chest. 'Are we going home now, Gregori?'

Why can't he kill the boy? Point the gun and shoot. End it. Shoot yourself after and be done.

'Gregori?'

Slit his throat then slit your own. Hang yourself. Drink poison. Swallow pills. End it. The boy is not natural.

'Gregori? Gregori? Gregori? Gregori? Gregori?' The boy says his name over and over, his tone so light and that of a child. His little legs swinging as they hang from the seat. His hair all tussled and his face golden from the sun. 'Gregori? Gregori? Gregori? Gregori? Are we going home, Gregori? Are we? Are we, Gregori?' The voice goes on, relentless and unceasing. A thing of perpetual motion that will never end.

'No,' Gregori didn't know he was going to reply but there it is. A word uttered and one the boy seizes on almost with triumph.

'Where then? Where are we going, Gregori? Where, Gregori? Where then, Gregori? Where are we going, Gregori? Where, Gregori?'

Kill him. Drive the van into a wall. Set it on fire. Burn it. Kill the boy.

'We go new home.'

'Yay,' the boy claps with delight.

Yes, that's what they need. A new home where the garden isn't covered in corpses and stains of blood from teaching the boy how to kill. Somewhere remote and private. Somewhere the boy can be a boy and not be unnatural. Get food and toys. Get clothes for the boy and himself. Get books and the things a child needs. Not weapons and knives but toys and books. Yes. Do not let history repeat itself. They took him as a debt and made him into a thing. They beat and tortured every last emotion from him until he was hardened yet entirely broken as an individual. They made him so brainwashed he could be sent anywhere in the world but would always return and wait for the next instruction.

He sees it now. His reason for being here. His skills are to keep the boy alive and safe so he can grow to be normal. Not a machine that kills but a free man that thinks and learns. Nothing can touch them. Gregori knows this. The undead hold no fear to him. He is Gregori. He was a killer but now he shall be a protector and in this he will seek to right a life of wrong.

His knuckles turn from white to pink again. His breathing comes slower. His mind settles. Let the boy be a boy. Protect don't kill.

'New home,' he grunts and nods as he glances to the boy and becomes aware of the stench of death coming from the back of the van. He brakes steady but firm to bring the van to a stop. 'Come, we go.' He drops down to walk swiftly round the front to the passenger door. His eyes up to watch and scan. Always watching. Always scanning.

'Come, we go,' the boy mimics and jumps down onto the road and looks round at the houses, 'are we living here?'

'No,' Gregori says and hesitates, suddenly unsure of the protocols of protecting instead of killing. Every bodyguard he ever encountered was killed before he ever got a chance to understand what they do. It must be a reversal of skill. No, not a reversal but a change of perspective. Like a thief advising on home security. How would he stop himself from killing the boy? He frowns at the thought. If he was coming for the boy the boy would be dead. How would he stop himself? He couldn't. He wouldn't be able to. His mind fills with a sudden image of himself fighting himself. Who would win? The other Gregori would win. The one that didn't have the weakness of the breakdown in the park.

'Gregori? Are we walking to our new house?'

He blinks and rids his head of the abstract notions that would never have come into his mind before today.

'No, new car.'

'New car?' The boy asks, staring up in confusion.

'We need new car,' Gregori says with a nod, 'this smell,' he points to the van.

'Can we have a blue one? No a red one...no a yellow one...I know I know we can get a blue and a red and a yellow one and and...'

'Come...' Gregrori starts to say.

'...we go,' the boy beats him to it with a delighted laugh. He reaches out to push his hand into Gregori's as they move down the centre of the road, swinging his arm and skipping along with a body bursting with excitement at just the thought of having a new car.

Gregori analyses every vehicle in sight. Checking each visually for power, handling, security, speed, performance, fuel consumption and load capacity but not colour. Colour is not relevant for this mission. Colour is important when you are either trying to blend in or trying to stand out and announce your arrival but this is not a mission. Let the boy be a boy.

'Choose.'

'Can I?' The boy blurts spinning round with his tongue poking out as he analyses every vehicle in sight, 'the blue one,' he says, pointing to a VW Golf.

'This one?' Gregori asks.

'Yes yes yes no no no, the red one...no the blue one...'

'Choose,' Gregori says, looking round at the houses and back down the street.

'Red one,' the boy says, choosing a diesel Skoda Octavia.

'This one?' Gregori asks, pointing across the road to a battered old mini.

'No!' The boy laughs, 'this one, Gregori.'

'This one?' Gregori asks, pointing to the blue VW.

'Gregori,' the boy squeals, 'the red one, Gregori.'

Gregori nods and looks through the windows of the Skoda. He

can force an entry and start the vehicle easy enough but why use force when you get the keys. He looks to the house the car is parked outside. This is England where people are weirdly fanatical about being able to park outside their homes.

'Come,' he takes the boy with him up the path to see the front door is hanging open with a thick wake of dried blood going down the garden paving slabs. He pauses, listening, smelling, sensing. Nothing here. He finds the keys in the kitchen and goes to leave then stops and looks at the boy. 'Food. What food you like, Boy?'

He goes through the cupboards pulling tins and packets out to be given either a nod, a shake of the head or a look of absolute disgust by the boy. Food gets bagged and carried to the car to be placed in the boot. They go to door to door. Pausing, listening, smelling and sensing before taking food from cupboards that gets put into bags that get carried out.

The Skoda is loaded and he gets the boy into the passenger seat and leans over him to fasten the seatbelt. By the time he gets into the driver's seat the boy is jabbing the radio while frowning.

'Make it work, Gregori.'

Gregori grunts and slides the key into the ignition barrel and turns to let the coils heat before starting the engine.

'I want music,' the boy huffs.

Gregori looks at the radio then at the boy with a whole new thought process entering his head.

'Please,' Gregori says, the word coming out like *pliz*.

'Make it work,' the boy ignores him, turning dials and jabbing buttons.

Gregori waits. His face betraying no emotion until the boy looks at him and he lifts one eyebrow of one bulging eye.

'Please,' the boy says.

'Better,' Gregori says. He presses the button for the radio and goes through the stations, checking for emergency broadcasts but only hearing static. He flicks from FM to MW and again goes through.

'CD,' the boy says, 'mummy had music on a CD,' he jabs at the eject button and waits for a disc to slide smoothly out from the thin opening but pushes it straight back in. The music system detects the disc insertion and automatically switches from radio to disc as the illumination shows the numerical digit for the first song. Gregori doesn't watch the stereo though. Instead his eyes stay fixed on the wing mirror and the infected woman standing outside the house further back down the road. She makes no effort to stagger after them but stares drooling and red eyed towards the red car.

He blasts air from his nose, finds the bite on the pedals and drops the handbrake to turn out from the row of parked vehicles as the speakers come alive with a thudding techno beat that makes the boy clap and laugh.

As the vehicle moves down the road that fills with the solid thrumming of an electronic beat so Gregori glances in the rear view mirror to see not only the woman walking out into the road but far back, in the distance, the hundreds from the park walking after them.

He grunts in response and speeds up. They will find a house. Isolated and rural. Somewhere small with a fresh water supply and a good view of the surroundings. The boy will be a boy. Not a killer.

Printed in Great Britain
by Amazon